D1453098

FEAR OF FALLING . . . UP

They left him there all afternoon, more than two hours, with eternity overflowing his eyes. When a teacher supervising the buses finally noticed the still figure and ran to let him down, David was raw with sun- and windburn. His ears and hands felt gone, chilled to utter numbness, as if they were no longer part of him. His eyes burned and the lids rasped over them, all tears sucked away by the dry autumn wind, the eyeball surface so desiccated that he felt as if someone had poured a sludgy glue into his eyes.

He had stopped screaming.

He was past screaming.

He had seen the hungry sky.

—from "The Hungry Sky" by Brad Strickland

Horror Anthologies Published by POCKET BOOKS

DEATHPORT, edited by Ramsey Campbell
FREAK SHOW, edited by F. Paul Wilson
HOT BLOOD, edited by Jeff Gelb and Lonn Friend
HOTTER BLOOD, edited by Jeff Gelb and Michael Garrett
HOTTEST BLOOD, edited by Jeff Gelb and Michael Garrett
PHOBIAS, edited by Martin Greenberg, Richard Gilliam,
  Edward Kramer and Wendy Webb
SHOCK ROCK, edited by Jeff Gelb
UNDER THE FANG, edited by Robert R. McCammon

PHOBIAS

STORIES OF YOUR DEEPEST FEARS

**EDITED BY WENDY WEBB,
RICHARD GILLIAM, EDWARD KRAMER,
AND MARTIN GREENBERG
INTRODUCTION BY ROBERT BLOCH**

POCKET BOOKS
New York   London   Toronto   Sydney   Tokyo   Singapore

An *Original* Publication of POCKET BOOKS

POCKET BOOKS, a division of Simon & Schuster Inc.
1230 Avenue of the Americas, New York, NY 10020

ISBN: 0-671-79237-7

First Pocket Books printing January 1994

10 9 8 7 6 5 4 3 2 1

POCKET and colophon are registered trademarks of Simon & Schuster Inc.

Cover art by Kirk Reinert

Printed in the U.S.A.

Copyright Notices

Contents

Contents

Contents

INTRODUCTION

Robert Bloch

"WE HAVE NOTHING TO FEAR BUT FEAR ITSELF."

President Franklin D. Roosevelt said it, more than sixty years ago, and it sounded logical at the time. But he was talking about the economic depression of the 1930s, not the depression caused by whatever pushes our panic buttons.

There is a wide variety of these personal panic buttons and all sorts of pressing problems to set them off. But for the majority of us, those buttons are usually dormant and are not activated by slight pressure.

Panic is an extreme form of fear, often groundless, an almost spontaneous and contagious group phenomenon. The early Greeks presumed it was inspired by or at least associated with Pan, the god of nature. Alarm caused by natural occurrences, such as violent thunderstorms in a forest wilderness or upon lonely mountain heights, was thus described as "panic."

I just threw that in to sound educated, which I am not. Nor am I particularly knowledgeable about panic's twin brother, fear. I do believe the two are not identical twins. Panic is generally and accurately described as blind and unreasoning, whereas it's quite possible to be fearful and still think clearly. Fear is merely one response to a threat to survival.

For years I felt what I perceived to be fear, so much so that I finally began to write about it in hopes of exorcising or at least understanding the emotion—if it is an emotion.

Only recently I've concluded that much of what I labeled fear can more appropriately be called anxiety. Anxiety is also a survival mechanism, but one that we all share. Anxiety sparks the alertness and alacrity of the other fight-or-flee members of the animal kingdom.

Fear has always had a bad press. To be "cowardly" is disdained in our branch of mammalian society, which reserves its praise for fighting rather than fleeing. It is more acceptable to be aware of potential or present danger. Thus I take comfort in being an anxious individual rather than a timid soul.

It's lucky for me I didn't reach such conclusions as a teenager, or else I'd probably never have written what I did. Nor would I be writing this introduction today.

Actually, I have no real credentials for doing so. I'm not a psychotherapist and have never undergone analysis. I didn't major in psychology for many reasons, one being that I never attended college. At seventeen it was already too late for psychotherapy to come to my rescue; I was already a professional writer, and there's no cure for that. I was writing stories that dealt with fear in psychological terms, even though at that time I didn't know the difference between Sigmund Jung and Carl Freud.

Apparently some portion of my work has evoked fear amongst readers, auditors, and viewers over the years, and if so, I've accomplished part of what I set out to do. What I didn't achieve was a true understanding of what I worked with; I lacked a genuine comprehension of fear. But then you don't have to be a nuclear physicist in order to fire a warhead. All you need to know is how to press the right button.

It's been a long time since I began raising hackles for fun and profit. And while there's still a lot to learn, I did tap into a few of the factors governing fear: apprehension, alarm, dread, terror, horror, trepidation, and whatever else can be dredged out of the thesaurus or the darkest depths of the human psyche. But the most significant discovery I've made about fear is that there's a lot more of it around these days than ever before.

Anxieties have abounded over the past half century, involving everything from crime in the streets to weaponry in the skies. The exact moment when these anxieties escalated into full-fledged fears is difficult to determine, but there's little doubt that the depressing elevation has taken place. Today it's not just Russia that has the power to destroy a nation. The criminal in the streets has become an increasing threat to us everwhere, including in our own home. Terrorists destroy innocents at will and at random. Fifty years ago the serial killer was an exotic rarity. Parents were never worried that their youngsters might be murdered by other youngsters in the schoolyard or the classroom, or steal cars and guns for drive-by shootings. Customers weren't afraid that the drugs they bought at the corner drugstore might be poisoned. There was no talk of the greenhouse effect or nuclear waste; certainly no concern that we could become victims of cancers caused by the very air we breathe.

And for every danger we did recognize there was a ready form of protection. The government stood between us and the threat of thermonuclear war, the police would deal with the "criminal element," Mommy and Daddy were there for their kids to run to, and of course there was always the ultimate haven of religion.

Today our faith in government has eroded, and police protection is as uncertain as the prompt arrival of an ambulance or fire truck after dialing 911. The "criminal element" is not confined to mean streets nor in the insufficient number of penal facilities. In many households Mommy has to work, and there is no Daddy. So no wonder parents *are* concerned. No wonder that Mommy and Daddy (whoever and wherever he is) have come to place less and less reliance on each other. Families can no longer be relied upon as assured sources of security; the only stable family relationship remaining is the one between Cain and Abel. Religion seems to have lost its power to heal and console. Many now seek salvation in substance abuse; the young snort or shoot up against the fear of shoot-outs, their parents pop prescription pills, the elderly trip out on tranquilizers, in or out of Bedpan Heaven.

Thus fear proliferates and seemingly prevails. At just what point it will become uncontrollable is anyone's guess. But if it does, present hallucinogenic home remedies will be ineffective; there is no panacea for panic.

Now most of us continue to cope as best we can. But there's a segment of society that cannot cope with a problem worse than anxiety, fear, and panic combined. These people are suffering from phobias.

According to definition, a phobia is an obsessive, persistent, unrealistic fear. Its cause, psychiatry tells us, is the displacing of internal unconscious conflict to an external object symbolically related to the concept.

If defining displacement is a problem, the same sources explain it as the unconscious transference of an emotion from an original object to a more acceptable substitute.

The most common and simplistic example, I suppose, would be a fear originally connected with penises that has been transferred to herpetophobia, the fear of snakes.

Phallic symbolism is easy enough to interpret in this instance. But what obvious counterparts can be found in nomatophobia, arithmophobia, or chronophobia—just three example out of the scores of phobic states that have been observed and categorized? Why would anyone be obsessed with fears of names, numbers, or the concept of time? How and where did the fright originate in the ordinary world?

These are the questions that have impelled the writers included in this anthology to explore the mind-set of phobias' victims, people who dwell in dread, entangled in the toils of inexplicable terrors.

By so doing, they are perhaps coming to terms with their own fears—and allowing you to confront your private

Introduction

apprehensions. There are few of us who can truthfully claim complete freedom from fears that seemingly have little or no foundation in reality. But for the most part, we reserve our reactions to appropriate phenomena such as fire, flood, earthquakes, and other natural disasters; we respond to the danger of disease germs, certain forms of insect and animal life, poisonous or contaminated food and drink. Such concerns are cautionary, not compulsive; we do not live in a world of imaginary perils.

Again we return to fundamental questions of why and how phobias take possession of seemingly ordinary people in ordinary situations—a possession that at times appears to be almost demonic. "Displacement" is a very scientific-sounding label, but is it enough to explain the plight of tens of thousands of bedeviled phobics who create their own private hells?

Invading these private hells constitutes a challenge in itself—one that psychiatry still confronts with some uncertainty.

Exploring and mapping those hells is an even more formidable task. The time-honored tools of the trade may not do the job.

Recently released studies indicate that fear may have a physiological basis in a genetic deficiency. Plainly put, they posit that some people suffer apprehension for lack of a gene that could supply them with the proper endocrinological antidote. In other words, cowardice is a matter of chemistry.

Should this prove to be the case, then courage must be chemical, too. Many flags must stop their waving if battlefield heroes are merely responding to the same mindless glandular stimulus as the cape buffalo. And conversely, the fearful are no more psychologically responsible for their reactions than the antelope whose lack of a particular genetic endowment causes it to retreat from what the buffalo would attack.

All of which serves only to complicate the situation for those who attempt any scientific approach to the study of phobia. Since first categorized, more than two thousand different phobias have been distinguished and discussed by supposedly qualified medical authorities. If we cautiously reject both the expertise of the practitioners and the validity of their findings in many cases, there still remains a striking unanimity in the description of symptoms.

And even if we extend skepticism to its extreme and arbitrarily toss out ninety percent of those two thousand different classifications, we are still confronting two hundred separate and distinct phobias, observed over the course of the past century in tens of thousands of patients from all parts of the world, united only in the similarity of their dreads.

Bear in mind also that these instances represent only a tiny fraction of a terrified total who never sought aid from or were observed by psychotherapists.

With so little known, mental health practitioners can scarcely be said to have entered the phobics' private hells; indeed, from where they stand, they're barely beginning to feel the heat.

But their plight is mild when compared to that of the writers who contributed to this anthology. These talents do more than merely brave such hells—they must first *create* them. Then they enter the minds where terror reigns, the bodies shackled and imprisoned by fear.

This, I assure you, calls for a great deal of courage.

It is not pleasant to sit alone in a room and force oneself to focus upon the fantasies of the disturbed and the distraught—to see what they see, or imagine they see—to feel what they feel and, in effect, do what they do. While watching them, one temporarily *becomes* them. It's not a task for the timid. But with artistry and insight, that is what the authors in this anthology have dared to do, and skillfully so.

In so doing they are inviting us to accompany them on a journey into realms where hallucination is often translated into grim reality. Some of the steps you take will lead to agitation and torment; some, hopefully, to grateful relief in the recognition that there are perhaps certain secret and suppressed fears that do not haunt you alone. The control of

Introduction

such fears is aided by understanding—an understanding gained from those who unhappily lack the capacity to cope with them.

The authors in this anthology share this rare gift of understanding, but it's not necessarily the type of gift that comes wrapped in a pretty pink ribbon. To fathom the fears of others one must first confront one's own, and this is a price all who are represented here have paid. The fantastic tales they tell attest to their talent, but the sources of these stories come from within the deepest recesses of the human psyche. To write horror one must recognize its face, and for that purpose the tool with the closest cutting edge is the mirror.

Franklin Roosevelt's "nothing to fear but fear itself" is applicable to a common phenomenon known as *phobophobia.*

Many of us who pride ourselves on being quite impervious to imaginary perils nevertheless acknowledge the threat of succumbing to some phobia. If the stories that follow in these pages can offer insight and understanding to dissipate such apprehensions, then they will have served a secondary purpose.

But wait—does this mean that the gifted men and women who wrote them had another intention as well? Does it mean that their *primary* goal in creating these tales was to entangle your minds and emotions with those of the terrified victims they bring so vividly to life? Is it possible that their aim was to ensnare you in a web of fear until the illusions of their stories take on a life of their own? Did they actually set out with the purpose of frightening you with accounts of diabolical deeds and dreads? In a word, are they trying to scare you?

I'm afraid so.

PHOBIAS

A FEAR OF DEAD THINGS

Andrew Klavan

On Friday evening Dr. Lawrence Rothman found a dead mouse in the bread cupboard and thought of Curtis Zane. The mouse lay curled on its side, the gray fur bristling on its back. There was no sign of what had killed it. Rothman felt a little hitch of disgust in his throat and withdrew his hand—he'd been reaching for the package of wheat bread when he saw it. His first instinct was just to shut the cupboard door again and pretend he'd never found the thing. He could work around it for the rest of the weekend easily enough. On Monday Lily, the cleaning woman, would come in and take care of it for him.

But again he thought of his new patient. He thought of Curtis Zane.

Zane had come into the Manhattan office just that morning, at the end of the morning, the last session before noon. He was a man in his early forties with steady eyes and an iron line of jaw. Good-looking, Rothman thought; dominant-looking; the kind of man women find attractive. Zane said he lived in the Village and owned and operated a

1

Andrew Klavan

trade magazine out of a loft down in SoHo. He managed
about seven people, he said, give or take a few steady
freelancers. He did not seem nervous as he talked, but
crossed his legs at the knee with decision and steepled his
fingers quietly under his dimpled chin. And when Dr.
Rothman asked him what the problem was he explained it
clearly in a firm, deep voice. Some of them liked to play it
that way, Rothman thought: as one professional to another.

"I have," Zane said, "a fear of dead things." He waved
one hand as if it annoyed him, as if it were flies. "Irrational,
terrible," he said. "Even paralyzing sometimes. Bugs—
dead bugs—birds, mice. Any kind of . . . *corpse* at all. I
can't even take my clothes down to the washers in my
building because there are always roaches, dead roaches, in
the basement, and . . ." Here, Rothman noticed with some
satisfaction, Zane could not pull off an ironic smile. A
shudder took him instead across the shoulders. "I can't
tolerate the sight of them."

Behind his desk Rothman sat still, his hands in his lap, his
face impassive. He let the silence stretch way past the
comfort level. But Zane was tough enough for that. He
waited it out. At last Rothman said, "Anything else? Are you
hypochondriacal? Are you afraid of dying yourself? Of
becoming, I mean, one of these dead things?"

Zane appeared to give this some thought. Then he shook
his head briskly. "No. No." And he broke into a rakish grin,
one side of his mouth going up, one eyebrow lowering. "I
guess that sounds kind of funny. But I've often thought that
people react more to the symbols of things than to the things
themselves. I mean, we react more to things—and people,
too—according to what they mean to us instead of what
they really are. Don't you think?" He laughed. "Anyway, it
would explain why people vote for the politicians they do.
And why they fall in love with the people they fall in love
with, too."

Rothman hoped his face remained impassive. He was
afraid he might have given way to a little pucker of distaste.
Already, he found, he disliked this man for some reason. His
bush-league insights, maybe, or maybe his take-charge atti-

2

tude; he wasn't sure. Whatever it was, Zane had set something nervous and unpleasant squirreling around in his stomach. Rothman wanted to move away from him. He wanted to swivel in his chair away from the confidence of Zane's gaze and jaw and gesture. He had to remind himself that he, Rothman, was the doctor; he was in charge. It was Zane who had the problem, who had come to him for help.

Rothman let out a controlled breath. Maybe he could just refer the man to someone else, he thought. He could say he wanted to send him to someone who "specialized in phobias," or some crap like that.

"I guess that's what psychiatry is all about, isn't it?" Zane went on, one guy to another, magazine-guy to psychiatrist-guy. "You show people what things symbolize to them—what other people symbolize to them. You tell them: Your wife represents your mother, your car represents your cock, and all that—and then they can get around their confused reactions, get down to the business of dealing with things as they really are. If things really are anything, that is." He grinned that pirate grin again. Before he could stop himself, Rothman squirmed a little in his chair. "I guess that's the problem right there. What if the symbols are the only reason we react in the first place: Your wife's your mother, your car's your cock. What if things in themselves, people in themselves, don't mean a damn thing to us, don't really exist for us at all?"

"I think for now," Dr. Rothman said, clearing his throat, "we should meet with each other once a week."

And so he tackled the mouse, the dead mouse, himself. He did not leave it for the cleaning woman. Because he was still the doctor here. He was not the one with the problem. Even if he was thick at the middle where Curtis Zane was trim and taut. Even if he was balding where Zane had wavy salt-and-pepper hair. Even if his shaggy, curly black beard did not entirely hide the face of the high school weakling who, in high school, he had been. . . . Even so, it was Zane who had come to *him* for help, not the other way around. So he swept the dead mouse out of the cupboard and into a dustpan. Then, quick, quick, quick, holding the dustpan as far away from him as he could, he carried the thing to the kitchen garbage can and dumped it in. Turning his face away, he lifted the garbage bag out of the can. Twisted it, tied it shut. Carried it, his face still averted, down the connecting hallway into the garage. And there he dumped it in the can and clamped the lid down tight. And that, he thought, dusting his hands off, was that.

Then he made himself a dinner of eggs and toast. Then he washed the dishes and put them away. And then he went to bed. And then he started to cry.

Actually, he started to sob. Actually, to bawl was probably the best way to describe it. Clutching his pillow, biting, gnawing the corner of it to keep from making those raw, gasping sounds he hated himself for. He cried as he had cried almost every night since Gerry had left him. Not only because she'd left him, although he did believe he loved her, but also, more specifically, because she'd left him for another man.

"I'm sorry, Lawrence, it was just something that happened. I met him through work. . . ." Gerry was a designer for a Guatemalan clothing manufacturer, so Rothman had immediately imagined her tilting limply against the chest of some cocky Latin, some casually smoldering caballero who was quietly amused at how easily the wives of these weak Yanquis . . .

"Don't," he'd said to her quickly. "You don't have to tell me. In fact, really, I don't want to know."

And Gerry fell quiet at once. Her eyes were damp with sympathy. She was genuinely forlorn for him. All in all, in fact, she was excruciatingly kind. Which only made Rothman choke on it the more. Because enough was said, with all her kindness, for him to get the idea. He listened for it. He was trained to catch it. "It wasn't you," she told him. "It was me, it was marriage, I don't know. There was always something *missing* for me. I was just . . . *unsatisfied* somehow. As if some part of me were always *unfulfilled* . . ." Gently she said these things. As if to comfort him. As if she were doing this to him with all the pity in the world. Like the nurse at his castration.

Well, he knew, with his history, it was bound to hit him hard. People under stress tend to crack along their fault lines, after all. But still, this nightly weeping—Jesus, after fifteen years of analysis, it made him doubt—lying there, twisting there, chawing on that pillow corner—made him doubt not only his own mental health, but the value of his entire profession.

And snuff, snuff, snuff, he went, his pillow sopping.

"Now when you experience this fear," he said, "when you see a dead cockroach in the laundry room, for instance, does anything come to mind, does it remind you of anything in particular?"

It was Friday again, and there, again, sat Zane. Aggressively thoughtful in the patient's chair. *Battling* his problem, *wrestling* with it, using strategy, brain power.

"Well, obviously, I've considered this a lot. I mean, my childhood. Right? That's what you're talking about. I've tried to figure out what it has to do with all this. I mean, it sure wasn't a very happy childhood. In fact, I would say it was downright unhappy."

"All right," said Rothman, encouraging him with a nod, with a mild roll of his hand—his practiced gestures. He was going through the motions to hide his dislike of the man.

"Right." And Zane actually began ticking it—his childhood—off on his fingers. "My father. A nobody. Some sort of factotum for the phone company. A gray man. Gray, gray man. Nobody." Finger two. "My mother. She just disdained him. She was merciless about what a failure, what a nobody, he was. A mean, snarling person. She terrified me." Three. "She cheated on him. The milkman, the mailman, the neighbors. Anyone. Everyone in town knew it but Dad. Maybe he knew it, too."

"Did you know it?" Rothman asked.

"Oh, yeah. Oh, yeah. I was downstairs in the playroom half the time it was going on. Mom made me promise not to tell. Said she'd cut my dick off." His pirate grin was quick, but just a little pallid this time. "I hope I'm not making your job too easy for you."

Rothman stroked his beard, hiding a small smile. He had to admit he was gratified by that last stroke, "making your job too easy for you," the hostility in it. For all this brusque display, the finger-ticking, the macho stuff, Zane was ashamed of the sordidness of his early life. He resented the fact that it had to come out like this. But, thought Rothman, stroking away, it always did in the end, didn't it? You got past the shell of people, the shape of them, their defensive loveliness or manliness, their sweetness, their courage, their wit—and there was always just a tarry hell of one kind or another, the shapeless gunk of pain held together by those defenses into something like a human form. There was no hiding it from him, not over the long run. It always spilled out onto his desk eventually. Bubbling, boiling with the anguish of childhood. Sooner or later. He just had to wait for it.

He did wait. And this time the silence worked. Zane pushed ahead bitterly. "She left anyway, my mother, when I was around eleven. My father had a sister I stayed with during the day, and there were baby-sitters. Just housekeepers, really. My mother I never saw again."

Dr. Rothman closed his eyes and shook his head in his usual gesture of uncommitted sympathy. He thought: This guy is going to need the full course, all right, five days a week by the time he's finished. He felt a strange mixture of satisfaction and discomfort at that.

"That's when I began to kill things," Zane said.

Rothman's eyes came open. He looked at the man across his desk, through the frame made by the upright pens in the calendar set Gerry had given him.

"Little things," Zane went on, with merely a rueful shake of his handsome head. "I remember I got an old board once and nailed some earthworms to it. My father liked to go fishing sometimes, and he said they didn't feel any pain, worms, when you put the hook in them. But they do, you know. And . . . what else? I coated a firecracker with sugar once, laid it near an anthill, and waited until it was crawling with ants, then . . ." An embarrassed shrug.

"Any . . ." Rothman cleared his throat. He'd heard this sort of thing before, often—but that didn't help somehow, not this time, not with Zane. "Anything else?"

"A squirrel. Once. Shot it with a BB gun. Stunned it. Then stepped on its head."

"Any . . ." He should have kept at him. He should have asked the question again. But he didn't. He coughed into his fist. "How did this make you feel?" he asked after a while.

"Well . . . not bad or anything, not guilty, at least not that I'm aware of." Zane frowned, considering. "I think it made me feel . . . calm, more than anything. Sort of firmed up inside. I mean, maybe it sounds crazy, but I think it worked as a kind of therapy for me. After it was over I always felt very clearheaded. Strong, directed. And, in most ways, I've been like that ever since." A manly chuckle here. "It's the secret of my success, I think. That attitude. It's always made me very popular, anyway. Especially with women. I always have been very, very popular with women." And the corners of his eyes crinkled handsomely as he gave Rothman a wink. "But I guess you know how that is," he said. "Right?"

Rothman wasn't sure why he kept coming up to the Connecticut house every weekend. The summer was long over, and this humorless, slate October they were having— it seemed to perch on the roof of the place like a great gray crow, with outspread wings the length and width and heaviness of the sky. Gerry was not here now to make a fire for, to pour a brandy for. And all their friends, their laughing houseguests, had turned out to be mostly her friends in the end. And even his happy memories of those old times were ruined for him, knowing that only he'd been happy then, and she . . . "dissatisfied," "unfulfilled." That night, that Friday night, he sat at the dining room table again, alone again, eating his scrambled eggs again, and wondered why he bothered to come here at all anymore. To sit here, mashing his eggs dully, like a toothless old man, a sexless old man. Reading his journals and his Xeroxed articles with distant interest and a muzzy mind. After a while he glanced up and just fell to empty gazing. Not much in the journals that could help him anyway, he thought. Necrophobia—the fear of dead things—was common enough, but it rarely became very intense or crippling. It hadn't inspired any massive amounts of literature, that was for sure. A few up-to-date articles, a couple of case histories, but most of the stuff he found was included in pieces that covered phobias in general. ". . . connected to hypochondria and the fear of death . . ." they said. ". . . associated with sometimes unrelated childhood traumas . . ." Nothing that would guide him in a specific case like this. He gazed out through the picture window at the backyard. He noticed he had neglected to have the swimming pool covered. The water was dark and brackish now, the dead leaves floating in it. A sad sight, a pool in autumn. He sighed, mashing the last of his eggs.

When he was done he carried his plates into the kitchen. He was even walking, shuffling, like an old man now. He'd have to remember to go out and buy himself a pair of baggy pants in the morning, and a flannel shirt. He scraped the plates into the kitchen garbage and rinsed them off. He tied the garbage bag and carried it down the hall to the garage. He flicked on the light and moved to the garbage can. He pried off the lid.

And he cried out. He jumped back.

There was a raccoon in there. Twisted on the bottom of the can. Dead. Its eyes glassy in their mask. Its pink tongue dangling over its bared teeth.

"Jesus," Rothman said. The smell had just now reached him. It was not bad yet. Only a faint, faintly tangy unpleasantness in the air. But it made him think of trash in the summertime gutters. Something that had lived was turning into trash.

Rothman set his garbage bag down hard. He put his hands on his hips and bent over, breathing in and out deeply. He had to fight to keep his disgust from turning into nausea. But he wouldn't even think of shirking this. He would not let it become a problem for him. The thing had crawled in there to get at his garbage, gotten itself trapped, and starved to death; now he had to remove it, that was all.

And in some ways it turned out to be easier than the mouse. All he had to do was get a fresh bag, fit it over the opening of the can, and then upend the can on top of it. The raccoon tumbled right down into the bag, although it did make an unpleasantly soft *phlump* as it hit the garage floor. He carried the bag down to the edge of the woods and squeezed in a little past the trees, brushing away the branches he couldn't make out in the dark. He set the bag down and stepped back from it. Bent over, reached out. Pinched the bottom corner of plastic delicately between thumb and forefinger, careful not to touch anything, any trace of any part of the thing that was inside. And then he lifted the corner, his arm outstretched, and the coon plopped onto the forest floor. Barely even visible, lying there in the night. And the lovable little creatures of the forest could just take care of the rest.

The nauseous jolt of first finding the thing came back to him later, though. That Friday, the session before noon. Even ensconced in his chair with its arms around him and its high wings shielding his head. Even with the stolid bulwark of the desk between him and Zane. The sensation returned, and he felt his muscles go tight and had to lay his finger across his mouth to cover his lips' working. He watched Zane but remembered finding the raccoon. He saw Zane's crags and jawline and flashing eyes, all the tics of his masculinity. . . .

That's when I began to kill things.

And he thought of walking into the garage again, of prying off the lid of the can.

I pried off the lid of the can, he thought.

"Doctor? Are you listening?" Zane said.

Rothman, of course, had been asked this far too often to be caught out. He answered smoothly, "Yes, I'm listening. Just go on," and he forced himself to pay attention.

Zane gave a nod and soldiered ahead. "All right. It happened Wednesday. I was coming home from *Borderlines*

—that's the name of my magazine. I was walking home, which is what I usually do. It was around eight o'clock, a little later. I was feeling fine. Striding along. Came around the corner at Fifth Avenue and Twelfth. And there was . . . God, it's ridiculous."

Rothman lowered his hands to his lap, really interested now. *I pried off* . . . he thought. But he forced his mind clear. "There was what?"

"This roach. This cockroach. One of those real New York specials, about the size of Staten Island."

"And it was dead," said Rothman when Zane paused.

"Yeah." Zane rubbed the back of his neck. "It really got me, too. I mean, normally, you know, I might've crossed the street, I might've even turned back and gone around to Sixth to avoid it. I mean, if I'd been with someone, I'm sure I would've just forced myself to look away, just stepped right over it so they wouldn't notice. But this time . . . No. Jesus. I don't know what it was. Maybe because I've been coming here, you know, exposing my feelings, maybe I was more sensitive to it than usual. But I tell you, Doc, it stopped me cold. I felt like the blood was draining right out of my feet, right into the sidewalk, I felt like I was glued to the sidewalk. I couldn't move. Backward or forward. I was that terrified. I just stood there. With the cold sweat all over my face. Staring at the thing. I couldn't even look away. It must've been—I don't know—minutes, three, five minutes before I . . . ran for it. I mean *fled*. Just went scampering back to Fifth, to that café around the corner there. I had to inhale a couple of martinis before I could even bring myself to go around the other way."

Rothman kept his posture relaxed, but he felt the juice going through him. He felt wired and sick, but his patented sympathetic-yet-impassive tone came automatically. "What were your associations? During those three to five minutes when you were confronting the dead roach. Were there any memories, any thoughts that came to you?"

Zane seemed to consider the question. And as Rothman watched, his stomach churning, Zane's attention seemed to drift away, his gaze to drift away to some lower corner of the empty air. "I don't know," he said, and his voice was dreamy, hollow. "I guess . . . I guess I thought . . . that *this* is what we are. You know? That everything else is just . . . bullshit. That it's just, like, some kind of play or something. Walking around, pretending to be somebodies, pretending to . . . sympathize with each other, and love each other, and live. It's like some kind of puppet show, a puppet show done with corpses. People are all just these corpses jerking around according to a pattern of electric pulses in their brains. Smiling and saying things matter, and saying they want cream in their coffee and will vote Democratic and love you, when all the time they're just these . . . things. These animated things. Temporarily animated things."

It was long seconds—silent seconds—before Rothman realized he was staring at the man, just staring at him, all queasy and electrified, his mouth sour and dry. He had to wet his lips before he could speak again. "And you're afraid of that," he said hoarsely, finally. "You're afraid that the people who . . . who love you will soon become . . . inanimate things. Dead things."

"Yes." In that mesmerized voice, that dead voice.

Rothman leaned forward in his chair, leaned far enough to rest one arm upon the table, and yet leaned carefully, as if closing in on something that might turn suddenly, that might strike out. "You know," he said, "in my business, we believe that the thing you fear is also the thing you secretly . . . desire."

It was another moment or so before this reached him, Zane. Then he blinked and came to himself. He raised his eyes to Rothman's. He smiled.

"Yes," he said softly.

That night—that night was hell. The house was hell that night. Rothman actually searched the place when he came in. He couldn't believe he was doing it. He wouldn't admit he was doing it, but the moment he came in he put his overnight bag down and went through the rooms. Cautiously opening the cupboards in the kitchen, kneeling on the living room floor to peer under the couch and the chairs. He checked the garage and the garbage cans there, the bathrooms and the medicine chest. He did not think, How could it have gotten in, if I pried off the lid? And he didn't think: She met him through work. That's what she told me. She met him through work. But while the night outside was very still, and there was no wind and there were no noises, he sensed a lowering urgency in the ink-blue dark, a sere, severe, almost imperious call to panic. At the windows, at the spaces in the sashes where the cool seeped in, he sensed it, it reached him. He could not keep from moving, moving from room to room, searching room after room until—well, until he just ran out of places. Until, that is, he couldn't put the real thing off any longer. And then he wound up in the bedroom, as he knew he would, seated with slumped shoulders on the edge of the double bed, looking at the phone. Glaring sullenly at the phone.

He had used the phone in his office after Zane left that afternoon. He had done it quickly, before Zane had a chance to get back to his magazine, to *Borderlines*. He had called *Borderlines*. A young woman answered cheerfully. Excuse me, Rothman had said, but just what sort of magazine is this exactly? And cheerfully the young woman had read it off to him: It's the magazine of the fashion and fabric trade between the Americas. Thank you, he had said. And he had hung up.

I met him through work. It was just something that happened. . . .

But there was no shock to it. He didn't go reeling backward, openmouthed, hand to brow. A diffuse instinct simply coalesced, and he had sat then as he was sitting now, sulking over the phone. Sulking and thinking: I'm not actually going to call her, obviously. Thinking: It's ridiculous. Thinking: A neurotic reaction. A sense of inadequacy. Manifestations in fantasy . . . and so on. Which was exactly why the night became hell for him, driving up to the house, reaching the house, standing in front of the house in the imperious ink-blue chill. The house, that night, was hell because there might be . . . *proof* in there. He didn't quite say it to himself. But that pressure of panic from the dark, that's what it was: He knew there might be proof, that there *would* be proof if he was right about it. In the cupboards, in the garbage can, under the chairs. Somewhere. And he couldn't keep from searching.

And afterward, when he had found nothing, nothing anywhere, he felt no relief. He simply sat on the edge of the bed with his options exhausted, and he glared at the phone, without proof, just knowing. He sat by the pillows into which he'd cried, sobbed and cried through the hours night on night until he was humiliated even before himself. He sat and sulked until it began to dawn on him—in one of those cloudy sort of half dawns that you don't even notice coming, that becomes just day after a while all unannounced—that he was not going to call her. That he was damned if he was, he, the more wounded party. He was going to get up and put his pajamas on instead, that's what. He was going to slide under the covers. He was going to lie there without tears. He was going to sleep, all comfy, in this sanctuary of his secret miseries—which was also, he realized now, the temple of his high and terrible rage.

In the morning he made himself a mug of coffee and took it out onto the deck. He sipped it, looking over the back-yard, and he saw the deer floating in the pool. He wondered, though only briefly, if he could have the police remove it for him. It must've fallen in and drowned, he would tell them, and he pictured its forelegs thrashing in the water as its sleek, graceful head went down.

The creature's corpse looked bloated and gaping, he noticed, as if it had been in there for days and days.

Curtis Zane did not come to his next appointment, and the last time Dr. Rothman saw him was that evening on Park Avenue as he was walking to his car. The cold was really bitter now. The doctor's ungainly figure was hunched up inside his overcoat. His bulbous nose was red and runny. His chin and beard were pressed down against his chest. He was thinking about Zane, naturally enough, and about the deer in the pool.

It had been easy for him to get rid of the deer, emotionally easy, and he thought that was strange. He had gone to the hardware store for a rope and gloves, but he'd still had to grapple with the creature in the end—and yet he hadn't really cared. He'd grabbed hold of the deer's left foreleg right where it joined the torso, and he'd felt the yield of the flesh through his gloves, felt the flesh bloated drum tight under the sodden fur. The trek down into the woods had been breathless work, but easy, not terrible at all—and that just seemed very strange to him; he had been thinking about it a lot all week. All week, in fact, it had been the same. The thing that was happening, that was going to happen: It was not dreadful to him, not terrible. It was all just very, very strange, and strangely unmoving, as if he had eased without noticing it into an inner state of gray, a state like ashes. It reminded him of that moment by the phone. When he had lapsed so gently into the knowledge that he would not call her. Just as gently, maybe even at the exact same moment, he seemed also to have glided through the borders of something essential, something that had seemed solid but was really only mist. It seemed to him, after long consideration, that he had stepped out of the bubble of his central self, and it had burst, silently, and he had become . . . ashes, walking. . . .

A movement to the side of him made him look up. He stopped, panting. In a doorway, there was Zane.

The man looked robust enough, but dreamy. In a charcoal overcoat, his salt-and-pepper hair stirred by the wind, he cut his usual substantial figure. But just his unexpected presence there, hard to believe, and maybe also his distant smile made Rothman blink. He confronted his patient with no knowable emotion. He just sniffled and waited and wiped his nose with his glove.

"Look," said Zane. He held his hand out. "Look."

Rothman didn't look down right away. He would have liked not to have looked down at all, but the man was standing there, holding his hand out, and so he did, finally.

A large cockroach lay in Zane's palm, lay on its back, its six legs pointed upward, shivering, probably with the wind.

A Fear of Dead Things

Rothman grimaced with distaste and turned away.

"Look," said Zane. "I'm better now."

Rothman hurried on up the avenue.

Small and hunkered in the indifferent dark, the house stood before him when he stepped from his car. Not horrible, not even mysterious. Just a container really, he realized; four walls and a roof built around the empty air. As he came up the walk he could muster only the most miserable sort of suspense: the fear of being startled. And even that much surprise seemed unlikely to him. He let himself in through the front door and headed up the stairs at once.

He turned on the stair light and the upstairs hall light as he went, but the bedroom was still almost completely dark when he came into the doorway. He reached around the sill nervously and snapped the light on in there.

He did start a little when he saw her. And yet she lay in a natural position in the bed, just as she might have lain when they were living together. The covers were pulled up almost to her throat to hide her nakedness. One arm was flung out over her husband's pillow, one rested, a little stiff and clawlike, atop the counterpane. Her head was turned to the side, her black hair trailing out in back. Her eyelids, a little purple in the gray face, were gently closed as if she were sleeping.

For a minute or two Rothman stood there heavily, observing her with a sullen, sidelong look. But even then some unformed energy, not quite excitement or fear or rage, was urging him to move, to move now, move anywhere, so that he seemed to himself at once inanimate and a creature of pure behavior. He felt, that is, like a thing, but like a thing doomed to take action.

He went back downstairs and headed out to the garage to get the shovel.

SNAKES

Jane Yolen

IT'S SNAKES WITH ME," MAVIS SAID, "THOUGH FOR THE LIFE OF me I can't think why."

"Sublimation," her cousin Peg volunteered in a voice that made it sound like a deadly disease, cancer or AIDS.

"No," Mavis said absolutely. "I'm not afraid of snakelike things. Not ropes or worms or spaghetti or—"

George looked alert at last. "What about lizards?"

"Ugh!" Peg shivered dramatically. "Snakes with legs."

"No." Mavis was thoughtful. "I rather like lizards. It's the legs, actually."

"Penises, then," Sandy pronounced.

"She rather likes them, too!" said George.

Peg giggled. "Mavis—or Sandy?"

"Both!" Sandy's boyfriend Bill said.

They all laughed then, even Jack, though his laughter was a bit hollow and lasted much longer than anyone else's, as if he had something to prove. Peg wondered briefly, and not for the first time, if Mavis had been unfaithful to him. As a girl Mavis had never stuck with any one boy.

Snakes

They were at that time in a party when conversation has run down and Peg introduced games as a last desperate measure to keep everyone occupied and away from the liquor, especially George. She had suggested Phobias, and they had taken to it eagerly. Well, at least the women had.

"No," Mavis said, "just snakes. And I can't think why."

"Me, too," Sandy said airily, making them wonder if she was just being supportive as usual. After all, she had also confessed to hating spiders like Peg and bees like Jack. "Can't even watch TV shows with snakes on them. Remember that opening of 'I, Claudius,' Bill?" She said this to her boyfriend, but it was obviously meant for all of them. "Remember? Horrible!"

"I can't even look at their pictures in books," Mavis said quietly, but at that point the only one who heard her was Jack.

Now if this had been a murder mystery, Jack would have been sitting quietly in the armchair, glass in hand, contemplating ways to import snakes, either deadly poisonous ones like mambas into their bedroom to bite her, or ordinary ones because Mavis had a heart condition and if he dropped it into her bath she would be frightened to death. Or if this were the start of a horror story, the gigantic serpent Ourorobous would have been coiled up inside the walls ready to devour the entire party except for Mavis, whose phobia had called it up. Or if a fantasy, Mavis would descend into a kind of madness in which she saw everyone about her changing inexorably into snakes.

But it was simply a party game, and Mavis, on the way home in the car later, remarked to her husband, "I am really tired of Peg and her games. I never thought I'd say it. I mean, we've been best friends forever, as well as cousins."

"She's harmless," Jack said. "And she does have her hands full with George."

"He's better, actually."

"He won't be better unless he stops drinking altogether. It's that kind of disease." Jack had always been a bit of a prig.

17

They drove on a little further in silence, each thinking about George in a particular way, and neither of them being very kind to him, when Mavis cried: "Jack—look out!"

He swerved to avoid what they both thought was merely a bag of garbage on the road, but when they had gone a bit further Mavis said, "Jack . . ." There was a tenderness in her tone.

"I know. I know." He backed up slowly.

The bag had moved. It was closer to the side of the road, and there was no wind.

Jack backed the car up until his headlights illumined what was now lying in the roadside gully. Getting out, he signaled Mavis to stay in the car. But she didn't pay any attention as she rummaged around in the glove compartment for the flashlight. As soon as she found it she jumped out of the car and ran toward Jack and the gully. But she kept her eyes in a squint so as not to have to look directly at the body, for that was what it was, a body in a shapeless black coat and not a bag of garbage at all.

When they were both close enough and Mavis shone the light directly down on him, the man rolled over and sat up. He had a gun in his hand. Giggling, he said, "I'm hijacking you to Cuba."

"We don't want to go to Cuba," Mavis said. She turned to her husband. "Jack—we don't want to go to Cuba."

"He's drunk," Jack pronounced. "Or worse—stoned."

"Both," the man said. "But I still want to go to Cuba."

"Why Cuba?" Mavis said, trying to sound reasonable. "Why not Miami?"

"Too many Cubans there," the man said, and he giggled again. "And I am taking the lady with me. I like her sense of humor."

"Jack," Mavis cried.

Jack began to protest, though to Mavis it all sounded rather pro forma. Nevertheless, the man with the gun took it as a threat. He stood unsteadily and stepped out of the gully. In the middle of Jack's second round of protests the man hit him on the head with the gun. Jack fell down at once and didn't get up again. Struck speechless, Mavis couldn't tell—because the flashlight in her hand was beginning to shake—whether he was just hurt or dead. Or faking. She knew he had a very thick skull.

"Come on, funny lady," the man said, and he grabbed her arm.

"Don't—" she began, but the hand on her arm seemed to have choked off her ability to talk, as if he had put his hand on her throat rather than her arm. Sweat broke out on her forehead, and she could feel her heart racing, racing. She began to shake.

He dragged her toward the car, forcing her to climb over the driver's seat to get to her own. Her new silk print dress caught on the gearshift and tore down the side. It seemed to tear her throat open, too.

"Damn," she whispered.

"What did you say?" He no longer seemed drunk or high—just horribly menacing.

"Damn," she whispered again.

"Damn—meet Don." He giggled, as if she had just introduced herself.

Mavis began to cry, but silently. Her heart stopped racing and seemed to slow down. In fact, *everything* seemed to slow down. She heard his voice as if it were running on thirty-three instead of seventy-eight.

The man put the car into reverse and started to back out when Mavis, with a great and slow effort, reached over for the keys. The man slammed on the brakes and backhanded her expertly, and when she sank against the door, her cheek stinging, time began to go normally again. He gave another of his awful giggles and reached for the front of her dress.

"Don't," she said, clearly this time, but he didn't listen. He ripped the front of her dress down to her waist, then climbed over the gearshift to crouch on top of her. She could feel him grow hard against her, could feel his hand reaching under to unzip his pants.

Frantically out of control, almost ecstatic in her horror, she realized she still held the flashlight in her right hand. She clubbed him hard three times, and when he sank down she pushed him off. The gun lay on the floor where he'd dropped it. She thumbed off the safety and emptied it six times into him. Then she clubbed the back of his head, his shoulders, and especially his hands and the fingers that had touched her. Touched her. Touched her. If she had had the energy, she would have turned him over and hit him—there—as well. But she was suddenly weak. Dropping the gun, she just settled back against the car door and had a good loud cry.

Eventually Jack stumbled out of the gully and made his way to the car. "Oh, my poor darling," he said when he saw the awful mess. He opened the door for her and put his arm out that she might steady herself on it, but he did not try to hold her, did not try to comfort her physically in any way. He knew better than that. Her fingers on his arm perched so tentatively, they might have been birds for all the impression they left.

Mavis had no fear of snakes. None. None at all. In fact, she had just, rather expertly, that very morning, picked up a poor harmless garter snake he was about to dispatch with a hoe. She had done it with great care and tenderness. She couldn't stand to see the animal hurt. But she was—so the doctors said—erotophobic. She had an unnatural and hysterical fear of sex.

Jack smiled grimly. Too bad the gunman hadn't controlled his impulses. Mavis was a beautiful woman, but . . . and Jack rubbed the back of his head, which ached, just as it had the first—and last—time he had tried to make love to Mavis on their honeymoon.

Snakes indeed.

HOUSEBOUND

George Alec Effinger

Monsters in the closet terrified Jennifer O'Casey when she was seven years old. Well, there was only one monster, but it was enough. Jennifer didn't know its name, but she knew what it looked like. It looked like a big hulking monster, huffing and puffing way back in the blackest dark.

As Jennifer got older she learned to use her imagination. That was why, when she was ten, she realized that a monster in the closet was a dumb idea. No, any monster worthy of the name would clearly lie in wait beneath her bed, ready to bite off any foot that dared touch the ground, or any arm left carelessly dangling over the side. And Jennifer understood that the bed was big enough to shelter *many* monsters, instead of the stupid single monster in the closet.

Something had to be done. After a year or so of sheer bedtime horror Jennifer hit on the idea of forging treaties with the monsters. They were evil, but they were also reasonable. Or so she figured.

The first treaty stated that she was safe from the monsters as long as the bedside lamp was lit. The second treaty said that after turning off the lamp Jennifer had till the count of ten to get under the covers and to safety. The third treaty was a concession to the monsters. Jennifer would remain safe all night as long as the sheet and blanket were drawn up tightly around her neck, and she had to keep her hands and feet inside.

Jennifer slept every night this way, with the covers clutched in her small fists and held tightly across her neck even in the most stifling weather. She didn't break the treaties until she was twenty-four years old.

Six years later, while shopping in the Piggly Wiggly near her home, Jennifer began feeling strangely nervous and queasy. She thought she might be getting sick. As the minutes passed she tried to ignore the uncomfortable feeling. She thought she might have eaten something bad or triggered an allergy she hadn't known about before. She tossed some frozen manicotti into her cart, then found herself gasping for breath. She was having some kind of attack, and she was frightened. All she could think about was getting home, to safety. She said the hell with the rest of the shopping list, turned her cart, and headed to the checkout lanes.

The decision to bail out of the Piggly Wiggly and go home didn't make her feel any better. She guessed she was making a tremendous fool of herself in public with her anxiety and panicked reaction. She just wanted to be in the shelter of her car, on the road to her house. Instead, the shoppers in front of her dawdled and wrote checks and did everything they could to increase Jennifer's discomfort.

At last she put her groceries on the checkout belt, paid the money, and carried her purchases to her car, a cream-colored 1977 Fiat, the single most indefensible expenditure in her life. She loved the Fiat, but she felt no better behind the wheel, headed for home. She felt acutely nervous, aware of the myriad things that could happen to her in traffic. She pictured herself dying in dozens of different ways, and her own driving became timid and tentative. She knew other drivers all around her were cursing her, but she was unable to escape her sense of helplessness, her gut feeling of horrible dread.

Housebound

When she arrived at her apartment building she hurried from the car, leaving the groceries behind on the seat. She rushed to her front door and unlocked it with trembling hands. Once inside she felt a wave of calmness sweep over her. She was home now. She was safe.

Still, her body was quivering with unrelieved tension. She paced anxiously from the living room to the dining room to the kitchen. It would take a while to expend all that nervous energy. In the meantime, she thought, maybe she could use a drink.

Jennifer rarely drank this early in the day, and she never drank alone, but she counted this as a special occasion and decided that anything that would mitigate her panic should be counted as medicinal.

She made a gin and tonic and drank it down in two gulps. She sat down on the davenport and waited for peace and forgetfulness. The minutes passed heavily. She got up and made two more gin and tonics. Not long after she drank them she began to feel a warm and blurry sedation creep over her. Two more, she decided, and she went back to the kitchen. She remembered nothing after that. She awoke several hours later, half on and half off the davenport, with her cheek pressed against the cushion.

There was a pool of saliva near her mouth. That was the worst thing about this whole episode—she'd been drooling. A Mount Holyoke girl like Jennifer should never be caught drooling, not for any reason at all.

Her bones creaked as she climbed back on the davenport. She had to think this through. What had brought on the panic attack in the Piggly Wiggly? She'd felt perfectly fine when she went into the grocery store. Maybe it was a warning of some kind, some tabloid newspaper kind of premonition. She desperately wanted to understand what had happened—only not yet. She had a terrible headache and an upset stomach from passing out drunk. Jennifer found it difficult to keep her mind on anything at all. Most of all, she wanted to sleep.

When Jennifer awoke the next morning she had only a small headache. A couple of aspirins would take care of it, she thought. She stayed in bed much longer than usual, still trying to figure out what had happened to her in the Piggly Wiggly. After a while she decided that knowing the truth was unimportant, as long as she didn't have another humiliating attack in public.

Good, she thought. She was proud of her self-diagnosis. The bad news was that to prevent any further emotional displays she'd have to turn into a virtual recluse. She didn't dare go out, because she was almost certain of what would happen if she did. She could have the Piggly Wiggly deliver food, but what about work? The advertising agency where she was an account executive would never allow her to work at home.

Putting those decisions off for the moment, Jennifer decided it would be a major victory to accomplish anything as complex as taking her clothes off and standing under a hot shower. She wanted to feel the water wash away the last of her fear.

It was when she realized that washing her hair was just too much to worry about that Jennifer realized she might be in some trouble. She dried herself off and climbed back into bed. She felt an odd tingling in her hands and feet. In her head there was a horrible feeling that none of this was real.

She got out of bed and went downstairs to the kitchen. She was hungry, but putting together a meal was totally beyond her. The bottle of gin was right where she'd left it, on the counter. She poured about six ounces of it into a large plastic cup, then filled it the rest of the way with tonic water.

She gulped a little right there, to calm her nerves, because she was afraid that she'd spill the glass in her wobbly state. She managed to get back upstairs without any misadventures. She put the gin and tonic on her nightstand, grabbed the television's remote channel changer, and got back in bed. Ha, she thought. Now she had everything she needed for a happy life, and all within reach. She glanced at the television; it was tuned to a network animal show. That was just fine with her. It was too much trouble even to flick through the stations to see what else might be on.

Days passed like this. She gave up on inventing new lies to

24

tell her boss and took an indefinite leave of absence. She was living off her savings, and when that ran out . . . well, she didn't want to think about it now.

As the days became weeks she had to admit that her behavior was not normal. Calling her friend Amanda was the most difficult thing she'd ever attempted.

"You're right about one thing," Amanda said. "Your behavior is not normal. I think you should think about seeing a therapist."

"Yes," Jennifer said, "but—"

"Don't start with your objections, Jenn. To me they'll just seem trivial, but I know they're very real to you. You know that I'm subject to severe depressions, and that I hate it when someone comes up to me and says, 'Hey, just cheer up.' God, do I hate that."

"Don't you see?" Jennifer said. "You're telling me to go out and find a shrink or something. My whole problem is that I can't *leave* the house to find a therapist. Now, if you know of one who makes house calls—"

"It's not that funny, Jenn. I'm not a professional, but I do know that you're going to have to make some effort, even though it may be very painful."

Jennifer paused. "I was hoping there'd be some magic pill someone could prescribe to instantly cure my anxiety. Lithium or something."

"Another reason to find a therapist, Jenn. Maybe there *is* a pill that would help you. I don't know; the only way to find the truth is by confronting your fears long enough to get you through an interview with a trained specialist."

"I'll think about it, Mandy, but—"

"You know you're not going to feel better until you stop saying 'but' all the time."

"I know you're right."

"Good girl, Jenn," Amanda said. "Get out your phone book and make a few calls."

"I'll do that," Jennifer said, "but—"

"Bye, Jenn. Got to go."

And then Jennifer was listening to the dull burring of the dial tone.

Talking with Amanda had made her feel much better, but the good feelings fled as soon as she hung up the telephone. She knew intellectually that what her friend had told her was the truth. Emotionally, however, she couldn't face it.

Not, Jennifer corrected herself, without a little fortifying. It was just about time for the liquor store to send over another bottle of gin. No hurry, though; she had an untouched bottle of vodka to get her through tomorrow. Realizing that she didn't have to worry about panic attacks, she relaxed, took out the telephone directory, and called the number of a psychiatrist not far from her home.

The receptionist said, "Are you a new patient, or have you seen Dr. Metz before?"

"I'm a new patient," Jennifer said.

"Well, you need to be evaluated first. Can I put you down for next Friday? Ten o'clock?"

"Part of my problem is that I'm unable to leave the house. I was wondering if Dr. Metz—"

"She needs to see you in person, you know. Do you think you could overcome your fear if you were with a friend? He or she could drive so that you'd be freed from that anxiety."

Jennifer bit her nails. Amanda might be willing to drive her to the appointment. They'd been friends since college. "Yes," she said, "I think I could manage that. Next Friday, at ten?"

"That's right," the receptionist said. "We'll see you then."

Next Friday morning Amanda arrived in her station wagon to drive Jennifer to the doctor's appointment. Jennifer was waiting for her in the kitchen. Beside her on the counter was a mostly finished bottle of vodka, a tray of ice cubes, and a bottle of Rose's Lime Juice. She was just this side of plastered. Amanda looked at her disdainfully.

"Hell, Mandy," Jennifer said. "If I'm going to let you bully me into seeing this woman, give me a break. I'm sure the doctor's seen cases like me before."

"Maybe so," Amanda said, "but I haven't. And what I see isn't pretty."

Jennifer gritted her teeth to prevent her from saying something that might damage her relationship with

26

Amanda. After her recent behavior, Amanda was about the only friend she still had. Jennifer wanted to tell her that constant bullying made her as angry as Amanda got when someone told her to "just cheer up."

"Well," Amanda said, "are we going or aren't we?"

"Do I have a choice?"

"Yes, you have a choice. Your choice is between going to this appointment and starting to get help on one hand, and this sorry drunken life you've made for yourself on the other."

Jennifer glared at her friend, then came to a decision. She picked up the phone and dialed the doctor's number.

"Dr. Metz and associates," the receptionist said.

"Hi. This is Jennifer O'Casey. I've got an appointment for this morning at ten o'clock. It looks like I won't be able to come in today. Can I reschedule?"

She could hear the tapping of the receptionist's pencil as she looked through Dr. Metz's calendar. "The best I could give you would be next Thursday at two."

"That's quite a while from now. You don't have anything sooner?"

"I'm afraid not."

Jennifer said, "All right. Thursday at two."

"Okay," the receptionist said. "We'll see you then."

"Thank you." Jennifer hung up the phone.

Amanda stood in the middle of Jennifer's kitchen. She said, "You're testing me, aren't you? You're trying to prove how miserable your life has become by chasing away all your friends. You're denying yourself help that you truly need. And you're trying to push me away, to see how much I'll put up with before I, too, walk away from you. Well, I'm going to. If ever you feel up to going to an appointment, give me a call. You have the number. In the meantime, fear or not, this is pretty ridiculous behavior." Amanda turned and went out the front door.

Jennifer watched as her friend pulled out of the driveway. Her own car was there, too, sitting reproachfully. She knew she could get the help she needed if she could just make herself go out again, but the very thought made her shudder.

It wasn't that she was afraid of open places. It was that she was horrified at the threat of making a fool of herself in public again. Realistically, she was afraid of being afraid, afraid of succumbing to a panic attack with all those people watching. . . .

Almost a week passed. In those days Jennifer woke up covered with perspiration. She just wanted to be asleep, and when she saw the clock in the morning she always groaned and rolled over. Some days she got up only long enough to use the bathroom and then went back to bed. On Thursday morning she got a call from Amanda. "Hi, Jenn. You want to go the appointment today? Or are you going to poop out again?"

"I'll . . . I'll go today. I just want this awful feeling to go away."

"Good girl. I'll come pick you up in fifteen minutes."

"Thanks, Mandy." After she'd hung up the telephone Jennifer looked around her apartment. Garbage was piling up in the kitchen, and dirty dishes were everywhere. She hadn't felt like doing the laundry, either, for some time. She saw how terrible her house looked, but she didn't have the energy to clean up before Amanda arrived. She wondered how much liquor she could get down before the doorbell rang.

Amanda just stood in the doorway, looking around the living room and saying nothing. She wrinkled her nose in disapproval. She knew enough, however, not to criticize Jennifer.

"Whose car shall we take?" Jennifer asked.

"Mine, I thought," Amanda said. "That way, in case you have another panic attack, you won't have to worry about getting home."

"Thanks, Mandy," Jennifer said. "I really do appreci-ate—"

"That's okay, Jenn. But let's get going, all right?"

"Sure," Jennifer said. She gathered up her house keys and stuffed them into her purse. When she came to the threshold she froze.

"You're making progress already. Now give me your

hand, and we'll go to my car. You've done that a million times, haven't you?"

"Uh-huh," Jennifer said warily. She could feel her heart pounding. She realized she was breathing in short little gasps. She felt a panic attack coming on. "Maybe this wasn't a good idea, Mandy. What if I have an attack right out there on the street?"

Amanda looked at her closely. "Jenn, I know what you're going through. Believe me, I know. I also realize how tough this must be for you. If you want to feel normal again, you're going to have to do it the hard way."

Jennifer's mouth was dry, and she could hear a loud buzzing sound in her ears. "Yes, okay," she said. "I don't like this at all."

Amanda smiled sympathetically. "Just hang on. In a few weeks you'll be feeling all right."

"God, I hope so," Jennifer muttered. And then she was strapping herself into the front passenger seat with no idea how she'd gotten there. Her hands were shaking, and she closed her eyes. She was grateful that Amanda was there with her. She was absolutely sure she could never have come even this far on her own.

"How are we doing?" Amanda asked when they arrived at the small medical complex where Dr. Metz had her office.

"Fine," Jennifer said. She was startled to hear her voice. It sounded like a croaking frog. As she followed Amanda to the elevator the feeling of unreality became ever stronger. Soon she'd be sitting in the doctor's waiting room—trapped.

"Ms. O'Casey?" the receptionist said. "Would you please fill out this sheet for our records?" She handed a clipboard and pen to Jennifer.

This much I can handle, Jennifer thought. She dreaded seeing Dr. Metz. As Jennifer filled out the doctor's form she felt a silly fear that Dr. Metz had caught her doing something forbidden and now was about to execute Jennifer's punishment. Dumb, dumb, Jennifer thought.

She sat there for some time, completely involved with her own problems. Soon she noticed how hard she was holding

Amanda's hand, and she tried to relax. "It won't be so bad," she told herself. "And when I go home I'll already be under treatment. It won't be so bad."

Cold, unforgiving time passed. Jennifer tried to interest herself in one magazine article after another, but she soon realized that she was reading so intently in order to keep her anxiety at a comfortable distance. She began to tremble again when she understood what she was doing. It was kind of a vicious circle—first she was afraid, then she began to hide from the panic, and then she understood that her panic was *so great* that she needed to hide from it, and that just proved how real and intense the anxiety was.

"Dr. Metz will see you now," the receptionist said. Jennifer felt a shower of discomfort as she stood up. Her whole body was tingling in an unpleasant way.

Amanda stood and gave her friend a brief smile. "Don't worry, Jenn," she said. "I'll be here when you're through."

"Thanks, Mandy," Jennifer said in a hoarse voice. She let the receptionist lead her to an examining room.

"Dr. Metz will be with you soon. Make yourself comfortable," the receptionist said.

The examining room was large, with several shelves of books, a desk, and a comfortable black leather couch. She fidgeted a moment, then sat down on the couch.

Dr. Metz came in suddenly. She was a tall woman, prematurely gray in a rather attractive way, but all business. She glanced through the basic information on Jennifer's chart. "Yes, well," the doctor said, "what has brought you here today?"

Jennifer really hoped that Dr. Metz wasn't going to begin by minimizing her fear. She began by telling the doctor how it had all begun with the panic attack in the grocery store. Dr. Metz sat at her desk and slowly nodded her head. Jennifer discovered a new concern: Should she tell the doctor absolutely everything or hold something back?

"Do you understand the nature of your fear, Ms. O'Casey? You're describing what we call agoraphobia, a fear of open spaces, but you probably don't realize how complex and interconnected the root causes of your anxiety are. Over the years I've managed to help many people overcome their phobias. Some people come to me paralyzed by a fear of cats, of spiders, of heights, of flying—the list of possible phobias is very long. Yet a good half of those patents also say they suffer from agoraphobia."

"I don't understand," Jennifer said.

"It's very simple. If a person is afraid of snakes, for instance, he will stop going to places where there is a chance of seeing a snake. Soon this fear is generalized; the patient stays home for days, weeks, even years at a time. His house is a fortress against that which he fears."

"Are you telling me that my panic attacks could be triggered by something else entirely, maybe something in my past?"

Dr. Metz frowned a little. "I'm definitely not a Freudian, which would lead me to locate the roots of *all* your phobias and neuroses in your childhood," she said, "but his work does give good and valuable insights into this sort of problem."

Jennifer laughed nervously. "I was hoping you could just write out a prescription for me, and that would be the end of it."

"I'm sorry, Ms. O'Casey, but it's not that easy. No, if we're going to work on this together, we have to come to a common understanding of why you feel panicked. We may have to open old wounds, and sometimes the therapy is more difficult than the neurosis. You're going to have to trust me, and likewise I need to trust you, too. If you keep canceling appointments, I'm afraid there's little I can offer. It all depends on how committed you are to freeing yourself from the agony of emotional bondage. Do you follow me?"

Jennifer looked down at her feet. "I understand, Doctor. To be honest, I'm not certain that I'm strong enough."

"Fine," Dr. Metz said. "As long as I feel you're making an honest effort, I'll be willing to be here as often as you need."

"Thank you, Doctor. But isn't there some medication that would make it just a little easier?"

Dr. Metz sat back in her swivel chair. "I could, you know, write a couple of prescriptions. One for an antidepressant.

That will take a few weeks to begin working. In addition, I could give you a mild tranquilizer to handle short-term panic attacks. But—and this is a large 'but'—it's no good trading one kind of emotional crutch for another. You've been drinking, haven't you? Much more than usual, I'd say. These medications, while effective, have their own sinister aspects. For one thing, they're habit-forming, and I don't want to cure your phobia and then have to treat your drug dependency."

"I've always been pretty good with medicines," Jennifer said.

"We'll see. Here's a prescription for Tofranil, which is the antidepressant, and one for Xanax, the tranquilizer. If you have trouble with side effects or anything, call the office here, and we'll try something different. Now, as to your next appointment, same day and time next week?"

"Yes, that would be fine."

Dr. Metz walked her to the door. "Let me know if the medications give you any kind of problem."

Jennifer just nodded. She still had to face the ride home, and—good God—the stop at the pharmacist. She began feeling overwhelmed again.

Amanda must have sensed Jennifer's mood, because she put her arm around Jennifer as they walked to the elevator. "You'll lick it," Amanda said.

"Thanks for the encouragement, Mandy," Jennifer said. "Right now I feel like the earth is going to open up right in front of me, and I'll tumble down all the way to hell."

"Let's just get your medicine and go home. Maybe next week *you* can drive."

Jennifer gave her friend a weak and unsteady smile. "Why don't we just take things one step at a time?"

"Sure," Amanda said.

Over the next several weeks Jennifer kept her appointments with Dr. Metz, although she didn't feel as if she was making any progress at all. During one of their conversations Jennifer admitted that the most terrifying day of her life had happened when she was ten years old. Her father was at work, her mother was out shopping, and a fire started. The neighbors called the fire department, and the fire was brought quickly under control, but she had been traumatized. She never forgave her mother for not being there when Jennifer needed her. That's why Jennifer had decided never to have children, because she knew she couldn't always control what happened in their lives. She would feel guilty every time she had to leave them in someone else's care.

"Perhaps that's it," Dr. Metz said thoughtfully. "Maybe that's the root of your distress."

"I don't know. If that's the case, why did it happen when it did? Why didn't I feel the panic before, in all the years I've been living on my own?"

Dr. Metz shrugged. "I can't say, Jennifer. Maybe something triggered a long-buried memory. An odor, perhaps. You may have gone into the Piggly Wiggly and passed by the barbecued ribs, and just the right song was playing on the Muzak. It would take a lot of delving."

"But I am making progress, aren't I?"

"You're making fine progress, Jennifer, but I wouldn't go around patting myself on the back just yet. I explained to you how long a struggle it would be. Do you think it's time for you to come alone to our sessions?"

"Yes," Jennifer said, not the least bit confident.

"Just remember to stay as relaxed as possible. One other desensitizing exercise you can do is to imagine the very worst thing that could happen at every juncture. Imagine yourself getting into your car. I'd think that wouldn't pose a serious problem for you now. But turning the key and backing out of the driveway? Your serious fears might prevent you from taking back your own life."

"You don't know how difficult it is," Jennifer said.

"It so happens that I *do* know how difficult it is. I went through a period that lasted a full year, during which I couldn't bring myself even to get my mail from the mailbox."

Jennifer opened her eyes wider. She had come to think of the doctor as rock-steady and perfectly competent. "You?" she said.

"After my husband died. Do you see? It can happen to anyone. Now, if you want to make further progress, you're going to have to take small steps. You're going to have to win through to peace by confronting every stressful aspect of your life. Picture yourself accepting the challenge of getting here on your own. Imagine all the terrible things that could happen. If you work through all that, then it should become easier for you to travel about. You'll have already created scenarios far more horrible than anything that might happen in real life."

Jennifer was dubious. She wasn't sure that she could follow Dr. Metz's advice. It sounded too much like sympathetic magic to her. Live through the worst that could happen to her? Jennifer wanted something else entirely. She wanted a magic pill or a wave of a wand to free her from her escalating pain and anxiety. All right, she could admit that there were no magic pills or therapeutic wands. She'd hoped that she'd gone through the hard part, yet it seemed that every time she'd vanquished one fear, two more sprang up. At the end of the session Jennifer was deeply distressed. It seemed to her that there was always another hurdle she'd have to get over.

A few months ago it had been a joke. But life was hard. You could just read the T-shirts and find out what the rest of her generation felt about stress, fear, and helplessness. What had once been mildly amusing now appeared to be bitter truth. This made her attempt at therapy even more ironic, because she didn't really have much faith in Dr. Metz's planned renovation of Jennifer. She thought it was awfully simple to sit on the other side of the desk, nod meaningfully, and deposit a hefty check after every visit. That was not very difficult; Jennifer imagined they could train chimpanzees to do the same.

Then, yet again, Jennifer realized that she couldn't make light of this situation. She knew that unless she did what Dr. Metz suggested—confronted her fears—she'd be permanently paralyzed by them. Yet wasn't it too much to expect from her in this state?

"All right," Jennifer said to herself later that week, lying out beside her apartment building's swimming pool. "I'll just get some sun, maybe some exercise, and then I'll be better able to face Dr. Metz." She felt guilty because she hadn't performed any of the mental exercises the doctor had suggested to her.

Jennifer recalled the four stages on the way to emotional security. The first part might be the most difficult: facing up to the worst of her fears. Easier said than done, she thought. It meant no more drinking, no more hiding in bed. She couldn't fight a problem while she was still denying it even existed.

Lying in the sun, Jennifer tried to picture herself going back to the Piggly Wiggly. She imagined every step of the way, and all the bad things that could happen to her. She had conquered her fear of driving—she'd been back and forth to Dr. Metz's office alone for some time now. Of course, her fearful mind told her, she'd just begun thinking of the doctor's office as an extension of her home, a safe and secure haven. What she needed to do was extend that feeling until it took in the whole world. That was the hard part.

Later, during her appointment with Dr. Metz, she admitted that at times she could look at her fear of leaving home, and then she knew it was all stupid. There was nothing terrifying about a grocery store. No one had shown any hostility toward her there. At other times she was firmly in the grasp of another panic attack at the simple thought of the Piggly Wiggly.

"I really need your help, Dr. Metz," she told the therapist.

"I'm glad to help any way I can, Ms. O'Casey. Your true progress will begin when you realize you *don't* need my help, that everything you need in order to feel better is already there. I'm here just to show you how to fashion your own treatment."

Jennifer smiled with feigned humor. "The problem is that I can understand what you're saying on an intellectual level. I can even agree with you. But on a raw emotional level . . ." She just shrugged.

"Let me ask you a question, if I may," Dr. Metz said.

"Of course."

"Your mother . . . would you say she was strict with you?"

"She was strict, yes," Jennifer said, "but she was no demon. She just had very strong ideas about what my behavior should be like."

Dr. Metz nodded. "And did she punish you? Physically?"

Jennifer didn't have any idea what the therapist was driving at. "Yes, she punished me, but she didn't often hit me. She had other methods."

"Depriving you of something? Grounding you, that sort of thing?"

Puzzled, Jennifer let out a breath. "Yes, more along those lines rather than actually hurting me."

"One more thing before we end this session," Dr. Metz said. "You're carrying around a lot of guilt in addition to your agoraphobia, aren't you?"

Jennifer was astonished. "I suppose I am, but how did you know that?"

"It's common among phobia sufferers. You mentioned once that you resented your mother for not being with you when the house fire took place. You feel guilty about that resentment. You feel guilty about involving your friend, Amanda, in your problem. You probably feel guilt about leaving home because you're afraid something awful—a fire, a burglary, *something*—might happen in your absence. You no doubt have guilt feelings about other matters, too."

Jennifer thought for a moment. "Yes, you're right, I think. My trouble is that I can sit here and fully understand what you're saying, even agree about the sensible explanation, but I still know that I'd suffer a panic attack as soon as I set foot in that Piggly Wiggly."

Dr. Metz closed her notebook and looked directly at Jennifer. "Maybe at this stage that would happen. I think you need to do some more work on desensitizing your fear in your imagination. I know that there are a million tiny things that could bring on an attack. You could break a bottle of something in the grocery store, or you could

36

temporarily misplace your keys—all things that you could handle perfectly well before your attacks began."

"Sometimes I have trouble even imagining those things without panicking."

The doctor nodded to show that she understood perfectly. "But that's just what you need to do. You should be totally relaxed, at home and safe. Then you can begin imagining what might happen if you went to the Piggly Wiggly. That's the next stage in your therapy."

Jennifer nodded. She'd expected something like that.

"Remember," Dr. Metz said, "plain fear can't hurt you physically. I want you to face up to it, let it completely wash over you. Let the fear have its way. Experience a panic attack and then notice that if you practice the relaxation method, the panic will gradually go away."

Jennifer gave another weak smile. "It sounds impossible."

"It may seem so now, but it's something you have to do sooner or later."

On the way home alone in the car Jennifer thought about what the doctor had said. She saw the logic in what Dr. Metz asked. She promised that she'd really begin to work at the relaxing and imagining routines—tomorrow.

The next morning Jennifer felt a little better. She put on her swimsuit, grabbed a towel, and went down to the pool. She spread the towel on the concrete apron and lay down on it. She felt the warm sun on her legs and back. She closed her eyes and pretended that she was at the beach. She imagined waves of cool water rushing up and covering her feet, then draining back, taking with them all the tension from her ankles down. When her feet were relaxed she imagined that the waves came in as far as her knees, and so on until every muscle was as relaxed as possible.

Jennifer began visualizing the Piggly Wiggly store as clearly as she could. She was amazed to see that, while she was still nervous and edgy, she suffered no panic attack. She thought about her real fear—not the grocery itself, according to Dr. Metz, but a fear of having fear in the store. That made her feel worse, so she relaxed her muscles once more and allowed the anxiety to do its worst.

It wasn't so bad, actually. In fact, she felt capable of dealing with panic on that level. When the anxiety had completely disappeared she decided to test her shaky peace of mind.

She took her towel with her as she went back to her apartment. She looked at the telephone. She reached out for it, drew her hand back, then grabbed it and called Amanda's work phone number.

"Amanda Romano's office," a secretary said.

"This is Jennifer O'Casey. Is Amanda available?"

"She should be. Hang on a minute while I try to find her."

Jennifer listened to an easy-listening version of "Layla." She thought she'd rather have silence when she was put on hold. She believed that rock 'n' roll should never be played soft and mellow.

"Jennifer?" Amanda asked. "Is that you?"

"Morning, Amanda. I was wondering if you could spend some time with me today. I want to see how far I've gotten with my therapy."

"That's great, but I can't go with you until after work. We're swamped around here. Maybe I could drop by your place later."

Jennifer said, "That'll be fine, Amanda. And thanks."

"Hey, you're my best friend, you know. Now I've got to run. See you later."

"Bye, kid." Jennifer thought she'd try going to the Piggly Wiggly with Amanda later in the afternoon. Before that, however, she decided to see what would happen if she went somewhere neutral. The post office. She needed to buy some stamps anyway.

The house was safe, the car was safe—now she'd find out if the panic attacks happened only in the Piggly Wiggly or if she was completely trapped by her phobia. If this isn't confronting your fear, Jennifer thought as she dressed, I don't know what is. She locked her front door and went to her Fiat. She still felt no particular anxiety.

That's good, she thought. Maybe she'd find out that this healthy feeling had driven her panic attacks away entirely. It was wrong to set herself up for a big letdown, yet the positive attitude couldn't be anything but therapeutic.

When she arrived at the post office she pulled into one of the parking places. She let the engine run and the radio play while she went through the imaginary beach relaxation routine. Finally there was nothing left to do but go into the post office and get in line. She turned off the radio and killed the engine. Then she marched bravely to the entrance.

There was a line of nine people ahead of her. She read a few posters, looked at the pages of men and women wanted for federal offenses, admired some new stamps. It felt very normal. Jennifer was immensely pleased with her control. She couldn't wait to tell Dr. Metz about it.

She bought a book of stamps and went back to the lobby, happy about her victory, wanting to extend it as long as possible. She wondered what to do next. She could go uptown and have lunch—all by herself, like any normal adult. She felt as if she could do anything she wanted now.

Almost anything. The Piggly Wiggly still haunted her. She didn't dare try going there on her own. That was why she'd called Amanda.

Jennifer was further pleased to realize that she didn't have to get drunk to feel comfortable. At first the fears and guilts had mounted up to a daunting level; now the happier, more stable moments were accumulating just as quickly.

About six o'clock that evening Amanda rang the doorbell. Jennifer let her in. "Guess what I did today," Jennifer said.

"Did you do what Dr. Metz suggested? Go out and sit in your car and imagine a trip to a public place?"

"Better than that," Jennifer said. "I sat in the car, drove it down the street, and then went downtown to the post office."

"Wonderful, Jenn!" Amanda said. "I'm really proud of you. Did you go inside?"

"I sure did." She held up the book of stamps like a tiny trophy.

"Well," Amanda said, "that's some progress. Why did you want me to come over? You're not going to try the—"

"The Piggly Wiggly."

Amanda's face showed grave concern. "It might be too early to jump in the deep end."

"That's why I asked you to come with me."

"You think you can handle it?"

"I handled the post office just fine, didn't I?"

"Yes, but—"

"No buts," Jennifer said. "I'm determined."

"All right, if you think you're ready," Amanda said. Her expression told Jennifer that her friend was doubtful. There was only one way to find out.

Amanda drove, just in case Jennifer had another anxiety attack in the Piggly Wiggly. On the way there Amanda glanced at her passenger and said, "How are you doing so far?"

"So far so good," Jennifer said. She was practicing her relaxation technique.

Jennifer did feel good. That lasted until Amanda parked the car in the grocery store's lot. It was like a sudden lightning stab of fear. Amanda could tell there was something wrong. "You're anticipating, Jenn. Don't make up extra worries for yourself."

"You're right, of course. I'm afraid that I'll be afraid." She took a deep breath, held it, then let it out slowly. "Well, let's do it."

Jennifer was surprised by how weak her legs felt as she climbed out of her friend's car. She realized that she was trembling all over.

"Take your time and relax," Amanda said.

Jennifer only nodded. There was only one thing to do, or else admit defeat. She clasped Amanda's hand as they walked toward the entrance.

"There's nothing threatening in the parking lot, is there?" Amanda said in a soothing voice.

"No." Her mouth and throat were unusually dry.

"Let's go in, then."

Jennifer nodded. Her face was covered with perspiration. She had to grab hold of shelves because she was afraid that she'd faint otherwise. She was in the store for less than a minute before she fell into a complete, paralyzing panic attack. "Let's go," she said in an unsteady voice.

Amanda helped her out of the store. "We're outside again," Amanda said. "Do you still feel the anxiety?"

"Yes."

"Well, let's just go home then and make some dinner."

"All I've got is macaroni and cheese."

"Fine," Amanda said. Jennifer didn't say a word on the drive home. On top of her fear in the store she felt the humiliation of having her best friend witness a full-blown attack.

At her next session with Dr. Metz Jennifer described in detail the day of the post office and the Piggly Wiggly. She no longer felt free to go out by herself. Her second panic attack had persuaded her that her behavior couldn't be trusted.

"I'm very glad that you made the effort to venture out," Dr. Metz said. "The trip to the post office was a good idea. I can't say the same for the grocery store. Now, there is a technique called 'flooding,' in which the patient subjects himself to the worst of his fears, with little or no preparation. Sometimes this 'once and for all' solution produces favorable results. Sometimes, as in your case, it can be disastrous. You seem to have regressed to the point where you were when you first came to me. I wish you had called me before attempting to flood your emotions by going to the Piggly Wiggly. I would've said that you're not quite ready."

"Will you continue to help me?" Jennifer said in a pitiable tone of voice.

"Of course I will. Try to master your feelings as you did when you went to the post office. When you've progressed to the point at which you decided to take your life back again, we'll work slowly on your fear of the store."

"If it's only the store I'm afraid of," Jennifer said, "maybe I'll just start shopping elsewhere."

"That's one solution. It doesn't satisfy me, however. It's like putting a bandage on a broken leg. I won't be happy until we've achieved a complete cure, and I think deep down you feel the same way."

Jennifer just nodded.

"Fine," Dr. Metz said. "You must know there's hope. Well, we begin again."

"Thank you, Doctor," Jennifer said. This time she really did know there was hope.

HOT WATER

Kristine Kathryn Rusch

"YOU SURE, HONEY?" STEVE ASKED, HAND ON THE BRASS doorknob. The foyer was dark and a bit too warm, carrying the day's heat. "The Sandersons invited you, too."

Louisa brushed his curling hair out of his collar and straightened his suit jacket. "It's okay," she said, trying to keep the impatience from her voice. Steve wanted to include her, but this time she didn't want to be included. She had been waiting for this night. "I've had a long week. I just want to be alone and relax."

"All right." He kissed her, almost missing her mouth, and pulled her close for a brief moment. "I'll be back around midnight."

She put her hand on top of his and pulled the oak door open. "No hurry. I'll probably be asleep when you get here."

He kissed her again, on the forehead this time, and walked out. She followed him onto the porch. Twilight had just settled in the valley, giving the trees a gray, shadowy edge. A cool breeze made the branches rustle. The frogs had started their evening chorus from the pond halfway down

43

the driveway, and from overhead a bird gave a good-bye chirp.

"Wish I were staying here with you," Steve said. "It's a great night."

She smiled but said nothing. She had been waiting for this evening alone for almost two weeks. She wanted nothing to spoil it. Steve squeezed her shoulder, then hurried down the wood stairs to the flagged path. They had only been in the house a few months, and it still needed work, but Louisa loved it. If she strained, she could hear cars passing on the road over a mile away, but that was the only sound of civilization—except at midnight, when the distant whistle from the mill announced the arrival of the third shift.

Steve hurried down the walk and opened the door of their car, a champagne-colored Porsche covered with dust from the gravel drive. He had been threatening to pave the driveway and to buy a truck, claiming that the Porsche was too expensive to suffer the nicks of tiny rocks churning beneath the wheels.

Someday he would decide the car was too expensive to drive.

The car roared to a start and made its way around the curving slope of the drive, through the trees. Louisa leaned against the wobbly wood railing and watched as the taillights grew smaller along the mile-long gravel drive.

No lights shone in the valley. The house just down the hill had been abandoned years ago. The three neighboring houses—the ones she could see sprawled on their individual twenty acres—had the clean look of a place with owners out of town. On Labor Day weekend she could count on everyone being away.

She sighed and stretched, feeling the knots in her back pop. She couldn't get more alone than this.

Still, she needed darkness. She slipped back inside and pulled the heavy door closed behind her. Then she shut off the porch light and the light illuminating the huge foyer.

Her hands were shaking.

The only way to conquer fear is to face it. Her therapist's voice echoed in her head. Roger wanted her to do this. He wanted her to take charge of her life. *Now that you know why the fear exists, you can control it. It doesn't have to control you.*

Right.

She glanced at the stairs. Up there was her office, the safest place in the house. She could go there and grab a book, climb into the easy chair, and while the hours away.

Or she could stay down here and face herself.

She walked to the kitchen, avoiding the bathroom and its mirror. The kitchen light was still on, illuminating the hand-carved cookie jar she and Steve had bought on their honeymoon. Dishes dried in the rack, the long knife Steve had used to carve the beef resting on its side next to the plates.

Everything looked normal here. Everything was normal, except her. At least Steve had patience. He loved her. He had known even before they married that she would never take off her clothes for him, that she couldn't stand to be naked in front of anyone. They made love in the dark with her nightgown pushed around her waist, his gentle fingers stroking her breasts through the fabric.

He loved her, but she could see in his eyes that sometimes he wanted more. Just once he wanted to see her, all of her at the same time.

She flicked off the light switch over the phone. The fluorescents held their light for a moment, then went dark. She walked into the breakfast nook and stared through the glass-paned doors at the hot tub.

Even with the lights off she could see it clearly, a big ungainly structure sitting in the middle of her backyard. A deck Steve had built circled it, with a rack to one side for their towels. He liked sitting nude in the water. He said it was one of the most sensual experiences in the world.

Her heart pounded in her throat. She hadn't been this nervous since the first time she had made a sales presentation nearly six years before. Roger had helped her overcome stage fright. Now he was helping her with this.

You need to face your fear, he said, each week. Next week she wanted to go into his office and tell him she had.

She stepped back from the door and pulled her T-shirt off over her head. Her hair got caught in the neck, and for one suffocating moment she couldn't get free. She struggled, then pulled, willing to rip the shirt to free herself from the fabric. Finally she was out, and she flung the shirt away from her.

It fluttered like a bird in midflight and landed gently on the sofa. Her body shook. She hadn't been that trapped since (he grabbed her and threw her against the sand, the hot granules digging into her bare back. He wrapped his towel around her face and arms, pinning her in place—) No. She wouldn't remember that. He had no place in this house. His memory, and the memory of his touch, were the things she was trying to get rid of.

She took a deep breath and made herself calm down. Then she slipped out of her shorts and panties, leaving them in a pool on the floor. She wrapped a towel around her torso, stepped into her thongs, and opened the back door.

Cool air caressed her skin, raising goose bumps. She loved the mountains. No matter how hot it was in the day, the nights were always comfortable, the breeze always fresh. She closed the door behind her and stood on the wooden back porch, letting the night woo her with its promise of secrecy.

She didn't feel naked yet. The towel was enough protection. An owl hooted nearby, adding its voice to that of the frogs. At the base of the driveway a car swooshed past, its sound little more than a reminder that other people lived in the world. The trees rustled around her as the wind caught the leaves.

Natural sounds. Safe sounds.

She took a deep breath and walked down the creaky wood stairs to the stone pathway Steve had built. The stones tilted to the left, down the hill, and she had to hold her arms out to maintain her balance. The towel shifted precariously against her skin. She grabbed the top with one hand and nearly fell. Only Steve seemed able to walk across the stones without stumbling. She walked the rest of the way on the grass.

The tub made a low humming sound, so faint she heard it only when she was up close. Sometimes it clicked off, and she was left in complete silence.

Dew had formed on the tub's plastic cover, leaving little trickles in the dust. The edge was cool to her fingers. She grabbed a side and pushed it back, not willing to take the entire cover off. She had tried to put the cover back on by herself once and had pulled a muscle in her back.

Steam rose off the surface of the water, and the biting scent of chlorine filled the air. Her heartbeat sped up, and her breath came in shallow gasps. Almost there. Almost.

The wooden stairs leading up to the deck were sturdier than the steps on the porch. Steve had built the deck out of cedar, and the faint woodsy scent mingling with the chlorine made her think of him. She clung to that thought as she did to the railing, maintaining her balance, giving her strength.

When she reached the top of the deck she stopped, hands clutching the towel to her breasts.

The mountains across the valley were inky shadows against the dark horizon. No cars passed. Even the white glare from the mill was missing—it had shut down for the holiday. Occasional bursts of steam obscured her view like tiny clouds. Crickets had joined the frogs, and the breeze had an extra bite away from the house.

Alone. She was alone.

Carefully she undid the knot holding the towel in place. The air kissed the sweat between her breasts, and her body went rigid.

(He had smiled at first, friendly as she was, another nudist on a nude beach. The alcove didn't seem private. Over the rocks she could see her friends playing volleyball. But her screams mingled with the cry of seagulls, masked by their laughter, and no one found her until hours later, huddled in a small sunburned ball, nearly dehydrated from the sun.)

She had been wrong to go for heat. Heat would bring the memory back. Heat would make things worse.

Excuses. The memory was back and would haunt her each time her skin was bare. Every morning before she got in the shower she saw his face. She didn't want to see his face anymore.

Face it. Face your fear. Once you face it, no one will ever be able to hurt you again.

She hung the towel on the railing and immediately sat down at the edge of the tub, her feet in the water. The warmth made her toes ache, but she ignored it and slid inside, feeling covered by water, not quite as visible as she had been a moment before.

She didn't move for a long time. Then she tilted her face toward the sky. She was doing it. She was sitting alone, under the stars, naked. Absolutely naked.

Free.

A tiny feeling of elation pushed aside her fear, and she breathed into it. Free. She smiled and then stood. The chill tickled her heat-covered skin; she had never felt so sensual, so alive before. She ran her hands along her wet skin. He had had no right to touch her that way. Touch felt good.

It felt good.

And she was free.

She didn't know how long she had stood there, letting the breeze caress her in places her husband had never seen. The moon had moved across the sky, and wispy clouds appeared to the west.

Steve would be home sometime soon. And she would be waiting for him. Completely, gloriously nude.

She slipped back into the water and let its warmth relax her. Roger had been right. It had been so easy, but it had taken so long to get the courage. Even then, she knew. One false statement on Steve's part, one wrong move, and she would have to do it all over again.

Unless she prepared herself. Unless she sat in the darkness and thought all the problems through. He would be startled, surprised to find her in the tub. He might comment on that. He might say her name softly, in a voice filled with awe. He might ask if she was okay.

A twig snapped. She stiffened, heart pounding. The sound had come from the front of the house. She swallowed and listened closely. A faint rustle. Soft movements in the bramble.

Deer.

A week after they had bought the house the tub had finally been clean enough and warm enough to use. Steve had taken off his suit, looking glorious in the moonlight. She wore hers as she slipped into the water. They had held hands underwater and stared at the stars for what seemed like hours before they heard something behind them.

She had tried to sit up, but Steve had held her still. "Deer," he whispered. He put a finger to his mouth and turned carefully, without disturbing the water. Then he touched her shoulder and pointed. A doe stood just behind them, upwind, ears twitching. Finally she ignored them and began eating from the apple tree at the edge of the yard.

Deer.

Louisa made herself take a deep breath. Of course she was on edge. She would be until she got used to being without clothes again. Once she had been able to be naked with strangers—at a nude beach, up in the hot springs, at hot-tub parties when she worked in California—then it had all disappeared in the space of an afternoon, while she screamed, with hot granules of sand digging into her back.

She was safe now.

It was over.

She was free.

She leaned back in the water and rested her head on the tub's plastic side. By the time Steve got home her body would be shriveled and wrinkled. She smiled. Then he couldn't judge it. Then he couldn't decide that the woman he had married had one of the uglier bodies on the planet.

A light went on in the house.

Louisa sat up, water sloshing around her. Steve wasn't home. She would have heard the car. She would have *seen* the car coming up the drive. There were no timers on the lights, because they felt no need for them. No one could see the house from the road. Sometimes they even went away and left the house unlocked.

Someone was inside.

A stranger was inside her house.

A man crossed the foyer. He was bigger than Steve and more muscular. His shoulders, in shadow, looked like they could carry the world without dropping it. Another, smaller man followed him.

A light went on in the living room.

What were they doing? Waiting for her? No. The house was dark. They thought no one was home. They were looking for something. But they hadn't brought a car, probably so that they wouldn't be caught on that circular driveway. No car. She would have heard it. Something they could carry. Not the Dali in the living room nor the Degas in the den.

(Although they could cut the paintings out of the frames and roll them. Carrying tubes would be easy, even in the dark.)

The safe held extra money and her jewels, mostly her costume jewels. The real ones were in a safety deposit box in a bank downtown.

Except for the emerald. The antique emerald her grandmother had given her. The one the photographer for *Smithsonian* had photographed for the article they were doing on family heirlooms. The one that had been reproduced in papers all over the state.

It certainly wasn't the most valuable jewel they had, but it was the most famous.

They must have been planning this for a long time. She had thought she had heard a car earlier, down by the abandoned house, but Steve had said she imagined it.

Steve was wrong.

Her heart pounded in her throat. They were in the living room. They didn't know she was there. If she eased the lid back over the tub and crouched under it, she would have enough air to last for several hours.

But that might make too much noise. She was probably better if she didn't move at all.

(Then they would find her and pull her out and hold her on the cedar boards, the wood digging into her naked back—)

No. She had to get away now. But her clothes were inside, and Steve had the car.

Steve. What would happen if he came home while they were in the living room? It would take them time. The safe was behind the heavy oak bookcases. They had to take the books out of the cases, move the cases, and figure out the combination.

(Mixed birthdays—her month, Steve's day, the combination of their years: 6-10-56. Impossible to guess unless they knew. Unless they had a stethoscope like in the movies, a man who ran an emery board against his fingertips so that they would be sensitive—)

She was panicking, thinking nonsense instead of finding a way to save herself. The Holts lived half a mile down the drive. They rarely locked their house. She could go inside, use their phone, have the police catch the men in the act.

And she would be safe.

They didn't know she was there. They wouldn't know she had escaped.

Deep breath. Deep breath. Move quietly. Do not stir the water.

She moved her hand underneath the water and braced herself against the seat. A shadow fell across the living room window, but no one else moved in the foyer. She brought her other hand out and grabbed the lid.

Water dripped, sending echoey pings through the yard.

Her heart rate increased, but she didn't move. They couldn't hear the pings, she knew, because she could never hear anyone in the hot tub unless the windows were open, and now they were all closed.

She stood. The cold breeze raised goose bumps on her body—

And she froze. She couldn't get out. They would see her. They would see all of her, and—

She had to. She had to. It was the only way to save herself.

Maybe she could crawl back in. It wouldn't take too much effort to pull the lid down, and she would have enough air for hours. She would be safe there, and no one would see her. No one would notice that she was nude. . . .

Another shadow moved across the living room window. She sank back into the hot water. In a minute they would turn on the outside light and see her. She wasn't safe. Not here. Not now.

Face your fear, Roger had said.

If only he had known.

Her body was shaking so badly she was making little ripples in the water. Out. She would only be naked for an instant. Long enough for her to grab her towel, wrap it around herself, and get off the deck.

But to get to the driveway from there she had to either go down a path beneath the living room or walk through six feet of brush. Snapping twigs and crackling branches. They would hear. They would find her.

She had to try.

She eased herself out of the water again, eyes closed, imagining Roger's face, hearing his voice with its calm confidence. *Face your fear, Louisa. That's the only way it will disappear.*

Her torso was out, breasts exposed to the night air. The breeze kissed the water droplets. Her shaking had grown.

Face your fear.

She braced her hands on the side of the tub and pulled herself up until her buttocks rested on the lukewarm plastic. Then she slid back, feet still in the water, until the plastic turned to wood. The cedar of the deck. She reached over, grabbed the towel, and wrapped it around herself.

Then she opened her eyes.

A man stood in the kitchen, staring out the double-paned doors. Staring at her.

She held back a scream, finally understanding how the doe had felt when she approached the apple tree. The man picked up a knife and set it down, then opened the cupboards.

He hadn't seen her.

He couldn't see her. The kitchen light was on. He couldn't see what was going on in the yard. In the darkness.

She pulled her legs out of the water, careful not to make a sound. With her right hand she tied the towel in place. With her left she grabbed her thongs and slid them on her wet feet. She glanced at the house and the path. Lights from the kitchen and the living room illuminated it. If someone looked out, he would see her, crouching. Besides, that way was the opposite direction from where she wanted to go. She had to go down. Away.

She climbed off the deck and paused for a moment, wondering if she should put the lid on. Too much time. And too much risk of noise. She had to get away. She had to disappear before they realized that under the towel she was—

She wouldn't think about it.

The dry grass crunched beneath her feet. Each step sounded like a peal of thunder. She went around the large oak tree, using it for support as she slipped into the bushes.

Her towel caught on a thorn, nearly pulling it loose. She yanked, and the bush shook. She waited. Nothing changed inside the house.

She took a few more steps down. She could see the gravel glinting in the moonlight. Up the driveway stood the carport with nothing in it. They had parked somewhere else. They had planned this.

They thought she was gone, with Steve, until midnight.

She let go of the oak tree and grabbed a blackberry bush, wincing as thorns bit into her palm. A few more feet and she would make it. A few more feet and she would run for her life.

A twig snapped beneath her thongs.

"Jesus!" a voice boomed from the house. "What was that?"

Another voice responded, and then the voices grew silent again. She huddled, knees against her chest. No doors opened. No one came down.

She was okay. As long as she didn't step on anything else.

She made herself count to one hundred before moving again. She stayed low, letting the blackberry bushes protect her. Nothing snapped beneath her feet. She crossed the expanse of grass until she reached the gravel—

—which shuffled like an explosion against the silence of the night.

Another light went on in the house. She swallowed heavily. They would find her. They would find her and hold her—

She kicked off the thongs and ran down the side of the road, on the unmowed grass. Rocks pierced her bare feet, but she willed it not to hurt. It wasn't going to hurt. It couldn't hurt.

The back door opened.

"—told you I heard something."

And the porch light went on.

"Good God. There's someone here."

"No. There's no car—"

"Lid's up. The damn tub's steaming. And there's footprints."

She reached the fork in the driveway. Her bare foot landed on gravel and slid out from under her. She fell, gravel moving her forward. A grunt escaped her, and pain ran up her left side. Rocks had embedded themselves in her legs and buttocks—

(like grains of sand)

—but she made herself stand up and keep running.

"Down there!"

The men crashed through the brambles. She ran downhill, gaining speed with each movement. One wrong step and she would fall on her face. Gravel flew behind her, and her feet felt like lacerated sores.

"I'll get the car. You see if you can spot him."

Not the car. If they had the car, they would find her. But she had reached the bottom of the hill and the clearing. She only had a few more yards before she reached her neighbor's house.

"Leave the damn car. It's too far away. There's nowhere he can go."

Other footsteps followed her. She rounded the corner and vaulted the gate, losing her towel. She stopped, reached for it, but couldn't grab it. The tall man was crashing down the road, looking even bigger in the moonlight. He saw her.

It was the towel or escape.

A whimper left her throat. She needed that towel, needed the cover, needed—

—the phone. The police. Help of some sort.

She took a deep breath, left the towel where it fell, and ran up the dirt walk and onto the porch.

Please let the door be open. Please.

She grabbed the knob and yanked. The door opened, and she nearly stumbled backwards. She went inside and pulled it closed, locking it behind her.

The phone was on the kitchen counter. She had used it once before hers was installed. She grabbed it, thumbed the buttons, counted, and found 911.

It rang once.

"Nine-one-one, may I help you?"

"Yes. Men have broken into my house. They've chased me down to the neighbor's. They're coming up the walk now. I need someone out here as fast as possible."

The doorknob rattled. She stepped back, fear making her entire body cold.

"—located at 6611 Aker Road?"

Her neighbor's address. "Yes. He's at the door. Can someone hurry?"

"There's a car in your area."

A face pressed against the glass of the sliding patio doors. Shit. She hadn't checked the locks on any of the other doors. Even if the door was locked, all he had to do was break the glass.

"Please hurry," she said. "Please."

"Someone will be there as fast as possible, miss. In the meantime, stay on the line—"

She set the phone down and groped behind her. Damn. She should have paid more attention when she was down here. Knives on the sideboard? No. But she needed something. Anything.

She reached up, and her hand brushed something metal above the stove. Skillets. Cast iron. Heavy. She pulled the biggest one down as he yanked the patio door open.

He held up her towel. "Forget something?"

55

She froze, seeing not him, but the man who had grabbed her on the beach. A big man, bigger than this one, smiling. She couldn't see his face now, in the dark. But he was probably smiling, too.

Her breath was coming heavy, her chest heaving. She had to move. Had to. He had already seen her naked. He had already done the worst he could do. Help was on the way. All she had to do was hold him off until it arrived.

A tinny voice echoed from the phone. He came closer, shaking the towel. "Thought you were smart, didn't you? Thought we would never find you. Wet feet leave footprints, miss."

Her arms ached from holding the skillet. She backed up until the wood counter dug into her back. She was breathing through her mouth, the air whistling between her teeth.

"Scared, huh? You got nothing to be scared about. Not yet. Not till my partner gets here."

He hadn't seen the phone then. In this dark corner of the kitchen he probably could barely see her at all. He came forward, waving the towel the way a bullfighter waves a cape.

"Hope you're pretty. I like pretty women."

Pretty. He had said that before. On the beach. She could smell him, the sweaty, oniony scent of an overweight man. He would touch her, and this time sand wouldn't dig into her back. The counter would.

And she was naked, just as she had been the first time.

"Got you trapped," he said. He reached out, and she swung the skillet at him, catching him full on the side of the head. The metal rang. He grunted and fell against the counter. The towel landed on her feet, the soft weave tickling the skin. She kicked it aside. He moaned again and reached for the counter to pull himself up. She brought the skillet down, harder this time, and he collapsed against the floor.

A voice was yelling outside. A man's voice. She held the skillet against her shoulder like a bat and stalked to the door. The other man stood in the driveway, his body silhouetted in the moonlight. He glanced in all directions, unable to see her or his friend. He was shouting his companion's name—a word she couldn't quite catch.

And then she heard sirens.

He wouldn't find her if she kept quiet. But she had to protect herself. She had to make sure the other one wouldn't wake up. She walked back in the kitchen. He hadn't moved. He huddled in a near-fetal position, one arm trapped under his head. She crouched over him, skillet poised, like a child about to smash a bug.

The tinny voice still spoke from the phone. Even though she couldn't hear the words, the sound comforted her. Someone was there. Someone was listening. The sirens grew louder. Flashing red and blue lights illuminated the kitchen. Something dark streaked the side of the counter. The man's hair had matted against his skull. His breath was raspy, difficult, as if his nose were plugged.

The door behind her opened, and a light came on. She stood and whirled at the same time, skillet clutched tightly in both hands.

A policeman stood there, hands out. "It's okay, ma'am. I'm here to help."

She didn't move. He came across the carpet slowly, facing her as he walked. He knelt beside the man and touched his matted hair. His fingers came away bloody. Two other policemen came in the doorway.

"He's breathing," the first policeman said. "But we'll need some help."

One of the others went back out the door. The first policeman stood. "We caught the other man on the road. You're safe now. That was some pretty quick thinking."

Her arms trembled under the skillet's weight. She didn't want to let it go. It was her protection. He came closer, reaching for her.

"It's okay. You're safe now."

"Your husband's outside," said the other policeman. "We met him as we were turning into the driveway. He wants to see you."

Steve? She felt as if she were surfacing from a very deep

sleep. Everything had to be okay if Steve was there. She loosened her grip on the skillet, and the policeman took it away from her as if he were afraid she would use it.

"Come on," he said gently. "You're safe with us. Do you have anything . . ."

For a moment she didn't know what he meant. Then she glanced back at the man on the floor. His left hand lay flat on the towel. She shook her head.

He nodded to the other policeman, who went into the bedroom. He returned carrying a pink chenille bedspread. With one hand he extended it. She took it and wrapped it around herself, wondering at the need for it. Would it embarrass them if she went outside naked?

"You hurt?" the first policeman asked.

She shook her head.

"Your husband's outside," the second one repeated.

They wanted her out of the house. Away from the man. That was good. She didn't want to be near him anymore. She had shown him. She had finally shown him that he couldn't hurt her, that he had no more power over her.

The night air was colder than she remembered. Five squad cars had squeezed into the small lawn, one parked on the baby pool near the swing set. Uniformed men huddled outside, talking. Steve stood with them until he saw her.

"Jesus, honey."

He came over and put his arms around her. She realized for the first time that she was trembling. He caressed her face, then stopped when he touched the bedspread. It had slipped so that it clung to her like a cape.

"You're not wearing anything. Did he—"

His voice broke. She knew what he saw. More months of therapy. More months of darkness, of hesitant touch.

"No," she said.

He took his hands off her as if he had been burned. She stepped back into his arms and leaned her head on his strong shoulder. "I mean," she said, "that he didn't touch me. He didn't touch me at all."

His body felt good against her bare skin, the rough cloth of his suit giving her comfort she didn't know she needed.

The bedspread fell, and as he reached for it she stopped him. He finished the hug, clutching her tight, and then bent down.

"You need this," he said, and he wrapped the spread around her.

She didn't need it. Not like he thought. Not ever again. Roger had been right. She had faced the fear and conquered it.

And no one would ever be able to hurt her again.

SILENT PACE

Jerry Ahern and Sharon Ahern

Sleep and Death, two twins of winged race, of matchless swiftness, but of silent pace.

The Iliad, Book XVI

I DON'T WANT TO KNOW YOUR NAME!"

Coughlin smiled. "Dr. Clemmens, you're faced with three possibilities and nothing more. Knowing my name or not knowing it won't make any difference to your fate. Trust me."

"My family and friends were expecting me. The police will find us. I demand that you—"

Coughlin cupped his hand over her lipsticked mouth. "You have no living family and no close friends other than your professional colleagues. You won't even be missed for another two days with this being Friday night. And once it is realized that something may have happened to you, the police won't even have a clue as to where to start looking for you. Dr. Clemmens, those three possibilities? Let me explain them instead of wasting time with idle chatter. You can willingly help me to relieve the anxiety that is destroying my life. As a psychiatrist, you're also an M.D. Remember your Hippocratic oath? If you choose to ignore your moral obligation, please believe that I can force you to take it more seriously."

Dr. Clemmens strained against the ropes that bound her into the folding chair. She tried to scream, but Coughlin merely pressed his hand more tightly over her mouth and continued speaking. "I'm a professional contract assassin, not a kidnapper. You'll have to forgive my technique when I chloroformed you in the parking garage and brought you here, but normally I just kill people. At times, however, I've been associated with teams of men whose job it was to extract information from someone prior to his death. I've watched these sorts of people work often enough that I know their methods. Imagine how painful it would be if I began tearing off your pretty fingernails one at a time with a pair of pliers, Dr. Clemmens. You wouldn't like it. If it matters, neither would I.

"So you can either help me willingly without all that pain and suffering or help me eventually anyway. There are more horrible things I can do to you than you could imagine, Doctor. It's all the same to me."

Coughlin took his hand from her mouth.

Dr. Clemmens didn't scream. Perhaps she'd realized it would be useless to do so. There was no one in the house besides themselves, and she had to have noticed as he brought her there that there were no other houses for miles around. She sucked in a deep breath, exhaled slowly, then asked in a slightly trembling voice, "What is my third option? You said there were three."

"That third possibility is the one that should keep you going. It's your one chance to live, that you'll be able to outsmart me and escape!"

Her blue eyes were rimmed with tears, some of the tears beginning to stream down her cheeks. Her makeup was smudged and had been since she'd awakened about an hour into the drive. Her shoulder-length, wavy blond hair needed brushing, too. Her suit was wrinkled, its skirt halfway up her thighs, and the knee was out of her left stocking. "Why do you want to kill me? I've never even met you before."

"It's nothing personal. I need help, the kind that only a

61

psychiatrist of your considerable abilities can provide. I've researched you, and you're the best there is. Unfortunately for you, however, in the process of helping me you'll learn too much about me. So I can't let you live afterward."

"I wouldn't say a word! Honestly. The doctor-patient relationship is confidential, so you'd have nothing—"

"I can't afford to take that chance. So you rest awhile, I'll fix something to eat, then we'll get started."

"How can I rest? Like this?"

Coughlin smiled. "Learn to cope. You'll be more comfortable later, I promise." He walked out of the bedroom, flicking off the lights, then closing and locking the door behind him. This was all for psychological effect. Dr. Cynthia Clemmens had to realize that her position was utterly hopeless, that her only chance lay in helping him and somehow defeating him during the process.

Coughlin entered the kitchen, took a beer from the refrigerator, then set about making some dinner for them both. While researching Dr. Clemmens's personal habits in order to efficiently accomplish her kidnapping he had discovered that they had something in common in their appreciation of Italian food. For that reason he was making lasagna.

In recent months Coughlin had become intimate with the gamut of late-night talk show personalities. Reading, in which he had indulged both eclectically and voraciously since his childhood, was now taboo unless the material was so wildly erotic that he became sexually aroused merely at the thought of it. With conventional fare he nodded off. Coughlin had even abstained from his favorite and somewhat sleep-inducing cabernet sauvignon in favor of beer. Any nice red wine would have been ideal with what he was preparing for his and Dr. Clemmens's dinner, but he couldn't risk it.

He avoided sex entirely unless he was certain that the woman would both stay with him during the night and awaken him in two hours. By trial and error Coughlin had determined almost precisely how much sleep he could allow himself in order to stay alive and how much time he needed to keep awake in order to sleep soundly.

His exhaustion from lack of sleep made him cranky, but he would allow himself only two hours of sleep out of every twenty-four. And although he had to frighten Dr. Clemmens into helping him, he had to remain somehow sympathetic in her eyes and couldn't let his worsening temper show.

Coughlin had first become aware of his fear of sleep after killing his best friend Lenny with a single 7.62mm NATO mil-spec sniper round at three hundred twenty-five meters. A tough shot. Lenny had turned police informant, and Coughlin was given the contract; business was business.

Meticulous research was just as vital to the success of a professional killer as were state-of-the-art weapons. Coughlin researched the malady that plagued him, learning that it was called hypnophobia.

The classic hypnophobe feared sleep because it mimicked death; but those who did not sleep inevitably died. His was the classic dilemma: He was damned if he slept, damned if he stayed awake.

Phobias, Coughlin learned, were usually seated in some deeply buried and unrememberable psychotrauma. Normally, however bothersome, phobias were simple affairs. The brontophobe, for example, feared thunder. This was irrational, of course, because thunder in itself was only a moderately loud noise, as benignly natural as the tapping of the wind-driven rain that was striking the kitchen windows.

And phobias were, by and large, reactions to generally avoidable situations. If one was alloraphobic, one could avoid cats by staying out of pet shops and alleyways and living in a building that didn't allow animals.

The possible manifestations of hypnophobia were the fears of dreaming, sleepwalking, sleeptalking, or loss of control. Or death. Dreaming, which had once been relaxing to him, was now, however pleasant in content, a signal to his subconscious that he was near death, and it was thus to be avoided. To his knowledge, he neither walked nor talked during sleep. And Coughlin was always in control.

Coughlin's hypnophobia centered on an irrational fear of dying. Through self-analysis and research he was certain of this. Only those persons for whom life was otherwise inescapable torture craved death; conversely, most people avoided contemplating their own mortality, crowding out thoughts of death with the daily routine of life. However, the sleep/death-centered hypnophobe's entire existence was focused on nothing but his inescapable fear.

Phobias were often conquerable through psychotherapy, but the conventional doctor-patient relationship to which Cynthia Clemmens had referred was not open to him. Regardless of its supposed sanctity, Coughlin could not risk exposing his past deeds to a doctor, as the result would be the realization of his greatest fear: ritual death through state-sanctioned execution by lethal injection, gas, or electrocution.

Coughlin's work had begun to suffer, his finances had dwindled, and his life had become an eternity of weariness. He had no choice but to kidnap the practitioner who would heal him, then kill her, mercifully and quickly.

Dinner almost completed, Coughlin returned to the bedroom, stopping first in the hallway for his olive-drab mechanic's tool case and the matching duffel bag, slinging the latter over his shoulder. As he entered the bedroom he could hear Cynthia Clemmens whimpering. He flipped on the light. Her eyes stared back at him, almost animal-looking in their terror.

He approached her chair. She recoiled. "Dinner's nearly ready. I know you like Italian. I made lasagna."

"I'm not hungry."

"But you'll eat, or you'll be punished. You see, I need you healthy and well so that you can make *me* healthy and well again."

"You say you want me to help—"

"I'm a hypnophobe with a death fixation. See the circles under my eyes? The red rims? Two hours every twenty-four is all I can risk, and it's killing me."

She licked her lips as he set the bag down on the table near

64

her. "It could take months or years to help you to get out of that."

"It won't take that long. In my currently exhausted state my susceptibility to hypnotherapy should be very high. I've already done a considerable amount of introspective analysis, Dr. Clemmens. We'll pinpoint the immediate cause of the problem in no time."

"That's not the hardest part of—what is that thing?"

She was looking at what he held in his hands. As Coughlin started putting it around her neck she began to scream. "This won't hurt you, nor will you achieve anything by screaming, Dr. Clemmens. Screaming is something I find extremely irritating, however." She closed her mouth and didn't make a sound, but her body shook violently, and as he closed the collar around her neck the tendons there went taut.

"What—"

"Isn't too tight, is it?"

"But—"

He closed the lock and pocketed the key. "Let's take this a step at a time, Dr. Clemmens. Then we'll have dinner. The collar is fabricated from two thicknesses of eight-ounce cowhide with a flexible metal strip between them. If you got hold of a knife or a pair of scissors, you might be able to cut through the leather—although I doubt it—but you'd never cut through the metal. This same collar is used by one of the world's top antiterrorist agencies to restrain rottweiler attack dogs, so I wouldn't think you should bother trying to break it, either. The lock on the buckle is pick-proof. A really good locksmith might be able to open it, but you'd break half the world's visible supply of hairpins and never get it."

"Why are you doing this to—"

"Security, Dr. Clemmens. As I was about to say, the plastic-sheathed cable I'm locking to your collar"—he attached the cable with a second lock identical to the first—"has a break strength of seven thousand pounds. It's chiefly used in aviation and marine applications. There's one hundred feet of it. But don't worry. It's extremely lightweight, so it shouldn't be a burden to you." Coughlin walked toward the door, knowing that her eyes followed him. He uncoiled the rest of the cable from the duffel bag, then locked the loose end to an eyebolt set into the floor. "This bolt passes through the floor and into a concrete slab beneath it. The concrete was allowed to dry around the bolt, so there's no sense wasting your energy trying to get free this way, either."

"Then I'm not the first person you've kept prisoner in this house, am I? Am I?"

Coughlin held the keys to the locks in his right hand, closed his fist around them, and looked Cynthia Clemmens square in the eye. "I'd tell you that was none of your business, but then you'd only waste time trying to get it out of me under hypnosis. So to answer the question, you are not the first human being to be held prisoner in this room. This house belongs to certain so-called organized crime figures with whose names I'm sure you'd be familiar. Do you want more information than that?"

"No—yes."

"Ambivalent, aren't we, Doctor? That's a sign of anxiety, if I'm not mistaken. But fine. Every organization has its personnel problems. Didn't you wonder why the floor in this room is covered with ceramic tile rather than carpeting? An easily cleanable surface was needed. Some people have been killed in this room, but only after they've been punished for their sins. Let's leave it at that, shall we? But I've spent the night here many times, Dr. Clemmens. Rest easy; the place isn't haunted."

"You vile son of a bitch!"

Coughlin laughed. "Glad to see you're in good spirits! One other thing before we eat dinner. There is no telephone in the house. You may have noticed the phone in my car. Even if we happened to be in range so it could be used, the garage is one hundred yards from the house. Your tether is one hundred feet. I'm going outside to put these keys in that car. If you killed me, Dr. Clemmens, you'd have no means of getting out of this house, ever. This is private property.

The taxes are paid for the coming year. There's about a week's worth of food in the house for two people to eat well. If you rationed it carefully, you might make it for four weeks. If you cannibalized my body—"

"You beast!"

"As I was saying, the flesh from my body might get you through another few weeks. In six weeks, at the outside, you'd begin to starve. In eight weeks you'd be dead, in a far less pleasant fashion than I have in mind for you. And any chance you might have of outsmarting me and somehow making it out of this alive would have vanished."

Coughlin walked back to the chair and began to untie her. "Flex your legs and arms for a while before getting up. Dinner's on a warming tray, so it won't get cold. I'll look forward to seeing you in the kitchen—we're not formal here—in about three or four minutes." And he glanced at his watch. Her slightly purpled hands reached up toward his face, then balled into fists and hammered down against her own thighs. She cried.

Coughlin left to go to his car.

Cynthia Clemmens might try to kill him, he thought, to snatch his gun from his holster. He hoped she believed what he'd told her; the truth was usually powerful logic. She would never leave alive regardless of what happened to him.

When he returned to the house she was waiting for him in the kitchen. Her face was washed, her hair brushed (he'd left suitable items for her convenience in the hall bath), and she offered to serve him dinner. Coughlin was amused by her predictable behavior, knowing that offering him her body would likely be next. After she cleared away the dinner dishes she got him another beer and asked if she could have one, too. "Certainly," Coughlin told her.

She was standing beside the refrigerator when she said, "You can have me. I mean, I know you can take me. You're bigger, stronger, but it would be nicer for you if—well, you don't seem like the kind of man who'd prefer doing something like that by forcing somebody."

"Dr. Clemmens—"

"Cyn—that's what everyone calls me." She had her beer,

had a glass in the other hand, and walked back to sit across from him at the kitchen table.

"Cyn. If you'd like us to have sex, I'd like that, too. Very much. But the keys to your restraints are still in the car, not in my pockets. If you take my gun"—he patted the weapon holstered at his right side—"it won't help you to escape. If you kill me, you'll die anyway. You can't shoot through the cable. If we make love, no matter how good you are to me, I still have to kill you when this is over."

"I know that."

"And you still want to?"

"Only a fool doesn't make the best of a bad situation. I want to know your name now."

"Jim Coughlin."

"Jim. My place or yours?" She laughed, and the laugh seemed genuine. That worried him a little. If Cynthia Clemmens flipped out, her death would be for nothing, and he'd still be trapped in sleeplessness.

"The couch."

Coughlin took her by the hand and led her into the living room. Dutifully she stood before him while his hands worked open buttons and zippers and hooks, stripping her naked. When he was through she dropped to her knees before him. Coughlin was at once thrilled by the thought of what she began to do and simultaneously embarrassed for her, that she would so debase herself.

As she opened his zipper Coughlin warned her, "If I fall asleep afterward, don't let me sleep more than two hours. If you do, and I don't die in my sleep, I'll hurt you."

"Yes, Jim."

Coughlin closed his eyes.

Making love with Cynthia Clemmens was extraordinary. Her hands, her mouth, her body were more skillful than any prostitute's had ever been, than any woman's had ever been. It was possible that being his prisoner, living under the threat of certain death, was a sexual turn-on for her. Yet, as Coughlin began drifting off, he reminded himself that she was there to deal with his psychological problems—it wasn't supposed to be the other way around.

Dutifully she awakened him two hours later. Even if he hadn't been wearing his wristwatch, he would have known from the loudly ticking clock on the mantel and from how he felt. He was just as weary as he had been before, and his body was bathed in the sweat of fear. But he was able to keep his eyes open. It helped that she was sitting across from him, wearing nothing but her bra and panties. "May I sleep for a while, Jim? Then we can get started helping you."

"Sure, Cyn."

While she slept he watched television. Off antenna only, reception was rather poor and channel selection limited.

Even though he had to remain otherwise sleepless, there was no sense in making the woman uncomfortable. He let her sleep for a full eight hours, checking on her several times just to make certain that she had not become fatally entangled in the cable leading from her collar. Like most women, she looked incredibly peaceful and even more beautiful when she was asleep. She awoke naturally a few moments before he would have roused her.

Cynthia Clemmens asked once if the collar could be removed while she showered. Jim Coughlin gave his regrets, advising her that the leather was treated with waterproofing and would dry quickly enough under the hairdryer he had provided for her use.

Their first session began at eleven in the morning. "If we wish to do this, Jim, then I'm going to have to hypnotize you."

"You know I expected that. Just please remember how useless it would be for you to kill me or otherwise bring about my death."

"I'll remember. Before we start with that, though, what do you think is the immediate cause of your problem? You said that you thought you knew."

Coughlin lit a cigarette. He exhaled. He was very tired. "There was a police informant I killed, up in Detroit."

"How did you do that—kill him, I mean?"

"Impersonally. I shot him in the head with a single bullet from a rifle. I couldn't even see his face. The problem was that I knew him. His name was Lenny Pavesi. We did time

69

together when we were kids. He was a nice guy, always a friend to me. I've killed people before that I knew—don't get me wrong. But that was something that just happened in the moment—"

"In hot blood, rather than cold blood?"

"Something like that, Cyn."

"Aren't you afraid that even if I'm able to help with your problem, you'll experience the same thing after you kill me? I'm asking this professionally, not personally, Jim."

He shrugged his shoulders. "It could happen, but I'll cross that bridge when I come to it."

"I see. So. Killing him. What did it precipitate in you? Feelings of remorse? Tell me."

Coughlin inhaled smoke deep into his lungs, stared at the cigarette's hard, glowing tip. "The way I figure it, I'd never really personalized death before. I lost my mom when I was just a little kid, and my dad lived a long happy life and died of old age. The guys I'd killed in 'hot blood,' as you put it, were acquaintances, nothing more. After I killed Lenny, however, I started thinking about how we'd never get together for a drink again, or split a pizza, or spend Saturday night screwin' our way through every babe we could get. I think Lenny's death made me realize my own mortality."

"So you attribute your self-diagnosed death-centered hypnophobia to this single act. Right?"

"Yes, I do."

She smiled indulgently, tugged his bathrobe closer around her body. "Jim, you have to understand something. I respect your intelligence a great deal. That's the honest truth. But a layman indulging in psychoanalysis—especially of himself —has poor odds for success. I've specialized in working with the subconscious through hypnosis for well over a decade, Jim. By way of example, if I survived this somehow —and I've accepted the fact that I won't—but if I did, let's say I became a hit man. Isn't that the term?"

"One of many, Cyn."

"If I did, though, go out and kill people, would you expect me to be proficient at it, even given that I'm reasonably intelligent and a fast learner, and assuming that I had a natural talent for it? What would my abilities be as compared to yours? How long have you been killing people?"

"Twenty-three years, if you count the war. I was a sniper. And no, you'd probably stink at killing people."

"So don't be offended when I tell you that I think your problem is rooted much more deeply, Jim. Indeed, your friend Lenny's death may be the immediate cause, and hypnophobia may be the actual diagnosis, but the ultimate cause is what we'll have to get at. And I guess we don't have very much time. So let's begin. I want you to put out your cigarette, settle yourself comfortably in the chair, and just relax, breathing normally but evenly. Will you do that?"

"All right. Just please remember, Cyn, what will happen to you if anything happens to me."

"I'll remember, Jim."

He clicked the play and record switches for the tape player beside him. "And I'm recording everything in each session. If you implant any posthypnotic suggestions to free you or anything like that, it won't work. I know enough about hypnosis to know that a person cannot be forced into an act that violates his basic nature."

"You couldn't hypnotize me, for example, and turn me into a murderer? Is that what you're saying, Jim?"

"Yes."

"Theatrical hypnotists make people cluck like chickens or bark like dogs, of course. However, that can only be done while the subject is in the trance state. But you're right, clucking or barking isn't the same thing. And for you, releasing me and placing yourself at risk would be a violation of your most basic nature, your instinct for survival. So I could no more force you to release me while in the trance state or as the result of a posthypnotic suggestion I'd implanted than I could make you shoot yourself. Anyway, in the past I've always considered it grossly unethical to manipulate someone's mind to my will. Believe me, I've accepted the fact that I'll almost certainly be murdered by you. I really have accepted it.

"And I've considered my options," Cynthia Clemmens went on. "I could keep you in the trance state and take your gun. I could figure out how to make the gun shoot. If I shot you, I'd be stuck here, unable to escape. Of course, I could kill myself after I killed you. But I'm not capable of suicide. I've thought about that ever since you left me in the dark all tied up and went off to make dinner. And suicide or your murdering me are the only ways I can avoid an even worse alternative, death by starvation. Tape to your heart's content, Jim. You won't detect any plots, I promise you."

"I'm sorry to have to kill you, Cyn, but it will be quick and painless."

"Will you tell me first?"

"If you want me to," Coughlin said honestly. "It might be easier on you if I don't, though."

She smiled. "Do you always shoot your victims?"

"Not always. I've killed in other ways." Cynthia Clemmens seemed to be considering something for a moment. "What's on your mind?" Coughlin asked.

"We were lovers last night. This will take several sessions at the very least. I'd like us to be lovers again, as often as we can. And when you do kill me, do it in the same way that Othello murdered Desdemona. Do you know what I mean?"

"I understand, Cyn. And fine, we'll do it that way."

She was playing with the belt from his robe, her fingers moving nervously over it in her lap. "Will that be quick and painless for me, Jim, to be strangled with a kiss?"

"There's a way of doing it. 'I that am cruel am yet merciful; I would not have thee linger in thy pain.'"

"Then you do understand." And she smiled at him. "Now, we'd better get started," she said brightly. "There are various methods for hypnotizing someone, Jim. Some people use lights, some people use no props at all. I prefer the latter method."

"Go for it."

"Use your dimmer switch for the overhead lights. Lower them almost completely."

Coughlin worked the remote dimmer with his index finger.

"Jim, I want you to focus on my fingertips. I'm going to keep them right here in my lap. Watch how my fingertips move, so slowly, so gently, like leaves rustling in the wind. I want you to relax, to feel your muscles relaxing one by one. Take a deep breath in through your nose and let it out ever so slowly through your mouth, as if it's starting at the tips of your toes and coming up along your legs and your abdomen and finally up to your chest. And your shoulders feel relaxed. And so does your neck. Your feet are on the floor, your hands are in your lap, but they aren't moving. Your heart rate and your blood pressure are dropping. Your eyelids are dropping, too. They're so heavy that you can't keep them open anymore, and you're so totally relaxed that your eyes will remain closed. You're warm, aren't you, Jim, but not hot, just comfortable? And you're so peaceful. Even though your eyes are closed, you can still see my fingertips moving, very gently moving. And within my hands there's a light. You can see that light. Can you see it, Jim?"

"Yes."

"I want you to picture yourself moving into that light, and once the light totally surrounds you—it's pleasantly warm and the most peaceful sensation you've ever known—once that light totally surrounds you, I want you to tell me."

The light was warm, and he felt more relaxed than—he couldn't remember ever being so relaxed.

"The light, Jim, as you become accustomed to it, you see colors in it, don't you?"

"Yes."

"Yellows and blues and greens, very soft, easy to look at, peaceful."

"The colors are moving around me like clouds."

"One of the clouds is just ever so slightly pink, isn't it?"

"Yes," Coughlin told her. The pink cloud was the most beautiful cloud, and it surrounded him while he spoke to her, telling her his most intimate secrets, his memories sometimes making the light become dim, making the pink cloud begin to dissipate. Then there was her voice—the cloud was in her hands, the light was her light—and the cloud was as it should be again, and the light was bright and warm, and he was at peace.

He heard the clapping of her hands, three times. The first time was like a soft, distant roll of thunder, the second time louder, stronger, and the third time—"I—"

"You're out of it now, Jim. How do you feel?"

Coughlin laughed. "Better than I've felt in months, maybe better than I've ever felt." He looked at his watch, then at the counter on the tape recorder. It featured a continuous readout and would run into six digits until returning to zero unless reset. Memorization of numbers had always been easy for him—bullet drop figures, license plates, anything —and Coughlin had committed to memory the elapsed numbers on the counter as they corresponded to fifteen-minute intervals of time. He reasoned that if she paused the machine in order to plant some sort of secret seed in his mind, the numbers would be out of sync. They were not. If they had been, a few seconds with his calculator would reveal how much time was unaccounted for. Several minutes at least would be required if she were going to trick him. "Did we make any progress?"

Cynthia Clemmens leaned back in her chair. "Yes, Jim. There's something repressed that we're starting to get at. Actually, our progress is remarkable."

"How soon before we can try again, Cyn?"

"Let me see your watch."

Coughlin unclasped the watch from his wrist and passed it over to her. "Mine's a Rolex, too. And I could use my watch, when you get around to it. It helps me to keep track of the session."

"I've got it in the car with your purse. And there's the clock on the mantel in the living room. We could bring that in here." The dining room was Spartan in the extreme, devoid of all decoration except for a vase at the center of the table and the two overstuffed chairs in which they sat by the window. "I can get your watch for you now."

"No need to bother. We won't try again for several hours. Maybe tonight. All right, Jim?"

Coughlin smiled, telling her, "You're the doctor."

They spent the afternoon in her room's bed rather than on the couch, Coughlin feeling more energetic in his lovemaking than he had since killing Lenny in Detroit.

And Cynthia Clemmens was beyond anything Coughlin had ever imagined possible in a woman. At one point she asked that he bind her with the ropes again, but tie her into the bed this time, not a chair. He bound her. Her fingers, unable to reach him, curled into claws and lashed out; her teeth snapped at him as her body undulated beneath him. And he was spent more completely than he had ever been. He fell asleep.

"Jim? Jim?"

Her voice. Coughlin opened his eyes. "Cyn?"

"The therapy's starting to work. We're not there yet, but it's really starting to work! I could see your wristwatch. You slept for three hours." He sat bolt upright as she said it. Then Cynthia Clemmens laughed. "I would have let you sleep longer, but my hands are going numb."

"Aww, Cyn, I'm sorry!" He began untying her immediately. She showered while he made dinner. She discouraged him from wasting time on something complicated, so he warmed up the remaining lasagna and made garlic bread to go with it. She had a beer, and so did he, resting, talking while she cleared the table and began to wash the dishes.

"You don't have to do that, Cyn."

"A lot of people assume that because a woman devotes the major portion of her life to a career—well, that she doesn't like the simple things anymore, like doing for a man."

Coughlin lit a cigarette. Killing her would be the most difficult thing he had ever done in his life. But he would do it.

After a time they drifted into the dining room. Before they started he ran out to the car—the ground was still wet from the previous night's rain—and retrieved her watch. It was a very sensible-looking watch, the face black, the case stainless steel, the band of the Jubilee style, composed of alternating links of stainless steel and gold.

The session went very long this time, but when he awoke he felt even better than he had the first time. As Cynthia Clemmens reported on their progress he compared the time to the tape recorder's counter numbers. All was in order, and Coughlin felt almost guilty for having bothered to check. "Your mother died when you were quite young, Jim, as you said. But everyone thought you were too young to understand it at the time that it happened. Isn't that true?"

"You know how adults think about kids. My parents were good people, good to me. After Mom died Dad took really good care of me."

"We're getting very close, and I feel stupid telling you, because as soon as we have the cause, I have the feeling we'll be able to take care of your problem relatively quickly. One thing I really do regret, Jim."

"Look, I'm sorry—"

"No. I don't mean that, the part about killing me. I only wish that we could somehow report what we've done here. The progress we've made needs to be shared with the psychiatric community. Sleep deprivation seems to accelerate the progress that can be made under hypnosis."

"Can't do it, Cyn."

"I know that, but we might really be able to help some other people suffering from your problem, or from similar phobias."

"Sorry." Coughlin lit a cigarette. "When's the next session?"

"I'd say you should go for a two-hour sleep session, maybe three. I'll watch your eyes and awaken you if you start to dream. Then I'm going to get some sleep," she told him, smiling.

"You're beautiful. And I think I love you. But none of this will change anything."

"I know." She stood up, leaned over, and kissed his cheek.

When the second session of the fourth day ended and he

had perfunctorily checked his watch against the counter numbers, Cyn said to him, "If I'd thought of it, I could have asked you before. Would you like me to cure your smoking habit? I can, you know."

Coughlin laughed. "No, but thanks anyway. How are we doing?"

"Well, I'm an imbecile for telling you this, and I hope it doesn't mean you'll just get up out of your chair and shoot me, but I think we've got it."

He leaned forward in his chair, and she drew back from him. "No! Relax. I promised you it'd be painless."

"And to strangle me with a kiss."

"Yes, with a kiss. And it'll be a little while yet." Coughlin hated lying to her. "Tell me—I mean, tell me all about it, and—"

She smiled. "All right. But let's at least have this night together, Jim. Okay?"

"I promise, Cyn." And he wasn't lying.

She nodded her head slowly. "When your mother died you were actually in her room, but you don't consciously remember it. You got up out of bed and came in to see her because you were frightened and couldn't sleep. She was asleep—probably dead, but you thought she was only sleeping—and you tried to wake her. You couldn't awaken her no matter how hard you tried, Jim. A few hours later—and the only thing I'm guessing at is the time—your father discovered that she was dead."

"They always slept together until she got sick. I remember that."

Cynthia Clemmens nodded. "He told you that your mother was only sleeping, then put you back to bed. When you woke up the next morning you found out that she was dead. Somehow, when you killed your friend Lenny— someone you really cared about—and personalized death, your subconscious dredged up from your childhood that association between sleep and death. Lenny was so like you that you realized your own mortality in a way you never had before, as you thought. But the key to it was seeing your mother asleep and learning that she'd really been dead."

"You mean I'm cured?"

"I think so."

"Swear to God?"

She laughed, nodded, repeated, "Swear to God. You're no longer hypnophobic."

"And—I feel funny asking this, but—"

"Will killing me trigger it again? No. Unless I'm dead wrong." And she looked down into her lap. When she looked up into his eyes, her eyes were tear-rimmed, as they had been that first day. "Your problem—it was a little more complex, but your diagnosis was right. Your hypnophobia is cured."

"Thank you." Coughlin licked his lips. "Look. We skipped dinner. How about something special? I've got some steaks."

"I won't be very hungry, but I could eat a little, I guess."

"Want a beer?"

"Maybe later. I mean—"

"Relax! There'll be a later." He stood up, raised her from her chair, and kissed her hard on the mouth. "You may not believe this," he said, "but I really love you." He released her and went off to start dinner.

She joined him in the kitchen after a while, laughing when she told him she liked her steaks bloody. She had a beer and got him one. He made baked potatoes in the microwave oven. They ate in the kitchen. Had they used the dining room, he would have been able to hear the ticking of the mantel clock, and he didn't want to think about time.

Coughlin didn't want to kill this woman, but he knew that if he didn't murder her that night he might not do it at all.

By midnight they went into the bedroom. "I want to ask you something," she said as she took off her bra.

"Please don't ruin this," Coughlin almost whispered.

"No, Jim, I wasn't even going to ask you to remove my collar. I think I'd feel naked without it." She looked down across her body and laughed. "Well, you know what I mean. No, it's just a little favor."

"If I can," he answered truthfully.

"After you kill me, take my watch and keep it to remember me by. Maybe it won't be so bad to be dead, but it would be awful to be forgotten. My parents are gone. Well, you know that. And then my husband died two years ago."

"A street mugging. I know."

She whispered, "He was at one of those automatic teller machines, and—"

"Hey, don't talk about it. You'll only make yourself cry."

She bit her lip, nodded. Without looking at him she asked, "Will you take it? Will you remember me, Jim?"

"I'll always remember you. I swear to God."

And they both laughed. She undressed him and drew him under the covers with her. He pushed the cable leading from her collar out of their way as he took her into his arms.

Her ferocity that night was beyond anything he had experienced with her before. It was as if life filled her more than he ever could. Coming was the greatest moment of violence he had ever known. Cynthia Clemmens's hands grasped his face, holding him, her lips hard against his, her tongue raping his mouth. Coughlin's hands drifted over her body, stopped at her breasts, her shoulders, her neck. He kissed her so hard that it hurt as his fingers closed tighter and he threw his weight with his shoulders and the life left her in an instant.

"Just like Othello and Desdemona, just like I promised." Coughlin let her head fall back against the pillows. "I really loved you, Cyn." As his thumbs lowered Cynthia Clemmens's eyelids he remembered his other promise. He raised her left arm. Her flesh was still warm, alive-feeling. He opened the clasp on her watch and slipped the band from her wrist. He looked at the time. A little after two A.M. He yawned, glancing at his own watch. Almost quarter till two.

Coughlin raised up to his knees. His breathing was coming hard. He picked up his cigarettes and his lighter. He hadn't smoked all evening. He lit up. "Shit!" He spat the cigarette onto the floor, his throat starting to fill with vomit. He picked up the cigarette. There was a burn scar on the floor tile. Coughlin brought the cigarette to his lips.

Again he began to feel as though he were about to retch.

Coughlin stabbed the cigarette into the ashtray, then ran from the bedroom into the kitchen. The clock on the microwave read the same as his wristwatch. The living room. The clock there read the same as his watch, the same as the microwave. He stared at her watch.

"Would you like me to cure your smoking habit? I can, you know," she'd told him.

Coughlin leaned heavily against the mantel, looked at the couch on which they'd made love that first night. "No. No, damn it!"

He started into the hallway, ran its length to the bedroom, looked at her there on the bed, a smile on her face even in death. "You didn't, damn it! Did you?" Coughlin grabbed his pants, pushed his feet into his shoes, grabbed up his gun.

He ran, not bothering to stop at the closet and get his trench coat, but running from the house, running the one hundred yards to his car. "Keys, where the fuck are the keys?"

Coughlin didn't have his car keys, remembering that he'd left them in his trench coat pocket. The car was parked beside the shed, and there was wood stacked there for the fireplace beneath the living room mantel. Coughlin picked up a log and smashed it through the driver's-side window.

Despite the glass, the instant he had the door open he flung himself down behind the wheel, flipping her watch onto the seat beside him. His hands moved along the steering column, finding the wires near its base. In less than a minute he had ignition. But Coughlin didn't care if the engine turned over. All he wanted was power. His eyes riveted on the dashboard clock as it came alive, then shifted to her wristwatch.

Her watch and the dashboard clock matched almost to the minute.

"The tapes."

Coughlin was up and running again, still carrying her watch, his gun cold against his naked abdomen.

It would have to be the last tape, he told himself. On his knees before the recorder near the chairs by the dining room window, he pressed the rewind button. He heard himself talking. She wouldn't make it easy.

His eyes on her watch—the real time—he kept rewinding the tape, stopping every few seconds, listening, going on, back in time to find the message she would have left for him to hear.

At last he caught it. ". . . think that I've accepted the inevitability of my death, Jim. Don't feel bad for killing me, because I was telling you the truth. After my husband was killed I wanted to kill myself, and I couldn't. I could have killed the man who stabbed him to death for twenty dollars, but I couldn't kill myself. You did me a favor. So maybe it was wrong of me to repay your kindness this way."

"What way, Cyn?"

". . . to prove to you that I could do it, so you wouldn't doubt. If you haven't wanted a cigarette yet, don't you wonder why? Posthypnotic suggestion, Jim. Just like the one I gave you so you'll never be able to sleep again without seeing your mother dead there in her bed, and when you look very closely into her face you'll see me. Then you'll open your eyes. Every time sleep comes to you you'll awaken instantly. I didn't lie, telling you you're no longer hypnophobic. You won't have to fear sleep, because you'll never sleep. How long do you think you can survive without any sleep at all, even your two hours, Jim? Another psychiatrist? I don't think so. I'm the best. Remember? It could take months, maybe years to get deep enough into you to cancel what I planted there. Want to survive by being drugged into unconsciousness? And maybe you'd still see your mother, and me, and the dream would go on forever.

"I'd suggest suicide, Jim. In a roundabout way, if you're listening to this, it worked for me, didn't it? Funny thing is, Jim, I think I love you, too. Sleep tight." And then she was asking him questions again, as if what she'd just said had never been said at all, their regular hypnotherapy session never interrupted, querying him about all the people he had killed, about Lenny.

Coughlin stood up, letting her voice play on from the machine as he walked back toward the bedroom.

He stopped at the foot of the bed. He shook his head. "I have to hand it to you, Cyn. And I really did love you, anyway."

He put her watch back onto her wrist, touched his lips to her face. Her skin was cold.

Coughlin lay down beside her and took the gun from his belt. He cocked the hammer. He placed the muzzle beneath his jaw. "Good night, Cyn. I misjudged you. You would have made a fine hit man."

Coughlin closed his eyes as his thumb jerked back the trigger.

THE UGLIEST WOMAN IN THE WORLD

Valerie Frankel

Y OUR BREASTS ARE LOVELY," SAID MITCH. "I DON'T KNOW why you think otherwise." He smiled as handsomely as any short, balding, mustachioed man can and reached across the table to touch whatever part of my body was within reach. I instinctively jerked away. Instead of lowering his hand, he let it hang in midair, waiting. I shouldn't have said anything, I thought before I reluctantly brushed my wrist against his fingertips. There was enough bone there to not be too erotic. He lowered his arm, satisfied with this small victory. The young girl at the neighboring table put her hand on her boyfriend's knee and motioned toward us with the tilt of her pretty head.

"Maybe we should stop drinking now," I said.

"Why, are you sick?" he asked.

"I just don't want to drink anymore."

"Okay. We won't drink." Mitch picked at his dessert. His eyes traveled across the boundaries of our table toward the one next door. Her breasts were round and high, and she clearly loved them. The restaurant was too ritzy to allow for overt appraisal, but I noticed the way men looked at her throughout the duration of our meal. I'm always watching men watching women. Men are never watching me, but I don't care. I let myself wonder on occasion what life would be like if I didn't have the deformity. But I do, and I've learned to spend as little time as possible imagining the impossible. The jealousy, though, always finds a way to surface.

She wore a black bra underneath one of those sheer tops that are so popular these days. Her plumpness overflowed from the bra cups, and I watched Mitch try to discern whether that spot of brown was the top of her areola or just a strategic shadow. I'd already decided it was indeed the areola, and that she had particularly large ones at that. The kind that bring male groins to life. My own are pathetic shriveled quarters. They are shocking, like my attitude problem. At least that's my mother's opinion.

I let Mitch stare at her and then pushed my fork over the side of the table with my elbow. While fishing under the cloth to retrieve it I gave Mitch's lap a thorough inspection. There didn't seem to be any sign of activity, as if I'd know what to look for in a man. I reminded myself that Mitch, forty-five, was probably too old and infirm to get a hard-on from the mere sight of a pretty girl. But for all I knew, his small body might very well be churning with whatever rages it could produce in his approaching middle age. Maybe he'd fantasize about her later while we were screwing. I'd never know if he did. Fuck him, I thought. I hate him.

"We could have asked for a clean one, you know," Mitch said, pointing at my fork. I imagined plunging it into his jugular. The arc of red blood would look nice in the yellow light.

"Tell me more about your childhood, Mitch," I flirted. "It sounds fascinating."

"Look, Liz," he started, "I want to do this. I don't get why you're trying so hard to make me like you." His eyes hit me head on. "I like you already." He blushed slightly. I felt a wave of self-loathing. I needed a disguise. Mitch must think this is all so fucking funny, I thought.

"Let's order more wine," I suggested. Then, remembering, I said brightly, "I changed my mind. It is a woman's prerogative."

"More wine, then." Mitch smiled and signaled the waiter. I peeked at the couple next door. She had apparently lost interest in our awkward dealings and was having a lively conversation with her muscular companion, boyfriend, slave, dick, whatever. His eyes were so focused on her tits that I couldn't understand why she bothered to keep on talking as if he heard a single word of her babble. She gestured with her arms more flamboyantly than she needed to. I wondered if that was a personal quirk or her ploy to make her breasts bounce like softballs in a bathtub. Later on in the night he'd take her home and fuck the shit right out of her ass. I pictured this and felt disgusted. My gaze drew hers. My expression must have reflected my thoughts because she seemed to shudder slightly when we made eye contact. I do believe I've frightened the girl, I thought. I smiled inwardly and felt better.

I heard once that breasts are man's eternal quest. The women's studies professor who introduced that concept in her class suggested that men (man, males) are forever searching for their mother's tit to latch on to and suck the life out of. They'd thereby leave her drained, nothing more than an empty void with deflated milk sacs withering on her chest. At the time I heard this lecture—I was just twenty-one—I wasn't worried about all that. My own breasts were grotesque and deformed. Mutated and repulsive. No man would ever suck the life out of me and live to tell.

I was a late bloomer. The boys in my junior high school called me Buds. I didn't mind being a have-not then. The developing girls who were my friends always complained of pain and awkwardness. If they leaned over and brushed against anything—a door, a wall, a basketball, a father, a brother—they felt a self-consciousness and embarrassment like no other. They held books against themselves to cover their rebellious bodies. Bra straps cut into their shoulders and were snapped intrusively by boys after school.

By the time we reached high school that intrusive bra snap

had become the mating call of hundreds of frustrated teenagers. Baggy T-shirts were replaced with leotard tops that accentuated curves, swells, and blossoms. The boys took notice and, in turn, held books against themselves whenever confronted with the view of a nice set. My own set was still in lazy construction. This lack didn't draw any male attention, and I was fine with that. For one thing, male attention didn't seem like something to covet. I didn't understand what made a titty-twister so erotic or why the girls would squeal and giggle whenever they received one. I also didn't understand why I found myself filled with rage and jealousy toward the girls who had once been my friends. As for the boys who never were, I found them to be buffoonish, boorish, and childlike. And equally as enraging.

My psychiatrist has something to say about this (and everything else): My late development caused conflicting interest in sex and in the opposite sex. And, like many women, my self-worth is intrinsically tied to my opinion of my physical appearance. I hated the way I looked; I hated myself. In college, the focus of this hatred had fallen on my breasts, the clearest signal of post-adolescent femininity. By freshman year my breasts had finally grown, but they'd developed into horrific masses with mountainous fibroids and venous bulges. They were disgusting. I was so depressed that I stopped eating for a while—at least I lost the last of my teenage weight. But that didn't change the deformity. If I could have sliced off my tits and not bled to death, I would have. I took to wearing big sweaters to hide them. Not wanting to be found out, I took showers in the middle of the night. I never undressed in front of anyone. During the hot months I never hung out at pools or by the river. It was hard to talk to normal people—they couldn't understand my problems. I started to avoid roommates, classmates, anyone. And eventually everyone. Friendships had always been a bother anyway.

If any men showed interest in me—few did, I was such a loner—I'd tell them to fuck off. They wouldn't have wanted me if they knew my secret. I was doing them a favor, not that they deserved it. I watched the men in college make fools of themselves every day, swilling beer, hitting each other, throwing up in public. I hated them. The women not only tolerated their behavior, they encouraged it by pooh-poohing cutely and wearing little clothing. I grew to hate the women, too. Especially the ones with nice breasts.

Mitch and I left the restaurant an uncomfortable ten minutes later. We never got the wine, but Mitch paid for it just the same. In the cab to my place in the Village he said, "I'm buzzing like a bee."

"Is that good?" I asked. I often drink a few glasses of wine with my dinner at home. I felt nothing that night.

Mitch responded, "Good versus bad stopped being a concern for me when I hit thirty-five." He looked at me, and the lights of the city night flashed across his ever-expanding forehead. If only he were a different person, I thought. Then maybe this wouldn't be so hard.

"You don't look much older than thirty-five," I lied.

"I wish you would stop with the flattery, Liz," he complained. "You know how I feel, and I know how you feel. You think I'm doing you a favor, and that's what's the most insulting. But don't worry. I'm not trying to get out of this. I want this for myself." He seemed genuinely hurt, which confused me. I tried to figure out why he'd be insulted by my appreciation. People make no sense. He faced away from me. For a crazy second it seemed like he was crying. Mitch is too sensitive for me, I decided. The last thing a deformity like me needed was to worry about someone else's feelings.

"I haven't had the best luck in love," Mitch confessed when he turned back to face me. Any evidence of tears had vanished.

"Like I've had luck with men?" I asked.

"I'd like to tell you about my past."

"Forget it," I stated. I'd heard around the real estate office where we work that he had had an ugly divorce from his wife and a maddening affair with a younger woman immediately afterward. Curiosity made me listen, but when the gossip got more detailed I'd tune out. I really didn't want to know about any of them. That they'd ever know anything about me made me murderously angry.

"I don't know what you've heard," Mitch started.

I interrupted him. "If anyone at the office finds out about us, I'll kill you," I said, and I smiled. I am not a violent person in practice.

"People like to talk about their experiences, Liz," he said. "It's human nature. And I want to tell you about mine. It'll make us feel closer to each other."

To shut him up I slid over the taxi backseat and leaned on him. That made us feel closer, at least physically. He gave me a soppy look and kissed me.

The taste of foreign tongue is supposed to be sensual, like a lick of honey or the lingering scent of garlic on fingertips. As our kiss deepened I felt my entire body ice over as if I'd fallen into a fishing hole. My leg muscles clamped with tension; my lips twitched with nerves. Mitch mistook these changes as signs of my excitement. I don't know how on earth this is going to work, I thought. He put his hand on my neck. It made me sick.

"Don't stop, Mitch," I said.

"I've always wanted you," he confessed, and I felt sicker.

"Me, too. You." His hand slid down to my shoulder. Our lips were still touching, his tongue running across my teeth.

"You love to tease," he breathed, and I didn't understand what he meant. Teases are loose women. I was tight as a drum, everywhere. I pushed him away. "What's wrong?" he asked.

"Can't you wait until we get to my apartment?" I bitched. "This is the longest cab ride in history." I turned toward the window and away from Mitch. I picked out faces and bodies as we crept through the busy streets, searching for the man who could make it all different. Mitch was not the one, but he'd have to do. I'd made my decision, and it would have to stick. Forty-four-year-old virgins like me don't have many choices.

* * *

The Ugliest Woman in the World

My mother is flat-chested and toothpick-skinny, no hips, tiny waist. She's sixty-five years old with long silver hair that looks good when she twists it into a ponytail in the summertime. My father, sixty-nine, a professor of biology at Rutgers University, always told her the ponytail looked ridiculous. His favorite swimwear is a striped Speedo bikini and a baseball cap. My mother used to brag to her friends that he could get away with it.

My parents have a pool with a black bottom at their house in New Jersey. I remember on one summer day, it must have been ninety degrees, Dad decided to skinny-dip in front of me and Mom. She squealed with delight, the whole time telling him that it was inappropriate for me to see him naked. I was fifteen. In lieu of a nice set of breasts I'd developed a weight problem. Flesh rolled across my stomach, and my upper arms jiggled if I waved. My shrink thinks that I put on all that weight as a teenager because I subconsciously hoped some of it would increase my bosom. It didn't. She also thinks that I wanted to ensure disinterest from boys. I was afraid of rejection, so I cut off the possibility, she said. But she's wrong. We all strive to find out the one thing we're good at in life. Even then, I knew that being rejected was my personal forte.

I never invited friends over to swim during those summer days. I was embarrassed by my weight, my nonexistent breasts, and my obsequious parents. The one time I did convince a diminutive girl named Joni to come over, my parents went overboard to make her feel at home. I hated them for it—after all, I hardly perceived any effort on their part to make me feel comfortable in my home, skin or otherwise. My mother argues my fear of bringing home friends was completely unfounded. And yet she's the one who insists on footing my shrink bills.

On the day of Dad's nakedness I dived to the black bottom to retrieve a drowned salamander. I placed the tiny body on the hot white cement border of the pool. My mother told me to throw it out, it was disgusting. My father swam over and took a look. The professor said, "It's dead, all right. Toss it in the bushes."

I said, "But salamanders are amphibious."

"Sure," agreed Dad. "But that means they are born in water but need air to survive as adults. This bugger is grown-up enough to be dead."

"But what if it never surfaced? What if it stayed underwater forever?" I asked with genuine curiosity.

My father gave my mother a what-have-we-done-wrong look and said to me, "If you were attractive, the stupid things you say would actually be charming." My mother pooh-poohed him and told him to put on some clothes.

Mitch and I arrived at my one-bedroom apartment, and he suggested we take a bath together. He thought I was tense and that I needed to relax. I'd trusted him enough to tell him that the time had come to rid myself of my virginity. I'd hinted at the condition of my breasts, but I didn't want to scare him off. Maybe after the sex I'd flash him so he'd be sure never to come back. No man has seen my breasts. I pitied Mitch for being the potential first.

My gynecologist is a small-breasted woman. On my first visit with her I vehemently refused to remove my bra for the breast exam, and she has since stopped asking. She did tell me that sleeping with a bra and showering with a bikini top weren't the healthiest practices. I also dress in the dark and have no mirrors in my apartment save the one above the sink in the bathroom. These are my security measures. I have fainted before from the sight of my naked breasts and almost hurt myself. My shrink is also a small-breasted woman. I was referred to her by my gynecologist. I wondered at the time if there was a small-breasted women's network.

I have never had a boyfriend, and on the few occasions when I have been kissed by a boy or man I have never taken off my bra. Inevitably, they'd leave me in frustration. One said, "I never wanted you anyway." My shrink said that was a projective comment. I don't know if I agree. She also said that I use my breasts, "the symbols of female adulthood," in order to stay out of the grown-up world. As I've said, she has opinions on everything and proof of nothing. She's never seen me naked, after all.

The one time a man put his hand under my dress was only a month ago. That was Mitch. It was at a bar. I went along with a group of people from the office to have a drink at the margarita place that had just opened across the street. They always ask me to join them out of politeness. I don't usually go, but I allowed myself to be convinced. For a minute I wondered if it was because I knew Mitch was going, but that would mean I cared, and that was impossible. We all drank, and I excused myself to go to the bathroom. Mitch was waiting in the hallway for me when I came out. He pushed me back inside and kissed me. I was afraid he'd try to touch my breasts, and when he went for my ass instead I was relieved. I slapped him across the cheek and called him a motherfucker. He was smiling as I walked out.

After work I usually just go home to my two cats. I make elaborate dinners that take hours of preparation. I enjoy my wine, and I watch a lot of television. I'm a member of an adult video club. A new tape arrives in the mail each week—the postal system saves me the embarrassment of going to rent them. I started to watch them a while ago to see what it is I'm not doing. Now I depend on them. Although the thought of doing those things myself is humiliating, I must admit that the primordial part of me gets incredibly turned on. The scenes with many men on one woman seem to be the most effective for me. I'm sure my therapist would say that's proof of my desirability doubts. She doesn't know about the tapes.

I don't hate the actresses for their perfect breasts. In a weird way, the women in pornography are like friends to me. They know my biggest secret—that I masturbate to their images with my feet on the coffee table and a pillow between my legs. When I come a flash of blue explodes behind my eyes. Sometimes I take a Valium and just float through a viewing. The cats hate it when I watch videos. They feel neglected and pull books off the shelves. I throw the old video in the garbage when the new one comes. I'd hate for a guest to discover my little vice. Then again, I never have guests.

"No baths," I said to Mitch. "That's too intimate."

"There's a lot going on in there," Mitch said, and he touched my hair.

He meant inside my head. I'd already offered him my virginity, and now he wanted to penetrate my mind as well. I'm the first to admit I may be an excessively private person, but asking for my thoughts was too much. "Maybe you should go," I said. "I don't want to talk, and if that's all you want, then get out."

He sighed. I couldn't shake the idea that he should be having a tougher time willing himself to stay in my apartment, with me, alone. There was something wrong with him, I was sure.

"Men will fuck anything," I said to myself out loud.

"You don't have to take off your clothes if you don't want to," he responded. "You're self-conscious, I know. It's okay if you don't want to take off your clothes. I won't either."

"Let's just do this, all right?" I hiked up my skirt, pulled down my stockings, and leaned over the armchair in my living room. I waited in horror for his touch, but it didn't come. I straightened up and turned around. Mitch was sitting on my wool-covered couch, picking pills and looking extremely uncomfortable.

He didn't face me when he protested, "I won't do it like that."

"I can't make this any easier for you," I said through my teeth. My impatience with him grew. "Do you think I like it that I'm a virgin?" I asked.

"I think it's sad that you are," he commented.

"We were talking about me."

"I don't want it to be like this," he said. "You deserve romance. Wine and music. Soft lighting."

"That's bullshit for scared adolescents," I argued. "I want to get fucked, Mitch. And if you can't do it, maybe Stan will." Stan was another guy from the office. He had beaten Mitch out for a promotion, and Mitch hated his guts. He sank farther into the couch when I mentioned Stan's name. I felt a twinge of excitement and power. Hostility rose in me like juice being poured into a long tall glass. Mitch remained, dejected and vulnerable on the couch. Leave it to me to pick the one guy in the world who won't just do his business and get the fuck out.

The two reasons why I decided to go ahead and lose it: defiance and curiosity. My life that has taken me nowhere. I've lived in New York City for twenty years and have witnessed so many horrible things that I've given up any thought of happiness for myself. I don't know if any standard definition of happiness would be for me anyway. The one thing I refuse to acknowledge is that I'm scared. My shrink thinks that the reason I've cut myself off from the world is this fear of rejection business. If I play, I'll pay, and I can't afford it emotionally.

At our last session she even dared to suggest that my breasts are totally normal-looking and that the deformity is only in my head. She also thinks that I haven't been cursed with overactive hostility hormones. Maybe, she said, the anger came in typical, human amounts, but instead of releasing it, I directed it inside myself. The theory continues: I honed the hostility, fed it, shaped it, and have grown to depend on it to keep myself apart. I believe my deformity and my separateness make me special, yadda, yadda, yadda. And the virginity thing, she said, is fear plain and simple. Fear of what, I asked. She wouldn't tell me. And that's when I decided to do it to prove her whacked-out theories wrong. Plus, after a couple years of video watching, I'm curious about how it feels.

I was ready, and Mitch had better get ready soon, I thought, or I'd have to kill him. I asked him sweetly to follow me into the bedroom, my favorite room of the two-room apartment. I had a lovely duvet cover with a hand-painted rose pattern. I dropped perfume on my pillow before sleep and dreamt I was running through a giant garden with flowers and cats all around.

I sat on the foot of the bed, and Mitch sat next to me.

From up close I noticed the beads of sweat spotting his forehead and the strands of gray in his mustache. I placed my hand on his chest, closed my eyes, and kissed him. I called images from pornography to the surface and focused on them. As my body lay back on the bed with Mitch's weight heavy on top, visions of blow jobs, come shots, and scissored legs danced in my head.

Any time he neared my breasts with his hands I'd move them away. The weight of his body on them was fine, but actual finger contact would be too humiliating. We kissed and touched each other. My breathing deepened, and my heart jumped in my chest. I felt blood rush down my belly, and I heard myself moan. I'm actually enjoying this, I thought, and I felt a combination of surprise and disappointment.

We'd been rubbing against each other for a while when Mitch started removing my clothes. I pushed his hand away when he tried to remove my bra. "Everything but that," I said strongly but sweetly, trying not to ruin the mood. He didn't respond. I opened my eyes for a moment, and he was already naked. His body didn't impress me, even though he was the first naked man I'd seen in person save my father. His penis resembled the ones I'd seen in porn, but the three dimensions made it foreign, unknown. I reached out and touched it. It felt like a piece of metal covered in silk. I closed my eyes again and envisioned all my young video friends as they licked and sucked and begged. We hadn't even approached intercourse when I started to see blue.

Mitch ruined everything by squeezing my breasts. I didn't expect the pain. It came suddenly and completely. I could barely breathe. I pushed him away with whatever strength remained and then doubled over in agony. It felt as though the wind had been stomped out of me. I cupped my deformities gently and rocked back and forth on the bed, gasping for air. He did this to me, I thought. He hates me.

"My God, what's wrong?" Mitch's voice seeped into the bubble of my consciousness. "Are you all right?"

"I hate you," I managed to get out. Speaking increased the pain, and I doubled over again and rocked.

"You're hurt," he gathered. "Let me see it. Maybe I can help." He approached me and touched my shoulders. I jerked away. He became insistent.

"Just leave me alone," I spat. "I hate you."

He ignored my protests and pried my hands away from my chest. I was too weak to fight him off, and I must confess that I didn't mind the idea of him seeing my naked deformity. That'd show him, I thought. I leaned back and let him remove my bra. The pain was still intense, but the thought of revenge made it hurt less.

The bra fastened in front. Mitch straddled me on the bed and released the snap. The bra cups clung defiantly to the deformities. I looked up at Mitch's face. The spots of sweat had become little rivers flowing down the sides of his head, disappearing in his sideburns and reappearing again on his chin. He's enjoying this, I thought. He can't wait to see.

Mitch slid his finger underneath one of the cups. He slowly pushed the bra away as if he was afraid to do so. I felt a moment of panic and wondered if this was unfair. Maybe I shouldn't let him see, I thought, but it was too late. He'd done it. I lay completely naked on my bed. Mitch hovered above me. The room was silent and motionless, save for the blare of car horns from the street. The moment was here, and I was glad. I watched his face as he looked at my exposed deformity. I waited for his expression of shock and horror. It didn't come.

Neither of us moved or spoke. Mitch didn't turn away from my breasts once. His breathing deepened as I held mine. After what seemed like hours he leaned over me and began kissing me again, as if nothing had happened. He was even more passionate than before. The terror subsided momentarily, and I wondered, Is this what it's like to be normal? Is this how whole women feel while their bodies are being ravaged and adored? I started coming to a likable understanding about sex and advertising. But that was when the realization struck me like a battering ram. Mitch was one of them. One of the guys I'd read about in the porn catalog. Mitch liked this. He liked mutants. He got turned on by us. He was a sicko. A twisted pervert. He probably rented those videos full of amputees and burn victims. And he was on top of me, stroking, stroking, kissing and licking. I fought nausea. I begged him to get off me. Only after I started beating him on the back with my fists did he move.

"What's wrong now?" he asked breathlessly as the sweat continued to stream down his face.

"Get out of here, you pervert," I yelled.

"What?"

"I know what you are," I accused. "You repulse me." I crawled under the rose-patterned covers and gathered them across my chest. I wouldn't give him any more cheap thrills.

He stared at me and shook his head. "I don't get this at all," he said. His expression was a combination of sad and angry.

"Just get the fuck out of here. I won't tell anyone about you," I promised, hoping that would make him leave. Then another startling revelation struck me: He might rape me, I thought. He'll force himself inside me and tear me apart. He'll hurt me again. I covered my face with my hands. I couldn't watch. "Please, just go," I begged, and I started to cry with fear.

He didn't say anything, but I heard the jangle of a belt buckle and the zip of a fly. I continued crying for a few minutes. I thought I heard the door click shut. When I had the courage I got out of bed to make sure.

The cats rushed at me as I walked naked through the living room. They raced between my legs, and I almost tripped. I went into the bathroom and splashed water on my face. Some of it dribbled between my breasts. I took a deep breath and looked down. The water left a mark on my skin. That was different, but my breasts were the same. The bumps and lumps, discolored and angry, throbbed with a life of their own. Giant veins radiated in crisscross patterns from the shriveled gray areolas with their sharp purple nipples. The whole mass hung from my chest like dried-out bunches of grapes. I felt darkness cloak my mind, but I fought it bravely. I figured a Valium might help. I took a few extra for good measure.

I decided to draw myself a bath. While the water ran I

stared at my breasts in the bathroom mirror. Their shape seemed to change every few seconds. Once I was past fainting, the spontaneous mutations were almost transfixing. I tested the water when the tub was full. It was a little too hot, like a swimming pool in summertime. I eased into the water. The heat on my naked breasts burned at first, but I got used to it. I let my head rest on the back of the tub. The Valium kicked in, and I thought about bugs and snakes and ugly things. I closed my eyes and let myself slide down under the water. That's when I lost consciousness. I blew out air bubbles and dreamed about how long I could stay alive like this. A few minutes later I started inhaling water. A few minutes after that, brain damage was irreparable. A few minutes after that, I was dead.

Epilogue

Liz's mother couldn't reach her on the phone, nor could her shrink, or the people at work when she didn't show up or call in sick, so the police went over to investigate the next day. They found the body in the tub. Liz would probably have been surprised to hear the words of one of the officers as they fished out her corpse and placed it on the bathroom floor. "Another single woman suicide," he said. "It's a damn shame—she had a nice pair of knockers."

HEAVEN SENT

J. M. Morgan

OLD MRS. SEDGEWICK WAS AFRAID OF DEATH. IT WASN'T dying that scared her. She knew about pain and lingering illness. Living with cancer had taught her about suffering. If death would bring an end to this ongoing torment of her life, she would welcome it. But it wouldn't. She knew that. It was death itself that scared Eleana Sedgewick. Death, and what would come after.

"I'm a wealthy woman," she told her retinue of doctors and nursing attendants. "I can afford all your drugs, blood transfusions, and surgery. You do what will keep me alive. Understand?"

One or two doctors had tried to explain the situation. "You're dying, Mrs. Sedgewick. There's nothing any of us can do to prevent that. All of our efforts at postponing the moment of death by these desperate measures will only prolong needless agony for you. It's time to let go."

That doctor was "let go," taken off her case within the hour.

The fools didn't understand. Any kind of life was better than what awaited her. Eleana Sedgewick wasn't positive there was a God, or a heaven, but she was sure there was a hell.

"How are you today, Mother?"

Her son, Burton Sedgewick, was a useless man like his father. Eleana had kept the family's research and pharmaceutical company going all these years. She'd been the brains behind the financial success of Sedgewick Laboratories.

"What do you want, Burton?" She was feeling irritable, the pain in her side slicing through her with every breath. Damn him for bothering me now, she thought.

"I came to see how you were feeling, Mother."

"Liar." He came to see if she was dead. Not yet. He and his greedy sister Christine would have to wait a little longer to get their hands on their mother's money. Eleana and her lawyers had drawn up an ironclad will. Nothing except her death would allow Burton or Christine the right to a single penny of the Sedgewick estate.

"Are you in pain? Is there anything you need?" he asked solicitously.

Was there anything she needed? Oh, yes. "Life."

It was hard to hold on. She had been fighting for so long. What did any of them know of real suffering? *How are you feeling? How are we today, Mrs. Sedgewick? Is there anything you need?*

"I brought someone to see you, Mother. He's a Catholic priest, but that's all right. He says it doesn't matter that you're not of his faith. He visits all the sick people at this hospital. I've been telling him about you, about our family. Talking to him has helped me. Father Joe's so good at understanding what troubles people, Mother. He thinks he might be able to ease your fears and bring you comfort if you let him."

He wants to hear my confession, Eleana thought bitterly. In hell, priest.

"Get out." Pain crawled up her abdomen, tearing away bites of living flesh. She pushed the plunger of the morphine syringe strapped to her side. The medication was self-dispensed as needed. Lately she had needed it more and more often. Had to be careful and hold back, even when her body screamed for relief. It was possible to overdose on the drug. An overdose would mean death. And death would mean . . .

"Hello, Mrs. Sedgewick," said an unfamiliar voice. "I'm Father Joe Battallia."

"Go to hell." The biting teeth were tearing her apart this time. Ripping at her guts. Her thumb rested on the plunger, every nerve in her body begging her to push a second release of pain-killing morphine into her vein. No! she thought. Dammit, no.

"I wondered if I might just visit with you for a minute," said Father Joe.

She could hear chair legs scraping over the floor. He was sitting beside her, making himself comfortable. If she could move, she thought, she'd show him what she thought of his collar and his church. Thought he knew something she didn't. Thought he had the answers. Maybe she *should* tell him her confession. She'd like to see the look in his eyes. What would he think then?

The morphine began to take hold. She could feel her body smooth out like a flat surface. The space of ease would only last a few minutes. Just enough time to gain strength for the next time.

She glanced around the room. Burton was gone. The young, fresh-faced priest sat close beside her bed. He had dark hair that fell in boyish strands over his forehead, and soulful puppy-dog eyes.

"They breed ones like you in the seminary?" It was the longest sentence she'd spoken in days. Damn clever, too. Made her want to laugh. Laughter was a pleasure she could no longer afford. It took too much energy.

"Mrs. Sedgewick, if you'll let me, I believe I can give you peace about what is coming."

"Oh, you can?" she said. She knew what was coming. This boy priest had nothing to do with it. "How?"

"I've been talking with your children."

"Two fools."

"I'm told they love you very much," said Father Joe.

They loved me once, she thought, but that was a long time ago. They were children, and that was before I took over the business for their father. For an instant she remembered how it had been when Burton and Christine were young, and when she was simply Thomas's wife, and their mother.

Time had changed everything.

"Do you believe in God, Eleana? Or an afterlife?"

She shrugged. "I believe in hell."

"But not in heaven?" he asked, frowning.

That always stumped them, the preachers who wanted her soul. Father Joe wasn't the first to have tried his mystic mumbo-jumbo on her. She knew the routine. He would talk to her about faith, and God's love, and Jesus.

Instead he asked, "Have you ever heard of near-death experiences?"

It was the word "death" that interested her. She shook her head, and Father Joe began talking. For the next hour he talked. He told her stories of people like her, some young, some old, both the sick and the well, those who had died and were brought back to life by doctors. He told her what had happened to these people after death, and what they had seen.

While he spoke, Eleana forgot her pain. She forgot she was sixty-seven, twenty years a widow, and a woman guilty of far more sin than anyone knew. For that brief time she heard only Father Joe's clear voice, and the promise of his words.

"Those people found a new life waiting for them after this one," said Father Joe. "Some were not religious. They hadn't come to know God, but they were lifted into a shining light, like the others, and all pain ended. They knew only love and peace. Call it whatever you want. That place is where we all go when we die, Eleana."

"You believe this?" She studied his eyes. He seemed simple and honest, with the innocence of a child.

"If I didn't," he said, "I couldn't be a priest."

She considered this. Was it possible? Would pain and fear drop away like unwanted weights at the end of her life?

Would she, like the others in his stories, lift toward the light? She didn't know. Eleana Sedgewick was too shrewd a businesswoman to stake her future on an untested theory.

The morphine had dulled her constant pain to a tolerable throb at the base of her spine. If she didn't move, she could speak without too much discomfort.

"Now I'll tell you a story, priest."

He smiled, a boyish, condescending little grin. "All right," he said. "I'll listen to you."

He was placating her, but she didn't care. It didn't matter if he thought she was a senile old woman, only that he listened and understood what she was saying.

"I was widowed over twenty years ago," she began. "When Thomas died, control of the company came into my hands. I knew very little about drugs and running a pharmaceutical laboratory."

"That must have been difficult," murmured Father Joe.

"Yes," she said. "It was. There was very little money. My children needed things I couldn't provide for them, school, security. Thomas left us nothing except the company. It was all I had to save us."

"I'm sure you did what you thought was right. In those circumstances it would have been easy to make mistakes."

He was trying to make this simple for her, but he didn't understand.

"We lost money and gained money. Never anything to sustain us for long. Finally we were about to lose our home. I was becoming desperate." She took a long breath, felt the first sharp twinge of the pain returning, and knew she must hurry to finish before the morphine stopped working.

"One day a worker came into my office. He was one of our employees, a lab technician. He had made a discovery that I knew would change the course of everything in my life. What he brought me was a drug for treating the CXT virus."

"My parents told me how rampant the virus was in their generation," said Father Joe. "A real killer. They lost friends and relatives to it."

"Everyone did," said Eleana. "My husband . . ."

"Oh," said the priest. "I'm sorry."

"I bought all rights to the drug and dismissed the lab worker from our company. He tried once or twice to claim ownership of his miracle drug, but I had the legal documents on my side. Our company made a fortune. The virus had struck so many families, and our drug was the only treatment that helped. It extended the lives of the sick, the dying. It bought them time."

"That was a blessing," said the priest. "You gave them hope."

"Yes, hope." Eleana repeated the word. "There was hope, but they continued to die. The old, the young men, the mothers with their babies. Eventually they all died."

"You can't blame yourself for that. You did everything you could to fight for their lives. God didn't give you the way to save them."

"But he did," said Eleana. "He did . . . in the discovery of a vaccine against the virus. A scientist brought the formula for the vaccine to me. He showed me proof of its merit and value. The vaccine prevented the CXT virus from taking hold in humans."

"You were part of that?" asked Father Joe. He was staring at her with admiration in his eyes. "I remember when the vaccine was released. My parents were so relieved. I was in my first year of high school."

"No," said Eleana sharply. "That vaccine was produced much later, through another company. Not ours. The story I'm telling you happened twenty years earlier."

It took him a moment to digest what she was saying. She could read his reactions as they changed on his face. "You mean . . . you had the vaccine in your possession, and you held back its use? For twenty years?"

She gave a slight nod of assent.

He pushed his chair back—she heard it scrape across the linoleum floor—and stood up. "I don't understand," he mumbled. Then, in a louder, firmer voice, "I don't understand why you would do such a thing."

"Money," explained Eleana.

He seemed astounded. "People were dying of the virus. You had it in your power to save them, and you kept silent about the vaccine? And for money! My God! Wouldn't selling the vaccine have given you money?"

"Not a quarter as much as we made on the drug to treat the illness. The drug was needed for the patient's entire life. It was much more profitable. A vaccine would have prevented all that. The company would have taken a loss. I couldn't allow it to happen."

"This is unbelievable!" said the priest. His eyes were angry. He no longer stared at her with compassion or the love of humanity. Now he stared at her with horror and disgust. "You willingly let those sick people die. For twenty years you let them die so that you could make more money. That's a terrible sin."

"Yes," said Eleana, "it is. And that is why I am so afraid to die, priest."

She needed more morphine. The pain reliever had worked for such a short time. Now she was breathless with hurt again. She began shuddering, her thin fingers clawing at her back and belly, where the torment was centered. Inside, she was being torn apart.

It had taken so much of her strength to tell her story to this man with the childlike face. Why had she bothered? The agony she was enduring was a result of too much talking, too much remembering. Her body twisted into contorted shapes on the bed, frantic in its pursuit of relief.

"Mrs. Sedgewick," called the priest. She could hear him at her side. "I'll get the nurse for you."

"No!" she cried, and she gripped his hand. "Tell me, priest. When I die . . ." She tried to speak, but the tearing came again, and she screamed. Then, in a whisper, "Tell me," she gasped.

His face was ashen. She pulled him close so she could see into his eyes. They spoke a truth that his lips would not.

"I—you"—he stumbled over the words—"you must ask God's forgiveness."

She screamed again. Pain was all she knew.

He tried to pull away, but her hand gripped his harder. "Let me go!" he cried. He jerked back suddenly and wrenched his hand free. She could hear his chair fall over and hit the floor. "I can't help you," he told her, his voice strident as a yell, but a restrained whisper. "There's nothing I can do . . . or want to." He stumbled toward the door.

Her screams followed him.

At the door she heard him say, "Turn to God, Mrs. Sedgewick. Only God can help you."

She didn't see him go. Nurses rushed into the room. One of them, a heavy woman, held Eleana down while the other forced the plunger of the syringe, releasing a flow of morphine into Eleana's vein. They restrained her arms, keeping her from digging at her stomach with her fingernails, from clawing her back, until the screaming stopped.

It was too soon for the morphine, she knew. The drug would carry her toward death. It would carry her toward that fear she had seen in the priest's gentle eyes. She could feel it spreading over her.

A weight of unconsciousness pressed at Eleana's mind, but she heard one of the nurses say, "I'm tired of running after this old crow all day. Give her another dose of the stuff, and we'll all get some rest."

Eleana tried to shout *No!* But she couldn't make a sound. She felt the second injection. Her voice drifted to that place of drugged silence, and in a moment or two her mind followed.

For a time there was nothing. She hovered in a vast darkness. The quiet was leaden. Nothing touched her. Nothing moved. Her body was caught and held in a seamless void. It was not sleep, but emptiness. She drifted . . . drifted.

The sound startled Eleana. It was insistent, a repeating buzzer of loud, irritating noise. Impossible to ignore. It came again and again, dragging at her.

Beyond the repeating blare of the buzzer she heard an urgent play of voices. Some were shouting. It was as if she were underwater, trying to hear something just above the surface. It was getting closer . . . closer . . . and then the surface broke into bright, hurtful shards of light. She was yanked into consciousness. Awake. And pain returned.

Eleana tried to scream, but there was something heavy pressing down on her chest. The weight had forced all the air from her lungs. Her eyes were open now; the faces came into focus. Nurses. Doctors.

"Shut off that damn code blue!" yelled Dr. Westin. He was staring into her face. "Eleana!" he said sharply. "Eleana!" Couldn't he see her? He was looking right into her eyes.

I'm here, she wanted to call out to him, but the weight pressed harder. Please. Don't let me die.

"Get a crash cart in here. Intubate her."

A long tube was roughly forced into her mouth and down her throat.

"Fibrillation!" said a nurse. "We're losing her."

"Paddles!" demanded Dr. Westin. "Clear!"

Eleana felt the shock hit her body. Two massive fists striking her chest. The force of them lifted her off the bed.

"Again!" said Dr. Westin. "Clear!"

Don't let me die, she thought.

The smash of fists came again. She felt the brutal slams into her chest and side. The rush of current shot through her, and again her body jerked.

"Flat line," said the nurse at the monitor. "She's gone."

I'm not gone! Eleana struggled to say. Only her eyes could speak for her: Look at me! I'm still here.

And then she wasn't.

It happened that quickly. One instant she was encased in a body that had stopped working, and the next she wasn't there anymore. She popped free. Something in the body that had held her to it released its hold.

She looked down and saw herself, the shell of what she had been, surrounded by ten or more doctors and nurses. Dr. Westin was hitting her chest with his fist. She watched but felt nothing.

"Paddles!" she heard Westin call.

"Doctor, we've lost her," the nurse said gently.

"Give me the damn paddles!" he shouted.

Eleana didn't feel the electric current this time. She felt nothing. And then it was clear to her—all pain was gone. There was no sensation of pain, and the heavy weight on her chest had lifted. She was free.

Dr. Westin was still trying to revive her. "One amp of lidocaine!"

She heard and saw. And then she felt herself drawn away.

At first there was only the knowledge of lifting, moving toward something. There was a rush, hurrying through a dark space. The space enclosed her but wasn't frightening. There was nothing in her that was causing the forward movement. Something was taking her.

A clean light pooled above her. She saw the outline of it first, the white radiance of a circle, and then the brightness filled in. The light was without heat or glare. She felt herself being lifted into it. Something in Eleana responded, in recognition of this perfect light, and she felt a peace settle over her.

There was no fear. No pain. There was only love.

Love, pure and clean, wrapped around Eleana Sedgewick and comforted her. A joy rose in her that was of such profound strength, she could not name it. She *was* joy, and goodness, and light.

"Eleana."

A woman stood beside her.

"Who—who are you?"

The woman's face was graceful, gentle, and as non-threatening as any face could ever be. "I'm Anna."

"Anna," Eleana repeated. As she said the name, the light opened, and she saw a green pasture of rolling hills before her. Beautiful flowers dotted the grassland, pinks, blues, yellows. Just in front of where she stood, a clear river flowed.

"It's perfect." The words came from her like a prayer. "Take me there." She tried to step into the water, but Anna touched her arm.

"No, wait," said Anna.

On the sloping hillside, across the river from Eleana, stood a large gathering of people. Young and old, men and women, they walked to the edge of the water and looked across at her.

"Who are they?"

"These many are the lives you cut short," said Anna.

"I didn't . . . I've never seen any of these people."

"No, you didn't see them, but their lives might have been spared by the vaccine you held back. Each of them died before their intended time, because of you."

Eleana never thought to argue with Anna. The truth was standing there for both of them to see. In that instant she understood the guilt of all she had done.

"They're here now," she said. Nothing could be better than this place. "Let me go where they are."

"No," said Anna. "You may not join them. They have found peace."

Eleana wanted peace. She wanted desperately to cross the water and step onto the grassy hill where the others stood. "Please," she begged, "let me stay."

As she spoke she felt herself pulled away from the river, and from the many lives her greed had touched. She felt the light fade, and the image of the woman lessen and finally disappear.

She heard Anna's voice say, "For your sins you are consigned to everlasting—"

Falling. Darkness rushed up at her as she plummeted through the distance. Her arms stretched out to touch the seams of the space, but there was nothing . . . nothing. It was a terrifying void, and Hopeless was its name.

She fell, finally seeing muted shapes below her. A glaring brightness. Sound. A pounding rhythm. One shape was more defined than all the others. As she watched, that shape seemed to open.

Gasping for breath, Eleana Sedgewick dropped back into her body. Pain shot into the core of her being. Savage, brutal pain.

"I've got a pulse!" someone shouted.

"She's breathing on her own," said another.

Eleana heard the triumph in their voices. She knew where

she was. Back in her body. Back in the world. She had lived, and the doctors and nurses were congratulating one another on their success.

"This old lady's terrified to die," said a male LVN. Eleana remembered his voice. He was the tall young black man who had brought her lunch one afternoon. "I heard her talking to a priest. She's carrying some heavy guilt, man. Heavy. You guys grabbed her right out of the jaws of death."

Let me go! Let me die. Eleana tried to talk, tried to tell them not to fight for her life, but there was an oxygen mask over her nose and mouth.

No one listened. Pain filled her mind and her soul. None too gently, she was transferred to a hospital gurney and taken to CCU. There, guarded by monitors, a round-the-clock nurse, and every conceivable means of physical support, Eleana Sedgewick revived and won her bout with death.

Monsignor Joe Battallia lowered himself carefully into the chair of Holy Family's confessional. Confessionals were nicer these days, two deep-cushioned chairs instead of the hard benches of the old booths. Now there was a room. Priest and penitent sat opposite each other and spoke face-to-face. A lot had changed in the forty years since he had been ordained.

This was a quiet Saturday. It was after Easter, and still months before Christmas. There wouldn't be many people who felt the need to confess their sins on such a beautiful weekend afternoon. Given a choice, he wouldn't be there either. This was a day to go fishing or take a walk through the autumn woods. The days of his life were numbered, he could feel that; and the idea of locking up early, closing the door on the confessional this once, and taking that walk through the woods was tempting.

It was the very old and the very young who came to confession on days like this. Neither had anything of any great weight to confess. They were driven to it either by their parents' will or by another force, their own fears.

The door of the confessional opened. The monsignor noted the red light indicating that someone was kneeling on the opposite side of the small screen. A few people still preferred the old way. They needed a barrier between themselves and the priest.

"Do you wish to make a confession?" asked the monsignor.

"I have a story to tell you, priest."

The voice that gave him this strange greeting was old indeed. He could hear age in the tone, like dried leaves crackling. And there was a certain breathlessness. He couldn't sy whether it was male or female.

"I'm listening." Many people preferred not to use the traditional form of confession. For some it had been so many years since they'd made their last confession, they had forgotten the words of the litany. For others it was more comfortable simply to talk to the priest the way they would tell their problems to a friend. "Go ahead," he encouraged the speaker, wishing he could address the unidentified voice as either a man or a woman.

The story unfolded. As the monsignor listened to the words, and to the voice like paper moving over sand, a line of cold sweat beaded his top lip and his brow. He'd heard this before . . . the worst experience of his priesthood was replaying itself. Suddenly he felt how isolated he was in this room, how alone he was with whoever was behind the screen. I am old, he thought, and vulnerable.

But the voice was old, too. The voice was far older, from the sound. And that fact frightened him.

Was it the same story? How could that be? Impossible.

"Are you confessing the sin of another?" he interrupted. "Your mother's, perhaps?" He remembered that woman. She had been the terror of his dreams for many years after that day at the hospital. He had forced his memories of her to the back of his mind, but now they rose like unclaimed souls.

"No, priest. My mother is long dead."

He was ashamed at the relief he felt at hearing those

words. As far as he knew, that woman had died without absolution of her sins. His fault. If he had been more confident as a priest, or if he had understood human nature better, he might have found a way to save her. It was a memory that still haunted him. He had failed her, and if his fears were correct, he had let her fall through his grasp into . . .

"There was a woman," he began, "a long time ago, who told me something like what you're telling me now."

"Not something like," said the voice. "The same."

He didn't want to be there anymore. He wanted to walk past that screen and escape into the open body of the church. Fear swam in his veins, in the hard beating of his heart, and in the trembling that had overtaken him. A terror began to build in him that he would have to see the face behind the screen.

"Who are you?" he whispered.

"You know me. I am the one you lost."

"I didn't," said the priest, knocking his chair over as he stood up. "It wasn't my fault." He knew this had to be a dream, a horrible nightmare. "I told her to turn to God."

"You abandoned me."

"No, no, I tried to help." He was more afraid than he had ever been in his life. The woman he had seen in that hospital so long ago must be dead these past forty years. If that was true, who was in the confessional with him now? Who, or what?

"I feared death."

And then he knew. All doubt left him. This *was* the woman. Her ghost. Her spirit that had never found peace. Guilt, for his part in her loss, overwhelmed him. "How can I help you?" He was badly frightened, but willing.

A wail, long and high, pierced the deathlike stillness of the room.

"Jesus protect us!" the monsignor cried. He couldn't move. His legs felt paralyzed and solid with terror. If she came at him now, whatever was behind that screen, he could do nothing to save himself.

The shriek came again, filling the small room with the sound of unending torment.

He heard the scraping of the wooden screen as it moved. Slowly. Dragging across the floor.

"Oh, God in heaven," the monsignor cried, "help me."

And then the screen was pulled aside. A frail old woman stood before him. The one, yet not exactly the same.

"Mrs. Sedgewick?" He breathed the name like a sigh.

"You called on heaven, priest. Behold, I am heaven sent."

Monsignor Joe Battallia could make no sound. His pulse raced into a loud roar within his ears. A pain started below his rib cage and traveled across his left shoulder to his back. It widened there, hitting again and again, like a fisted hand.

The old woman came closer. Her skin looked thin as tissue paper. "I feared death. For my sins, heaven was denied me. I was sent back to endless life and suffering. I cannot die," said Mrs. Sedgewick, "though I would give all I have to be freed. This is my hell. Until my time of penance has passed I must remain here," she said. Her breath was foul as she leaned close to his face.

"I am death, priest, and I have come for you."

He couldn't answer. He was feeling a darkness begin to swallow him. The pain in his back had turned into agony, and his legs buckled beneath him. He fell, his body folding onto the hardwood floor.

He could barely hear her now over the loud pounding of his heart. And then the pounding stopped. In that silence were the last words Monsignor Joe Battallia heard on earth.

"Remember me as you climb toward the light . . . for I am heaven sent."

It was a quiet Saturday afternoon. Few parishioners came to the confessional. It was late in the day when another priest of Holy Family discovered Father Joe's lifeless body. Only one old woman remained in the church. She sat in the pew directly opposite the confessional, as if she had been waiting for her turn.

"You must have been here a very long time," the young

priest said to her. "I'm sorry. Monsignor cannot hear your confession today."

Mrs. Sedgewick rose from the pew, and with the careful movements of the very old and the very sick, death walked from the dim recess of the church . . . and out among the living.

THE WORST PART

Lawrence Watt-Evans

SOMETIMES HE TRIED TO TELL HIMSELF THAT THE WAIT AT THE gate was the worst part. Why they called it a gate at all he wasn't sure—the damn thing wasn't a gate, it was a tunnel —and the combination made him think of the gates of hell.

That was all too appropriate an image—a tunnel down into the hell of an airliner's cabin, with its sadistically narrow seats, its fetid pressurized air, the hard, ugly plastic everywhere.

The wait wasn't really the worst part at all. It was bad, it was very bad, but the *worst* part . . .

Well, it just kept on getting worse. The long, horrible wait in that dreary holding pen, strewn with other people's newspapers, and then the march down the tunnel like prisoners into their cells, squeezing through that right-angle right turn where the crew greeted everyone with their phony smiles and where, off to the left, he could see into the cockpit, could see all that ominous black machinery with its colored lights, obviously too complex for anyone to actually understand and control properly.

And then down the aisle, waiting while people stuffed

heavy luggage into the overhead compartments, standing there sweating and stinking of fear while those idiots blithely tried to jam in as much as possible, so that it could all fall down on him later, and then they'd bend themselves into their horrid little seats and let him pass so that he could find his own horrid little seat and squeeze himself into it.

Grope for the seat belt, near panic for a moment when one side seems to be missing; visions of bouncing around the cabin, head battering against the reading lights and attendant call buttons as the plane veers and swoops. Then find the belt, buckle in, and worry about whether he'll ever be able to get it open again or whether he'll sit there, trapped and struggling, while the cabin fills with smoke, with flame, with water, while the other passengers all slide out to safety and he sits there, strapped down and waiting, and they don't hear his screams over their own relieved laughter. . . .

And his knees hit the seat in front of him, his head doesn't fit comfortably on the headrest; half the time they're flying, the attendants block the aisle with their silly drink cart so he can't reach the lavatory or the exit if there's an emergency.

And the takeoff, the engines screaming so that it hurts to think, the wing deforming itself as he watches out the window. What if those flaps come loose? Can those little metal struts really hold it all together at six hundred miles an hour? My God, *six hundred miles an hour,* how can *anything* hold together, how can anyone control it, at that speed?

Six hundred miles an hour, thirty thousand feet up, that's *six miles up,* six miles with nothing but empty air below them, nothing holding them up but those bits of metal, those hydraulic struts that hold the wings together, the wings he can see bouncing and shimmying like diving boards that someone's just used for that six-mile plunge, the wings that could tear off or fall to pieces at any moment, and the plane would turn and plummet earthward, falling six miles out of the sky. Six miles would give him time to watch, to think, to see that he was going to die. He'd have all the time he needed to think it over; he'd be able to see the ground screaming up at him, and he wouldn't be able to do a thing, he'd be strapped in his seat while the plane was in free-fall, like the biggest damn roller coaster you ever saw going down a six-mile drop, only there's no curved rail to swoop him back up—he'll go down and down and *down* until he hits the hard earth and his neck snaps and his bones break and his blood sprays across several counties. They'll be picking pieces of him out of cornfields and hedges, and everyone will read the newspapers and see just another statistic, and they'll never think of the shock of impact, the incredible pain, the burned black flesh when the jet fuel ignites.

And if the wings hold up, if the pilot doesn't go mad and dive just to see how big a crater he can make, if the pilot doesn't die of a stroke and send them plummeting, if the engines don't explode, if the fuel doesn't spill away into the air as a toxic cloud settling over the countryside and leaving them powerless, if the whole thing doesn't catch fire from the friction of that incredible six-hundred-mile-an-hour speed and smother them all in smoke, if the pressurization doesn't fail and leave them all gasping in unbreathably thin air, eyes bugging out and hands clutching throats as they suck at air that isn't there, drowning in near-vacuum like fish out of water . . . if none of that happens, then they'll reach the airport where they're to land, and they'll drop out of the sky *deliberately,* falling down through those six miles of nothing and trusting the plane and the pilot to catch them at the last minute and land them safely on the runway, not to plow into a building somewhere; they'll hit the ground still traveling two hundred miles an hour, and those engines that have been screaming for hours will suddenly roar into reverse, sucking in everything as they try to stop the plane's headlong rush to disaster, and the tires will squeal and shudder as they scrape along the tarmac, and he'll sit helplessly in his seat, his life in the pilot's hands, waiting for the impact with the terminal, with another plane that's on the runway by mistake; waiting for a tire to blow, a strut to fail, for the plane to buckle sideways and drive wreckage in through the window at him.

And *that* was the worst; after that, it would be over, the

panic would subside, his stomach would relax—he might need to vomit, he had once or twice—and he would get off the plane shaking only slightly, and he'd tell himself, There, it wasn't really all that bad; he'd tell his friends that he was okay, he didn't like flying but it was no big deal, there was nothing to be scared of. He knew all the statistics, the facts, the reasonable, rational attitudes, and he would convince himself that he believed them, that they applied to him, that he could fight down his fear and control it.

He knew that his fear wasn't rational, not really, and he was a rational man. He'd relax and he'd *forget* how awful it was, he'd forget and he'd agree to do it *again,* he'd buy a ticket to fly somewhere else, and then when it was too late to back out he'd start remembering again, the panic would start to gnaw at his belly, his throat would dry and tighten, and rationality would fall away. He'd *know* that he was going to die this time, that *this* would be the plane that fell flaming from the sky, and it would be worse than ever before. Every time it was worse; every time he told himself he was over his fear, and every time it was *worse.*

But every time he *forgot* that, forgot what it was like and agreed to fly again, and that brought him back here, right where he was, sitting at that gate to hell, Gate C3 for Flight 1108, his palms sweaty and his fingers shaking as he tried to control his fear. He looked down at them, tried to will them to be still, to be steady and calm and brave.

"Jack?"

He looked up, startled, and his eyes wouldn't focus at first.

"Jack Hartman? Is that you?"

"Sharon?" The neatly attired young woman in the dark green skirt and jacket stood in front of him, looking down at him, a purse hanging from one shoulder and an overnight bag held in front of her; he blinked up at the heart-shaped face with its uncertain smile.

"It *is* you!" she said, and the smile became steadier. "Jack, it's been years!"

"Yeah," he said, vaguely aware that he should smile back, that he should have said something clever, or at least semi-intelligent, rather than the stupid monosyllable. He should have given some sign that he recognized her and remembered her and was glad to see her.

He couldn't; he was too full of fear, too busy worrying about his impending death, his certainty that his plane would crash.

"Are you all right?" she asked, the smile vanishing; she dropped the overnight bag and sat down in the seat beside him, leaning toward him.

"I'm okay," he said.

"You're pale," she said. "I mean *white.*"

"I'm okay," he insisted. "I just don't like flying, and I get nervous waiting."

"Oh," she said, and the tone of her voice wasn't the derision he feared, but it wasn't comforting, either, it was simply puzzled. He started to turn away, then stopped himself; that would be unforgivably rude. She was trying to be helpful, she was concerned about him; it wasn't her fault if she didn't understand something as irrational as his fear of flying.

"So what are . . . how are you?" he managed to say.

"Oh, I'm fine. Are you sure you're okay?"

"I'm fine, really—just don't like flying."

"But you—you were never scared of anything, Jack. You're afraid of flying?"

The look in her eyes took him back a dozen years, to high school, when he and Sharon's older brother Greg had been pals, teasing Greg's kid sister at every opportunity, but she'd still hung around, staring at Jack with admiring eyes.

That admiration was still there.

He stared at her, amazed and glorified; if he'd ever thought about it at all, he'd thought it was just a little-girl crush, that she must have outgrown it long ago, but here she was, a grown woman, looking at him with that same wide-eyed intensity.

No one had looked at him like that in years.

"It's been a long time," he said.

"Oh, I *know,*" she said. "It's been *too* long! I kept asking Greg to write to you, or call you, you know, just to keep in touch. I didn't think I should do it myself, you know how that is. . . ." Was she blushing slightly? He almost thought she was.

"I should've written myself," Jack said.

He didn't really mean it; he and Greg had drifted apart, and neither of them had been much interested in staying in touch once Jack moved away. Some friendships lasted, some didn't, and his friendship with Greg had been one he outgrew.

But Sharon obviously hadn't outgrown her interest.

He started to ask what she was doing there, then stopped himself. What *else* would she be doing at an airport gate with an overnight bag? She was waiting for a plane—for the same plane he would be riding.

They would be flying together—maybe they could arrange to sit together. That would be . . .

That would be horrible. He would be white-faced and gasping for air, and she would be laughing at him. She'd see him for the coward he was, and that admiration would leave her eyes forever. His goddamned phobia would do what years of separation had not.

But maybe her presence would help. Maybe he could hide his fear, fight it down; after all, for several seconds, while he looked at her face, he had managed to forget that he was waiting to board the airplane that would carry him to some horrible, humiliating death.

And maybe . . .

"So you don't mind flying?" he asked.

"Oh, I *love* flying!" she said. "Watching the ground fall away, sailing through the sky—I *love* it!"

Hardly a fellow sufferer, he told himself mockingly. "I don't," he said. "Bad food, cramped seats—I hate it."

"Oh, that's silly. It's not so bad," she said. She blinked. "Oh, is *that* what you meant, about not liking it? I thought it *scared* you!"

He forced a smile and said nothing.

"I should've known you weren't scared," she said. "You were never scared of anything. What are you doing now, anyway? Are you married?"

She blushed again, he was almost certain—she must have realized just how blatant her interest was.

"No," he said, "not at the moment. What about you?"

"Never," she said.

"I remember you worked at that drugstore; you still there?"

"Of course not! I have a *real* job now!"

They chatted, and for first seconds, then minutes at a time he forgot his fear. Color came back to his face; his hands didn't shake as he adjusted himself in his seat, as he patted her hand. While she told him about decorating her apartment on the cheap he found himself thinking that maybe this time, maybe *this* time he could hide his fear; maybe if he had her beside him to talk to he could forget about fire and smoke and falling and asphyxiation.

And maybe when they landed he could ask her out somewhere, if he hadn't made a fool of himself on the flight.

"Now boarding, rows sixteen through twenty-three," the gate agent announced over the PA, and Jack groped reluctantly for his briefcase; Sharon snatched her overnight bag out of his way.

Together they walked toward the entrance to the jetway, still talking. At the door she stopped, and he stopped as well, assuming that she must be sitting in one of the rows further forward, the rows that hadn't been called yet. A momentary surge of panic flooded through him at the thought that they would be separated on the plane, that she would not be there beside him to help him stay calm but would see him when he burst out screaming in terror.

Surely, though, they could trade seats around somehow. He knew that if she was beside him, the flight wouldn't be so bad.

At least, not until the crash.

"All seats now boarding," came the call.

"I guess I'd better say good-bye," she said, stepping back, away from the gate.

He stared at her, thunderstruck. "Aren't you coming?" he croaked.

"Oh, no!" she said. "I wish I was." She giggled. "I'm

120

sorry, I guess I didn't explain. I'm just here to meet Greg—his plane's delayed. It'll be arriving over there in another twenty minutes or so." She pointed at another gate, Gate C5.

"But the overnight bag . . ."

"This?" She hefted it. "Oh, this is Greg's; it got checked onto an earlier flight by mistake. I'm sorry, I should have explained. Good-bye, Jack. Write sometime, why don't you?" She was receding somehow, backing away from him, and he was drifting down into the jetway, down through the gates of hell toward the plane that would carry him to fiery destruction, and he could not turn back, could not reveal himself to be a coward to her as he watched her carried away from him, lost forever. He could feel the blood draining from his face, could feel his hands trembling more than ever. His last hope was walking away.

She turned and waved.

"Have a good flight!" she called, smiling.

And that was the very worst part of all.

SLIME

Jon A. Harrald

1

MAN, I GOTTA TAKE A LEAK SO BAD, MY BLADDER FEELS close to burstin'—like one of them paint-filled scumbags I used to chuck off the roof when I was a kid, watch 'em splat blood-red on the sidewalk. But I ain't going into the crapper, man—not in the middle a the night.

Not with *them* scurryin' around there in the dark.

Rather hold it in till morning. Rather wet my fuckin' bed. And it's all that fuckhead Jabba's fault. It's like he made me as messed up as him—put the fear into me. Not the same fear. But just as bad.

And all I ever did was try to help him.

Funny, all I gotta do is shut my eyes and I can still see it clear as a movie, that day in Coopér Park long time ago—like six years or somethin'. Summer just started, school's out maybe a week, but already it's hot as a bitch. Step outside your buildin', sunlight bounces off the street, stab you straight in the eyes. Sidewalk bakin', feel it right through the bottom of your sneakers. Air all thick and smelly, like garbage cookin' in the heat.

Slime

That was the day it all started.

It was like ten in the mornin' when we hit the street, me and Jabba. No one called him that then, of course. That came later. His real name was Jabrowski. Funny. Never heard no one use his first name, 'cept maybe teachers and shit. Lawrence.

Anyways, so we're outside on the stoop, and I see the block's totally empty, no other kids to play with, so I says, "Let's go to the park," and he says, "Sure." He hasta half cover his mouth when he says it, 'cause all this spit kinda bubbles out from the corners. He's got this problem with his teeth or somethin', but he can't afford to get it fixed.

Tell the truth, he was pretty gross-lookin', Jabba. Far back as I knew him, which was like in kindergarten, he was always real fat. Not solid fat, like some kids, but all soft and blubbery. Poke him in the stomach, your fingers sink right in like he's the fuckin' Pillsbury Dough Boy or somethin'. Got this real porky face. Little brown eyes, like someone stuck a coupla Milk Duds in the dough. Pig's nose. Fat little mouth, lips kinda stickin' out, all pink and slippery. And real sweaty all the time, like he never took a bath or nothin'.

Just from lookin' at him you could tell he din't have too many friends. I just hung with him sometimes when nobody else was around, mostly 'cause him and me lived in the same building—same floor, as a matter of fact—and my mom was friends with his mom and told me to be nice to him.

Even with Jabba draggin' his ass it took like maybe two minutes to get to Cooper Park, cuttin' through the alley to Lacey Avenue, then across the big empty schoolyard and over to Wicherly Boulevard.

Even back then I'd seen lottsa pictures of these big parks they got out west, like in Kansas or wherever, and I knew Cooper Park was pretty dinky by comparison—just a strip of patchy grass with a lotta dog shit and garbage layin' around, a coupla broken-down wood benches, and some dusty-lookin' trees stickin' up here and there. But you know how kids are. To us it looked like a fuckin' forest.

So we get to the park, which was totally empty, too, 'cept for this wino bum lyin' on one of the benches like a shitload of greasy rags someone dumped there. Smelled like shit, too. Jabba right away says, "Let's play Indiana Jones," which was kinda dorky. But there wasn't no other kids to play with or nothin', so I figured what the fuck.

"Awright," I says.

"Okay," he says. "Let's pretend we're in the jungle and there're these headhunters chasin' after us, an' if they catch us, they'll cut off our heads and shrink 'em." And you can tell he's all excited—his eyes're all shiny, and he's flutterin' his hands all over the place, and the spit's sprayin' outta his mouth.

"Okay," I says. "I'll be the headhunter, and you be Indiana Jones. You run for the trees and try to make it to the other side before I catch you. 'Kay? Ready? Go!"

He gives this squeal, then turns around and starts humpin' for the trees, his fat ass bobblin' like he's got pillows stuffed into his jeans. I figure I'll count to ten, then take off after him. Otherwise I'd of caught up to him in about two seconds.

So I count one-Mississippi, two-Mississippi till I get to ten, then I go tearin' after him, makin' these loud whoopin' noises like they do in those old movies where these Indians or whatever are attackin' the good guys. Jabba's just about made it to the little clump of trees when I start, but he's movin' so slow, I'm almost on top of him before he knows it.

"I'm gonna shrink your fuckin' head!" I shout, reachin' out my hand to grab him.

Jabba shoots a look over his shoulder and lets out this real girly scream, and he tries to pick up speed as we go barrelin' into the shade, and I can just feel the neck of his T-shirt under my fingers, and then suddenly—wham!—he goes flyin'. His toe musta caught a tree root or somethin', and down he goes, crashin' into the dirt like a fuckin' ton of bricks.

I'm goin' so fast I gotta jump over his fat body to keep from trippin' over him, and there's a tree straight ahead of me, and I put out my hands to keep from smashin' into it face-first. I stop myself with my hands, then turn around to see what happened to Jabba.

For a second he just lies there on his stomach like he's dead or somethin'. Then he shoves himself to his knees, makin' these gruntin' noises like it's a real strain to lift all that fat.

"You okay?" I says, takin' a step toward him.

He's starin' down at the front of his T-shirt, which is all covered with dirt and little bits of grass and shit, and somethin' else, too, a little lump of somethin' all dark and thick and shiny which I couldn't tell what it was, though the thought goes through my head that maybe he's landed on a fresh dog turd.

Just as I start to point to it and ask him what the fuck it is he lets out this terrific scream, scrambles to his feet, and begins hoppin' around and wavin' his hands like a madman. Even in the shade I could see how white his face looked.

"Hey man, you okay?" I begin to say again.

But his screamin' cuts me off. *"Gettitoffme! Gettitoffme! Gettitoffme!"* He's still dancin' around, and his hands are shakin' so hard it's like he's bein' 'lectrocuted or somethin', and now he's both screamin' *and* cryin' at the same time— totally freaked out. I can't tell if he's hurt himself or what, like maybe he landed on a piece of broken glass and that dark, shiny stuff is blood. Shit knows, there's plenty of broken bottles lyin' around the park, what with the winos and all the kids hangin' out there on summer nights, chuggin' beer.

And then I take a closer look at his shirt and I see what it is—this gray-brown gob of slime kinda drippin' down his shirt like a giant lump of snot. It's a mashed-up slug. You see 'em crawlin' around the park where it's shady in the summer. Jabba musta landed on one when he hit the ground.

He's still doin' his wildman dance. *"Gettitoff me!"* he screams, his voice gettin' higher and screechier all the time.

"Hey, man, I ain't touchin' that," I say. I can feel my lips kinda curled up, all disgusted. It looked pretty fuckin' gross, man, lemme tell you.

Suddenly this stink hits me, and I look down. There's this spreadin' puddle around Jabba's feet, and I can see the inside legs of his jeans are all dark.

I bark out this laugh, I couldn't help myself, man. "Hey, Jabba," I says. "You pissed your fuckin' pants!"

Jabba just freezes for a second, and the look on his face was kinda hard to describe but like the kinda thing you see in horror movies when someone opens the wrong door and sees the most awful, scary, grossest thing you can think of. Then he lets out this tremendous babylike yowl— *"Wahhhhhhh!"*

Next thing I know, Jabba's tearin' ass out of the park toward our block, still shriekin' and cryin' and shakin' his hands in the air.

I stood there a sec, surprised at how fast he could go when he wanted to. Then I followed him back home.

2

Jabba kinda disappeared after that, but I din't think too much about it. I just figured he was maybe hangin' around his apartment, 'cause like I said, he din't have too many friends or nothin'. Or maybe he was like embarrassed to show his face 'cause he'd acted like such a pussy.

Then, maybe a week after that day in the park, I come home one afternoon from the schoolyard where me and a coupla the guys was shootin' hoops, and as soon as I walk through the door my mom comes stridin' up and hauls off with this slap—bam!—right across the side of my head. Man, I'm seein' these little tweety birds flutterin' aroun' my head like in the cartoons. Then she grabs me by the hair and starts hollerin': "Whatcha do to him?"

"Ow! Leggo!" My hair feels like she's rippin' a bald spot right on top.

She gives another yank, real hard. "Whatcha do to him, ya little bastard?"

"Who?" I scream. I'm doin' my best not to cry, but I can't

help it—the tears are just squirtin' outta my eyes. Man, it hurt like a motherfucker.

"Jeanette's kid!" she hollers.

"Jabrowski?"

"Yeah."

"Nothin'," I scream. "I din't do nothin'!"

She finally lets go, and I go stumblin' back away from her, rubbin' the top of my head with one hand and tryin' to wipe my tears and runny nose with the other.

"Jeannette says the kid's been sick ever since you and him went out to play together last week," my mom yells. Her bathrobe's hangin' open, an' I can see one saggy tit.

"I din't do nothin'," I say, all whiny and sniffly. "We was playin' in the park, an' he tripped and fell on somethin', a slug or somethin', an' he got real upset an' ran home."

"Jeanette says he's just been layin' around in his room all day long, like he's afraid to come out," my mom says. She ain't yellin' anymore, but she's still talkin' in this real mean voice like I'm the one to blame. "And he's been havin' these real bad nightmares, wakin' up screamin' every night."

I shrug. "I din't do nothin'," I say again.

She shoots me one more nasty look like I'm a piece of shit she just scraped off her shoe bottom and says, "Go and see how he's doin', and tell him you're sorry."

Jabba's mom opens the door, and the first thing that hits you is the stink, like they got a big pot of sauerkraut that's been cookin' on the stove for a coupla weeks and they ain't opened a window the whole time. I can feel my nose wrinklin' up like when you get a whiff of a real smelly fart, but I try to keep my face from showin' how gross the place smells.

So she invites me in and says she don't know what the hell's wrong with her kid. He hasn't got outta bed for a whole week, she says, but he ain't really sick or nothin'. She points down the hallway to where the door is shut and tells me to go right inside the room.

So I walk down this little dark hallway, past the kitchen

and the crapper, and I push open this door. And man, the smell in the hallway wasn't half as bad as what Jabba's room smelled like—like old sweat socks and crotch rot and somethin' else real nasty, too, like there's a dead fish layin' around somewhere. The room is all like in shadows, 'cause the blinds are down, just maybe a few little slices of light cuttin' through the slats and hittin' the bed where Jabba's layin'.

So I walk over to the bed, and I suddenly realize that it's not just Jabba's room but also where his mom sleeps, 'cause I can see her dresser with all this lipstick and shit on top and her underwear half stickin' outta the drawers. And I can make out in the bed right next to him that the sheets are all messed up and the mattress's got this big dent in it from her body. Weird.

Jabba looks up at me, and I'm standin' close enough to the bed that I can see how his eyes look all sunk in, like someone that ain't slept in a week, and how his mouth got this crusty shit in the corners from where he's been rubbin' away at the drool. Tell you the truth, he din't look too hot.

So I says, "Hey, how're you feelin'?"

Jabba blinks a coupla times and runs his tongue over his lips but don't say nothin'.

"My mom says I should tellya I'm sorry," I says.

He kinda shrugs his shoulders.

"You sick or somethin'?"

He shakes his head.

The smell in there is makin' me feel kinda crappy. "I guess I better go," I says. "Catch you later." I head for the door, but even before I reach it Jabba calls to me in this weird croaky voice. So I take a step back to the bed, and he says, "Don't tell no one, okay?"

"'Bout what?"

"You know. 'Bout my bein' so scared."

"No problem," I says. For a minute he don't say nothin' back, so I figure it's okay to leave, but suddenly he's talkin' again in this real soft whispery voice, more like he's talkin' to himself than to me. I gotta bend a little closer to hear him.

Slime

"I hate it. Hate thinkin' about it—thinkin' about feelin' it or touchin' it or lookin' at it." And now I can see these streaks of wet runnin' down his cheeks, and his voice is all like strangled-up and quivery. "I think maybe I'm goin' crazy."

"What're you talkin' about, man?"

"You know," he says. "At the park. What I touched."

"The slug?" I says.

"No," he says, and now he's cryin' so hard he can hardly say the words. "The slime."

3

Lookin' back on it now, I can see where I shouldna opened my mouth, 'specially after Jabba told me not to. But I was like—what?—ten years old or somethin'. You know how it is. You're hangin' with the guys, shootin' the shit, and before you know it, you just let it slip out. I guess the problem was who I let it slip out *to*.

I let it slip out to Buddy Deemer.

You know that song "Bad to the Bone," 'bout this guy that's like *born* evil? That's Deemer, man. Kid was a fuckin' psycho from the time he was crawlin'.

Funny thing was, to look at him, you would of thought he was like some kinda dweeb. He had this face looked like a little baby—big blue eyes, one of them little turned-up noses, and this soft-lookin', very light blond hair, almost white and real curly. He was always littler than the rest of us, too—real short and shrimpy, like he never got enough to eat. Which was strange, 'cause his old man was a butcher, and you figure he's always bringin' home steak and shit to put on the table. But I dunno. Maybe he was too cheap or just din't give a shit. He was a pretty mean son of a bitch, Deemer's old man.

Nothin' like Deemer, though. You wouldna believed some of the stuff he done—and this was when he was just a little kid. Like this time a buncha us was walkin' along an' we

129

hear this real soft meowin' sound comin' from under a car,
so we go over to look, and there's this real little kitten sittin'
in the gutter like it's just been born or somethin'. So Deemer
right away pulls off one a his sneakers, strips off his sweat
sock, picks up the kitten, stuffs it inta the sock, then he
walks over to the apartment buildin' and just starts
poundin' his sweat sock against the wall. And all this blood
and shit starts leakin' through the sock. And Deemer just
keeps poundin' away—pow! pow! pow!—like he's ham-
merin' or somethin'.

So after maybe a minute he stops and looks inside the
sock, and his face is all like red and sweaty, and his eyes look
real weird, man, like glassy or somethin', and he's got this
real strange smile on his face—like someone who's just shot
his rocks off.

Creepy, man.

No one fucked too much with Deemer. You just couldn't
tell what he was gonna do next.

So like the summer's over and a buncha us are hangin'
around the schoolyard durin' recess, and like I say, I dunno
exactly how it happened, but before I know it I'm tellin' the
story 'bout Jabrowski and the slug.

Deemer cracks this smile like he just heard the funniest
joke in the world. "So the asshole fell on a slug?" he says
with this weird giggly laugh he has.

"Yeah," I says. "Got it mashed all over his shirt."

Deemer looks around at the other guys. "Jabrowski *looks*
like a fuckin' slug," he says, and everybody cracks up.

"Yeah," says Tommy DiNardo. "He looks like that ugly
motherfucker from the *Star Wars* movie—what the fuck's
its name?"

"Jabba!" Billy Palmer yells out.

"Hey!" Deemer says. "Jabrowski! Jabba!"

That's when everybody started callin' him that.

"Shit," Deemer says. "We oughta find a slug and shove it
down his fuckin' pants. See how he likes it."

"It ain't just slugs," I says. "It's like anything slimy freaks
him out."

Deemer don't say nothin' to that, he just gets this weird

look in his eyes like he's lookin' at somethin' no one else can see, somethin' goin' on inside his brain.

So then the talk moves onta somethin' else. Tell you the truth, I was feelin' a little sorry I ever said anythin', and I was hopin' Deemer would just forget about the whole thing.

I guess I din't know Deemer that well back then.

Two days after I told Deemer 'bout the slug I'm sittin' at this table with a buncha the guys in the school lunchroom. Deemer's sittin' across from me, chewin' on a sandwich and listenin' to the jokes and shit goin' on around him. But I can tell his eyes're scannin' for somethin'. And suddenly I can tell that he's spotted it.

I look over my shoulder, and there's Jabba walkin' along carryin' this tray with his lunch on it—this little milk carton and a plateful of the usual cafeteria shit, mashed potatoes an' Salisbury steak an' bread-n-butter. He's lookin' for a place to sit down an' eat.

It was the first time I seen him since that day in his apartment. He looked pretty much the same—big fat slob wearin' these super-dorky clothes that looked like they came from like forty years ago.

"Watch this," Deemer says to the guys at the table, and he gets up from his chair. I look at him and see he's got somethin' in one hand—one of them little white metal boxes that Band-Aids come in, with the top that kinda flips open.

Jabba's just about to sit down at the enda this table when Deemer comes walkin' up like he's bein' real friendly.

"Hey," he says. "Howzit goin'?"

Jabba just kinda looks at him and don't say nothin' for a while. He prob'ly never spoke to Deemer before in his whole life. Finally he says, "Okay."

Deemer looks at Jabba's lunch, which Jabba's still holdin' on the tray. "Mmm," Deemer says. "Your lunch looks good."

Jabba just kinda looks down at the food and shrugs.

"I got somethin' that'll make it taste even better," Deemer says. "Here."

That's when he takes this metal Band-Aid box, pops open

Jon A. Harrald

the top, and kinda shakes it over Jabba's food, like the way you shake salt out of a shaker. Only it ain't salt that spills out onta Jabba's food. It's a buncha big, fat, slimy earthworms.

Man, you shoulda heard the scream that comes outta Jabba. Jabba's scream is so loud it just shuts everyone up for a second. He throws his tray straight up in the air, and everything goes flyin'—the milk and the food and the plates and the worms—and then it all comes crashin' back down all the fuck over the place. And Mr. Pitman, who's doin' lunch duty that day, comes tearin' over to see what's wrong.

Deemer's already back in his seat by then, laughin' his fuckin' head off. Meanwhile, Jabba's just standin' there cryin' and shakin', and everyone's starin' at him and makin' fun of him, and Pitman's standin' over him shoutin', "What the hell's wrong with you, Jabrowski? Can't you even hold onto your lunch tray?"

I felt a little bad about Jabba and thought maybe I should say somethin' to Pitman or somethin'. But, I dunno. I guess I din't want to piss off Deemer. I was hopin' that would be the end of it—like maybe he got it outta his system or whatever.

But it wasn't the end of it. It was just the fuckin' beginnin'. It was like Deemer had this *thing* against Jabba, which was real weird, 'cause, you know, Deemer just kinda ignored Jabba before then. But from then on he just wouldn't let up.

Every day, almost, it was somethin' else. Deemer got all this real gross slimy crap from his old man's butcher shop an' just did all kindsa shit with it. Like one day Jabba'd reach inta his book bag, and there'd be this greasy loada chicken guts that Deemer'd shoved in there when Jabba wasn't lookin'. Or Jabba'd go to sit down in his chair, and just before his ass hits the wood Deemer'd reach over and stick this little plastic Baggie fulla all this globby yellow pig fat under him. And Jabba'd just plop himself down on it without lookin', and the Baggie would bust, and he'd get all this squishy crap all over his pants and go flyin' off his seat, squealin' like *he* was the pig.

Slime

Sometimes Deemer din't even bother with all that animal crap. He'd just come sneakin' up on Jabba in the hallway before class, dig a big glob of snot outta his nose or cough up some mucus, and smear it on the backa Jabba's neck.

I thought I should maybe say somethin' to Deemer—you know, like tell him to chill a little—but I dunno, I guess I din't want him to think I was like a wimp or nothin'. So he just kept doin' stuff to Jabba. It finally got so bad that Jabba stopped showin' up for school, and I guess his mom musta complained or somethin', 'cause a buncha us was called inta the principal's office.

Mr. Farr was the principal. He was a big baldin' bastard with thick motherfuckin' glasses like Coke bottles. So he has us standin' there in his office, and he's stormin' around and wavin' his hands and goin' on and on 'bout how horrible it was, all the stuff we was doin' to Jabba—he din't call him Jabba, but his real name, Lawrence. And how it would be horrible to do it to anyone, but it was 'specially bad to do it to Jabba 'cause he had like this problem.

So Farr asks us if any of us know what a phobia is, and Deemer kinda raises his hand and says, "Like a real bad fear," and Farr says, "That's right," and that Jabba got somethin' called, I forget the word exactly, but it kinda sounded like "mix-o-phobia" or somethin', meanin' he freaked out when he touched anythin' slimy. And how what we was doin' to him could cause him "serious emotional damage."

So then he yelled at us some more and told us how if we kept on doing this stuff to Jabba we'd get suspended, and he made us swear we wouldn't do it anymore, 'specially Deemer. Deemer kinda stood there with his head hangin' down and promised he wouldn't do no more stuff to Jabba.

So the next day Jabba's back in school, and Deemer walks up to him in the schoolyard durin' recess while everyone's kinda hangin' around watchin', and he says, "I'm sorry, let's shake hands." So Jabba just kinda looks at him for a minute, real suspicious, then finally holds out his right hand. Deemer sticks out *his* right hand and begins to shake, only

133

it's more like he's squeezin' Jabba's hand real hard, and Jabba's face suddenly goes real white, and he starts screamin' and tryin' to pull his hand away, but Deemer grabs onta his wrist with his other hand and won't let go. And now Jabba's really shriekin' and cryin', and suddenly I can see he's pissed his pants again, like that time in the park, only this time in fronta almos' everybody, the whole school practically.

That's when Deemer jumps back and comes runnin' towards us, laughin' like a maniac, while Jabba goes barrelin' outta the schoolyard, wailin' away like a police siren or somethin'.

"What the fuckja *do* ta him?" Tommy DiNardo says.

Deemer's laughin' so hard he can't even talk, so he just lifts up his hand, and we can see there's all this slimy shit runnin' down his hand—like the clear part of a raw egg, except thicker, like jelly.

When he calms down enough, Deemer tells us what it is. It's a cow's eyeball from his old man's shop. Deemer dug it outta the cow's head with a spoon and hid it in his hand. Then he squeezed it inta Jabba's hand until it popped, and all the slime oozed out onta Jabba.

4

Deemer got into a shitload of trouble for that one. His old man got called into the principal's office, and Deemer got suspended for a week. When he came back you could tell from the bruises his old man had beat the shit outta him.

For a real long time after that Deemer kept away from Jabba. But you knew he was still thinkin' 'bout him. You could see it in the way his eyes got real mean and hard whenever he looked at him. Or sometimes you'd be standin' next to Deemer in the schoolyar or somethin', and he'd catch sighta Jabba walkin' by, and he'd whisper in this real nasty voice, "I'm gonna get that motherfucker." And you knew he was plannin' somethin' bad.

But then all this time goes by and nothin' happens. Leastways not with Jabba. Deemer got inta all kindsa other shit. Coupla times he even got picked up by the cops for one thing or another. Meanwhile Jabba kept pretty much to himself. You'd never see him hangin' around or talkin' with other kids, not even the real nerdy ones. Before you know it, a coupla years go by and alla us are in junior high. And all this time Deemer's still lettin' Jabba alone. So much time goes by that you figure Deemer's just forgot 'bout Jabba.

But one thing 'bout Deemer—the fuckin' guy never forgets 'bout nothin'.

The real bad thing that happened next was in ninth grade. By that time there was these girls that useta hang 'round with Deemer and the resta us. Real pigs, mosta them, 'specially this one that really had the hots for Deemer. Randi. Man, you shoulda seen the tits on her.

Deemer was still a real short guy for his age, but he'd bulked up a lot from liftin'. He still had this weird baby face—real smooth skin, curly blond hair, fat cheeks, and this little mouth like you see on them angels in church. But all you hadda do was look in his eyes an' you knew he wasn't no angel. There was somethin' crazy in those eyes, man. Scary-crazy, 'specially when he was pissed off about somethin', which was like mosta the time. Anyways, this Randi was like all over Deemer. She'd do anythin' he ast her. So the school year's endin', it's like late May or early June, an' I'm suddenly noticin' somethin' very weird— Randi's hangin' around a lot with Jabba, like talkin' to him in the schoolyard or walkin' with him after class. And she's always like standin' real close to him, lettin' her tits brush up against his arm. I can't believe my fuckin' eyes.

Jabba, he's so outta it, he don't even know Randi's one of Deemer's girls. You can see by his face when he and Randi're together that he's just feelin' real happy. Prob'ly the first time in his whole fuckin' life he's ever even *talked* to a girl.

I'm wonderin' what the fuck's goin' on, so the next time I see DiNardo, I ask him.

"Ain't you heard?" he says in this whispery voice, like it's this great big secret. "Deemer's workin' on this surprise for Jabba."

"What kinda surprise?"

He waves his hand like I should talk quieter, then he says in this real low, excited voice, like somethin' really great's gonna be happenin', "Randi's been comin' onta Jabba. He thinks she really likes him. They're s'posed to go out to the movies on Sattiday night, then she's gonna take him to the park and start makin' out with him. The resta us is gonna be there with a little surprise. Deemer set up the whole fuckin' thing. Wanna come?"

I think about it for a minute. "I got stuff ta do," I says.

"Too bad," he says. "It's gonna be fuckin' great."

I think about sayin' somethin' to Jabba, and I almost do, but Deemer always seems to be aroun', so I never get the chance. I'm startin' to feel real sick an' tired of Deemer, the way he's got everybody shittin' in their pants. And I'm feelin' real bad 'bout what's s'posed to happen to Jabba. I keep hopin' that maybe the other guys won't go along with it.

But they do.

I get the whole story from DiNardo the next Monday morning. The way he tells it, it's aroun' midnight when Jabba shows up in the park with Randi leadin' him by the hand. She leads him over to this little patch of grass, not too far from that clump of trees where Jabba'd fell on that slug when we was kids, then she lays down on the grass next to him. It's real dark, but there's this streetlight at the edge of the park right there, so there's enough light so Deemer and the resta the guys can see what's goin' on. Deemer and the other guys're hidin' in the trees where Jabba can't see 'em.

So right away Randi starts makin' out with Jabba. She puts his hand on her tits, and she starts rubbin' him through his pants and all. And after a while she starts to unzip his fly and all, and DiNardo's tellin' me that Jabba's like all embarrassed, and Randi has to like fuckin' *force* him to let her pull off his pants. DiNardo's totally crackin' up when he's tellin' me this, like he never seen nothin' so funny.

Slime

So finally there's Jabba lyin' there with his pants and underpants down aroun' his ankles, and Randi's givin' him this hand job, and Jabba's gettin' more 'n' more excited, and he's just about to pop his rocks when Randi kinda jumps back.

And that's when Deemer and all the guys come chargin' outta the trees with these plastic bags fulla this shit which they dump all over Jabba. And Jabba, he just goes wild while Deemer and Randi and the other guys kinda dance aroun' makin' fun of him.

"Prob'ly ruined him for life," DiNardo says, laughin' away. "Prob'ly never let a girl near him again."

I ask DiNardo what was in the bags, and he told me.

You know how lettuce and that kinda crap gets when it rots, how it turns into this green-black slime that smells worse'n shit? Well, Deemer and the other guys got all this lettuce and crap from the grocery store and stuck it into these plastic bags and left it outside for like two weeks till it turned into this shit-smellin' slime.

Then they poured it onta Jabba.

5

It's maybe a week—no, more like two—after I heard from DiNardo about what Deemer and the rest done to Jabba. Thursday night, last week of school in June. I'm comin' home late from the movies—one of them pictures starrin' Chuckie. You know, that psycho-doll that goes aroun' killin' all these people. So I figure I'll take a shortcut to my buildin' by shootin' through the alley that runs between Lacey Avenue and my block.

It's real dark in the alley, but, you know, I crossed it like a million times since I was a kid, so I ain't scared or nothin'. Every now an' then you run into some creep shootin' up shit or somethin', but nothin' I can't handle.

So I'm like halfway through to the other side when this big dark shape suddenly comes outta the shadows on my right, and this arm gets a choke hold on my neck, and I feel this gun barrel shoved up hard against my head, and this real raspy voice says, "I oughta kill you, you motherfucker," and I feel this spit sprayin' all over the backa my neck, and I can't hardly believe it but I realize right away that it's fuckin' Jabba.

"You're stranglin' me," I says in this real choked-up voice. I never knew how strong the fat motherfucker was. It felt like he was crushin' my fuckin' throat.

He slides his arm away, but he keeps the gun stuck up against my head, right behind my left ear.

"I oughta splatter your fuckin' brains for what you done to me," he says.

"What're you talkin' about, man?" I says. My voice comes out kinda trembly. I ain't never had no gun stuck into my head before, and lemme tell you, it don't feel too great.

"You know what I'm talkin' about," he says. "The park. That bitch. Deemer an' the rest of you." I can hear him breathin' real heavy behind me—pantin', like. And I can feel the gun kinda shakin' in his hand. Man, it's scarin' the shit outta me, knowin' that all it takes is one twitch of his trigger finger and—blam!—my skull's all over the fuckin' pavement.

"Hey, man," I says, real serious, "I wasn't even there. I tried ta stop 'em, man."

He don't say nothin' for a while, then he says, "If you knew they was plannin' it, why din't you warn me?" There's somethin' funny in his voice. It's still real angry, but there's somethin' else there, too—like hurt or somethin'. Even though what I'm mainly feelin' is scared shitless, I suddenly feel kinda bad 'bout not warnin' him or nothin'.

"Hey, Jabba, man," I start to say, but he cuts me off, real angry, and shoves the gun a little harder against my head.

"Don't call me that," he says.

"Okay," I says real quick. "Sorry." My mouth is all dry—no spit. I take a deep breath and say, "Hey, man. Whyn't you put down the piece and let's just talk about it, 'kay? Can I turn around?"

"Awright," he says after a coupla secs.

Slime

I turn around face-to-face. By now my eyes can see pretty good in the dark—good enough to see the gun he still got pointed right at me, this nasty-lookin' 9mm job.

I try to talk to him real friendly. "Where'd you get the piece?" I says, noddin' down at it.

Jabba kinda glances down at it, then back up at me. "You kiddin'? Buyin' a gun in this neighborhood's like buyin' a fuckin' Mars Bar."

"Well, you don't wanna use that thing on me," I says. "I'm on your side, man."

He don't say nothin' for a while, just kinda looks at me real hard. I can't really make out his eyes in the shadows—but man, I can *feel* 'em.

Finally he says, "We'll see. Let's go. I got somethin' to show you."

It don't take me long to see where he's leadin' me. Across the parkway, on the corner of Colgate Street and Price, there was this old abandoned buildin' that'd been empty for like years and years.

He din't have his gun out no more—he had stuffed it inta his pants underneath this sweatshirt he was wearin'. I thought about makin' a run for it, but I wasn't too crazy 'bout the idea of his maybe yankin' out his burner and takin' some potshots at me in the dark. There was somethin' else, too—I was kinda curious 'bout what he wanted ta show me. But when I saw where he was takin' me, I wasn't too happy about it. I hadn't never been inside that place 'cept durin' the day. The thing was, the old buildin' looked real spooky in the dark, like this giant haunted house or one of them creepy castles you see in Dracula movies.

So I says to Jabba, "We ain't goin' in *there*, are we?" But he just tells me to shut my fuckin' trap. I tell you, man, I ain't never heard him talk that way before. It was like he was this whole different person.

We get to the buildin', and Jabba leads me aroun' to the side where there's this entrance that goes down ta the basement. There's this pile of trash lyin' by the entrance,

139

and Jabba squats down and kinda digs around behind it and comes up with this flashlight he musta stashed there. Jabba flicks on the light, points it at the entrance, and tells me ta get movin'.

Lemme tell you, man, it's *scary* in there—like goin' down inta some giant's mouth or bein' swallowed or somethin'. And it smells real creepy, too—like all wet and moldy. And you can hear things scrabblin' all aroun' you—rats and shit. And when Jabba's light hits the walls you can see all these big motherfuckin' waterbugs crawlin' around—like these giant cockroaches with wings.

I'm drippin' sweat and thinkin' maybe I might even like black out or somethin', and just then Jabba grabs me real hard by the shoulder and points his flashlight off to the left. I see there's this doorway with no door or anythin', just a black openin' in the wall. And Jabba says, "In there."

It's this old storeroom or somethin'—you can see these old broken crates lyin' aroun' in the corners and a buncha trash, like broken bottles and crushed-up paper cups and stuff. Cement floor's all cracked and dirty, with little black puddles here 'n' there. Somethin' touches my head, and I give this little shout and jump away, but when Jabba hits it with his beam I see it's just this loose wire danglin' down from the ceilin'.

So then Jabba steps over ta this one wall, and I can see there's like this hole in the wall, big enough for someone to crawl into. Broken plaster all over the floor in fronta the hole. There's this pile of bricks maybe three feet high leanin' against the wall, and a bag fulla somethin' like cement.

And Jabba kinda waves to me like I should come up closer to him, and when I do he shines the light inta this hole, and I bend over to look, and I see there's all this stuff lyin' in there on the floor—this big coil of rope and a roll of duct tape and somethin' small an' shiny that when I look closer I see it's this pair of handcuffs.

So I look up at Jabba, real surprised. And he's just standin' there with this crazy smile on his face, and lemme tell you, that flashlight's makin' his face look real spooky,

like he's wearin' this orange Halloween mask or somethin'.
So I start to ask him what the fuck this is all about, but even
before I do, he goes ahead an' gives me the answer.

"That's for Deemer," he says.

I ask him what's he mean, and he starts goin' on and on
'bout how Deemer's been torturin' him for so long—that
was the word he used, *torturin'* him—and how he ain't
gonna take it no more, and how he's gonna kill Deemer.
Only he ain't just gonna shoot him or nothin', 'cause that
would be too fast. So he goes on ta tell me 'bout this plan
he's been thinkin' 'bout. Only now he's really gonna do it,
on accounta what Deemer done to him in the park. It's
somethin' he got outta this book, this story called "The Cast
a Somethin'" by this famous writer called Poe. It's about
this guy that gets revenge on this other guy by stickin' him in
a hole in a basement and brickin' it up and leavin' the guy
there to die real slow. And that's what he's gonna do ta
Deemer. So I ask him how he thinks he's gonna get Deemer
ta come down there.

And that's when he says, "I ain't. You are."

I stare at him like he's crazy, but he don't notice, he just
goes on an' tells me what I'm s'posed ta do. I'm s'posed ta
tell Deemer that I heard that Jabba's like run away from
home and is hidin' out in the basement of the abandoned
buildin'. Jabba figures as soon as Deemer hears 'bout it he'll
sneak aroun' an' try ta pull some shit on Jabba. Only
Jabba'll be there waitin' for him.

I listen to all this, then I says, "I don't know."

And then Jabba grabs me aroun' the throat—and shit,
that fucker's *strong*. It's like my throat's in a fuckin' vise.

So he's standin' there almos' chokin' me ta death, and
meanwhile he's shoutin' how I gotta help him, how I owe it
ta him, and how he'll kill me if I don't. And that we gotta get
rid of Deemer, the guy's a fuckin' monster that deserves ta
die, an' on an' on. And it's weird, 'cause it's like he's
threatenin' me, but it's also kinda like he's beggin' me.

So I finally yank his hand away, and while I'm standin'
there kinda gaspin' for air all these thoughts are goin'

around in my head, like how maybe I *do* owe somethin' to Jabba, and how Deemer's got like this hold over everybody, and fuck him anyway, he ain't nothin' but a goddam psycho.

So I'm finally able ta talk again, only my voice comes out real funny, like a fuckin' frog or somethin'.

But what I says is, "Okay."

The next mornin' is Friday, and before school I see Deemer hangin' around the schoolyard smokin' a cigarette like usual, only there's all these other people hangin' around, too, so I wait till I catch him alone later on around lunchtime, and I tell him what Jabba told me to. And it's just like Jabba says. Deemer asks me, how do I know? So I says I heard it from my mom, who heard it from Jabba's mom. Deemer's eyes kinda light up, and he smiles that creepy smile of his.

Then he says maybe he'll pay Jabba a little visit later on.

I don't crawl outta bed till aroun' twelve o'clock the next day, which is Sattiday. I just throw on these clothes an' head outside and start goin' 'round the neighborhood lookin' for Deemer. I'm half hopin' Jabba din't go through with it and I'll run inta Deemer like usual, hangin' around the school-yard or at Rudi's Pizzeria. But the other halfa me is hopin' I won't.

So I run inta DiNardo and Palmer and ask them 'bout Deemer, but they ain't seen him. I come across Randi and a coupla her friends, but they ain't seen him neither. After a while I head over to Crowell Avenue and look inta the window of Deemer's old man's butcher shop. I can see Deemer's old man behind the counter, whackin' away at this big piece of meat with this humongous butcher knife.

But I don't see Deemer nowhere.

I'm all nervous an' jittery, but I make myself wait till night, 'cause I don't want nobody ta see where I'm goin'. But as soon as it's good 'n' dark I head for the parkway. I'm runnin' full speed, so I'm sweatin' like a pig by the time I get ta Colgate, an' my heart's thumpin' so fast against my chest bone it's like I got somethin' alive trapped inside there, like a rabbit or somethin' that's tryin' ta get out.

The street's totally empty like it always is at night. I got one a them flick-my-Bic cigarette lighters in my pocket, and I pull it out and snap it on.

Then I head down inta the basement.

Right away I'm in this crazy, twistin', solid black tunnel again. I don't know where the fuck I'm goin', just followin' the hallway this way, that way, right turn, left turn. The wall's real tight an' narrow on either side of me, and that cold, moldy smell's fillin' up my nose. Every now an' then I stop an' listen, but all's I hear is rats scurryin' and water drippin' and this weird kinda raspy sound which it takes me a few seconds to realize is my own breathin'.

I keep goin'. My shadow's real big on the wall, like this big black monster slidin' along right beside me. Then up on the left I think I see the openin' inta the storeroom.

I kinda creep up on it, listenin' real hard, expectin' ta hear like moanin' or somethin' comin' from where Jabba's got Deemer bricked up behin' the wall. But I don't hear nothin'. The sweat's drippin' inta my eyes, makin' 'em sting. I reach up with my free hand and wipe 'em dry.

Then I step inta the storeroom.

And that's when this hand shoots out and grabs me by the neck, and I let out this real loud yell and drop my lighter. And just then this flashlight lights up, shinin' straight inta my eyes, an' I can't see shit for a minute. I lash out with my fist, but all I feel is air. The guy musta seen it comin'.

He lets out this growl and swings his flashlight like a club. But I get my hand up and block it, then lash out again. This time I connect. He grunts and drops the flashlight.

The next thing I know, the two of us're rollin' 'round the floor, fightin' and wrestlin' and cursin'. But after a while I'm flat on my back, an' the fucker's on top of me with his knees diggin' into my chest, and I can't hardly breathe. The flashlight's lyin' on the floor right beside me, and he reaches down ta pick it up, and I can see in the light what I already guessed. That it ain't Jabba kneelin' on my chest.

It's fuckin' Deemer.

"Come ta help your buddy kill me?" he says, only it sounds more like a snake hissin' or somethin'.

"Get offa me," I say. "I don't know what the fuck you're talkin' about."

He stares down at me for a minute, then slides offa me.

"Get up," he says.

I get to my knees, breathin' hard, and wipe some blood from my nose. After a while I stand up facin' him.

"What the fuck're you doin' here?" he says.

"Just come ta see how Jabba was," I says. "I don' know. I felt kinda sorry for him—you know, hidin' down here in this place."

"Felt sorry for him, huh?" Deemer says. "You know what that fucker was plannin' for me? He was plannin' to bury me down here, man! Alive!"

"You're shittin' me," I says. I hope to hell I sound like I mean it—you know, like I'm surprised and all.

"No, I ain't shittin you," he says. "Only I guess he still don't know Deemer, man. I sneak down here, and the fucker jumps out an' pulls this burner on me. But he's so fuckin' excited he don't even notice I'm hidin' this big piece of pipe behind my back. Before he knows it—bam!—the fucker's out cold." Deemer's kinda chucklin' now, like it's all this real funny joke. "When he wakes up, *he*'s the one with the fuckin' cuffs on him. Then I give him a little treat."

"Treat?" I says. I can feel like my hands and legs're startin' to shake a little, just from the way Deemer says it.

He smiles and points his flashlight over to the floor, right by where the wall's got that big hole in it. I see Jabba's body lyin' there on his back with his arms underneath him.

"Go on an' take a look."

I'm tremblin' pretty bad by now, but I take a few steps over ta the body. The thing is, I can already tell Jabba's dead, just from the way he's lyin' there.

"Go ahead," Deemer says. "Look closer."

He's aimin' the flashlight at Jabba's face. I bend down and look.

His eyes're what I notice first. I ain't ever seen eyeballs so big. They look like they're poppin' right outta his head—all white, like Ping-Pong balls or somethin', with just little black holes in the middle.

Then I see his mouth.

It's stuffed with somethin' that kinda looks like puke, this thick slimy shit, all yellow an' green an' chunky. Only it's got all these little brown pieces all mixed up in it. It takes me a second ta realize that the brown stuff is bug parts—pieces of wings an' bellies an' legs an' shit. And the yellow-green shit is like the stuff that comes oozin' outta bugs when you step on 'em.

Deemer comes up right behind me. "Cockroach cocktail," he says into my ear. "I caught a whole buncha them big fat juicy waterbugs and mashed 'em all up in a cup and made him drink it. He wasn't too happy about it, but I held his nose till he opened his mouth and forced it in." He gives out this soft little giggle. "You shoulda heard the sound that come outta him. Then he died."

I'm still starin' at Jabba's mouth. Just then one of the bug legs begins ta twitch like it's still alive. I feel the puke start ta rise up from my stomach, and I rush over to a corner of the storeroom and barf my guts out while Deemer stands there laughin' an' laughin' an' laughin'. . . .

I can't talk too much 'bout what happened after that. I don't like ta think about it. Deemer made me strip off alla my clothes, then he stripped off his. Then we used these big knives and cleavers an' shit he got from his old man's butcher shop and cut up Jabba's body inta little pieces and stuffed 'em inta these big plastic bags Deemer'd brought over. Then we wiped off all the blood from our bodies and got dressed again and carried the bags back to Deemer's old man's shop and dumped 'em in the dumpster in the alleyway. The next day the garbage trucks just hauled it all away.

That was like three years ago. No one never found out what happened ta Jabba. Everybody just figured the story was true—that he run away from home. The old buildin' got demolished, and all the blood and shit down in the basement was buried under a million tons of old bricks.

Deemer ended up bein' sent to this mental institution, but not for killin' Jabba. He got sent there for stabbin' his old man with a butcher knife durin' a big fight they had. The old man died the next day. But the judge din't send Deemer to jail on account of him bein' a minor and also 'cause his old man was abusin' him. He'll prob'ly be out in a coupla years or so.

And me? This real bad thing happened. I couldn't stop thinkin' about that stuff in Jabba's mouth, and after a while I couldn't stand ta look at any kinda cockroach or nothin'. It got so bad I was like screamin' and breakin' out inta tears whenever I spotted one. The school finally sent me ta this shrink, who said I had what Jabba did, like this phobia, only mine was just with cockroaches. But that's plenty bad enough, man—'specially if you live in *this* neighborhood.

That's why I can't go inta the crapper, man, not in the middle a the night. That's when they really come out, hundreds of 'em, scurryin' all over the walls an' the floors an' inside the bathtub. I can almos' *hear* 'em crawlin' around in there.

And man, I just lie here and pray that the night'll be over, and I wish that fuckin' Jabba hadn't never been born.

LAST THINGS FIRST

Jack C. Haldeman II

THIS IS HOW IT STARTED, WITH A SINGLE ENTRY IN A NEW SPIRAL
notebook. The cardboard cover was blue. It had narrow
lines.

17 FEBRUARY: SAW FIRST ROBIN OF THE YEAR.

Who would have guessed where such a humble beginning
would lead?

Bob Sanders was not the kind of man to keep a journal,
but he was terminally bored and had picked up the notebook at the checkout counter of the local Wal-Mart while
buying his usual month's supply of toilet paper and paper
towels. It was, as they say, an impulse.

Ah, impulses. They have toppled governments, cost politicians their careers, ruined many a marriage. All in the
blink of an eye. A thoughtless word, a wink at the wrong
person, a moment's indiscretion, a blue notebook: The
whole ball of wax gets blown all to hell. It happens.

Bob was far too young to be bored with life. He'd put in
twenty years with the Government Accounting Office as a

147

low-grade clerk. Twenty years and out. Full retirement. He'd started right after high school, so he was only thirty-eight when he retired. Far too young to be bored. Far too young to pick up a blue notebook on an ill-advised whim.

He had lived a simple and frugal life for those twenty years, and the day after he retired he moved to Florida and bought himself a decent concrete block house on a canal. It was close to the concrete block houses on either side, but if he sat under the avocado tree in his backyard he couldn't see his next-door neighbors, only the canal and the houses on the other side. For about two weeks he liked the canal, his little bit of nature.

But the canal had been dredged out of sand, and most of the nature he saw was of the dead and bloated, belly-up variety. The water did not circulate. A Styrofoam cup would float for days in the same place. The only fish that weren't dead were catfish. Not a lot to look at.

Still, it was a change from suburban Virginia, and for a few months he enjoyed things being different. After that, things got to be the same. After that, he got bored.

All the days looked alike to him. He was used to changes in seasons, but down here the changes were imperceptible. He tried to broaden his life with social contacts, but most of his neighbors were considerably older than he was, and he had never developed many social graces or interests anyway.

17 FEBRUARY: SAW FIRST ROBIN OF THE YEAR.

Bob sat under the avocado tree and grinned as he shut the blue notebook. Everything looked new, different, fresh. He had found his place. The notebook was filled within two weeks.

He noted almost every change. When the first avocado buds came out he made an entry. He marked the date of the first azalea flower and noted the blooming of the hibiscus with joy in his book. He carefully recorded the high and low temperatures each day so that he could tell the advent of ninety-degree weather and the start of the rainy season.

The weather reports he got on the television were not accurate enough for him, so he bought a home weather station. When he ate the first avocado of the year he got more pleasure out of noting the date than he did from eating it.

Three years later he got his first visitor. He marked the date in his book.

Sam Lane had worked in the cubicle beside Bob for five years. He was vacationing in Florida and decided to see how his old coworker was doing.

"Good to see you again, Bob," said Sam as his former acquaintance opened the door. "It's been a long time."

"I've been here one thousand three hundred and forty-eight days," he said.

Sam blinked.

"Three hours, sixteen minutes," Bob added, checking his watch. "Come in."

Sam hesitated, then entered the small house. Bob had always been a little strange, but this was creeping beyond strange into the realm of odd. Retirement did peculiar things to some people.

"Nice place," Sam said as he looked around the living room. It had a bachelor feel to it: overstuffed chair facing a TV set, coffee table with a few magazines on it, a couch that didn't look very used, a bookcase with about a thousand blue spiral-bound notebooks in it.

Bookcase? Notebooks? It was then Sam noticed the blue notebook hanging on a string from Bob's belt and the pencil behind his ear. He felt it best not to make a point of having observed this curious personal trait.

"Real nice place," said Sam. "Blue is my favorite color." Yow! Sam mentally slapped his forehead. Dumb move.

"Blue?" said Bob, looking around with a confused expression on his face.

"Super place you've got here, Bob," Sam said quickly. "Super. How about a tour?"

"Yes, a tour," said Bob. "Would you like something to drink? A beer? A soda? Some iced tea?"

"A beer would be nice. This Florida heat is getting to me."

"The average high for this month is eighty-seven degrees," said Bob over his shoulder as he fetched two beers from the fridge. "The record high for this month is one-oh-five, set in 1936. But 1936 was a remarkably hot year. Things start cooling down at the end of October, usually around the twenty-third. Here's your beer."

"Thanks," said Sam.

"My pleasure," said Bob, happily whipping the pencil out from behind his ear and opening the blue notebook. "First beer served to guest," he muttered, looking at his watch and jotting down a note. "Hot damn," he chortled gleefully. "And a Budweiser, too!"

"Uh . . . the tour?" asked Sam.

"Right. The tour." He dropped the notebook to his side and stuck the pencil behind his ear. "Follow me."

They went through a sliding glass door to a screen-enclosed patio at the back of the house. It had several plants and a fake plastic pond with three huge, fat goldfish swimming aimlessly around the imitation lily pads.

"Is that what you call a spider plant?" asked Sam.

"Sure is," said Bob. "And all these little guys are sprouts from the original plant, which I purchased on March twelfth two years ago. This fellow here was transplanted last April eighteenth, and this guy . . ."

Bob's face went white. He looked disoriented.

"I've got it here somewhere," he gasped. "Wrote it down in my own hand. I can find it. I *know* I can find it. I keep *good* records."

Sam gulped hard. Strange had passed clear through odd and was knocking hard on the door of bizarre with both fists.

"Nice fish," he said.

Bob beamed with relief. "Bought those fellas at the K-mart a year ago last June twenty-third. Was a Monday. My first fish."

"They sure look healthy," said Sam, eyeballing Bob with suspicion.

"One point five grams of rough-cut fish food at eight A.M. and four P.M. That's the secret for happy fish."

"I'll remember that," said Sam, backing away.

"You want me to write it down for you?" asked Bob, reaching for his pencil. "I'm good at writing stuff down."

"That's okay," said Sam quickly. "I'll remember it. Hey, what's out this way?"

"Backyard. The canal. Want to see?"

"Sure," said Sam, anxious to get away from the feeding regimen of oversize guppies. "Lead away."

They walked out back. Bob swelled with pride as he cataloged the dates of the first buds, first flowers, and first fruits of all the trees and bushes. Sam's mind was reeling, and it wasn't from the unfinished beer that had grown warm in his hand.

"Look at the lizard," said Sam, trying desperately to change the subject.

"That's Herman," said Bob. "Actually, he's a gecko. He disappears during the winter months every year but comes back when the weather warms up. Pretty consistent little fellow, too. Always appears the first week in April. He's been as early as the second but is never later than the fifth."

"When's the last time you see him?" asked Sam.

"Last?"

"Last," said Sam. "When is the last time you see him before winter sets in?"

"Last," moaned Bob, clutching his chest and staggering backward. "I never thought of last."

"I didn't mean anything," said Sam. "It's no big deal."

"No big deal?" shouted Bob, his face turning red. "Last things are as important as first things. Maybe even more important. I should have known."

He reached down and shook a small tomato plant by the throat, scattering cherry tomatoes all over the yard. "I can tell you the date of the first flower, first fruit set, and when the first tomato comes ripe," he shouted, the veins in his forehead standing out. "But can I tell you when the last tomato falls? No! I have been remiss, I tell you. Remiss!"

"Take it easy, Bob," said Sam, moving out of arm's reach. "Take it easy."

"That is precisely what I shall not do," said Bob. "I must be ever diligent."

"And I must be going," said Sam, backtracking like mad.

"Last visit by Sam," cried Bob, scribbling in his notebook as Sam made his hasty exit.

Bob sat down on the grass. Fear washed over him as the enormity of his task dawned on him. How in the world could he keep track of last things? So many things went by unnoticed, unrecorded. Had he seen a roach today? When was the last time he'd *really noticed* a roach? The last roach in the world could already have walked past him, and that data point would be lost forever.

The last mosquito bite? The last late newspaper? The last barking dog to keep him up? The last pass of migrating geese? The last dead fish floating in the canal? The last leaf to fall off his small oak tree in winter? And Herman! When would be the last time he saw Herman?

The only way to be sure was to write down everything as he saw it, and when he stopped seeing it, that would be the last time.

Bob got up and headed back into the house to call the office supply store for a case of blue notebooks. On his way in he looked at the lizard.

"Saw Herman today," he said to himself as he checked the time and wrote a note in his book.

Two years later Sam was in Florida for a business trip. On a whim he decided to drop in on Bob one afternoon and see how he was doing.

There was no answer to the bell, but when Sam twisted the knob the front door opened partway. Something seemed to be jamming it, so Sam pushed harder and eventually got it open enough that he could slip through.

Then Sam saw what was jamming the door.

Blue notebooks. Mounds of dog-eared blue notebooks filled the room. They cascaded from the fireplace and buried the sofa. Blue notebooks had completely covered the television and every other item of furniture in sight like cardboard kudzu run amok. At places the heaps of notebooks were six or seven feet tall.

Sam made his way to the back of the house, slipping on the notebooks that covered the floor.

The screen room was full of blue notebooks covered with mold from the humidity. All the plants were dead. There were three goldfish skeletons at the bottom of the empty plastic pond.

Bob was sitting in a chair out back, under a large umbrella, with a notebook in his lap. Every few seconds he would write in the book. There were loose stacks of blue notebooks all around him. A pallet with several thousand new notebooks sat within reach, covered with plastic. The lawn was littered with used pencils.

He looked up, and his face was haggard and worn. A brief smile tried to cross his worried face as he said "Sam" and took a quick note.

"Bob," cried Sam, "I—"

"Herman didn't come back this year," said Bob. "I last saw him on October twenty-second at four-fifteen P.M. What do you think about that?"

Sam really didn't know what he thought about that. Bob had crashed through bizarre and left full-blown crazy behind in a cloud of smoke.

"It must be a comfort to know the date," said Sam. "Herman was one good lizard."

"Comfort?" snorted Bob. "It is more than comfort, it is *imperative* to record such things."

"If you say so, Bob."

"Fate is out there, Sam, just waiting for us to blink and not pay attention. I owe my life to you."

"I wouldn't say that," said Sam, who wanted no such responsibility.

"But you should," Bob said gravely. "You helped me face my greatest fear."

Sam didn't say anything, hoping desperately that Bob wouldn't tell him his greatest fear. No such luck.

"I used to wake up in the middle of the night," said Bob, "gasping for breath. I'd try to remember the last time I'd taken a breath and never could remember. Sometimes I'd even think I'd forgotten how to breathe. Do you know what I mean?"

"No," said Sam, truthful even in the face of out-of-control madness.

"It haunted me. It gnawed at my soul. I would be afraid to sleep at night for fear I would stop breathing. And that very fear would cause me to panic and forget to breathe. I'm sure you've felt the same way, being a sensitive man."

"Can't say that I have," said Sam, who figured that if worse came to worst, he could always make a break for it by swimming across the canal. It would probably be easier than climbing over the notebooks in the house.

"Well, you solved it for me," he said with a smile, jotting notes in his book.

"I did?"

"Sure. You showed me that if I kept good records, nothing could sneak up on me. There's a lot to that 'know thy enemy' stuff."

Sam took two steps backward.

"I mark them all down, you know," said Bob.

"Them?" asked Sam.

"Every breath," said Bob, inhaling deeply and taking another note. "They're all in these books. My last breath isn't going to sneak up on me and catch me unawares. I'm as safe as can be, and I owe it all to you."

Bob started cackling and coughing and writing like crazy in his blue notebook. Sam jumped in the canal and headed for the far shore.

Bob waved at him and made another entry in his book.

HAIR

Kathryn Ptacek

THE PROBLEM ABOUT BODY HAIR, MARGARET DELON DECIDED on Monday, was there was so damned much of it. And it grew back no matter how often you cut or shaved it.

Maggie spent many hours each day devoted to maintenance of her body. She made a disgusted sound. It sounded as if she was working on a car. An *old* car at that. Except that she wasn't old. Not really. But she was about to turn the big four-oh, and that made her feel positively ancient, even though most of the people she knew were much older than she and had no sympathy at all for her birthday pangs.

So she tried to stay younger than forty. She exercised in the morning before work and took a turn around the parking lot at lunch unless it poured rain, and when she came home she would do another hour or so of exercise. She watched her calories, fat intake, dairy products, and cholesterol, she gave up beef, bacon, and barbecue, she looked out for nitrites and salt, with the upshot that there wasn't a whole lot left to eat anymore. But that didn't matter—eating took precious time away from the hair.

In the morning before she got ready for work she would peer at her face in the mirror over the sink. She'd pinpoint the fine wrinkles that had appeared in the last year on her forehead and at the corners of eyes. There weren't many, thank God, but they were unmistakably there. She couldn't do much about them except to use cream on her face and not go out in the sun, which she never did anyway. Nothing aged a person—man or woman—more than the sun. Her mother never sat out in the sun, and look at her; over eighty now, she could have passed for a woman in her early sixties.

Her skin was dry in spots and oily in others, and she didn't know from day to day what would be where. She applied moisturizer to some areas and just prayed the others would be all right as she spread her beige-tone makeup across her cheeks and chin and forehead. At least she'd never suffered from acne or been besieged by freckles.

Her lips tended to chap, even in the summer—she licked her lips far too often, but she just couldn't break herself of the nervous habit—and she applied Chap Stick before she put her lipstick on. Lipstick dried her lips even more, but she wanted them to look nice, so she put the moisturizer on as an undercoat. Her mother always said a woman wasn't totally dressed until she put on lipstick.

Her nose was the same as always, long and narrow. If she'd believed in cosmetic surgery, she'd have had it shortened. But she didn't dislike her nose all that much.

Ah, but the hair . . . *that* she could do something about. She had noticed the fine bristles around her lips darkening in the past few years. She'd always been thankful that she didn't have a horrible black mustache the way some women did, but lately . . . well, it wasn't a mustache, but it *was* unwanted.

She clipped it with cuticle scissors and pulled out other errant hairs on her upper lip with tweezers. Her eyebrows had once been thick and dark; now they were arched, thin. She peered at the smooth skin below her brow, searching for a hair that might be about to poke through.

She also shaved her underarms and her legs daily. The legs

took a long time, because she shaved from the ankle to the top of the thigh each time.

And now, lately, the pubic hair had begun bothering her. She told herself not to fret, but that was impossible. The more she tried not to think about it the more she *did* think about it. Stray hairs poked out beyond the legbands of her panties, and it looked, well, so *messy*. She cut off the excess that stuck out, and that looked better, although it itched a little. She got dressed, took the baby to day care, and then went to work.

Midmorning she got a call from Donald that his car had broken down again, and he'd had it towed to the garage, and the mechanic didn't know when it would be ready, although next week looked good, and she'd have to come and get him at work.

She tapped her pencil against the desk as she chatted with him, and she stared down at her fingers and noticed the fine hairs growing there.

She frowned slightly and put the pencil down, and when she hung up she went into the ladies' room with her purse and slipped into a stall, closing the door. Inside her purse she kept a cosmetic bag Donald had given her for Christmas, and she kept her other cuticle scissors in there. Luckily there was a light fixture just above her stall, so she could see the hairs quite plainly. They were a golden brown and weren't really noticeable until you looked closely. But they were there. She knew that all too well.

Carefully she cut them away until nothing remained but a fine fuzz. She ran a finger over it, frowned. Too much stubble. She'd have to do something about it. Tonight.

When she got back to her desk she glanced at the clock and was surprised to learn she'd spent thirty-two minutes in the bathroom. It hadn't seemed that long.

She spent the rest of the afternoon looking over policy papers and shuffling things from one end of her desk to the other. No matter how much she tried, it seemed she would never see the wooden surface under all this paper again. She would start to get things caught up, and then more orders would flood in, and more policies and more memos piled up, and the strata of paper just grew higher and higher. Her "in" and "out" baskets were crammed, as was her wastepaper basket. It wasn't as if she didn't get things accomplished. She did; she just didn't do it fast enough. No matter how well she did something, it wasn't good enough.

Somewhere along the way she realized her groin itched, and she thought she must have left some stray hairs in her panties. She'd fix that later. If she couldn't control her paper and life, she could at least take care of the hair.

She was halfway home when she remembered Donald's call, made a U-turn, and headed back to his office. He was standing outside and looking perturbed when she pulled up. He always looked perturbed, she thought, as if *everything* that went wrong was her fault. He didn't say it, but then he didn't have to.

"Sorry," she said perfunctorily as he got in, slammed the door, and said, "It's about damned time. I've been standing out in the sun all this time."

She glanced in the rearview mirror before swinging away from the curb. "Why didn't you wait in the lobby for me? It's cooler in there."

"I didn't want to. People come up and talk to me as if I'm still in the office." He thumped his briefcase a couple of times, as if that settled the matter.

Maggie sighed. They had this conversation at least once a week. Donald's car was always breaking down. They couldn't afford to buy a new one right now, and so they had to make do. He'd wanted to trade cars with her, take hers, and let her have his, and she'd laughed. He had glared at her.

They didn't speak much on the way to day care. She waited while Donald went in to get the baby, and she wondered when he had begun to lose his hair; there was a bald spot at the back of his head. She'd better not tell him, she thought. He was sensitive enough about his appearance. God knew that would really throw him into a tizzy.

He returned a few minutes later with the baby, who was trying to tell him about her day. DeeDee was three, almost four, and would always be her baby, Maggie realized, even when the baby was thirty-three. She and Donald had been married thirteen years and had waited a long time for their daughter; God knew they'd tried often enough, but nothing had clicked for years.

She smiled at DeeDee, who dimpled at her, and Donald buckled her up in the backseat. The itching in Maggie's groin had grown, and she shifted.

"What's wrong?" he asked as he slid into the passenger seat. He made it sound more like a demand.

"Nothing," she said, smiling.

"Then why are you wiggling around?"

"Just a momentary itch."

"God, I hope it's not your period again. It seems like it's always your period."

Like most men, she thought, Donald didn't understand a woman's cycles, nor did he care to understand. It was just some sort of inconvenience to him, particularly if he was in the mood and she just wasn't because it was the first day and all.

DeeDee chattered about what she'd had to eat for a snack after lunch and how they had played a new game. Sometimes Maggie asked her a question; Donald only listened.

When they got home Maggie changed into jeans and a casual shirt while DeeDee got into her jammies. She started dinner for them and did her exercises while the food cooked, and then when they were ready to eat they settled down in front of the TV.

During dinner she reached over and squeezed Donald's hand. It was their special nonvocal signal, a sign that let him know she was ready for bed. Nudge, nudge, wink, wink. Donald belched. Maggie wasn't fazed; he did that a lot. He was a hard sell on sex, but she could usually wrangle him into bed. He was okay once he got there. She had been scared for years to take the initiative but had decided there was nothing wrong with that. God knew she couldn't always wait for him to make a move.

When the shows were over she gave DeeDee a bath and brushed the child's long, light hair.

Such pretty hair, she thought as she ran her fingers

through it. She had had hair like that once, so baby fine and baby soft. Innocent hair; hair that hadn't been teased and sprayed and curled and permed. New and fresh and so sweet-smelling.

"Ouch, Mommy, a tangle," DeeDee pouted.

"Sorry."

She'd had really long hair once, hair so long it hung below her butt. Her mother said it made her look like a witch. Ladies, her mother declared, don't have long hair. And certainly, her mother said on more than one occasion, ladies didn't keep their hair long after they reached the age of forty. Maggie's hair was shoulder-length in defiance of her mother. Her mother tsked whenever she saw it. Her mother wore short, uncomfortable-looking curls, and as far back as Maggie could remember her mother had had the same hairdo.

Maggie tucked her daughter into bed and then went into the other bathroom—not the one off the master bedroom, because Donald would complain if she were in there more than three minutes—and locked the door.

She didn't take long that night because she was looking forward to some cuddling. When she finally went into the bedroom Donald was already asleep, the remote control loose in his hand. She sighed and felt strangely relieved, took the remote from him, switched off the TV, and then turned off the light.

It took her only seconds to fall asleep.

She was late on Tuesday because she had to drop the baby off at day care and Donald at his office, and there had been an accident on the freeway. Her boss said he understood, but Maggie knew he just didn't, not really, because the man was single, and what kind of responsibilities did he have, for God's sake, and he always seemed to be looking at her, and she didn't know why, and the company was being reorganized in the next few months, and not for the first time she began to wonder if there would be a place for her in the new setup, particularly if she came in late or called in sick those times when DeeDee had to stay home.

Hair

Her groin itched all day, and whenever she went into the restroom she scratched and scratched, and the hair felt coarse and, well, peculiar. She tugged at a few hairs, winced at the pain. There was nothing she could do there.

Back at her desk her fingertips found the fuzz on the back of her hands. She placed her palms down on the desk as she read a report—anything to keep from playing with the hair.

All the way home Donald bitched about work. He had been chewed out by his boss; one of his coworkers had accused him of snitching on her to the company head; and there was a new comptroller coming in the next week who was rumored to be a real ball-breaker.

The baby hadn't had a good day either, and she had the sniffles.

Maggie didn't talk about her day because she didn't think Donald would want to hear about it. Whenever she tried to tell him about her office worries he cut her off, saying he had problems, too; she wasn't the only one. She never said she was.

Maggie's groin itched unbearably.

"What's wrong? You keep twitching. You got a bug down there or what?" Donald asked.

"No." She tried to smile seductively. "I'm just a little itchy for someone."

He glanced out his window. "Yeah, just what I wanna do, Mag. Get fucked at work, and then come home and get fucked some more."

She almost slammed on the brakes then and told him to get out, but the baby was in the backseat, crying and wanting to get home. So she just pressed her lips together and made a precise turn into their driveway.

Once inside, she told him he could get dinner ready while she got the baby ready.

"But I've had a hard day at work!"

"So have I."

She walked out of the room and got DeeDee ready for her dinner and then bed.

When she came back in, there was no sign of dinner, and Donald had left, taking her car. She hated it when he did that. She didn't like not knowing where he'd gone. What if there was an accident? She supposed that in that case the police would get in touch with her, and she closed her eyes, not wanting to think about that.

She made macaroni and cheese, they watched a Disney tape, and she read DeeDee a story. By then it was ten, and still Donald wasn't home. She tucked DeeDee in, kissed her, then went to sit in the living room and wait.

By eleven he still hadn't returned, so she went into the bathroom. She stripped and looked at herself in the full-length mirror. She lathered up the soap, daubed it along her groin, took out her Lady Bic, and began shaving. The pubic hair came off in brown curls. She gathered it up carefully and tucked it inside a tissue and then threw the tissue into the wastebasket, putting a crushed Kleenex box on top.

Now her mound was smooth. She ran her fingers over the unfamiliar bare spot and tried not to giggle. She almost looked like a little girl again. She got out some aloe cream and carefully massaged it into the shaved skin; she didn't want razor burn in the morning.

Then she sat down on the closed toilet and began trimming the hairs off her toes. There weren't many, and she'd never had any on top of her foot, like some of her friends, but still. This made things so much nicer ... so much neater.

She shaved her underarms and her legs again, and when she looked at her wristwatch, which she had set on the side of the sink, she could see that nearly two hours had gone by.

She spread more cream across her body, feeling its cooling gentleness.

Then she looked at her part and along her temples for the white and gray hairs she knew were there. She plucked them as best she could. She knew one day there would be too many to pull out, and then she'd have to resort to dyeing her hair.

She remembered that in the Elizabethan days the fashion for women had been high, smooth foreheads, and they had tweezed the hair from the hairline back several inches to achieve that strange mode. She wondered what that would be like and touched some of the hairs there.

Just a few, she told the worried image in the mirror, and she plucked a neat dozen hairs. Her hairline was faintly pink, but the soreness would go away in minutes, she knew.

Not bad. Maybe she could do more tomorrow.

She cleaned up the bathroom, put on her nightgown, and went into the bedroom.

Donald was in bed, his back toward her side of the bed. She slipped in.

"Do you want to talk about it?" she asked.

"Talk about what?" he muttered.

"Our fight."

"We didn't fight."

"Our spat, then."

"I went out, okay? Let's leave it at that."

"Where did you go, Donald?" The light was off, and she was lying on her back, and she could see the lights of a car outside move across the ceiling of their bedroom.

"Just out, okay?"

"No, it's not okay. I was worried. I didn't know where you were. What if something had happened? To the baby?" She felt like crying, and she didn't want to, not now. She felt as if she should apologize to him, but she knew she shouldn't. She hadn't done anything wrong.

"Well, nothing happened, okay? I got home, and I'm all right, and you're all right. Okay?"

Except, she thought in the silent darkness of the bedroom, we're not all right.

"Are you doing something different with your hair, Maggie?" Ryan, her boss, asked on Wednesday. "It looks good. Not that it didn't before," he hastened to add.

She almost smiled. She *was* doing something different with it; somehow he must have noticed she'd plucked the hairs from her forehead, but she couldn't very well say that, now, could she?

"No, I don't think so, Ryan." She laughed a little nervously and thought it sounded like a titter. Good, that ought to impress him, she thought sarcastically.

"I really like it." He leaned against her desk and watched her.

She shifted in her chair. He made her nervous. She liked him well enough, but he was her boss, after all, not her friend. She wished he would go away and let her work. He was about five years younger than she, with pale blue eyes and dark blond hair and a tan. Sometimes she had wondered how far his tan went. Did he have tan lines? She didn't like thinking like that. He was her *boss*, for God's sake. A male boss, and they were always the worst.

"Well, gotta get back to the grind. Bring that Anderson account in when it's done, okay?" He smiled, waved, and went back down the hall.

The Anderson account. Momentarily her mind blanked. The receivership. Oh, yeah. Now where was it? She sifted through papers and folders, not finding it. It had to be there, she thought. She never threw anything away. But where could it be? She checked her files in the drawers, then located it in the bottom drawer of her desk. She had actually filed it. Could it be that she was getting efficient in her old age? Hardly, she told herself. Must have been a mistake.

Old age. She shuddered and glanced through the Anderson file. It looked fairly up-to-date, but she still had one more action to complete on it.

She picked up the phone and made a call.

After lunch she took the file into Ryan's office. His fingers touched hers as she handed the folder to him. He smiled. She swallowed.

"Fine. Let me look it over, and I'll let you know."

"Okay."

She went back to her desk and sat there for a long time, not looking at anything.

Donald had the car that day, so he picked her up, and they went home. They didn't talk much. They didn't discuss the night before.

She made dinner again, and Donald complained. He didn't like to try different kinds of food, but he bitched about having to eat the same old thing time after time. Can't win for losing, she thought sourly, and she scratched her forehead.

After dinner he turned on the TV loudly, and DeeDee helped her clean up. Actually, DeeDee made a mess, but Maggie would never criticize her when she was trying to help. It was important to encourage children. She had never been encouraged to do these things on her own. She wanted DeeDee to be able to do things for herself, not to depend on anyone . . . not to depend on a man.

When she went into the living room Donald was on the phone, but he got off hastily.

"Who was that, hon?" she asked as she plopped down on the couch.

"Wrong number," he said offhandedly as he switched channels.

"Oh, yeah?" But the phone in the kitchen hadn't rung. He had made a phone call. And ended it quickly when she came into the room. She didn't want to be suspicious, but . . .

"Who is she, Donald?"

"What?" He didn't look away from the Weather Channel.

"The woman you were talking to."

"I wasn't talking to a woman. I told you it was a wrong number."

"You pig," she said, and she got up. In the bathroom she locked the door and stared into the mirror. She thought she looked tired. She *was* tired. She touched the circles under her eyes. Bags, Donald would call them.

She stripped off her clothing and realized she hadn't exercised. It was too late now, she thought. Tomorrow.

She'd never really noticed, she thought as she peered into the mirror, that there were tiny hairs along the edges of the aureoles of her breasts. Now why, she wondered, do we have hair there? She took out the tweezers and quickly dispatched the hairs. It only stung a bit.

There was hair everywhere; she was as hairy as a gorilla, she thought, and she shuddered. Now that was an attractive picture. No wonder Donald didn't want to sleep with her.

She shaved her legs and underarms again and noticed that

her upper lip needed trimming; then she decided to check for gray. She didn't know why she did this, because it just depressed her. She was finding more each session, but if she didn't keep doing it, they'd just get away from her. Her pubic area was stubbly, so she took care of that, too. She used the tweezers. That hurt a little.

The pain of tweezing didn't bother her as it had when she'd first started plucking her eyebrows, when she was eleven.

She plucked some more hairs from her groin and rubbed cream on the offended area.

Then she yanked out some more hairs from her forehead, which was a little wider than it had been. But not that much, she decided. Not enough to notice. She wondered what Ryan thought he'd seen.

She shrugged and turned off the light and went to bed, and in the bedroom she could still hear the TV from the living room where Donald sat.

Thursday morning she got a call that her father was being rushed by ambulance to the hospital. She told Donald that he and the baby were on their own and that she was taking the car.

"How will I get to work?" he asked her.

"Call your friend for a ride," she suggested as she kissed DeeDee, grabbed her purse, and went out the door.

"No, I'll drive you," he said, and he dropped her off at the hospital.

Her mother sàt in the waiting room, looking very bewildered.

"What do they say, Mom?"

"What do who say, Margaret?" Her mother thought nicknames were vulgar, particularly for young ladies. Maggie wondered when her mother would realize she wasn't a young lady.

"The doctors, Mom, the doctors."

"Don't snap at me, young lady."

"I'm not snapping at you, Mom."

"You were too."

"What did the doctors say?"

"I don't know. They won't talk to me."

Maggie nodded. Her mother had just sat there and waited for Maggie to arrive, to take care of things, as she had done all of Maggie's life. She had always let Maggie's dad or Maggie do things. After all, a lady didn't dirty her hands.

Maggie glanced sideways at her mother. It wasn't quite seven in the morning, but her mother was dressed as if she were going to the opera. Had she, Maggie wondered, carefully applied her makeup while her husband got sick?

She asked the emergency room nurse about her father. He was being attended to, the woman said. Later she tried to talk to a doctor, but he couldn't talk because there'd been a car accident out on the highway and the injured were being rushed to the hospital.

It was nearly two hours later that Maggie learned her father had suffered a heart attack. He was being moved to the coronary care unit; they would be able to see him later. The prognosis wasn't good.

Her mother broke down, weeping into her violet-scented handkerchief when she heard the news.

Secretly Maggie felt relief, then was appalled at her reaction. This man was her father, after all. And it was because he was her father that she didn't want him to have any more to do with her life. And yet . . . she thought she loved him. She did. Didn't she?

"It's all your fault that he's sick, that he's d-duh . . ."

Her mother couldn't say the word. Savagely for a moment Maggie wanted to shriek: "Dying, dying, dying, that's what he's doing, Mother, *dying!*" But instead she sat quiet, playing with the hairs on the back of her fingers.

"You don't visit like you should, and your father frets, and it's been such a burden on his heart, and he misses Deirdre so. A grandfather shouldn't be deprived of the pleasure of seeing the only grandchild he'll ever have."

"He's not deprived, Mother. You both see us once a week. I can't get over any more because of my job. You know that."

"Your job." The words were a curse. "Is that more important than your father's health?"

Maggie bit down on her lip. Yes, she wanted to say, but she couldn't. She'd read somewhere that a woman's view of men was formed by the relationship a girl had with her father; she had known from early on that she was doomed. She was afraid of him, afraid of Donald, afraid of them all. She had prayed when she was pregnant that she would have a daughter, and her prayers had been answered.

"Margaret, you aren't listening to me." Tears had left pale streaks down her mother's powdered cheeks.

She wasn't about to get into it with her mother, not here, not about this. "I have to make a phone call." Her mother's weeping intensified as Maggie walked away.

She found a public telephone and called Donald's office. "I just thought you'd want to know about Dad," she said when he came on the line. "He's had a pretty bad heart attack. It's not good; the doctors say he could die anytime, but—"

"Look, Mag, I really can't talk. I'm late for a meeting as it is. Give your mom my love, and tell your dad I'm thinking of him." The line went dead.

"I will, if he lives," she said slowly as she hung up the receiver. She turned and looked around the lobby, at the ladies in pink at the reception desk, at the neat stacks of magazines, at a man drumming his fingers on his knee.

It was at times like this that she wished she smoked. Or drank. Or both.

She asked the ladies in pink where the restrooms where, and she went in and stood before the badly lit mirrors and took out her cuticle scissors and began cutting her hair. As she sawed away at the strands she remembered how her dad used to take her out for ice cream on Tuesday nights when her mother was at her ladies' club and how he would come into her room later, before her mother came home, and— she thought of how he would probably die, and she would be rid of him, and she would miss him, and she cried and cut and cried. She hacked off a good two inches or more and then began the extended process of evening it. Snippets fell below her collar and made her itch, but she didn't care.

Hair

There, she thought when she was done; she looked much better.

She went back to where her mother sat, still weeping into her now-soggy handkerchief, and she waited until the doctor told them they could go upstairs now, and the hair down inside her blouse itched, and her groin itched, and the hair on the back of her hands made her itch, too.

Thursday afternoon she came in to work, and Ryan asked her how her father was doing.

"Not good. I'm going to see him again tonight."

"My dad had a heart attack about ten years ago; it can be rough. Let me know if there's anything I can do, okay?"

She nodded, aware that she was trembling, and thanked him, and when he had left she stared at the paper on her desk and felt trapped. There were so many papers on her desk, more than there had been the day before, and she didn't know what to do with them, not when all she could think about was her father and how close to dying he'd come, and how Ryan was so understanding, and Donald didn't give a good goddamn. It had been a mistake coming into work, but she hadn't known what else to do. She couldn't go to the hospital and sit with her mother for hours and hours. She couldn't stay home. She had to do something. Or at least that's what she'd told herself.

As she began filing she realized she hadn't exercised that morning, and she hadn't exercised last night, nor the night before. She was slipping, she realized. Definitely slipping. And that was bad, real bad. She rubbed the stubble on the back of her fingers and wondered if anyone could see her mustache through the makeup.

Later Donald called and said he wouldn't be able to pick her up; she'd have to get home on her own.

"What about DeeDee?" she asked.

"You'll have to do that, too."

"Just how the hell am I supposed to without a car?" she demanded.

"Call a friend," he said, and he hung up.

She looked down at her desk through a shimmering of tears. Now she was stranded. Like the time her dad had forgotten to pick her up after her piano lesson and she had waited until it was dark and so cold and then begun the long walk home. She could call a taxi, she supposed. She looked through her wallet. She had six bucks. Not enough for a cab to the day care center and then home.

"Problems?"

It was Ryan.

"My husband can't pick me up tonight. And I have to get my daughter from day care."

"I can drive you home, Maggie. It's no problem."

"Ryan, I don't want to be a bother—" she began.

"What's the bother? It's not like you're demanding this. I'm volunteering."

There was probably some bus she could catch, she thought, although she didn't know the schedules, and she'd have to call the day care people and let them know she would be delayed, and just what the hell was Donald doing that he couldn't pick them up tonight?

"Well . . ."

"Come on. I'll get a chance to meet your daughter finally. I feel like I know her, but I want to meet the real thing."

"Okay."

"Fine. We'll leave around five-thirty or so. Is that all right?"

She nodded. That would get them to the day care place just about on time, she realized. She went back to work and ignored the itching in her groin.

They left just a few minutes later than they'd expected and picked up DeeDee, and Ryan insisted on taking them to dinner. They went to a diner, and Ryan said he thought DeeDee was beautiful, just as beautiful as her mother, and he smiled at her when he said that.

Maggie smiled, but her face felt stiff, and the hairs on the back of her fingers seemed to crackle. She rubbed them, felt only stubble, and wondered how he could think she was beautiful when she was as hairy as an ape. Wasn't that what her father had called her once? His little monkey?

"Something the matter?" Ryan asked. He was busy showing DeeDee how to flip a packet of sugar across the table.

"No."

They had coffee, and DeeDee had a small bowl of vanilla ice cream, and then he drove them home.

"Do you want to go to the hospital? I could take you," he said when he saw the empty driveway.

"Thanks, Ryan, but I should get DeeDee in bed. I'll call and see how my dad is doing. If anything had happened, I'm sure Mom would have called." At least she hoped her mother would have called. And where was Donald at this hour, nearly seven-thirty now? Out with some bimbo from his office?

"Thanks for everything. I really appreciate it. See you tomorrow." She gathered up DeeDee and waved to Ryan, who waved back, and then she went inside.

She gave DeeDee a bath and tucked her in, then sat in the living room and told herself she ought to do her exercises, but she just didn't feel like it, and she realized she hadn't taken her vitamins either. She should get up and get them, she thought, but she just didn't feel like it. She rubbed the back of her fingers, felt the damned stubble again, and wished that Donald would get home.

It was nine now. Still no sign; he hadn't called.

Ryan had been very kind to her today, she thought. Very understanding. He would probably fire her next week.

No, she insisted, he wouldn't do something like that. He was too nice. He was concerned.

He was after something.

That had to be it. No one does anything for free, her mother always said.

And hadn't that been the way of all men in her life? Her father, Donald, Ryan?

Hadn't she seen how he had looked at DeeDee during dinner? He would take a bite of his hamburger, and then he would look at the little girl who was chattering about the puppy that her teacher had brought to day care that day.

She didn't like the way Ryan looked at her daughter, not

one bit. It made her think of how her father had looked at her when they had the ice cream together.

She licked her lips, and went into the bathroom, and closed the door only a little bit. She wanted to be able to hear DeeDee if she should call out.

She shaved her legs and armpits, and her groin, and trimmed some of the hair on her arms, even though it had never bothered her before. For a few minutes she stared into the mirror and shuddered at all the hair she saw. She decided that her hair wasn't quite the right length, and she got her hair scissors out and cropped away until her hair was chin-length.

Better, much better, she thought. She plucked her eyebrows and decided they could be a wee bit thinner, no, thinner than that even, and the hairs around her lips were coming back again. She took care of them.

Then she discovered some fine hairs on her tummy, around her navel, and she plucked them. That sort of tickled, and she almost laughed aloud.

She touched her upper arms and realized she had hair there as well, hair so fine she had never really noticed it, but tonight it bothered her, and so she took out her electric shaver and switched it on and sheared the hair from her arms.

She looked at her bobbed hair and thought she could do better. She cut more off, and it fell in chunks to the bathroom floor. Then she turned on the electric shaver. When she was done she rubbed her hand over the unfamiliar skin and thought how good it felt.

Then she went into the baby's bedroom and bundled her up in her arms and brought her into the bathroom. DeeDee rubbed her eyes and asked sleepily what she was doing.

"We're going to make you pretty for Daddy when he gets home," Maggie said.

She turned on the electric shaver, and the long blond curls fell to the floor, and DeeDee began crying, and Maggie told her to hush, young lady, because there was nothing to worry about anymore.

THE HUNGRY SKY

Brad Strickland

O N A CLEAR MONDAY MORNING, AT THE AGE OF FORTY-TWO, David Walford bought the first airplane ticket he had ever purchased. He had been afraid, not of flying, but of—well, of something else.

It had started when he was six, on a windswept midwestern playground, with dust in his eyes, gusts fingering his jeans and windbreaker, and the halyards of the flagpole beating a frenzied tenor tattoo. David should not have been there in the first place, his mother would tell him later. That summed up the Walfords' philosophy of disaster: Those people shouldn't have been there in the first place.

But there he was, a first grader, small for his age, in the side playground, watching the big boys toss a football, admiring its arc, its spin, its precise flight through the contrary airs of autumn. No one had told him not to leave the little kids; no one had warned him that the seventh and eighth graders played unsupervised while their teachers grabbed a smoke or slaved to grade papers. No one had hinted that watching the big boys was not safe, and the thought never came to mind. After all, he knew most of them already, Bits and Scooty and Teeth and Stumbling Bob and the others. You didn't grow up in a little town like Duncton Prairie without getting to know the neighbor kids, their big brothers, their relations.

Teeth was the one who noticed him. Jim Tietjens, Teeth to everyone on his paper route. "Hey, squirt," Teeth yelled, "whyncha go back where ya belong?"

David, not knowing the change that being one of the pack made in a big kid, grinned and waved. Another one of the big guys, his face red from wind and effort, looked back at him, laughed, and said something to the others. They laughed, too, and David wondered what was funny. He leaned back against the flagpole and felt the fevered beating of the flag clips against the pole: *ting-ting-ting-ting!* The wind stiffened the flag, ripped flapping explosions from it, *tattatattatat!* The backbeat for the metallic music of clip against pole.

Two or three of the big kids split from the group and sauntered over, one of them tossing the ball up, catching it one-handed as it spun down again. David knew two of them, Hunky Walanski and Chris Schultz. "Wanna play, kid?" Hunky asked, grinning with cigarette-yellowed teeth. "How 'bout it?"

David, overwhelmed with shyness, grinned back. "Sure," he said, reaching for the ball.

"Ah-ah-ah." Hunky pulled the ball up and away. "Tell ya what: Ya wanna go for a high one?"

"Sure," David said. The big boys made it look easy, chasing and catching the spinning bullet of a ball.

"Ya really sure?"

More boys drifted over, some of them grinning, some of them giggling. The wind was suddenly very cold, and David's face very hot. Something was wrong. He backed up, only to bump against the flagpole.

"He wants ta play," Hunky yelled.

Their hands were all over him, grabbing wrists and elbows, ankles, knees, stopping his mouth before he was sure he was going to scream. They lifted him clear off the ground and held him, a bug pinned wriggling on its back. Bits Bitowski and somebody else hauled down the crackling flag, fought Old Glory to a standstill, and—incongruously —folded her in the respectful lapping-triangle method Mr. Krankheit, the scout leader, would have approved. The flag disposed of, the hands went to David's belt. Two clicks, and the flag clips held him. Hands hauled the lanyard, and the clips lifted his weight away from the restraining hands of the boys who held him.

He was screaming now, but his shrieks lost themselves in the older boys' excited yells or tore away on the wind, scraps of sound whipped away from the school, away from any teacher who might hear and answer. The boys released from his burden seized the halyards and pulled, hand over hand, and David Walford ascended, dangling by his belt, feeling the cruel pressure of it against his spine. His back arched, heels and head dangling low, belly pulled high by the thin rope. High, higher, highest! The eagle on the gold ball at the top of the flagpole stooped to greet him. Then he was so close that even the eagle was out of sight, the sky was the only thing, oh, God, the empty sky, going on forever and forever, wind coming out of it, nothing in it, not even a cloud, just blue nothing, nothing forever—

They left him there all afternoon, more than two hours, with eternity overflowing his eyes. When a teacher supervising the buses finally noticed the still figure and ran to let him down, David was raw with sun- and windburn. His ears and hands felt gone, chilled to utter numbness, as if they were no longer part of him. His eyes burned, and the lids rasped over them, all tears sucked away by the dry autumn wind, the eyeball surface so desiccated that he felt as if someone had poured a sludgy glue into his eyes.

He had stopped screaming.
He was past screaming.
He had seen the hungry sky.

Or maybe it started earlier, when David was three. His father, a man with strong arms and warm, beery breath, liked to play the old game of terror with the boy, toss-him-up-and-catch-him. Shrieking pursuits through the yard, a giant's capture at the end of the race, and then the dizzy swing *up*, the agonizing eternal pause at the top of the arc, feeling as if he would never fall again, and then the stomach-dropping swoop *down*, and Pop's big hands would sometimes fool him and not catch him at shoulder level or even belt level but lower, knee-high, barely a foot and a half off the hard ground, and he would squeal for more, so up again higher!

And he was three, and his father threw him high into the air and yelled the whole time: "Almost hit a cloud that time, Davey! Let's see if we can get the next one! Grab its tail and take a ride! I'll throw you up to hook on the crook of the moon! Here you go, Davey, this time you're going so high you'll *never* come down!"

And the squeals of excitement became screams of terror. The three-year-old could see too clearly the endless upward flight, Pop dwindling below, now a laughing giant, now a figure the size of a child, now a grasshopper of a man, his booming laugh thinned by distance to a high, angry buzz. And now a man lost in the maze of yards, and yards lost in the puzzle of the town, town gone, too, like a magic trick. The earth, like the dented tin globe coin bank on David's dresser, round and blue, and then small like a cloudy marble, and then a point and less than a point. And him still rising, rising forever, thrown so high he would *never* come down.

Or say it started at any one of a dozen other times. David Walford could not say, not after months of counseling in his one year at college, not after years of self-questioning. He only knew it had started sometime, when his pop had tossed him high, when the big kids had hauled him up the flagpole, sometime. And by the time he was eighteen it was a problem. He noticed it during his first year in college, a southern school. His father disapproved of David's decision to go so far away for his education, but by then David needed to get away from his father, and from the big sky of the midwestern plains. The state university he chose had a gracious campus thickly overgrown with trees, ancient canopies of oak cobwebbed with Spanish moss, the dangling gray strands the locals called Old Man's Beard. The trees held off the sky there, supported its intolerable weight, protected him.

It did not matter to David that he had to work in the dining-hall kitchen to put himself through school, to make up for the money that his displeased father would not spend. The days spent in the choking soap-sweet humidity of the kitchen, the clatter and yatter of dishes and silverware riding the big trays into a huge green commercial dishwasher, the mounds of half-eaten food, all were penance. He knew of his difference by then, and he begged the world's forgiveness by scraping slop until his stomach lurched with nausea, by working extra hours when his clothes already oozed with sweat.

No penance could absolve him for the difference. He missed classes on some sunny mornings. He had no excuses. His grades slipped. A girl, a psych major, told him about the counseling available to all students. He went. He spoke to a woman as beautiful and neat and cold as a porcelain figure. She might have been thirty-five or a little older, with striking red hair worn in a severe and unstylish bun. Her eyes were green and direct behind black-framed glasses, and her manner was brisk.

"Tell me about your problems," she said.

He spoke haltingly of the fear, the difference. "It's the sky that does it, I think," he said. "I'm afraid. I'm afraid."

"Agoraphobia is a common enough fear," she said.

"No, it isn't that. I'm not afraid just of the outdoors, not of open spaces. It—it's silly, it's stupid."

"Your intelligence scores show that you should be doing much better than you are," she said. "If the fear keeps you from living up to your potential, you have to deal with it. Tell me what it is."

But he couldn't tell her, not at the first session, not for many sessions thereafter. Not until he was on the verge of flunking out of a very forgiving school. And at last her cool insistence drove him to blurt it out: "I'm afraid I'll fall up."

"I don't understand," she said.

He had talked of his father's game, of the flagpole day. He stammered about these things, trying to make connections, to offer reasons where none existed. A phobia, after all, is an unreasonable fear, an unreasoning fear, an unreasoned fear. "I'm afraid that gravity might not always work," he finished miserably. "I'm afraid that the world will turn loose of me, and that I'll fall into the sky, and the sky goes on forever."

"Do you have a girlfriend?" she asked him.

"No, no, you're missing the point," he pleaded.

"There is a condition," she said, "called homosexual panic."

No. He felt no attraction to his own gender, and in his fantasies his partners were women, always. No. The gravitational pull that held him was a poorly understood force of electromagnetism, not a homoerotic tug. He was not afraid of drifting from the world of manly men into an outer space of gay liaisons, but rather of falling, literally, from a very real world, into a very real sky. It was the world's grip, not his, that he feared losing. This much he knew, though he could not understand the why.

(Twenty-four years later, as he boarded the airplane, David thought fleetingly of the counselor and wondered what had happened to her, the bitch. Angry, not at her, but at the sky he was about to invade. Angry and fearful and thinking back.)

He left school that semester, quitting before they could expel him. The army wanted him then, because in a far part of the world the country was fighting a war. He passed the physical. He submitted to the humiliating shears. He stood rigid while a drill instructor pushed to within an inch of his nose and screamed spittle into his face.

He collapsed one morning when they made him run. He lay on his belly, hands clenching the grass, eyes squeezed closed, face pressed to the hot earth, and he stayed there through threats and even kicks. He spent days in the guardhouse, but he could not walk the perimeter at night, not when the empty black sky domed overhead. The army psychologists were not as cool as the counselor had been, but they were more direct. Four weeks after his induction the army let David go. Unfit for service.

His father wrote him a letter. Any son of his who was unfit for service was unfit to return home.

He was still in the South. He made his way to Atlanta, a city that passed for big down there. He found a job, a demeaning one, but work.

David Walford became a mole.

In the heart of Atlanta there is a building that holds (reading from the bottom up) six shops, twenty-four offices, and then apartments. Below ground level a tunnel, then a long stairway, then a long walkway, lead to a subway station.

The apartment building, new and ready for tenants, needed a janitor/handyman.

David did not often get drunk; he therefore qualified for the position.

His payment for a seventy-two-hour week was minimum wage, less a good chunk of money he paid as rent for a two-room-and-bath cubbyhole. The apartment he lived in might have been intended, at some remote period, as a small office. It was in the basement, and it lacked a window. David did not mind. He had a kitchen, a room in which to sleep, and a bathroom. He needed nothing more. Not a window. Certainly not a window.

For more than twenty years David remained a mole. From one year's end to the next he never cast a shadow by daylight. He ate his meals in the cafeteria (employees' discount) or paid a ridiculous amount to have groceries delivered to him. What he could not get in the shops that filled the first floor of the complex, he did without. His furniture was an eclectic mix, an archaeological record of the refurbishings done to the apartments over the years. Did a tenant replace his bed? Fine, David got the least broken-down one of the old ones. Did an apartment renter break a lamp and throw it out? David rescued it, worked with Super

Glue and pliers and screwdriver to rehabilitate it, and used it to read by, after crowning it with a shade from a wholly different, and more broken, lamp.

The mole. A woman tagged him with that name, a dissatisfied wife who always had trouble with the apartment: the refrigerator on the blink, the disposal, the air conditioner. Summoned to work on a clogged toilet, eight or nine years after he had taken the job of janitor/handyman, David found her undressed for poolside sunbathing. A black and red bikini barely contained her abundant tanned flesh, her skin so dark that she might have been dipped in honey and golden-roasted. He knelt in front of the toilet and prepared to release whatever it was that had stopped the pipe. He wormed a long, springy plumber's snake down the drain, past melted-marshmallow blobs of soaked toilet paper, past clumps of floating excrement. She sat on the edge of her bed, long tanned legs crossed, and watched.

The toilet had just begun to gurgle encouragingly, the tide to go out, when she suddenly blurted, "My God, you're the whitest person I've ever seen. Don't you ever get any sun?"

"No'm," David said. He had picked that habit up in the South, the respectful phonemes tacked on the end of a yes or no. No'm. Yessuh.

"God, I believe you. Let me see your chest."

The water level dropped. David worked the slimy plumber's snake out slowly, flushing a couple of times to rinse off the worst of the sludge, wiping the coiled-spring length with a stained cloth to take the rest off. He pretended he had not heard. He coiled the snake, put it back in its poly bag, packed his tools. He pulled a handful of toilet paper from the roll, wet it in the tub, swabbed at the drops on the floor, flushed the paper down. No stoppage. David washed his hands in the sink. "'S okay now," he mumbled, stepping out into the bedroom.

"Pull up your shirt." She was standing close to him. He could smell her, could smell the coconut oil of her suntan lotion, and beneath that the woman scent of her. "I wanna see." Impatient, she reached out, tugged his shirt up, revealing his white belly, just beginning to pouch out in an incipient pot. She laughed. "Jesus Christ," she said. "What are you, a goddam *mole?*"

David tucked the shirt back in. "I could lose my job," he said. "Standing here with you like you are. My shirt out."

She grinned and shook her head. "No, thanks. I like my meat more well-done. I swear to God, you look like you spent your life underground. Get outside more. Here, lemme tip you."

He accepted five dollars, muttered his thanks, and went back down to his apartment below the street, under the ground. And she, poolside or at one of the parties the residents occasionally threw, made some observation, some remark, and "Mole" he became to everyone. The phone would ring for him, and it was, "Mole, the goddam stove won't come on in five-fifty-four. See if it's a breaker or something, willya?" Or, "Hey, Mole, I got some stuff I need to move out. When can ya help me haul it down?" Or any one of a hundred other trivial errands.

Mole.

Living underground.

Not happy about it, but living.

In a way.

Years passed, and times changed. David got outside more, in a fashion. As the subway line lengthened itself, creeping north toward the suburbs and south toward the airport, occasionally he would take rides. He would board the train in the underground station across the street from his apartment, reaching it by the safe tunnel. He might ride to Peachtree Center, the deepest station, safe from the sky. He would get out, cross over, board the northbound train, and ride back home. His social life.

He acquired a television set, a hand-me-down from a renter. Nothing wrong with it, a sweet little color set, a nice little bedroom nineteen-incher. It was just that the tenant had bought himself a bigger and better TV and saw no reason to hang onto the replaced model. So David saw the world, in a way, though he had to watch carefully. Sometimes a flying show would come on, pilots jockeying jets through the wild blue, and then for an instant he would be there, tossed by his dad or floating belly-up at the top of the wind-fingered flagpole, and the sky would be beckoning him. Hook you on the crook of the moon. Never come down. The hungry sky.

Such moments froze him, clutched his lungs tight on the breath inside, squeezed his heart until it leapt like a wounded and dying bird trying to break away from a tormenting cat. Sweat crawled down his forehead and over his sides, ten or twelve creeping clear beetles trailing the rank scent of fear. Sometimes he got drunk after seeing the sky too quickly on the tube. He developed a pathetic defense by taping a three-inch band of aluminum foil across the top edge of the TV screen. It cut the foreheads off the cops and the comics, the babes and the broads, but it gave an upper border to the sky, and somehow that made it more bearable. And all those years the phone rang from hour to hour, and it was "Mole this, Mole that."

He met a woman.

Her name was Darlene, and she was a waitress from somewhere far south of Atlanta, somewhere where vowels were butter-soft and ready to be spread sweetly. Not a beautiful girl, certainly, not Darlene: too thin, stick legs, a long, pointed chin, mousy hair. But she had lively blue eyes and a good swing to her walk. She ate with him once or twice anonymously, both looking down at their plates, neither speaking. Then one evening while she took her dinner break he heard her say, "Hi, I'm Darlene. They call you Mole, don't they?"

He looked at her, but her blue eyes were wide and without irony. "My name is David." Flatly. Without accusation, without apology.

"Sorry," she said. I'm hurt, her tone said.

David drew a deep breath. "I guess I'm not used to people talking to me."

"Me neither. Lord, my feet hurt tonight."

"Must be a hard job."

"It beats what my mama does."

"And what's that?"

The Hungry Sky

Darlene grinned, a gotcha grin. "Has babies and cooks for my old man."

They talked. Darlene had left school when she was in the eighth grade, but she read a lot, she said. Her older sisters, both of them, had gotten pregnant one after the other down in some little hookworm county in south Georgia. Same guy. "I left before he got the chance to cut a slice of me," she said. "Figured I might as well see what the big city was all about. Found out. Startin' to think old Floyd looks pretty good after all." A grin, a don't-you-believe-it grin.

More meals together, more talk. Another month, and a hint from Darlene: "You know I ain't never been to a movie in a walk-in theater?"

He wondered, Can I do it?

He prepared for the event as a general would prepare for an assault. The MARTA subway map showed him he could zip just a station away and be within a couple of blocks of the Fox Theater. A couple of blocks beneath the sky.

It might work if the weather was right.

He invested. One of the shops in the complex had become a smart little leather-and-brass accessory store: briefcases, crystal decanters, pen sets.

Umbrellas.

Not a black one, because black was too much like the night sky, yawning and empty. Not a blue one, no, certainly not a merciless, cloudless blue. Red would do, a safe red, an inverted cup to hold him down, to hide him from the sky.

And then the weather had to cooperate. Had to.

Did, one Saturday night. Darlene was off at eight, and a special show (a thirties musical, black-and-white, Astaire and Rogers, but no dancers on the wings of airplanes) began at the Fox at nine. He asked. She said yes, fretted about the street clothes she had worn to work. He said, Nonsense, you look great. We'll take MARTA, okay? Sure. You change, I'll get ready, meet you here in half an hour.

Good God, his clothes.

Coveralls he had in abundance. Moles go in gray, and they never need anything else. But civvies—well, something might be done. He never threw anything away, and maybe

183

not all his college trousers had bell-bottom legs. He found jeans, not in bad shape. Tight, but he could wear them. He pressed them on the bed, using a hissing little steam travel iron he had bought in the accessory shop. A short-sleeved pullover shirt, red and white striped, with just a small hole under the left arm, maybe not noticeable if he carried the umbrella in his right hand.

Outside a summer's night, overcast, with a steady warm rain showering from low clouds, gray in the daytime but at night tinged bloody red or salmon pink by the reflected lights of the city. He took a quick glimpse to make sure it was still raining (What would he do if it were not? Sorry, Darlene, I got an emergency tamponectomy to perform on somebody's toilet—no, impossible).

They met, they walked to the station. Rode the train in company with bright-eyed young men and women laughing and jiving, older people staring straight ahead with weary displeasure. A woman in a wonderful sari, a red thumbprint on her aged-ivory forehead, exotic, serene as a jade goddess. David's breath came shallow.

The station, the climb up to street level. It's only a rainy night, he thought. Clouds. The umbrella. The sky is far away.

They walked quickly, with David almost dragging her. Streets turned to mirrors with rain, signs backward, upside-down, distorted, cars hissing by, the welcome rain tapping on the umbrella, pressing, holding him down. "David," she protested, laughing.

"Don't wanna be late."

They hit the box office at the right moment, and he bought the two tickets. He furled the umbrella as they walked into the theater. A long cavern of a foyer, then a plush-carpeted anteroom. Darlene had never seen anything so grand. And a roof overhead, real and solid and substantial. David's breath came easier. This was not so bad.

Darlene oohed over everything: the silhouette signs that signaled the men's and women's rooms, the uniformed usher who smiled at the two of them. They walked into the auditorium.

The Hungry Sky

It was a small crowd, an older crowd, people who wanted to see Fred and Ginger again the way they had seen them in the thirties. Murmurs of lifelong companionship, laughter escaping here and there, sudden little birds flushed fluttering from ancient copses. Darlene wanted to sit close to the front. David looked around, amazed. He had never been here before, had not really heard about it.

The Fox was a relic of the grand days of movie palaces. The auditorium was a Moorish courtyard with fake stucco minarets and onion domes framing the high-domed ceiling. The house lights were on, and David shook his head in wonder. "Can you imagine building something like this today?" he asked.

"I can't imagine anybody building it *then*," she said. "My God, some people liked to see the movies in style, didn't they?"

A velvet curtain, a rich wine color, hung over the screen. Latecomers bustled in. Darlene took David's hand. He felt hot with pleasure, ridiculous, a ten-year-old's embarrassment in a man more than halfway through his thirties. The lights went down and the curtain rose.

"Oh, David," gasped Darlene. "Look up!"

Someone had peeled away the ceiling.

The spice-box sky of night overhead, black, pierced with starholes leaking light. Hungry for him. He held on to the arm of his seat and clutched Darlene's hand so hard she squealed.

Somehow he stumbled out into the aisle, blundered blindly back, and got beneath the blessed overhang of the balcony before his heart could hammer itself apart. Even as he sobbed he told himself he was a fool. Illusion, it was illusion: tiny twinkling bulbs for stars, a ceiling just hidden in darkness, but really there, not gone. A fake sky, not a real one.

"Sir?" An usher.

"A little sick," David said. He pushed past the man.

Darlene found him in the concession area, leaning against a wall. She carried the umbrella. "David?" she asked.

"I can't go in there," he told her.

On the humiliating ride back he told her why.

"David, honey," she said, her tone wondering but sympathetic. "That ain't real. I mean, the earth won't just let go of you. You can't go floating away like, I don't know, like some ol' helium balloon or something."

Bal-loon, she said.

"I know," he told her. "I can't help it. Knowing that it's false doesn't make it less true."

She saw him home. He woke the next morning with her in bed beside him. He was elated and deeply ashamed. She tried to convince him. "Well, if the earth just turned you loose, then gravity wouldn't be working, honey. I mean, all the *air* would just fly off into outer space. I mean, even if you stay here in this little apartment, that would kill you, wouldn't it? So what sense does it make—"

I know, he said, over and over. I know, I know, I know. But knowing isn't enough. I just can't—

"Never you mind," she said. She held his head against her breasts. He wept.

(Would he have risked the flight if it had not been for the solace Darlene had given, and he had accepted, that night? He had other motives, surely, but would they have been great enough? No, surely not. Surely that awakening led to his boarding the airplane six years later, led to the heart-in-the-mouth backtilt of takeoff, the roar of the jets, the launch into the hungry sky.)

More years passed. Darlene fell out of his life. She found a better job, a less crazy man. He missed her, God how he missed her. His hair showed flecks of gray. Some nights he rode the subway north, south. Like a mole.

Then she called, in the middle of the night, out of the blue. "He beat me," she said. "Can I come and stay with you for a while, David, honey?"

Yes, of course. She was older, a little more worn, but her eyes were still warm. "If you didn't have this thing," she sighed.

Yes, damn it, he knew.

She had been with him a week, was planning to leave in a

few days, when the cream-colored letter came, a lawyer's return address. Mr. David Walford, regret to inform you, father's death, you and your mother, equal shares, must be at the reading of the will. It felt like reading about a stranger's death.

He called. His mother's voice was tired: I'm sorry about all that happened. He didn't suffer, it was a heart attack, one minute he was sitting at the table, then he just fell forward. About two hundred and fifty thousand dollars, I think. Well, he sold the hardware store, you know, and made some investments. I wish he had called you, too.

That was Wednesday. On Monday the will would be read.

In a midwestern town more than a thousand miles from Atlanta.

David thought feverishly. With two hundred and fifty thousand dollars he might have a shot at keeping Darlene. It was crazy: She had slept beside him in the narrow bed for a week, but they had not passed beyond touching. A man with two hundred and fifty thousand dollars might sleep with a woman, might find a way to live without having to risk the sky. Other people traveled, and they never had to face the fear of losing their gravity, of falling up forever. Going up so high they would *never* come down.

Maps again. The subway leg to the airport was complete. He could leave his apartment, travel to the airport, and arrive there without once having the naked sky over him.

The plane was the problem, and after that the trip to the lawyers' offices.

He made a telephone call. Yes, there was a sheltered cab stand at the midwestern airport. A roof over his head.

And what would it be from the cab to the front door? Ten yards? Twenty? Could he do it with his eyes closed? He still had the faded red umbrella. The hell with the weather; he could pop it up in the sunshine. Eccentric quarter-of-a-millionaire, who the hell could tell him he couldn't use an umbrella in the sun?

He would do it.

It would take every penny of his savings, but it could be done. He made calls. Yes, there was a flight Monday morning, and yes, the taxi ride would take no more than thirty minutes, and yes, the connections could be made. The airline reservation: round-trip. First class.

Darlene went out and bought him a suit, an off-the-rack job that did not look too bad. It felt stiff and odd, like a suit of light armor. All the better.

Monday morning after a sleepless Sunday night. The tunnel trip to MARTA, the train to the end of the line. The cavernous airport, the friendly woman at the desk, luggage, sir?

"No'm, I'm coming back tonight."

Eyes averted from the big windows at the gate until the boarding call for his flight, then through the accordion-fold gangway and onto the plane. Plenty of room in first class. His little oval window shade pulled firmly down. He was in the front row. If he looked ahead, he would not see out.

Dry mouth, hands tight on the armrests as the plane took off. Then one hour, two, of refusing drinks, of not looking up to meet the hostess's gaze because he might see out a window. The cabin tilted down, and he began to breathe easier. Now, he thought, I would see the ground if I raised the shade.

He fingered it. The ground coming closer, welcoming him back. Shelter. He pushed it up a fraction, saw green, smiled. Pushed it a fraction more. A checkerboard of fields and highways, still far below, but coming closer.

A shape rearing up, a shocked moment while he registered it: a small plane, close, too close, screaming up, the airliner suddenly dropping in a panic dive, an explosion, a tug—

Debris around him, tumbling. Cold, bitter cold, and vacuum sucking at his lungs, fiery gasping. The airplane below, a jagged hole in its roof, the smaller broken plane tumbling my God like a tossed toy—

David spun in midair, and there was the sky.

Waiting for him.

He could not scream in the thin air. The sky had him, had him. No sensation of movement, but his mind told him he was falling. No matter; he knew he was dead anyway. He rolled, turned cat-twisting to land on his feet, no, on his face, to die against the earth at least to shut out the sky to—

He did scream then, a final thin blood-flecked spray of a scream.

The sun-warmed earth, green and growing, beneath him.

The horizon, vast and round and rolling.

The whole world as far as he could see.

Receding as he rose.

AFTER YOU'VE GONE

Charles Grant

THE ROOM WAS QUIET MOST OF THE TIME. THE FLORAL SOFA was too thickly upholstered for its springs to creak; the rocking chair by the window was never used, seldom dusted; the carpet was turned twice a year to prevent worn spots from putting a sole too close to the loose cheap-wood floor; the lamps were switched on by a dial on the wall; and the television sat alone in the corner, its screen rarely lighted, its volume never on.

The ceiling was covered with acoustical tile.

The hinges of the doors were oiled once a week.

It was quiet, it wasn't peaceful, and Ron had no idea what he had done wrong.

He hated noise. Loud music infuriated him, loud voices made him cringe, and the last time his neighbor in the apartment overhead had had a fight with her husband, he had called the police to shut them up, though he hadn't had the courage to give them his name.

He supposed he was crazy. So what? It didn't matter. Other people had their phobias and quirks, from dogs to cats to horses to trains, and he didn't see any reason why he shouldn't be as normally crazy as anyone else. It kept things from being dull. In a perverse way it kept him sane.

But the peace he had hoped to bring in with the silence hadn't come, no matter how often he walked about in stockinged feet, no matter how many times he drew the heavy floral drapes across the panes to absorb the sounds of the traffic and pedestrians below.

No peace.

Only quiet.

And on Saturday morning he stood in the bathroom and wondered about it as he shaved, tilting his head from side to side, searching for the right angle to take care of his whiskers. There were times, fewer now than before, when he wished that sometime earlier, back when he was thirty, back when he was twenty, he had grown a beard or mustache, just to see what he looked like, to see if they'd do something for the angles, the hollows. But there were too many spots along his jawline where the hair didn't grow. People would have thought he had mange, or something worse. People would have laughed.

The sound of the water spilling into the basin.

The drip of the water still falling from the shower nozzle.

He shuddered and turned the faucet off, dried his face and combed his hair, went into the bedroom where he slipped on his jacket and carefully knotted his tie. A single shake of his head, a roll of his shoulders, and he stepped into the living room to stand and watch and listen and wait, senses straining to locate the fault in his design.

Five minutes later, the same five minutes every day, he lifted an eyebrow in a self-critical shrug before opening the drapes to let in the warm sun, before checking the kitchen to be sure he'd turned off the gas stove, before pulling on his topcoat and walking out to the hallway where he took the marble stairs down two at a time.

Elevators fell.

He only took them when there was no other way.

And on the street, turning left, hands in pockets, chin

tucked into his chest, he listened to the choral chaos of the neighborhood's voice, wincing at a scream, shuddering at a harsh laugh, reminding himself that it would be only one more year, two at the most, before he'd have the money to move out. One more year—please, God, not two—to buy the small house in the country. To buy the silence. To find the peace.

"Nuts is what you are," his boss, Patsy Apalleno, told him that afternoon as they took inventory in the stockroom. "You don't want to leave the city, Ronny, for crying out loud. You been here too long. Jesus, what the hell would you do at night, listen to the crickets?"

Ron laughed politely and made a note that ballet slippers were big again this season. Schoolgirls with lessons, housewives with sore feet. Never different. Always the same. Fashion in the magazines was never fashion on the street.

"I like it out there," he said, putting down his clipboard to help Patsy with a carton. "You don't get mugged, for one thing."

"No, you starve to death when your car breaks down." The older man laughed. "You're nuts, boy. You're nuts."

Ron only shrugged. He'd heard the same thing for the past five years—through his promotions, through his failed love affair with the Puerto Rican woman who used to work in the drugstore on the corner, through his fever-crammed struggle with walking pneumonia the winter before, when Patsy and his wife came to the apartment every night with casseroles and soup and newspapers and gossip. He had paled at the intrusions, the loud voices, the good-natured attempts to make the place brighter and more amenable to the sun, but he had accepted their ministrations because he hadn't been able to do it alone.

He never had.

He didn't know why.

Like the peace he couldn't mine from the silence he created, he had seldom been able to do things on his own when those things had to do with life beyond his home.

"Ron, I think I'm going to sit down."

He looked at the old man and smiled, watched the too-thin, too-frail, too-stubborn shopkeeper wander into the store and drop into one of the half-dozen empty chairs set in a row in the center of the floor. He looks old, Ron thought suddenly; it's what happens when you try to make a living in the city. He had no idea what the man's true age was, but he knew without asking that it was much less than someone would have guessed just by looking.

He sighed sympathy, and hope, and stepped into the washroom to see if he was getting old.

He wasn't.

He wasn't there.

"Patsy?" he called. He reached above him for the light chain, pulled it, and blinked.

The stains were there in the lower left-hand corner, the specks of cleaning fluid not picked up by a cloth, the crack just above center near the peeling white rim, the room behind him, his shadow on the wall.

But he couldn't see his face.

"Mr. Apalleno?"

He tilted his head side to side, stepped back, turned away, looked over his shoulder.

He wasn't there.

He was gone.

Jesus, he thought, and he ran into the store, air not quite filling his lungs. Patsy was at the counter, talking with a young woman who carried a shopping bag over one arm. She nodded, looked to Ron, and gave him a brief smile before picking up her change and walking out to the street.

"Ron," Patsy said, "where the hell you been?"

Ron frowned. "I called you."

"I didn't hear. Sorry. The lady wanted shoes for a wedding in Jersey. What the hell's so different about a wedding in Jersey?" He slammed the register drawer closed and stored the receipt in a shoe box under the counter. "I was sleeping when she came in. I think she thought I was dead."

"Can you see me?" Ron said.

Charles Grant

Patsy put his hands on his hips and shook his head. "No. I can't see you. You're the Invisible Man. Where the hell were you?"

"The restroom," he said softly, turning around toward the rear door. "The—"

"You got problems?"

"No, I don't have problems. Patsy, when I looked in the mirror I couldn't—"

"You stay in that hole for nearly an hour and you don't have problems?" Patsy blew out a breath that fluttered his lips. "Boy, you need a vacation or a doctor is what I think, should you care to ask my opinion."

Ron didn't hear him. He looked at his watch, looked through the doorway at what he could see of the restroom, and looked back at the man with a halfhearted smile. "I think you're right. Y'know, when I looked in that dumb mirror I couldn't see my reflection?"

Patsy opened his mouth to laugh, changed his mind, and stepped around the counter. "No kidding."

Ron nodded.

The old man tapped his arm as he passed, and Ron followed him through the narrow stockroom, stopping when the restroom door was opened and Patsy stood on the threshold.

"Well," Patsy said, "I'm still ugly as hell."

Ron looked over his shoulder.

He wasn't there.

"So are you," Patsy told him. "You look like a ghost."

He backed away, collided with the wall behind him, and stumbled out into the store. Wearily he dropped into a chair and closed his eyes tightly, massaged his forehead, tried not to think. But he knew damn well he hadn't been in there for an hour, nowhere close to it. A minute, maybe less, unless he'd blacked out.

"Y'know," a voice said behind him, quiet, rasping, gentle, "what you need if you ask me is time off. How many jobs you working, Ronny, huh? Two, am I right? Sometimes three, if you can get away with it?"

Not even a minute.

194

After You've Gone

"Tell me when the last time was you had more than one day in a row off. A month? Three?" A pause. "A year?"

He nodded. Close enough, but how the hell was an assistant manager in a two-man shoe store going to make enough money to buy a house? He sure wasn't. He had to work elsewhere whenever and wherever he could. He had to. To get out of the city.

"That's what I thought."

Shoes scuffling softly on the floor; the cracked sigh of plastic as Patsy dropped into the chair beside him; a sniff; a cough.

"So what I'm going to be is, I'm going to be a nosy old man, butt in, take you to the Island with me next weekend."

"Mr. Apalleno, I—"

"My granddaughter, she has a birthday, eh? She wears me and my wife out just looking at us, and she ain't even a teenager yet. By the time Sunday comes I'm a dead man. So you come along and drive us back, okay?"

Ron sat up and opened his eyes. "Mr. Apalleno, I appreciate the offer, but—"

"Did I tell you my daughter's not married anymore?"

The old man looked at him without turning his head.

Ron couldn't help but smile.

"You'll like her," Patsy said, "but don't go getting any ideas. I don't want no relatives of mine living in the goddamn country."

A chuckle was the best Ron could give him, but it was enough to put the old man back on his feet and behind the counter. Ron returned to the inventory, cursing himself for being so easily led, and actually liking it in an insane sort of way. Besides, he thought, the old guy was probably right. All work and no play and all that jazz would put him in the hospital sooner or later.

It had already robbed him of his reflection.

"We close early next Friday," Patsy told him as they locked up. "Bring a suitcase. Not too big; it ain't forever. You don't have to buy the brat a present if you don't want to. What the hell you get them anyway, I don't know, maybe a muzzle. That'd be nice. She'll talk your damn ear off."

195

Ron closed his eyes at a horn blaring in the street.

"C'mon, Mr. Apalleno, she can't be that bad."

The old man just grunted.

The horn, a taxi double-parked near the corner, sounded again.

Ron wished the driver would die.

He walked home slowly, glad for the sun that kept the autumn chill off the streets for one hour more. Soon enough it would be cold, and then the noises would grow sharp. Blades. Razors. They would drive him crazy.

That night he ushered for a glass-and-glitter theater in midtown, not caring about the movie as long as he was paid, out of pocket and in cash, once the ticket window closed.

Sunday morning he clerked in a bodega that sold newspapers he'd never known existed and couldn't read anyway because he had no Spanish.

Sunday afternoon he slept.

Sunday night he was back at the theater.

Monday morning he shaved, never taking his eyes off his reflection, and making sure for the rest of the week that he never had a reason to use the store's bathroom.

Wednesday morning a man in a stained trench coat stood outside the shop door and played a trumpet for quarters; he wasn't half bad. Ron held on to his guilt for as long as he could before racing from the store and chasing the man off. Yelling. Waving his arms. Threatening to call the police and run the bum's ass in.

Patsy sat him down, leaned back against the counter, and folded his spindle arms over his chest.

"It ain't the noise, you know," he said, one eye half closed.

Ron felt a headache stalk the back of his skull, but he nodded anyway. "It is. Believe me, Mr. Apalleno, it is."

"Nope. The noise isn't that bad. Not great, but not bad. It's the city."

Ron grunted. The old man didn't know. He just didn't know.

"It's simple," Patsy said. "You live here all your life, am I right? Sure. So you know you either get used to it, so you don't even hear it anymore half the time, or you let it get to you, like that bum with the horn." He jabbed Ron with a finger, lightly. "It's like a dog, you know? You let it know you're scared of it, it's gonna bite your damn leg off."

Ron almost laughed, but he coughed it away instead.

"A couple of days," Patsy said kindly, patting Ron's shoulder. "A couple of days and you'll see what it's like on the Island. You'll know what I mean. Now, I got boxes in the alley. You can sit there all day, you can help me out, it don't matter to me."

Ron helped.

The city screamed at him most of the afternoon, most of that evening.

Thursday night he sat on the sofa and stared at the suitcase waiting by the door.

He didn't want to go.

It wasn't that he didn't want to do the old man a favor. God knew he owed him, he owed him big; but he didn't think he could take the long drive—out of the city on the expressway, all those cars impatient and loud, into another town where the noise was different, but it was noise just the same no matter what his boss said . . . and what if the little girl was as boisterous as Patsy claimed? What if there were dozens of kids there, and all their parents? What if they had play horns and played tag and shrieked and tried to get him to join them?

What if he couldn't take it?

He leaned back and closed his eyes, right forefinger slowly massaging his temple.

Silence in the apartment, all the drapes closed.

You could get sick, you know, he told himself; you could get a bug, the flu, the old man wouldn't blame you.

You could.

He couldn't.

Besides, he'd already bought a box of chocolates for the girl—whose name, for God's sake, he didn't even know—and what would he do with it? He didn't much like candy; it would go to waste. He had to go.

He laughed quietly at his dithering, shook his head, and

pushed himself to his feet. Only a real nut, he thought, would come up with a reason like that—you have to go to a party because you already bought a present you wouldn't want yourself. Another shake of his head, a sigh, and he wandered into the bedroom. It was late, he had to get some sleep, but the night, the street, was peaceful, quiet, and he hated to waste it dreaming. Silence with his eyes closed wasn't really silence, it was simply dark.

He yawned. He undressed. He went into the bathroom and brushed his teeth.

Stared at his reflection.

"What's it like in there?" he asked.

His other lips moved, not making a sound.

That's what it was like.

He winked, bent over and spit, and looked up.

He was gone.

Instantly he snapped his eyes shut, squeezed them shut until his head began to tremble, began to ache, while his hands gripped the rounded edge of the basin, slipping a little, holding, slipping again until he let them slide down to the drain and his head came forward and pressed against the mirror.

It was cool; it felt good.

When he looked up the first thing he saw was his naked chest, ribs and all. His chin. His mouth, lower lip quivering. His eyes.

Jesus, his eyes were bloodshot and too damn wide, and why the hell wasn't he blinking, he had to blink, he'd go blind, wouldn't he, wouldn't he go blind, staring at himself like that, drooling from the corner of his mouth, why the hell wouldn't he blink, he knew how, for God's sake, Jesus Christ—

"Jesus *Christ!*"

He slammed his forehead into the mirror.

The glass shattered, the noise and shock driving him to his knees, where he rocked back onto his heels, bent over, hands on the floor, while he watched the blood fall to the ridged white tiles.

One drop at a time.

Without a sound.

He didn't feel a thing.

All right, he told himself; all right, it's all right, you just lost it there for a while, nothing to worry about, don't get excited. One step at a time; take it one step at a time.

He grabbed the sink and hauled himself to his feet, feeling like an idiot. A vaguely triangular gap in the mirror, just off-center, the missing piece of glass wedged behind the hot water knob. He tilted his head and saw the cut just at the hairline. Nothing horrid, he was lucky, and he took a damp cloth to it, clearing his brow of the blood before patting it dry and applying a bandage. Then he ran the tap until he was sure there were no minuscule bits of glass to get him in the morning, checked his brow again, and turned out the light.

In the dark all he could hear was the sound of his breathing.

In the dark he could see the digital numbers of his clock radio.

"Impossible," he whispered, sitting on the edge of the bed, squinting at the shimmering digits as if that would clarify his vision.

Two hours after midnight.

His right leg began to jump, and he clamped a hand on it, held it until it stopped; a tic pulled under his right eye, and he scrubbed a thumb over it until it stopped; he stared at the numbers while they smeared and ran, and he grabbed the sheet and dabbed his eyes until the numbers stopped.

All right, he thought.

"All right," he said aloud.

He stretched out, arms at his sides, toes pointed at the ceiling; he took himself step by step from the time he got up from the sofa to the moment just before he got up from the floor to examine the damage to his forehead and the mirror.

Even if he had crawled it wouldn't have taken him three hours.

Slowly, very slowly, he lifted his hand and touched the place where the mirror had cut him.

Slowly, very slowly, his hand fell to the mattress.

There was nothing there; skin unbroken, no lump, no bump, no sign of abrasion.

"All right."

Patsy was right. He was killing himself, and not just with fear. It was too many damn jobs, too damn much pressure, too many ways for all his plans to go wrong and fretting about every one of them, every day, all year long. It stood to reason, then, that something had decided to slow him down, calm him down, force him to see that the country was a dream he was working toward through a nightmare.

He'd be dead before he got there.

"All right, it's all right."

A deliberate and steady inhalation until his lungs ached and his face felt rimmed with fire; a deliberate and steady exhalation almost a whistle between his lips.

He sat up.

He smiled.

"Got it covered, Patsy, got it covered."

He returned to the bathroom and flicked on the light, shook his head at the bloodstain on the floor, dampened a washcloth and wiped the blood away. Then he cleaned the sink, the counter beside it, wrung the cloth out, and hung it in its place.

He didn't look in the mirror.

Either he was there or he wasn't, and it didn't make any difference.

He was all right.

He would quit all his jobs except the one with Patsy, readjust his timetable to relieve the pressures of false deadlines, and maybe even have a good time at the birthday party, meet Patsy's daughter, have an affair, fall in love, maybe end up on Long Island, what the hell, it didn't matter.

What mattered was, he wasn't afraid anymore.

Patsy was right again; born and raised in the city, how the hell could he be scared of it? He knew it too well.

But now, after tonight, he was sane, he was sober, he was back on his feet after too many years of hiding in places where other people couldn't find him.

After You've Gone

He grinned again as he padded into the living room.

He might even get to like the noise.

A quick laugh, a shake of his head.

Okay, maybe he wouldn't ever like it, but at least he could learn to tolerate it, work with it, make it not quite so painful.

And if he didn't, so what?

No more crazy than anybody else, right?

Right.

He pulled the drapes aside.

The sun was up.

The city was gone.

MR. DEATH'S
BLUE-EYED BOY

S. P. Somtow

DARRELL SACHSENHAUSER LOVED MONEY AND HATED CHIL-
dren. Children had always frightened him, even when he
was a child himself.

He did not know why, although by middle age he had paid
a great deal of money to therapists, analysts, and occultists
to find out. There were those who wanted to probe his
dreams, who elicited little but recurring images of wild,
fanged creatures with slitty eyes. They tried to regress him to
that singular trauma of childhood that always seemed to
motivate their clientele; but this client did not seem to have
had much of a childhood at all; he had sprung into being
sometime around puberty; they could find no mismanaged
potty training, no virulent rape, no devastating primal
scene. It seemed to the Freudians that the trauma must be so
deeply lodged that only a larger infusion of cash could draw
it out; and so Darrell Sachsenhauser, who loved money
more than he loved himself, went to the Jungians instead.

The Jungians tried to get him to confront his Shadow and
communicate with his Anima, only to discover that he

seemed to have neither. A variety of New Age therapists had a go at him, but they ended up telling him that he simply didn't want to change. And then there was a shamaness who told him that some enemy had worked a spell on him, and that he should bury a thousand dollars in a certain grave-yard by the light of the full moon; Darrell Sachsenhauser balked at that and so received no succor from the spirit world. The last straw had been Marilyn Firth, whom he'd run into at the Long Beach coin fair: beautiful in a shopworn kind of way, a former Jungian, now some kind of vaguely Joseph Campbellian counselor; she had tried to help him communicate with his inner child, only to discover that there was no inner child within him—a shell without an oyster, she'd called him in a fit of pique.

At least she had been good in bed. Surfers always were. They bucked and heaved in time to an imagined tide.

After he weathered his midlife crisis it occurred to him that the attempt to fathom his phobia had become increas-ingly subject to the law of diminishing returns; he gave up trying to find out why. He merely avoided children whenev-er possible; and when, as often happened in the course of his daily business, he could not do so, he kept his distance as best he could.

It was not necessarily as discomfiting a phobia as it might appear. Darrell Sachsenhauser lived in an all-adult condo-minium, and he took a circuitous route to the coin store in order to avoid passing the playground and the elementary school. However, there were times when they did cross his path. After all, the coin store was a public place. There *was* a sign in the window that read NO CHILDREN ALLOWED, but it was not, of course, enforceable.

One particular Sunday he had planned to close the shop early. The last customer was a snotty-looking child who was clearly not about to buy anything. Darrell wanted to count his money without having to experience the unreasoning terror he suffered in this child's proximity. He retreated to the farthest corner of the store, switched off a few lights, and began emptying the display cabinets so he could put the coins back in the safe. But the child seemed to sense where he was. When Darrell looked up he was right there, sniffing the dusty air like a rat.

"Scram," Darrell Sachsenhauser said. "Show's over."

The child had a skateboard under one arm and a T-shirt with neon-pink skeletons dancing against black. "Wow!" he said. "Is that, like, really a *billion* on that banknote? How much is it worth?"

In his thirty years as proprietor of a second-rate coin store in the northeast side of the San Fernando Valley, Darrell had gotten pretty fucking tired of that question. Nevertheless, having to concentrate on the stock answer distracted him from the terror. He rattled off: "It's *Notgeld*, emergency scrip put out by local governments during the great inflation that hit Germany after World War I. . . . A billion marks could buy you maybe a dozen eggs. . . . That's how Hitler came to power, by taking advantage of the economic—" He paused. The unease was creeping back up on him.

The kid just stood there. Feral. Ready to pounce. Beady-eyed, slavering. No teary-eyed moppet, but a monster, a vampire. Darrell mopped the sweat from his forehead. Damn you, disappear! he thought. *Retro me, Satanas!*

"You okay, dude?"

. . . and something clammy slithering down his spine. "Take it," he said. "You can take the goddamn thing for a buck if you'll get out of the fucking store so I can close up!"

"Fresh," said the child. "Gimme two of 'em, dude."

Darrell selected a worn City of Bamberg *eine Milliarde Mark* note and a crisp Heidelberg *zwei Millionen*, hurriedly inserted them into Mylar envelopes, and handed them to the boy. He tried to make himself relax with the thought that, even at the discount, he was still clearing a four hundred percent profit. You could buy German *Notgeld* by the carton. It was worthless. A novelty item at best. His pulse raced. Any minute now he'd be gasping for oxygen—

The door clanged shut. Darrell was safe.

He put away more coins. He turned off the neon sign. Smog-filtered sunset streamed in through the window bars. He coughed. It had been a narrow escape. Another minute or two and he might have fainted dead away, like the time his neighbor's nieces had come over to use the swimming pool.

Darrell packed up the last of the gold, a handful of two-by-twos containing Liberty half-eagles in shitty condition, slammed the safe shut, and lugged it into the toilet, where he had a secret panel behind the medicine cabinet. That was where he kept the real treasures: an Athenian dekadrachm of the archaic period, a roll of CC Morgans, a mint state Caligula denarius with an unrecorded reverse . . . coins that could one day put him in a mansion on Mulholland. Coins he had killed for.

He held up the dekadrachm, feeling its weight and the weight of its past. The face of Athena was in profile, but the eye was askew; it glared straight up at him. Time hadn't touched the coin since some Ionian merchant hoarded it away in a wine jug and buried it against catastrophe. Darrell had snatched it from right under the nose of that Turkish dealer in a Paris hotel. Then the dealer had died, somehow. Heart attack. Poison. Darrell couldn't recall.

Darrell held the Turk's death between his fingers, a chunk of metal with the face of a goddess.

There was a tap at the window in the front of the store.

Quickly Darrell put away his guilty pleasures. He locked the medicine chest and came out of the bathroom. There was a shadow in the doorway. He mouthed, "We're closed. Go away."

The shadow didn't leave. It was a slender figure in a leather coat, silhouetted in sunset and in the flicker of sushi bar neon signs. It was banging hard now. Any minute it would set off the alarm. Insufferable. But at least it wasn't another kid.

It was a sharp-featured young woman with a pageboy haircut. She pummeled the door with operatic desperation.

"Closed! Come back tomorrow."

A high-heeled patent leather boot jammed the doorway. *"Bitte. Entschuldigung, Herr Sachsenhauser. Sie müssen mir ja helfen."*

"I don't do any of this Old Country talk, lady. Just

English." Darrell could understand German perfectly, but he had no memory of ever having learned it.

"Mr. Sachsenhauser?" A limousine was waiting by the curb.

Darrell looked her in the eye. Could she possibly know about the trail of blood that led to the medicine cabinet in the lavatory of his coin store? Was she Interpol, maybe? But why so distraught? Why the heaving sex appeal? Surely anyone with a dossier would have known that his interest in women was confined to his regular Saturday night outing to Mrs. Chernikov's—quick, impersonal, and modestly priced.

"I have been searching for you for months, Herr Sachsenhauser." She handed him her business card.

It read:

Eva Rotwang
OFFICE OF THE MUNICIPALITY OF HAMELN, WESTFALIEN, GERMANY

"You've come a long way, lady," he said.

"It was necessary." Maybe she *was* with Interpol after all. But Darrell had never killed anyone in Germany. Or robbed a collection. No. He'd always kept his hands off Germany. The Fatherland, he supposed, although he had no memories of it. He started to fidget. "There isn't much time, Mr. Sachsenhauser. Your passport is in order, I hope? But of course it is; you travel a great deal."

"Am I going somewhere?" he said. Sensing his unease, she tugged at his sleeve and pulled him out of the store so that they stood face-to-face on the sidewalk. She no longer seemed distraught. She gripped his wrists. Her mid-calf overcoat and leather gloves were overpoweringly German. She seemed strong . . . so different from the wishy-washy Marilyn. She allowed him a moment to lock up and set the alarm system. Then the chauffeur ushered him into the backseat.

He protested that he had his own car, but no one listened.

The Rotwang woman followed. "Are you kidnapping me?" he said.

"No, of course not," said Eva Rotwang. In a few moments they were on the Ventura Freeway. She picked up the car phone and dialed, said, *"Ja, ja,"* a few times, hung up.

"Nach dem Flughafen," she said to the driver.

"Bullshit," Darrell said. "I'm not going to the airport. Do you have a warrant?"

Eva Rotwang pulled something out of her purse. "Do you recognize this man?" she said.

It was a Polaroid shot: a pretty nondescript man, actually, long, scraggly blond hair, not too thoroughly shaven—the caveman type. His cheeks were hollow, and his face gaunt. . . . It was an Auschwitz sort of a face . . . a skull.

Mr. Death, Darrell thought. But he had no idea who he was and said so. "Whatever you're looking for," he said, "you obviously have the wrong man."

"I don't think so."

Darrell peered at the photograph again as the freeway crossed the Santa Monica Mountains. They were speeding; these people were used to the Autobahn.

The man in the picture was wearing some kind of medieval costume, he realized, one side red and the other side yellow; maybe he was an actor. But still, it wasn't someone he had robbed or cheated. No, Darrell told himself firmly, I don't know him. And yet . . .

Eyes on a cavern wall, dancing in candlelight . . .

"The man insists on seeing you, asking for you by name. And he's very persuasive."

"How so?"

"Enough to cause the city of Hameln to send me here to get you . . . by hook or by crook."

"I don't even know where the fuck Hameln is."

"In Westphalia. Germany. But you know of it, *natürlich* . . . the rats . . . the Pied Piper . . . the thirty guilders . . ."

"Oh, you mean Hame-*lin.*"

"Ja, ja, Hameln. Hamelin is the anglicized version."

"Well, listen, Eva, or whatever your name is, this doesn't seem to have much to do with me, so if you're not arresting me, you might as well let me off at the next exit. I'll take a cab home."

"You don't understand . . . we'll pay you. We *need* you."

"Usually, in a kidnapping, it's the kidnappee who pays." They were really flying down the San Diego Freeway now. He reckoned they'd reach the airport in about ten minutes. Perhaps he'd be able to lose her there.

The Rotwang woman said, "If not for the sake of a reward, then at least do it for the children!"

"Now you've really said the wrong thing." She scrambled in her purse and produced several more Polaroids. They were all kids. Cute little blond things. Children in sailor suits. Children waving Nintendo Game Boys and Barbie dolls. Each image filled him with revulsion. They're only pictures, he told himself, but he found himself sliding toward the window. "Children make me nervous. It's a phobia of mine." He gazed at the billboards as they reeled by, strident in the purple-streaked smog of sunset. The Polaroids were all over the seat, and he caught the reflection of one of them in the window . . . eyes superimposed over the cityscape . . . floating in the void. Animal eyes. Hungry. Glowing in the dark. Devil eyes.

"I *hate* children," he said softly.

"In that case," said Eva Rotwang, "you won't mind coming to Hameln. There are no children there at all, you see. They've all vanished. And you're the only one *he'll* talk to about giving them back."

It was an old familiar dream . . . the cave . . . the cold. And the hunger. Seeping into his bones. And the darkness. The only sound a steady drip . . . drip . . . drip . . . echoing. Echoing. Drip. Echoing. Then slowly, out of the cold and dark, a faint light. Flickering. Ebbing now, sucked back into the limestone void. Ice floes that hugged the interior of the mountain. Dark. Dark.

Candlelight . . .

Flash! The glint of a razor-sharp incisor. A hint of drool. A death smile forming out of the dimness . . . eyes that burn crimson . . . eyes. Eyes. And then the laughter: squeaky, metallic, punctuated by the drip-drip-drip . . . and the cold. The cold. Eyes. More eyes. Eyes. Screeching.

The laughter of feral children.

Darrell screamed.

He felt a cold compress against his brow. "There, there." A familiar voice . . . one he had thought never to hear again. "My, my, our inner child's sure going through a shitload of anxiety today."

"Marilyn Firth?" said Darrell, coming to consciousness and finding himself in the first-class cabin of an airplane. "Get out of here, go back to Santa Monica, find some new yuppies to torment."

She stood there, resplendent in sari and—this was new— dreadlocks. The Indo-Jamaican look. Underneath it, still the middle-aged surfer woman from Santa Monica. "Now you listen to me, Darrell. You're not paying for my services, so don't have a cow. Me all taken care of, mon."

"Talk about an identity crisis," Darrell said. "You with your bleached hair and your Santa Monica sun-weathered face and your"—he noted that she had now become a dot head—"third eye."

"Hey, I found myself, okay? In Jamaica, on the rebound from you, I might add. More than can be said of you, you old miser."

Eva Rotwang was coming through the partition into the first-class section now. "What a commotion," she said. "Do you want me to ask for you some sleeping pills?" Darrell seemed to be the only passenger in first. "I see the doctor has found you."

"Yes. Give me a Valium or something. And get this witch doctor off the plane."

"Got a parachute?" said Marilyn, shrugging. "Relax! Money's no object to these people; they *desperate.*"

He looked at Eva. "What possessed you people to bring *her* along? Don't you know she's a total charlatan? Her psychic powers come and go, just like her quaint and colorful West Indian accent."

"Oh, you've no imagination, Darrie. . . . We're all spokes

in the great cosmic wheel. Karma, mon. Hey, we could have sex. Old times' sake."

"I'm sorry," Eva said. "Our records indicated that . . . you're not the most stable of individuals . . . and this woman was listed as your most recent therapist."

"And you didn't want me to flake out on you while I negotiate with your modern-day Pied Piper."

There was a long silence as the women looked at each other, each waiting for the other to do something. At last Darrell said, "Okay, give me the damn tranquilizer."

But the nightmare came back as soon as he closed his eyes. It was more vivid than ever. And this time he could not wake himself up, because he had taken one Valium too many. The children laughed all the way from Los Angeles to Hamburg . . . all the way through customs . . . all the way along the Autobahn . . . all the way to the office of the mayor of Hameln.

Sculpted wood paneling; frayed carpeting; on the ceiling, a baroque fresco of cupids, nymphs, shepherds, and the like.

They were sitting at an oval table. Each wore a business suit of the identical shade of gray, and each wore a dark blue tie. They were the city council: all male, all old, all tired. Darrell had not had time for even a coffee break; the two women ushered him in, standing on either side of him, as though he were their prisoner.

"Herr Sachsenhauser," one of them, bearded, perhaps a nonagenarian, began. *"Wie glücklich, dass Sie schon angekommen sind."*

"He won't speak German, Dr. Krumm," said Eva Rotwang. "Darrell Sachsenhauser: the distinguished members of our city council. Unfortunately, the mayor will be unable to attend this meeting."

"He is in hiding," said the old codger, and he introduced the others quickly by name; Darrell soon forgot who they were. Confusion was kicking in. They weren't Interpol. They had dragged him halfway across the world because they thought he could save their children. He, the one person in the world who could not be in the same room as a child without experiencing a mindless, uncontrollable panic.

A man in a butler's uniform came into the room, pushing a television set on a wooden cart. He positioned it at the head of the oval table, and Dr. Krumm finally remembered to invite Darrell to sit down. The seats were dark green leather, the central heating oppressive. The butler turned on the television, and one of the councillors activated a speaker phone.

"There he is," said Dr. Krumm.

It was the straggly-haired blond in the medieval costume. *"Er ist im Gefängnis,"* said one of the other councillors.

"You jailed him?" said Darrell.

"Of course we did!" said Krumm. "He could be serial killer or something like that. A madman preying on ancient legend."

The man on the screen looked up at them; a prison guard handed him a telephone. He seemed unsure of its purpose, but after a brief explanation from the guard he lifted the receiver.

"I want to speak to Sachsenhauser," he said in a strangely accented German. Even through the speaker phone's distortion there was something compelling about his voice. His eyes, too, were hypnotic, so sunken that they were encircled with shadow.

"Herr Sachsenhauser is here now," said Dr. Krumm. "Enunciate clearly, though; he hasn't spoken the *muttersprache* for a long time."

Darrell said, "Good morning, Mr. Death," in German, surprising himself by how easily it leapt to his tongue.

"Why do you call me that?"

"I . . . I don't know."

"It is not I who kill the children."

"What are you accusing me of?"

The stranger said, "Five hundred years ago your many-times-great-grandfather made a pact with me. I have come to collect the money. With, of course, the accumulated interest."

Dr. Krumm said, "Which comes to, Herr Sachsenhauser,

211

four quadrillion, seven hundred and twenty-two trillion, sixteen billion, four hundred and twelve million, six hundred thousand and seventeen marks and thirteen pfennigs!" And he handed Darrell a piece of computer printout on which were row upon row of figures . . . and that ominous final figure, 4,722,016,412,600,017.13, underlined and circled.

"These folks mad as hatters," said Marilyn Firth. "Just my kind of people."

Dr. Krumm went on, "We have a document that has been in the city archives for some centuries. It is an . . . ah . . . a sort of trust deed. It certifies that . . ." He put on a pair of horn-rimmed spectacles and rummaged in a file. Then he looked up in frustration. The butler came in sideways, bearing a silver casket; Dr. Krumm took out a Xerox of a handwritten document. "I'll translate it for you: 'In consideration of services rendered to the municipality of Hameln, the sum of thirty guilders, plus interest, to be collected no sooner than one hundred years from this date, with the children of the town, their bodies and souls, to be pledged as mortgage collateral . . . that this agreement be binding upon myself and my heirs until such time as the obligations therein be fully discharged, as witness of which I herewith commit my living soul and the souls of my heirs living or as yet unborn . . . signed this day by me, having been granted such authority by the citizens of the municipality of Hameln, Antonius Sachsenhauser, mayor.'" Krumm removed his glasses and looked expectantly at Darrell.

"What the hell is this supposed to mean?" Darrell said. "Anyway, everyone knows what *really* happened. . . . Oh, I don't mean *really,* I mean in the fucking fairy tale. . . . The piper *did* get paid . . . with those children . . . good fucking riddance . . . and . . ."

"Apparently not," said Dr. Krumm. "Apparently there was some kind of compromise. . . . The piper agreed to . . . ah, carry paper, as you might say in the mortgage business . . . and the balloon payment has come due."

An even more geriatric fellow, jabbing his finger in the

direction of Darrell's face, said, "You are the only traceable living descendant of Antonius Sachsenhauser, author of this document."

"Awesome," said Marilyn. "I mean, it's, like, a visitation from the collective unconscious. I think I'm in love!"

"Bullshit," said Darrell Sachsenhauser.

"Oh, but it's beautiful, mon," Marilyn said. "It's not just that Berlin Wall she come a-tumbling down; it's the wall between reality and illusion . . . the wall between mythic time and modern time. This is so cool I could piss myself."

"I'm not descended from any mayor of Hamelin," Darrell said. How could they possibly know such a thing when even he himself had no memories of childhood, of being *anybody's* heir? And how could a fairy tale come true? Was it all something to do with the childhood Darrell could not remember, the childhood that seemed to have been walled up within the same mountain walls that had hidden the children of Hamelin? It was too ridiculous for words. Yet here were all these decrepit old krauts, sitting around a table in a plush old office building, waiting for him to be their messiah. "It's beyond belief."

"And yet," said Marilyn, causing all eyes to turn to her, even the eyes of the madman in the prison cell, "and yet he does have this irrational fear of children."

. . . the cave . . . the cold . . . the laughter . . .

The old men all looked at each other, nodded, muttered, murmured, as if Marilyn's revelation proved everything.

"You will negotiate with the piper," said Dr. Krumm. "You'll be well paid."

"Your city doesn't have a good track record in paying for pest control," Darrell said. It was easy to fall into the reality of the fairy tale because all of *them* believed it.

"You'll like what we have to offer." The butler, suaver than ever, came in with another casket, this time gold. Inside, on a blue velvet lining, lay a coin. A dekadrachm. It was a twin of the one in Darrell's bathroom safe. Except that *this* one was perfect. The last such dekadrachm to be auctioned had sold for $600,000, but it had only been in EF.

Darrell reached out to touch the box, but the butler snatched it away. "You certainly know what I like," Darrell said, "but somehow—"

"There is, of course, also the leaden casket," said Eva Rotwang. The butler whipped it out and opened it, and Darrell saw what was inside: a photograph of a dead Turkish coin dealer in a Paris hotel. There was another photograph of a glass case full of ancient coins, with one conspicuously missing. There was a third photograph—a closeup of the glass case—a fingerprint.

"I'll be damned," said Darrell. "You *are* from Interpol." Eva smiled a little, then clammed up.

"This is *so* fucking mythic!" squealed Marilyn.

"You have twenty-four hours, give or take a few," said Dr. Krumm. "That's the deadline *he* gave us."

"What if he has nothing to do with the disappearance of your children? What if he's just some lunatic taking the credit and trying to blackmail the city?"

"That is possible. But walk our streets . . . look out over the town square from your hotel window . . . go to the playgrounds. You will see that there are no children in Hameln. *None!*"

And all the old men began to weep.

Darrell did walk the streets. There were indeed no children in Hameln. If, as their records seemed to indicate, Darrell Sachsenhauser had actually been born in Hameln, and had emigrated to America with his parents and aging grandfather sometime after the war, it was strange that he felt no twinges of recognition.

Darrell walked down cobblestoned alleys, past rococo churches, past squat apartment complexes and medieval storefronts. Toy shops were boarded up. In a pastry shop old women in black dresses sipped hot chocolate and glared at each other. In Los Angeles there would be times when Darrell was just walking down the boulevard to buy a magazine . . . feeling quite safe, quite at peace with himself . . . and then there'd be a shrill cry in the air . . . a child whizzing by on a skateboard, brushing against him, and his nostrils would get a sudden blast of that smell they had, an odd amalgam of ketchup and chocolate and sweat and Teenage Mutant Ninja Turtles bubble bath. The contact would last for a split second, and yet by the time he'd reached the newsstand he'd have become a nervous wreck, unable to remember what he had come for. Or sometimes just the dread that such an encounter might occur would be enough to reduce him to a gibbering idiot.

After an hour of walking he had yet to feel that dread. There was no turning a corner and suddenly running into one of the creatures sprinting toward school. There was no metal-tinged laughter.

There really were no children here. Darrell could breathe deeply without fear of sucking in their breath, their odor. After another hour or so strolling along the left bank of the Weser it occurred to him that this was the first time he had ever felt free from oppression. He walked with his head held high, unafraid. All cities should be like this city. He waved at passersby, but no one waved back. It was autumn, and moist rotting leaves fluttered along the narrow streets, and people walked with their eyes downcast. One storefront was plastered with dozens of Polaroids of children, with a banner that read, *"Wo sind die Kinder?"* and Darrell was tempted to shout back, "Who cares where they are?"

At length he found himself beside a souvenir stand that sold plastic Hong Kong rats and wooden flutes. There was no vendor. It stood beside a stone gate, an obvious tourist spot, though there were no tourists; a Latin inscription noted that this gate had been dedicated, two hundred and seventy-two years later, to the hundred and thirty children abducted from the town and immured within Mt. Poppen. Sitting down on a bench, feeding the pigeons with a bag of birdseed pilfered from another abandoned souvenir stand, Darrell could see the celebrated mountain itself, rearing up behind the town's skyline, an unharmonious blend of the sixteenth and twentieth centuries. He helped himself to a Pilsner. It occurred to him that they must be following him, and sure enough he could see the leathery outline of Eva Rotwang in the shadow of the gate; but he didn't care. It was wonderful to know such freedom from anxiety. The therapists hadn't been able to do it. Maybe there never had been anything wrong with him . . . just with the rest of the world.

"Pretty grim, huh." It was Marilyn, sitting down on the bench beside him, opening an apple juice.

"On the contrary," said Darrell, "I've never felt better in my life."

"Oh, you old solipsist! I didn't mean you, I meant this town."

"I don't miss them."

"Oh, don't be silly. How would the human race replicate itself without children? Your ancestor did the right thing, in a way . . . life expectancy was much shorter in the Middle Ages. You eliminate one generation, you kill the whole town." She wasn't putting on some accent now, which meant she was dead serious.

"You're buying this malarkey?"

"You take their money, you take their shit," she said. "Besides, when old Krumm there was telling you how the children were all gone . . . and you were just staring into the piper's eyes on the monitor . . . there was something in your expression . . . it didn't look like doubt to me. It looked like *recognition.*"

"Maybe," Darrell said. Two women dressed in black walked past, not looking at them. A man walked toward them wheeling a baby carriage, but Darrell felt no frisson at all. As the man went past them Darrell realized that the carriage contained only a Cabbage Patch Kid . . . and the man was weeping.

"I can totally tell what you're thinking," Marilyn said. "You've been inside that cave with the laughing children, and you're all shuddering inside—and now for the first time you feel the walls crumbling."

"Maybe," Darrell said again. But as he breathed the clean, pure, childless air he thought: I don't need healing.

"I think maybe it's time for you to try to touch your inner child one more time."

"I thought it had been scientifically determined that I *have* no inner child."

"There's no living being who doesn't have an inner child," she said. "I am a shape shifter in my own way, you see; I dart from mythos to mythos; yet the heart is always the same. But, it seems, not your heart; perhaps you aren't human after all. What were those photographs they were blackmailing you with?"

"Nothing. I killed someone once. I think."

"Eww! Let us explore."

And then, right there in the empty plaza, Marilyn Firth began to dance. At first it was only with her eyes; they darted back and forth to a music Darrell could not hear; yet after a while, as if by hypnotic suggestion, he thought he could hear a kind of rhythm in the cooing of pigeons, in the flapping of old newspapers in the wind, in the footsteps of the passers-by, heads bowed, who were too absorbed in the community's grief to be interested in the strange woman dancing. Marilyn danced, and Darrell watched her eyes . . . fluttering . . . glittering . . . strobing . . . suddenly she began to whirl. Her sari began to unravel . . . and unravel . . . and unravel . . . veils of sheer silk jetted out in all directions . . . she unwound and unwound and unwound herself, and still the silk seemed infinite . . . like a magician's string of handkerchiefs . . . billowing upward, twisting, weaving into mandala-like patterns against the gray sky.

I must be dreaming, Darrell thought. But the colors were more garish than any dream . . . crimsons and ceruleans and vermilions and apple greens and cadmium yellows . . . dancing . . . dancing.

"You never used to do this sort of thing," he said.

She didn't answer him, but he could hear her voice pounding in his head like the wind in a tubular wave. . . . I've learned a lot of new tricks, Darrie. And you've helped me. You've heard the cracking of the cavern walls, not me. . . . You told me you were ready. . . . Now take me. Take me into your dream. We will go together, so you need not be afraid. We will go together, and this time you will be awake, conscious, understanding.

Darrell still could not believe that this phantasmagoric display could lead to a therapeutic epiphany, but he could not help but be mesmerized by the streams of color as their patterns shifted and undulated. After a time it seemed that the silk was darkening, taking on the shades of the overcast sky. He could smell the wet limestone and the dust that had hung for centuries in the sunless air. And the cooing of the pigeons . . . wasn't it transforming itself into the mocking laughter of children . . . children with predatory eyes?

And Marilyn danced, and the cave walls coalesced out of the lowering sky. The veils rained down around him and hardened and turned to stone. And it became dark. And he could hear the drip-drip-drip of water. And he felt the fear for the first time that day. Until Marilyn's voice echoed in the chamber: Speak to me from your dream. Tell me what you see.

"There's a cave."

Yes.

"There's voices. Laughing. Cruel voices. The children."

This is a dream, Darrell, but it's a waking dream. And it's a journey. There are caves within caves, and the darkest cave is the one inside your own soul. Tell me what you see.

"I see eyes."

But wait a minute! There were more than eyes. There were names attached to those eyes. There was a *real* cave. Wasn't there? Darrell stood up, grew accustomed to the darkness that was shot through with streaks of phosphorescence. He turned a corner and saw—

The dead Turkish coin dealer, mummified, sitting up in his coffin, holding out the glistening silver dekadrachm and—

Deeper. Deeper into labyrinth. He steadied himself against clammy walls. There were cave paintings here. He could hear the pattering of rodent feet. Movement in the shadows. A pair of eyes. Nothing now. The laughter came closer. The hairs on the nape of his neck prickled.

Go on, said the voice of Marilyn Firth.

He didn't know at what point the cave became, not the metaphorical caverns of his recurring nightmares, but a real cave. He had stepped through the wall behind which he had sealed his childhood. Images of it were hurtling through his mind in a surreal montage—

The belt buckle lacerating his buttocks, the rhythmic refrain of *Pay the Piper! Pay the Piper!* and—

Mt. Poppen . . . the town square with the medieval gate, the tourists, the plastic rats, balloons, the mousetraps in the attic, weathered faces of dead parents, sneaking over the bridge and pissing into the Weser . . .

Grampa showing him his most treasured possession. It's a hammered silver coin, thirteenth century, some German principality . . . "I was disappointed because it was all tarnished. I wanted precious coins to be shiny." He laughed ruefully.

Saxenpooper! Saxenpooper! Childish voices ringing out in the clear summer air.

. . . another country. A cave. Children. He hadn't always been afraid of children, he realized . . . and this discovery filled him with awe. "There's a cave," he told Marilyn. "A real cave this time. It's in America. It's summer, a hot wild place, Montana maybe. In the summer I stay with Grampa. Or maybe my parents are already dead. Yes. I just remembered the funeral. A car crash."

Tell me what's happening.

"I'm a child. I've never been able to remember it before. . . . How big things seem . . . how slender my hands and feet. . . . I'm with my friends, Stevie Dunn and Mikey Austin and Johnny I can't remember his last name. We're dissecting a rat. It's neat. It was stuck on a glue board in Mikey's mom's sewing room. It's still alive, but barely. I just stuck a pin through its head, one of those shiny pins that come stuck in brand-new shirts. Okay, the rat's sort of twitching now. Its guts are neat. I didn't know there was so many of them. It's fun. Johnny says, 'Pretend like we're Mr. Death,' a child-murderer in this part of the state. . . . There's been a manhunt for months and months.

"Mikey says, 'Mr. Death slices off their heads. He eats their brains.' Johnny says, 'Bull. It's their livers.' Mikey says, 'Nu-*uh.*' And I just watch the rat twitching, twitching,

219

twitching, but finally I put it out of its misery by squishing its head with a rock. The odd thing is that I'm not scared of these children at all. I'm more scared of the rat, even though it's a helpless thing, and now it's not even moving anymore."

Go on.

Images came flooding now. "Stevie comes running. 'C'mon, Saxenpooper! There's something you gotta see.' It's deeper in the cave. Deeper. We follow him. We're in a tunnel. We have to go in single file. There's a little bit of light because the walls are glowing. Mikey remembers his flashlight, and he turns it on, and then it gets weird because of the beam of light that darts back and forth. There's graffiti scrawled on the walls. Skeletal figures. A medieval dance of death.

"The cave widens. There's candlelight or something. Flickering. First thing we see, crouching behind a low ridge of limestone, is a face. Larger than life. Painted on the wall. Its eyes are a clear deep blue, and it's holding a flute to its lips. It's a face that shows no emotion at all, but to me it's scary. It's a thin, pinched face, like a skull. I look a little lower and see that he's wearing a medieval costume, one side red and the other side yellow. And I can almost hear the music.

" 'Jeepers,' Mikey whispers. 'What is it?'

" 'It's a shrine or something. Or a human sacrifice place. Yeah.'

"Around the image of the piper are children. They're not realistically painted, but drawn the way a kid might draw them . . . a circle for a face, a wavy line for the lips, a sketched-in skirt or overalls . . . only the eyes seem real. You can't help looking into those eyes. They're the eyes of creatures who were human once, but now they've gone dead. The candlelight lends them a kind of life.

" 'Jeepers creepers,' Mikey whispers urgently. 'There's a bum in here.'

"We look at where he's pointing. There is an old man huddled against the far wall, and there's a candle on either side of him, and that's where the flickering light is coming from. And he's wearing a tattered piper's costume . . . and he has a flute in his hand . . . and he's trying to blow a tune. So I haven't imagined the music after all. 'It's Mr. Death!' Stevie says suddenly. 'This must be his secret hideout or something.'

"The old man is my grandfather. But I don't dare say anything. I'm starting to feel the fear now, for the first time.

"'Let's *get* him,' says Mikey. 'C'mon, there's four of us and only one of him.'

"'I bet this is where they're all buried,' says Johnny, the littlest.

"Mikey takes a rock and heaves it at my grampa. It hits him in the forehead, and he gets up, and I can see a spot of blood between the eyebrows . . . it doesn't seem to hurt him."

Oh! Cosmic! Mythic! The wounding of the Fisher King! The opening up of the third eye!

But Darrell had no time for the intrusive voice of Marilyn Firth. In all the time he had lived without a memory, without a past, the world had been populated with phantoms, two-dimensional figures. Oh, God, this was different. He could taste, touch, smell this memory.

Darrell? Darrell?

"My grandfather stands fully erect. He's holding up the flute like a talisman. Mikey and Johnny and Stevie are throwing stones like crazy now. They're screaming, 'Take that, you baby-killer . . . take that.' And my grandfather just stands there, tottering a little, there's a big gouge in his left cheek, and his arms are pitted and bloody. And Mikey says, 'He ain't much. Let's kill the fucker. Let's carve him to bits.' He takes a Swiss army knife from his shorts. 'Yeah,' Stevie says, 'let's do him.' And I'm watching all this, not participating, and I see the three kids converge on my grandfather and surround him, and they're pummeling him with their fists and bashing him with rocks and biting and scratching, and he's just standing there. Finally I can't take it anymore and I scream, 'Grampa,' and he looks up at me. The boys are surprised for only a minute, and then they go on beating up on him, I guess they're too much into it now to stop.

S. P. Somtow

. . . There's all this rage in them . . . their eyes are glowing. They're laughing as they kick him and punch him in the stomach. Finally I run down there, and I'm trying to pull them off him . . . and he just stands there, taking it . . . his eyes darting back and forth . . . as though there were hundreds of kids, all over the cave, kids with glistening fangs and slitty eyes . . . and I wrest the flute out of Grampa's hand, and then I bring it smashing down on Mikey's head, and I hear bone cracking. . . . I see blood trickling down his face. . . . I see a whitish goo squishing out of the fractured cranium, and . . . Stevie and Johnny step back. And I say, 'Grampa, Grampa,' and my two friends are chanting, 'Mr. Death, Mr. Death, Mr. Death.' And Grampa says to me, 'Now we have to go all the way.' Suddenly he's strong. He's like a demon. He grabs the two boys. He slits the throat of one of them, then the other. I help him, I hold them down. We pile the bodies up in front of the icon of the Pied Piper. We're soaked with blood. I taste the blood. The blood's all gooey and crusting on my skin and hair. And I'm crying and saying, 'What's going on, what are you doing here, why did we kill them, are you Mr. Death?'

"Grampa's weak again. He looks at me, and I see hopelessness in his eyes as he says, 'Damn kids. They're out to destroy you, body and soul, because of who you are. They know about the past. They haunt you wherever you go. They lurk in the shadows. They leap out at you from the darkness. Their eyes glow, and their teeth glisten. It's always been this way.' I say, 'Why, Grampa, why?' and he says, 'When the piper comes you pay him. You hear? *Pay him!* Then all this will end.'

"The dead boys are stacked in a heap. We don't suck out their livers or anything like that. We just light candles around them and leave them as an offering to the piper. The pictures of the children on the walls seem to draw life from the dead boys because now their eyes are animated. I can hear them laughing. My grampa puts his bloody arms around me and says, 'Forget, my blue-eyed boy, forget.' And I forget.

"Except for the nightmares . . ."

222

Darrell followed Marilyn's voice, out of the cavern within the cavern, back to the square beside the memorial gate. She sat down beside him, securely cocooned in her sari now. There was no evidence around them of any supernatural happenings. There were only autumn leaves skimming the cobbled pavement . . . and pigeons . . . and the sun setting . . . and the lengthening shadow of Mt. Poppen.

"What was that all about?" cried Darrell. "Was that true? Did all that really happen?"

"When was the last time you wept, Darrie?" said Marilyn, her arm around his shoulder, her other hand swabbing at his cheek with a fold of her sari.

Darrell said, "I don't know. Back then, I guess."

Marilyn said, "So maybe I am a kind of sorceress after all, and not the crank you think I am. Reality has warped itself around you so that you'll get to replay this ancient myth. You can be a fatalist, and you can say myths are eternal, the outcome can't be changed . . . or maybe you can face up to this Mr. Death . . . and find the peace that's eluded you all your life. Good?"

And Darrell Sachsenhauser returned to his hotel and slept all night without dreaming. When he awoke he had a plan.

Darrell asked Dr. Krumm's office to buy up all the *Notgeld* they could find. "You can even print more, if you have to," he said. "Just make sure it adds up to the four quadrillion or whatever it is."

"But it is worthless," said Dr. Krumm.

"That," Darrell said, "is in the eye of the beholder."

To Eva Rotwang he said, "When you threw him in jail did you confiscate any items?"

"Yes."

"Any flutes? Pipes? Shawms? Woodwind instruments of any kind?"

"A wooden flute."

"I'll take that with me, too."

They piled up the sacks of money in the piper's cell. Then they left the two of them alone together. Darrell faced the nemesis he had not known he had until the previous day; he

223

looked him square in the face; and he cheated him of his quadrillions.

Mr. Death examined the sacks of useless money with interest. "It's only paper," he said. "Astonishing."

"But paper with promises written on it," Darrell said. "And that makes it more than paper; that lends it a kind of magic."

"I suppose you're right," said Mr. Death. "I'm glad you understand that a bargain is a bargain."

The Pied Piper was a little man after all, despite the monstrous icon on the cavern wall. In real life, locked in the cell, with his two-day stubble and his unwashed joker's costume, there was nothing to him.

Darrell handed over the flute.

The piper broke the flute across his knee. Then, with his sacks of money, he vanished.

As Darrell left the prison, his new dekadrachm in a velvet pouch in his pocket, he heard children's laughter. It didn't bother him anymore.

Darrell had dinner with Marilyn in one of those riverside coffee shops: schnitzel, one of those desserts drowning in whipped cream, a lot of beer to wash it down. He told her, "You were right. I shouldn't be fatalistic about it. Guilt's not genetic. I didn't do anything wrong."

Although he thought to himself: I *have* killed people.

But what did it matter now? The flute was broken. The phobia was no more. Soon he would be back in Los Angeles. He would think of the trip to Hameln as one of those weekend therapy retreats he'd tried so frequently in the past . . . only this time it had worked.

"You really *are* a sorceress after all, Marilyn." A wind rose from the river and blew out their candles. A girl ran past, her pigtails flying. Darrell laughed.

"I'm not a sorceress," said Marilyn. "Whatever it was you did, *you* did. And if there's any price to pay, *you'll* pay it."

"What price?" He couldn't resist taking the dekadrachm out of his pocket, sliding it out of the pouch as the waiter relit the candles. "What's to pay? I got away with it. The way I always do."

Marilyn smiled and scratched the dot on her forehead. It wasn't a real dot at all, just a stick-on thing. She peeled it off and stuck it in her purse. Sensing his surprise, she said, "Hey, all the girls do it this way now."

That night she showed him that the sari, which had seemed endless, could in fact be completely unwound. They made love; he remembered how well she used to thrash about; tonight, though, it was he who thrashed with newly learned abandon, and she who, eyes closed, rode him, serenely, as though he were a surfboard and their bed the infinite sea. And then, as he drifted into sleep, she left him.

Later that night Mikey Austin stood by his bedside. He was still eleven years old, and his brain was still oozing from the crack in his head.

"Long time no see, Darrell Saxenpooper," he said. And he laughed that high-pitched metallic laugh that had haunted Darrell all those years.

But Darrell wasn't afraid. "Oh," he said, "a ghost."

"Come on," said Mikey. And his eyes glowed. And he gripped Darrell's hand in his death-cold fingers. "Time for you to go now."

"Where to?" said Darrell. "Is this a fucking dream?"

"No more dreams, Darrie." The cold of Mikey's touch was burrowing into his flesh and creeping up his bones. "You know where we're going."

He tugged, and Darrell found himself getting out of bed. Mikey walked quickly. They penetrated the wall of the hotel room and sank through the floor . . . they reached the town square. It was deserted, and there was a full moon, and the dead leaves glistened like tarnished silver.

"Come on! Quick! You don't have much time left," Mikey said. And he laughed again. And this time Darrell did feel a ghost of the old terror. But the cold had seeped deep into him, and he was too numb to shiver.

They reached the café beside the Weser. The tables and

chairs were overrun with rats. Rats darted back and forth over the flagstones. Rats swam to and fro in the brackish water. The only sound, save the sighing of the wind, was the pattering of rodent feet, for he and Mikey made no noise as they trod the cobblestones of the city.

They flitted through the memorial gate. They skirted the Autobahn for a moment. There were no cars. Then they turned uphill, toward Mt. Poppen. There was a winding path that narrowed, narrowed, narrowed, narrowed, narrowed, and the mountain loomed higher and higher until there was no sky, and still the pathway narrowed until it was a man-wide cleft cut into the face of the rock . . . and finally there was no pathway at all . . . there was only the mountain . . .

. . . and the darkness. The cold. And the hunger. Seeping into his bones. And the darkness. The only sound a steady drip . . . drip . . . drip . . . echoing. Echoing. Drip. Echoing. Then slowly, out of the cold and dark, a faint light. Flickering. Ebbing now, sucked back into the limestone void. Ice floes that hugged the interior of the mountain. Dark. Dark.

"Hey, there, Saxenpooper! Been a while!"

Flash! The glint of a razor-sharp incisor. A hint of drool. A death smile forming out of the dimness . . . eyes that burn crimson . . . eyes. A shock of blond hair and a slit throat. And the blood, drip-drip-dripping.

"Stevie?" Darrell said.

"You should've paid the piper with real money, Saxenpooper."

"Johnny?"

"There's a lot of us here, Saxenpooper. And there's only one of you," Johnny said. His voice buzzed in his severed windpipe.

"But I didn't put you here! *He* did. It wasn't me who made that bargain."

"There's only one bargain, and you all made it," said Stevie. "You and every Sachsenhauser and every man who can't come to terms with Mr. Death."

"You can cheat the piper, but you can't cheat yourself," said Mikey.

"You're our new Mr. Death now," said Stevie. "Neato."

Darrell looked around. The panic gripped him. He couldn't breathe. His pulse pounded. Darkness . . . and the eyes. Glimmering, glowering, angry. Then the laughter: squeaky, metallic, punctuated by the drip-drip-drip of children's blood . . . and the cold. The cold. Eyes. More eyes. Eyes. He could smell their breath . . . and the sweat and the junk food and the baby shampoo . . . as they surrounded him, touching him, sucking the warmth from his body with their icy fingers . . . and laughing. Laughing. Laughing.

This time it would never end.

NEXT DOOR

Nancy A. Collins

LET ME TELL YOU ABOUT THE MEREDITHS.

They used to live next door to us when I was growing up in Seven Devils, Arkansas. At least Mrs. Meredith and her boy, Aaron, lived there. I don't recall much about Mr. Meredith, since he was pretty much out of the picture by the time I was coming along.

At the time, I didn't realize there was something wrong with Mrs. Meredith. Being a kid, I tended not to pay that much attention to what adults did or didn't do, unless it was something no one in their right mind could ignore, like the time Mortimer Teagarden beat his pregnant wife to death for talking to a nigger.

Looking back on it, though, I realize now that the Merediths weren't exactly what you'd call normal.

To give you the full story, I have to go back a ways—back before I was even thought of.

My folks had lived in the house on Apple Street from day one, as it had belonged to my Grandpa Wilcox, who gave it to my mama and daddy as a wedding present. The Merediths lived next door, on the other side of a big wall

Grandpa Wilcox built with natural stone trucked in from the Ozarks.

The Merediths weren't the Merediths back then, though. Elspeth Hanes hadn't yet met Jake Meredith. To hear my mama tell it, Mrs. Meredith had been a right smart-looking woman back then. Golden hair, apple cheeks, sparkling eyes—the whole nine yards. She was a tad on the shy side, though. Something of a wallflower at school dances, that sort of thing.

My mama figured it was on account of the Haneses being Baptists that Elspeth was so unsure of herself during social occasions. I don't see how that would make any difference, though, since the worst hell-raising party hounds I ever met were raised foot-washers.

Anyways, Elspeth was a bright young thing as well as pretty. Seems she landed herself a scholarship to a prestigious all-girl college up north. Her folks were real proud of her, but Elspeth seemed more nervous than excited about going off to school. When it was time for her to take the train up north she got sick and had to sit out her first semester.

She finally did get around to leaving Seven Devils for school, but it wasn't six weeks before she was back—this time to stay. Seems once she got up to college she'd done little else but stay in her dorm room. The first couple of weeks she attended classes, but soon she wasn't even leaving the room to eat in the cafeteria.

The dean of her college sent a letter to the Haneses, and Elspeth's father drove up to fetch her in his Nash.

Elspeth was skinny as a wormy dog by the time they got her home. The Haneses weren't happy with the way things had turned out, but they loved Elspeth and didn't force the issue of her going back.

Once she was home she seemed to perk up and put on weight and become her old self again. She got a part-time job waiting tables over at Mable's Diner. That's where she met Jake Meredith.

By most accounts he was a good-looking, virile fellow with a mass of wavy brown hair. Had money, too. Every available woman in Seven Devils was out to put her brand on him. But it was Elspeth Hanes who captured his heart. (My one memory of Mr. Meredith is of a big man sitting on his own front porch, surrounded by a pile of expensive women's clothes, drunk as a skunk and crying like a baby, so it's probably not representative of what the man was really like.)

One day he came into Mable's for a chicken-fried steak and fell head-over-heels for his waitress. He wooed Elspeth proper, sending her flowers and buying her chocolates and taking her out for rides along the levee on Sunday afternoons. By the year's end they were engaged to be married.

Folks in Seven Devils got their first hint that things weren't exactly right between Elspeth and Jake when the news got out that they'd be living with her folks after the wedding.

Granted, a newlywed couple moving in with the bride's family isn't all that unusual. But Jake Meredith was hardly a poor man, not by any stretch of the imagination. He could have bought his new bride any house in town—or had one made to suit her every whim—but that wasn't the case.

The local gossips were going on about how Elspeth had been under the Hanes' skirts too long and maybe wasn't up to being a full-fledged wife and homemaker on her own.

The Merediths lived with Elspeth's folks for three years before things started to get strange enough for folks to comment on it.

Elspeth remained somewhat retiring, but she and her husband would go to the movies together and attend the dances at the American Legion every second Sunday. Then old man Hanes had himself a stroke and died while mowing the lawn one particularly hot afternoon during the summer of '55. No one's sure, but it's believed Elspeth was the first one to find him, collapsed facedown in a clump of lawn cuttings next to the push-mower.

Elspeth took her daddy's death right hard. My mama can still recall how she kept fainting during the funeral, her husband holding her by the elbow so she wouldn't swoon and fall out in the aisle during the service. Turns out she was pregnant with Aaron at that time, but no one had any way of knowing that, not even Elspeth.

Mrs. Hanes started coming over to our place for afternoon coffee about that time. She and my mama would sit in the kitchen, drinking Maxwell House like it was water, and chew the fat. I was sort of a participant in those coffee klatches, since Mama was carrying me in her belly at the time.

Mrs. Hanes was worried about Elspeth. She'd gotten moody something awful lately (which was to be expected in a woman in her condition, and what with her daddy passing away and all), but she seemed to be taking it to extremes. She'd moved her husband out of their bedroom on the second floor to the guest room downstairs, claiming that his snoring kept her awake. She also rarely left the house, either alone or with anyone else, unless it couldn't be avoided. And the whole time she would be away from the house she'd fidget and fuss and complain about how she didn't like wherever it was they happened to be and how she needed to get home soon.

"It's them hormones, Ernestine," my mama would tell Mrs. Hanes comfortingly. "I wouldn't get too worried. You know how women get when they've got a bun in the oven—especially the first time around. She'll get over it. Her feet probably hurt, that's all. Lord knows mine feel like hot water bottles stuffed full of rocks!"

"You're probably right, Doreen. But I wish she'd be nicer to poor Jake! The boy's done all but turn himself into a pretzel bending over backwards to please that girl!"

"I can't fault her there. Sometimes I can't help giving my Frank dirty looks! Bless his heart, he tries to help, but most times he just gets in my way!"

Convinced that Elspeth's behavior was simply a result of grief and raging hormonal imbalance, Mama and Mrs. Hanes would then turn their attention to more interesting topics—such as who was keeping Lucas Tyrell's wife company while he was out on the road selling tractor tools.

Aaron Hanes Meredith was born April 12, 1956, two days

after my own initial arrival in Choctaw County, Arkansas. I was born at St. Mary's Hospital in neighboring Dermott, over in Desha County, since Seven Devils (in fact, all of Choctaw County, for that matter) didn't have a real hospital.

Aaron was born at home, delivered by the same midwife who'd birthed half the white and all of the black families in town.

This was when things got passing strange over at the Merediths'. Once Aaron was born, Mrs. Meredith stopped going out with her husband. The one time he succeeded in talking her into leaving the baby with her mother, she got as far as the end of the front walk before she broke out in a cold sweat and started crying, then puked in some nearby azalea bushes.

My mama had to admit that Elspeth's actions were a bit unusual, even for a nervous new mother. Still, the community being as small as it was, folks tended to more or less turn a blind eye to certain behavior, which is not to say they didn't discuss it in private. Still, if Elspeth Meredith wouldn't set foot outside her front door except to go to church—well, that was just her way.

Mrs. Hanes enjoyed having a grandson, and she more or less raised Aaron the first eight years of his life. Elspeth spent most of her time either locked in her room or watching soap operas in the television room downstairs.

(I can still see Mrs. Meredith seated in a huge La-Z-Boy recliner, nervously switching from soap opera to soap opera during the commercials with one of those old-fashioned remote control channel changers, the ones that looked like the ray guns on "Star Trek." She seldom spoke in my presence, and when she did it was only to address questions to Aaron.)

After about a year of this Mr. Meredith apparently had enough of humoring her and decided to take things into his own hands. He was convinced that Elspeth was simply spoiled—her daddy had treated her like a princess all her life, and her mama was just as bad. Neither one had ever pressured Elspeth into doing anything she hadn't wanted to do. As far as Mr. Meredith was concerned, his wife was simply being mulish. So he decided to take the direct approach and literally carry her outside, kicking and screaming if need be.

I was in diapers at the time, so I don't recollect what actually went on. According to my mama, this awful shrieking sound started coming from next door. It didn't sound human at first—more like someone was skinning a cat alive. She and my daddy ran out to see what was causing such a ruckus.

My daddy looked over the wall that separated our backyard from next door and saw Jake Meredith toting his wife over his shoulder in a fireman's carry. Elspeth was screeching and yowling like a panther with its tail on fire, kicking and clawing at him the best she could. Mr. Meredith's face looked like it'd seen the business end of a rake.

Suddenly Mrs. Meredith got all quiet and still and stopped fighting him and started up gasping like a landed fish. Mama claims she must have been having some kind of fit—one where you can swallow your tongue if you're not careful. Mr. Meredith got real scared and rushed her back into the house. So much for the direct approach.

Jake Meredith was a good man, if somewhat simple. I'm not saying he was stupid, mind you. It's just that he had a hard time dealing with something he couldn't actually lay hands on and work out himself. Lots of folks are like that, especially where I was raised. They're good people with a fair amount of common sense, but whenever they come up against something like depression or alcoholism or tax bills they're at a genuine loss. So instead of figuring out how to fix things or go outside the community for help, they simply chose to ignore what is wrong. And after his abortive attempt to shake his wife free of her "blues," that's exactly what Jake Meredith did.

Jake used to come over every now and again and share a beer with my daddy on the back porch, and in a rare fit of candor he let on just how bad things were between him and the missus.

They'd been talking about something totally unrelated—

either deer hunting or how to overhaul an engine, that's
what most men talk about in Arkansas—when Mr. Meredith spat and looked my daddy in the eye and said, "You
know the last time I had any, Frank? Figure out how old
Aaron is, then count back nine months. *That's* how long it's
been!"

"That's a damn shame, Jake," my father replied, not
knowing exactly how to react to such personal information.
"You want another beer?"

I got to give the man credit, though. He stayed with her
longer than most folks would have.

Mrs. Hanes used to bring Aaron over to play when we
were little—she and Mama would go on about things while
me and Aaron would try and swallow those little Fisher-
Price people without the arms and legs. After an hour Mrs.
Meredith would come out on her back porch and start
yelling at our house, saying it was time for Aaron to come
home. If Mrs. Hanes didn't pack up and head back right
away, she'd start getting panicky and practically scream the
house down. I have no idea why she couldn't just use the
phone.

Aaron had just turned three when his daddy started
taking up with some gal in Hoptoad, just up the road a piece
from Seven Devils. While folks in town made a show of
being disapproving, no one was particularly surprised.
Rumors concerning Elspeth Meredith's disregard for her
"wifely duties" were pretty widespread by then.

There were serious screaming matches going on at the
Merediths' most every night. Elspeth might not have been a
proper wife to her husband, but she sure as hell didn't
appreciate him running around on her. Most of the fights
ended with Mr. Meredith storming out of the house, slamming the car door hard before he drove off, while Mrs.
Meredith stood on the porch, wringing her hands and
screeching like a tropical bird: "Jake! Come back here!
Don't you dare leave!" She never once moved to follow him
to the truck.

Mr. Meredith moved out for good just before Aaron's

fourth birthday. Over the next five or six years he'd make occasional visits to see his son, but those became fewer and fewer after Mrs. Hanes died and Elspeth was in sole control of both the house and Aaron. Despite all that went on between him and Elspeth, no one can say he didn't honestly and deeply love that woman.

Of the whole Meredith family, Aaron was the one I was the most familiar with. While Aaron was never my own best friend—that title fell to Ralph Allenton—I was probably his, simply because he never had any other friends, period.

Aaron took after his mother—pale, slender, fair-haired, oversensitive. He was a handsome boy, if somewhat strange. He was never one for rough-and-tumble games, preferring make-believe and let's pretend to baseball and touch football. He was kind of skittish—as if a magician had turned a baby bunny into a little boy and then forgot to return him to his true form.

Having known Aaron all my life, I didn't think there was anything odd about the boy. Granted, he could be a real crybaby at times, especially if you didn't want to do what *he* wanted to do, but my mother took me aside one day after Aaron had gone home in tears and told me I shouldn't be mean to him because of his mother.

"Why? What's wrong with her?"

My mama pursed her lips, trying to decide whether to explain the situation to me or simply tell me to just do as she said and not ask questions. "Aaron's mother's sick, Billy."

"Does she have measles?"

"No, sweetheart. She doesn't have the measles. But she *is* sick. . . ."

"Then why doesn't she go see Doc Drummond?"

"It's not that kind of sick, Billy. Just remember what I told you about being nice to Aaron, okay?"

"Even when he's being a whiny baby?"

"*Especially* when he's a whiny baby!" I could tell her patience was beginning to wear thin. "Do I make myself clear, young man?"

Having your mother tell you you *have* to be nice to

someone is always something of a mistake. And while I kind of liked Aaron, it was this special dispensation that kept me from being as good a friend as I should have been.

We entered first grade together at Choctaw County Elementary, and it was then I realized just how different Aaron really was—and always would be. Most of the kids who attended school were either townies like myself or the children of farmers and white trash that populated the rural routes.

Most of the boys in our peer group were chunky, beet-faced kids sporting buzz cuts who spent most of their time sorting out the pecking order that would hold throughout the rest of our school days in the dirt of the playground. It should come as no surprise that Aaron ended up occupying the lowest rung.

Up until the eighth grade, when he officially dropped out, every school day was sheer hell for Aaron. Ostracized by both the popular *and* unpopular kids, he spent most of his time by himself, secreted away in the library, where he read books during recess. I have to own up to the fact that I seldom stood up for Aaron. My own position in the pecking order was hardly what you'd call lofty, and I wasn't about to lower my caste by coming to his rescue every time he got picked on. What can I say? Childhood sucks.

Aaron was something of a sissy, at least by rural Arkansan standards, but he was essentially okay. What I mean by that is that while he was a wet blanket, he wasn't *weird*. I guess having his Grandma Hanes looking after him those early formative years had something to do with it. Then, in 1964, Mrs. Hanes had the first of her heart attacks.

That first one sent her to the hospital in Lake Village for two weeks. The second one, in early '65, put her in the intensive care unit at Southern Baptist in Little Rock for six weeks. The third one, just before Christmas of that same year, put her in Lovejoy's Funeral Home. Aaron was nine years old at the time.

It was shortly after the funeral I saw Mr. Meredith for the last time. I reckon he thought Elspeth might be lured out of the house now that her mother was dead and there wasn't anybody to do for her. So he went to Little Rock and bought several hundred dollars' worth of fancy clothes and perfume and jewelry at Pfeiffer-Blass and loaded it up in his truck and drove down to Seven Devils.

He parked out in front of his wife's house and unloaded all these fancy party dresses and frilly underthings and high-class French perfume on the front porch and waited for her to come out.

He waited one day.

He waited two days.

He waited three days.

On the fourth day he was still sitting on the porch, taking slugs from a hip flask. My mama made my daddy go over and talk to him, and I tagged along. My daddy walked up real slow and cautious, his hands in his pockets, watching Mr. Meredith like you would a dog that's got the shakes.

"Howdy, Jake."

Mr. Meredith grunted a hello and nodded his head kind of jerky. As we got closer I could tell Mr. Meredith was crying, the tears rolling down his face easy as rain.

"How long you plannin' on sittin' out here, Jake?"

"Long as it takes."

"She ain't comin' out, Jake. You and I both know that. Hell, she didn't even leave the house for her own mama's funeral."

"She'll send out the boy."

"Not as long as you're sitting there she won't."

Mr. Meredith nodded as if he understood what my father was saying, but he continued to drink from his flask. His eyes were so red they looked like they were ready to leak blood, his hands shook, and his jaw was black with bristles. Except for his clothes, he looked like one of the old hoboes that hung out down on Railroad Street.

"I love her, Frank. God help me, I still love her." He wouldn't look at my father as he spoke.

"I know, Jake."

Mr. Meredith levered himself onto his feet, wiping at his nose with his sleeve. He staggered a little bit but otherwise seemed way too sober for his own good.

"Guess I'll be going now." He walked across the lawn and climbed into his truck and drove off, leaving the things he'd bought for his wife on the front porch. No one in Seven Devils ever saw him again.

For the first time in his life Aaron was alone with his mama in that big old house. Without his grandma there to provide some semblance of sanity he started acting even stranger than before. At first I attributed his behavior to his missing his grandmother, but after a while I realized there was more to it than that.

Aaron picked up a nervous tic that made it look like he was winking with his right eye. The other kids at school started calling him Twitchy.

The last time I set foot next door was the summer of '66. Usually Aaron came over to my house to play, but for some reason we ended up over at his place that time. The inside of the house was filled with stacks of old newspapers, piles of movie magazines, and cardboard boxes full of old clothes and broken toys and household goods.

Mrs. Hanes had been a house-proud woman, so I knew the mess had to be Mrs. Meredith's doing. I asked Aaron where all the boxes had come from, and he told me that his mother bought stuff advertised on the TV all the time. Magic Peelers, Wonder Knives, Kitchen Magicians, *Liberace's Greatest Hits* . . . if operators were standing by, Mrs. Meredith ordered one of each, sometimes more.

We were playing Monopoly in Aaron's room (I was winning) when the door suddenly banged open, and there was Mrs. Meredith, staring at us like we were sacrificing babies to Satan. She was wearing a shapeless, drab housecoat and pink fuzzy bunny slippers, her hair pulled up in a loose bun behind her head. She looked more like Aaron's grandma than his mama. It's hard to realize she was only thirty at the time.

"What is *he* doing here?" screeched Mrs. Meredith.

"It's just Billy, Mama. I—I asked him to come over—"

"You *know* no one's allowed in this house! What if he steals something? What if he takes something that belongs to me?"

"Billy's not gonna steal nothing, Mama—he's been here before, remember?"

"People are always stealing things from me! Taking things they have no right to! Get him out! Get him out right this minute!"

Aaron was close to crying, whether out of anger or shame I couldn't tell. His lower lip trembled as he fought to keep control of his tears. "But Mama—"

"Don't talk back to me! You know the rules!"

And she was gone as suddenly as she had arrived. Aaron wouldn't look at me, his pale cheeks glowing red.

"Aaron?"

"You better go home now, Billy." His voice was tight with unshed tears. He still wouldn't look up from the Monopoly board.

"Okay. Sure. I don't want you to get in trouble."

Aaron sat there staring at Boardwalk and Park Place as if they held the secrets of the universe.

When I got home and told my mother what had transpired next door, she got madder than a wet hen.

"That woman has some nerve, accusing my child of being a thief! And after our family has gone out of its way to treat her boy decent! If that's how she feels about things, I don't want you in that house even if you were on fire and they had the only extinguisher in town!"

After that, the only time I saw Aaron was either at school or on the infrequent occasions he asked to come over to play. My mama did her best not to slight him, but from that day onward she stopped going out of her way to be friendly toward Aaron.

Aaron Meredith grew paler and more withdrawn as time passed. He spent most of his free time with his nose buried in books, and during the summer he spent more time inside the public library than climbing trees or swimming. I remember him telling me that he'd read everything in the Choctaw County Library at least three times by the time he was thirteen—not surprising considering it only had a hundred books on its shelves.

Sometimes I'd catch a glimpse of him in his backyard,

usually late at night. He'd go sit out under the pecan tree his grandfather had planted years ago and stare out into space. Sometimes I could tell he'd been crying. I kind of felt sorry for the boy, what with him having a crazy lady for a mama, but I was too confused and embarrassed by my own adolescence to try and reach out to him.

Mrs. Meredith pulled Aaron out of school in 1969, just after we entered the eighth grade. There'd been a fight involving one of the McFadden boys—a great hulking Neanderthal in Oshkoshes and shit-kickers—that resulted in Aaron's nose being broken.

By the end of the second week the school sent one of its administrators over to the Meredith house to see what was going on. Mrs. Meredith refused to let him enter the house, talking to him through the closed screen door instead. Since at that time Arkansas public schools did not have mandatory attendance after the sixth grade, there wasn't a lot anyone could do or say about the matter. Not that anyone involved with the school really cared if Aaron Meredith received a decent education, but appearances had to be maintained.

I rarely saw Aaron after that. Occasionally I'd glimpse him on his way to the store or running errands for his mother, but we rarely spoke. The few times I did see him in broad daylight he looked unhealthy, with skin the color of cottage cheese and bluish-yellow circles under his eyes. He looked like a chronic victim of unfriendly dreams.

By 1971 the Merediths had succeeded so thoroughly in sealing themselves off from the rest of the town, it was like they no longer existed. Every now and again there would be a sound from next door that would remind us that there was, indeed, someone still living there, but little else.

In March of '72, while returning home late from the picture show, my mother caught a glimpse of Elspeth Meredith in one of the upstairs windows.

"Maybe it was just the light, or the way she was standing, but that woman looked big as a house! Lord knows she doesn't get any exercise, but that's no excuse for letting yourself get *that* size!"

None of us thought anything about it at the time—until

late July of that same year. That was when Aaron showed up over at our house, asking for help. He looked like a scared rabbit, what with his mouth twitching and his eyes darting every which way as he spoke.

"I need some help—I—I think my mother's dead."

Mama told me to fetch my father and call Doc Drummond, then accompanied Aaron next door. Having done as she told me, I went over to see what was going on.

The inside of the Meredith house looked pretty much as it had the last time I set foot inside it, six years past, only more so. Most of the rooms were little more than storage areas for piles of newspapers and old clothes, with dust an inch thick covering the furniture you could still see. There were narrow paths that wound through the towering piles of refuse, much like the trails wild pigs make in the forest.

Mrs. Meredith lay in a Mrs. Meredith–sized clearing on her bed. The rest of the mattress was taken up with discarded issues of *TV Guide, Photoplay, Grit,* and *Fate* magazines and scabbed-over aluminum Swanson's TV Dinner trays.

There was a lot of blood and other gunk. My daddy's face was almost as white as Aaron's, and my mother was saying "Lord, Lord" over and over to herself in this stunned voice. Aaron was sitting on a chair in the corner, holding what looked like a bundle of bloody rags in his lap, staring at his mama's corpse like someone had just come up behind him and caught him with a ball-peen hammer.

That's when I heard the crying.

Aaron looked at the bundle of rags in his lap, then up at my mother, his face wet with tears. "I think she's hungry, Mrs. Wilcox."

My mother was finally able to take her eyes away from the bloody mess on the mattress and focus her attention on Aaron.

"Oh. Oh, of course. The poor thing." She hurried over and took the wailing newborn baby from Aaron. The baby was still sticky and red, with a big hunk of umbilical cord hanging from its belly button. When it cried it sounded just like a Siamese cat.

Dr. Drummond showed up not long after and pronounced Mrs. Meredith dead on the scene. Seems there'd been some kind of complication during the delivery, and she'd bled to death before she could send Aaron for help. Such a shame. She was only thirty-six.

Aaron named his sister Elizabeth Erin Meredith. She had the same fair complexion, light hair, and cornflower-blue eyes as her mother and older brother.

Of course, the speculation was pretty intense as to who the baby's father might be even before Mrs. Meredith was cold in her grave. Some said that Jake Meredith had returned while no one was looking in a last-ditch attempt to woo Elspeth back. Others thought that she'd surprised a burglar, who took the opportunity to rape as well as rob her. But I never once heard anyone suggest—at least out loud where the children might hear—that the man responsible might be a lot closer to home. The curiosity value alone guaranteed a healthy turnout at the funeral.

After the service was over I walked Aaron home. He was dressed in his Sunday best, little Elizabeth wrapped in his arms. He had been ill at ease throughout the funeral, but I assumed that was because his mother was dead, leaving him in charge of a new baby sister. But as we walked I could tell his discomfort came from simply being around people, and that he was making a heroic effort to be polite to me the entire time we were together.

When we got to the front door of the Meredith house I paused and stared first at the baby, then at my feet. "My mama told me to tell you that if you should need anything to, uh, just give us a call. . . ."

"Thanks. But I don't think that'll be necessary."

"Aaron?"

"Yeah?"

"What are you gonna do now? I mean, are you gonna go move in with your dad or what?"

Aaron looked at me as if I'd asked him if he was planning on jumping over the moon. "No! Why the hell would I want to do that?"

"I just thought that . . . what with the baby and all . . ."

"This is my house." The way he said it made me look him in the face. And what I saw were Mrs. Meredith's eyes. "I've always lived here. I always will. Always. It's where I belong."

And without another word he turned his back on me and went into the house, holding his baby sister tightly to his chest, as if fearful someone might try and snatch her away from him. That was the last time he ever spoke to me directly.

And that's my story. Or that's the part that I know anything about. Not long after Mrs. Meredith died my father landed a job that moved us out of Choctaw County for good. And since my grandparents passed away in '77, there's been no reason for me to go back to Seven Devils.

I assume Aaron Meredith is still living in his mother's house. What goes on between him and his little sister—the one that looks so much like him it's unnatural—behind the closed doors of their home is their business. I'm not saying what happened was good or bad, or that there was no other way it could have been handled. But you have to understand the dynamics of small-town living. If you start pulling on one loose thread, next thing you know you've unraveled the whole sweater. So it's better to leave things well enough alone, if you understand what I'm getting at. Who am I to judge the Merediths and how they go about their lives?

After all, it's just their way.

THE GRANNY

Richard Lee Byers

PETER HAD TURNED ON ONLY THE GOOSENECK LAMP. NO SENSE wasting electricity when he was alone in the office. A shift in the darkness drew his attention to the doorway. Two shadows, one standing, the other seated, were moving toward him. He could tell the seated one was old and sick from the way its head lolled and its scrawny arms dangled, and from the familiar, sour stink.

Johnny, the pudgy black orderly, pushed it farther into the room, to the edge of the lamplight. "Hi, Pete," he said, grinning. "I brought you some company."

Peter attempted to answer, but his mouth was too dry. He swallowed and tried again. "What do you mean?"

Johnny dug a Camel and Bic out of the pocket of his white tunic, then lit up. The whole hospital was a no smoking area, but he knew Peter wouldn't rat on him, and as long as he got rid of the cigarette before he reentered the emergency room, no one else would see it, not at one o'clock in the morning. "A Jane Doe," he said. "A granny dump. Somebody didn't want to take care of her anymore, so they left her outside by the ER door."

The Granny

"Look," Peter said, "has she been medically cleared? Because there's no point in me doing a psych screening unless she has. And you're supposed to call me to the ER to do them, not bring—"

Johnny held up his hand. "I know all that. But there's been some god-awful pileup on the Interstate. Ten ambulances are on their way, and we'll need all our staff and space to handle the patients they're transporting. So Dr. Ramirez said that you should baby-sit this one till we have time for her."

Peter shook his head. "No way. I'm not a doctor or a nurse, and I can't be responsible. Put her on Geriatrics."

The orderly glowered. "You can't put a patient on a ward unless she's been admitted. You know that. Now look, it's not like anybody's asking you to *do* anything, except phone ER if she has a heart attack. So don't be an asshole, okay?" He wheeled and lumbered out the door.

Peter silently cursed him, then, reluctantly, hands trembling, turned to inspect his charge.

The granny's brown-spotted scalp was bald except for a few wisps of white down, her face so wrinkled that it reminded him of melting wax. One corner of her mouth turned up, as if she was smirking at his discomfiture.

"Ma'am?" he quavered. "Can you hear me?"

No response. Which didn't mean she hadn't understood. Working on Psychiatry, he'd learned that sometimes patients perceived what was happening around them even when they didn't react to it, a discovery that echoed one of his oldest fears.

But surely this woman truly was the vegetable she seemed. And if she was unplugged from reality, there was no reason to talk to her. No reason even to think about her. He scooted his chair back around to face his desk.

For a few moments it was a relief not to see her. He even managed to write a little more in the case record he was updating. Then he began to feel the weight of her unblinking yellowed eyes on the nape of his neck. What was she thinking as she stared at him? What might she decide to do?

Something thumped.

He lurched around in his seat. The granny wasn't moving. He told himself that the noise had come from another part of the hospital.

Yet he wasn't sure she *hadn't* moved, that she wasn't subtly shifting even now. How could he be, when the room was so dark? He sprang up, scuttled around her, giving her a wide berth, and flipped the switches by the door.

The fluorescents on the tile ceiling pinged and flickered to life, revealing veins like blue worms, gnarled fingers, and jagged, uncut nails. Drool glistened among the bristles on the granny's chin, and her grimy quilted housecoat was so food-stained that it looked like an artist's palette.

She *wasn't* moving, at least not right this second, but she was almost unbearably repulsive. Peter hated her family for ditching her, but he didn't blame them. He wished his parents had had sense enough to do the same.

When he was six his grandmother had had a stroke. Afterward she'd been a vegetable, too, but instead of putting her in a nursing home his mom had insisted on keeping her in the house.

Perhaps because Peter had been too young to grasp what had happened to Grandma, she gave him the creeps. He hated her cryptic, seemingly spiteful silence, her inertia, and the cool, doughy feel of her flesh. At first he'd managed to help his parents feed and clean her anyway, but gradually his repugnance became outright dread, and he shook and wept whenever he started up the stairs to her attic bedroom. Eventually his dad gave him permission to stay away.

But it still bothered him, just knowing she was near. In fact, much as he'd hated being with her, it was almost worse never to see her. Because if she *changed* somehow, got more energetic or crazier or mad at the grandson who resented her presence, he wouldn't know until he woke up and found her standing over his bed.

Five years later she finally died, but by that time he'd begun to feel uncomfortable in the company of anyone old. In fact, he'd majored in education partly because he figured that a career working with kids would minimize his contacts with the aged.

The Granny

Unfortunately, he'd graduated in the middle of a recession, with state budget cutbacks and no teaching jobs. A friend had put him onto an opening for a psychiatric caseworker, counseling patients, making referrals, and providing evaluations for the ER two nights a month. Because he'd minored in psychology he was at least semiqualified, and his buddy's recommendation got him in.

The job had required working with a few old people, but not many; most of them wound up on Geriatrics, not Psychiatry. In broad daylight, surrounded by coworkers, he could handle it.

And damn it, he thought, he ought to be able to handle it now, too. It was past time for him to get over childhood traumas. He forced himself to sit back down in front of her. He was going to make a real effort to communicate with her, the way a mental health professional should. If he could find out who she was, it might help the hospital get rid of her sooner. Maybe he could even find someone to come for her tonight. "Hi," he said, speaking slowly and distinctly. "I'm Peter Bellamy. A social worker. What's your name?"

No reply.

He made himself smile. The muscles around his mouth felt stiff, the movement unnatural. "If you don't want to tell me right now, that's okay. You probably wonder why I'm asking. Do you know where you are?"

No reply.

"This is the Social Services office of Barton General Hospital." His hands started to shake, and he clasped them together. The quivering seemed to buzz down his arms into the rest of his body, and abruptly he felt intolerably nervous. Though it was poor interviewing technique—he ought to maintain eye contact—he jumped up and started pacing. "Someone brought you here because he thought you needed help. Do you feel you're having any problems?"

Still no answer. Her expression didn't change an iota.

"If you aren't, that's fine," he continued, hearing his voice grow faster and shriller. "If you just need to go home, we'll send you there. But we can't do that till we know where

247

home is. So if you can see your way clear to talk to me, it will help make things work out however you want them to."

No reply. No *movement*. And suddenly he wondered if she was dead.

As if in response to his thought a new stench filled the air. Jesus, not only was she dead, she was already rotting! He backpedaled till his shoulders hit the wall.

He knew his alarm was dumb. If she had croaked, he guessed it was sad, but it shouldn't scare him. A moment ago he'd been afraid she might do something weird. Well, if she was dead, she couldn't. But for some reason it was horrible not *knowing*.

He supposed he could find out. In fact, since he was supposed to be taking care of her, he'd better. Reluctantly he eased forward.

Up close her foul miasma all but choked him. As he slowly reached for her face he remembered how much he'd hated touching Grandma, partly because, even after his mom explained what had happened to her, he'd still feared contracting her condition. His hand jerked back.

Grimacing, he forced himself to reach again. This time he managed to stick his trembling fingers under her nose. The air there was still. Damn, he thought with guilty relief, she *is* gone. Then breath blew out of her nostrils, and at the same instant he realized what the new stench was: She'd shit herself.

His stomach churned as if he'd actually stuck his hand in her feces. He recoiled, and now at last he saw her move. The corners of her mouth pulled higher, exposing mottled brown teeth. As if she was laughing at him. As if she'd dirtied herself and lured him close to her nastiness on purpose.

But he knew, or at least wanted to believe, she hadn't really, so he struggled not to scream at her. Instead he scuttled to the desk, picked up the phone, and punched the ER's extension. If he told them he was afraid the granny was dying—and he really had thought so, hadn't he?—they'd have to take her back.

The phone rang and rang. Maybe his unsteady fingers had

hit the wrong buttons. He tried again, with the same result. Apparently the ER was too busy to pick up.

Or maybe there was no one there. No one anywhere. Maybe he and the granny were alone in the building.

No. That thought was nuts. His anxiety was like a whirlpool sucking him down into craziness. He had to get hold of himself. He dropped into his chair, put his head between his legs, and tried to breathe slowly and deeply. After a while he felt marginally calmer.

He realized he was lucky the ER hadn't answered. If he'd bothered them unnecessarily when they were swamped with real emergencies, if they'd seen him hysterical, he could have lost his job. And not only did he need it, but getting fired from a county position could keep him out of teaching permanently.

He'd just have to tolerate the granny until Johnny came for her. Just exert some willpower—

Something rustled. He squawked and started violently. His chair fell over, dashing him to the floor so he banged his elbow. Motionless again now, if, indeed, it had been she he'd heard moving a second before, the granny leered down at him.

I can't keep her in here, he thought. It's like Grandma: I can stand to have her close, but not in the same room. I'll put her in the hall, tell Johnny I checked her every five minutes. No one will blame me, not when they smell the stink.

He sprang up, opened the door, then forced himself to step up close behind the granny. The skin on his hands crawled, even though he only clutched the wheelchair's rubber grips.

He pushed hard. Her body swayed, her head flopped, and a strand of her cobweb hair brushed across his knuckles. He bit back a whimper.

As soon as they passed through the doorway he reflexively let go of the chair, then realized it was going to run her into the cinder-block wall. He grabbed it again, brought it to a halt, then darted back inside the office. He slammed and locked the door.

His legs went rubbery. He stumbled to the leather sofa, collapsed on top of it, put his hands over his face, and tried not to cry.

After a time a shadow momentarily dimmed the light shining through his fingers. His heart jolting, he bolted up and peered wildly about.

There was nothing to see. He was still the only person in the office. The door was still locked.

Obviously, the shadow was just his imagination. He slumped with relief, then a gray blob oozed across the milky window in the center of the door.

It isn't her, he insisted to himself. She probably can't even stand, or they wouldn't have put her in a wheelchair. And other people walk up and down that hallway, even in the middle of the night.

But the rationalizations didn't help. He was panting and felt as if the office was shrinking around him. Suddenly it was no longer a refuge but a box, a trap, with the granny lurking at the only exit.

The shadow slid back into the center of the glass. The knob rotated, clicking against the obstruction of the bolt. The door shivered as the person outside pushed and pulled it.

This is all right, Peter told himself, his pulse throbbing in his neck. It must be Johnny. I need to get up and let him in.

But he didn't, because the blur on the glass was far too thin to be the heavy orderly. And if it was him, or anyone on the hospital staff—anyone in his right mind, for that matter—why didn't he *speak?*

"Yes!" Peter shrieked, startling himself. "Who is it? What do you want?"

The shadow didn't answer. It just fumbled with the knob for another moment, then glided out of sight.

What was the granny doing now? Lying in wait to pounce on him? Looking for a weapon, or a tool to break in with? Stealing away? God, if he let her disappear, the hospital would fire him for sure! Worse, once he lost track of her, she could lunge out at him anytime and anywhere.

It was hellish: He desperately wanted to cower on the sofa,

but he *had* to see what was going on. Tears dripping down his cheeks, he crept to the door, unlocked it, threw it open, and hurled himself through, trying to move so fast she couldn't grab him.

He slammed into the wall and rebounded. His soles skidded on the recently waxed linoleum. As he flailed his arms for balance something jerked at the periphery of his vision.

He whirled, punching, then saw that the shape was only a strand of his own sweaty hair bouncing at the corner of his eye. The granny was slouched in the wheelchair, just as he'd left her.

Had she ever been out of it? Could he have imagined the shadow, and the doorknob turning?

No! He wasn't crazy, and he wouldn't let her *drive* him crazy! He made himself stick his shaking finger in her face. "I know what you're up to," he whispered. "Playing tricks."

She snorted in three quick breaths; it sounded as if she was laughing. He cringed.

He couldn't take any more. He had to get away from her, no matter what. He might have simply bolted if he hadn't feared that, left unattended, she'd skulk after him. He grabbed the wheelchair and raced toward the ER, slipping repeatedly, running as fast as he could go.

Her withered body bounced from side to side. She started croaking a syllable over and over: "Puh, puh, puh, puh, puh."

"Shut up!" Peter begged. "Don't *do* any more!"

He spun her around a corner. Her hand jerked up and seized his wrist, the jagged nails digging into his flesh. He screamed, thrashed, and his feet flew out from under him. The chair tumbled. His head struck the floor.

The next thing Peter knew, he was on his back, the granny on top of him, pawing. "Puh," she said, her viscid spit dripping into his face. "Puh."

He grabbed her forearms and rolled, putting himself on top. Sobbing, he reared up, straddled her, and began pounding his fists down. The blows smacked, stung his hands, crunched her nose flat.

"Puh!" she wailed, trying ineffectually to fend him off. "Puh! Puh-please don't hurt me! Don't hurt me! I want my daughter! I want my daughter!"

At first her yammering fueled his rage. But finally he grasped that she was *talking. Pleading.*

The malice and witchy ugliness disappeared from her battered face. Now she was only pathetic. A victim. *His* victim.

"I'm sorry! Sorry!" he babbled. "But it will be all right now! It really will!"

Blood poured out her mouth and nose. Her throat rattled.

Peter embraced her. He was still crying an hour later when Johnny returned.

THE SHAPE OF ITS ABSENCE

Billie Sue Mosiman

Cora Lee would not be taken away. The village of Paul, Alabama, had been her home her entire life. The house she lived in was built by her husband's hands, and where it stood, on ground she had scrimped and sacrificed to buy, was the spot where she had lived since her marriage at twenty to Barry Robertson. That made sixty-eight years invested on a triangle-shaped thirty acres of earth.

It was in this cool concrete-block house Barry had died, taken by cancer of the throat just seven years ago, leaving behind when he passed over the shape of his absence, and the house was where Cora Lee was determined to remain until she, too, was called to God.

What Cora Lee's middle-aged daughter could not seem to understand was that it was not simple willfulness that made Cora Lee refuse to be budged. There was more to her staying than the notion of home or the comfortable and familiar surroundings she had spent a lifetime accumulating.

There was a problem with the world beyond Cora Lee's property line. The shape *out there* was all twisted, stunted, distorted. There had been riddles without solution adrift in the world for a very long time. Men everywhere knew that the world was dangerous, more menacing than ever before since the dawn of time, and Cora Lee could not chance what might happen to her if she wandered beyond the boundaries of the place she loved.

"Mama, please," Diane begged. "You won't let any of us stay with you, and you won't leave for that nice room you could have in Evergreen's nursing facility. What am I to do?"

"Do? What you can do is leave your poor mother alone. You needn't worry me this way, Diane. I'm perfectly all right. I haven't lost my mind, despite what you and your brothers might think. Just because I'm old doesn't mean I'm ready to be put away and forgotten."

"I'd never forget you, Mama. And if you want reasons why you should go, what about the stove?"

"The stove? There's nothing wrong with the stove. How you do go on."

Diane sighed and reached from the sofa to touch her mother on the knee where she sat gently moving in the rocker. "You leave it on, Mama. You *know* that. Daniel came over the other day and found you napping on your bed while a skillet full of grease smoked and spit on the stove. You *forget,* Mama. We're so afraid something will happen to you, don't you understand? You shouldn't be alone now."

Cora Lee waved away the burning skillet with her hand. "One mistake," she said, blowing out air through her pursed lips to prove how futile, how weak the argument sounded. "I meant to fry some sweet potatoes, and I got sleepy. I just forgot that once; it's not a crime. I won't be put in jail for it."

"No one wants to put you in jail, Mama. The nursing home isn't a jail. It's a nice place with other people your age you could talk to. I've checked it out. It's clean and bright, and the nurses are real dolls. Besides, the forgotten skillet wasn't the only thing."

"I dare you to produce another!" Now Cora Lee rocked so furiously that wisps of white hair from the bun at the back of her head drifted toward her face and then back behind her, tatters of web netting her small ears.

"There was the biscuit pan. And the ham."

"Oh! Well, I still don't believe I was the one who took them into my bedroom and slipped them beneath my bed. You can't make me believe it. That's not something I'd ever do. It's not something I will take credit for no matter what you say."

"Did you or did you not search for the pan and the canned ham for days? Did you or did you not accuse one of Raffly's boys of having sneaked into the house while you were otherwise occupied, saying he secreted them under your bed just to spite you?"

"*Somebody* did it. And if I *ever* find some sneaking lowdown stranger messing around my house, I'll . . ." She left the threat unspoken, for it came to her she didn't know quite what she would do faced with that situation. However, she felt good and stubborn. Stubborn was a state that suited Cora Lee, and she thought maybe she'd stay in it until the sun set today. She'd not cross the line into the state of cooperation until her daughter stopped browbeating her into admitting to things she was not guilty of.

"That somebody was you, Mama," Diane continued. "You took those things and hid them under your bed—God knows why—and it was days and days of hysteria before you remembered and found them there. Remember? You wouldn't cook a biscuit until you found your pan. Remember, Mama?"

"I remember not baking biscuits, yes, I do. That's the only decent biscuit pan I own. But I didn't hide it. And I wanted that ham for Sunday dinner. I wouldn't hide a ham for an entire week. That's the silliest notion I ever heard out of your mouth. I didn't do it."

Diane shook her head and stood from the sofa. She moved in front of her mother, going to her knees, holding her mother still in the rocker by gripping the back of the chair. "Mama, you can't take care of yourself much longer. There'll be a fire. Or you'll misplace your heart medicine.

Then we'll lose you. I don't want to lose you, Mama, you're so dear to me. If you'd just let me come stay for a time. My girls are grown, I'm out of work right now, I have plenty of spare time to spend with you."

"You have your place. I have mine. Now would you like some coffee? I've made a good strong pot of coffee."

But she hadn't. When she went to the stove to pour cups for them both to drink at the dining table, the pot was empty, standing upside down, draining on the sideboard near the porcelain sink. She whisked it under the water faucet before Diane could follow her into the kitchen. She quickly filled the pot, dumped grounds in the percolator basket, and slapped the whole works on top of the flame. She prayed she could keep Diane busy talking—haranguing, to tell the truth—until the coffee was perked and ready.

How these oddities happened in Cora Lee's life, she could not fathom. Late one night when she could not sleep, a theory came to her. What if chaos had come to roost in her house? What if it had belly-crawled through the open doors when she wasn't watching?

She really had left that skillet on the stove; there might have been a grease fire hadn't Daniel come to visit just then. Might have burned up the kitchen before she woke. So okay, she made a mistake, it wasn't just the elderly who made mistakes, she could assure her children of that fact, and one little mistake did not make her an invalid in need of constant care. She hadn't by any stretch of the imagination, however, hidden her own pan and ham from herself. What was the point in that? It was nutty, and she hadn't done it. Now she thought she'd made coffee, felt *sure* she had minutes before her daughter was due to visit, but it appeared that she hadn't. She could not refute the evidence of her eyes.

It worried her that perhaps the chaos outside in the world inched each day nearer, intruding like a fog that seeped through walls, creeping ever closer to her personal realm, where before she had thought herself safe. It might not even be coming through the doors or walls; it might be waiting out in the yard, now and then flicking aside what was right and real to frighten her proper. She wouldn't want to bet it wasn't happening. It was the sole explanation that came to her.

Diane drank the scalding coffee before hurrying away. Her husband was due home; supper had to be cooked. Cora Lee didn't want Diane to come stay with her. Diane's husband Joe was a demanding sort, and he'd be over all the time mooching meals, casting poisonous glances at his mother-in-law for stealing away his good wife.

It was a certainty Cora Lee would not leave her home to live in Evergreen's nursing home. She'd rather be rattlesnake bit or have the house catch fire or go missing her biscuit pan for eternity than to sit around with a bunch of old folks gumming their food and talking about the past. Naturally, there in Evergreen—even on the road that led to Paul, much less on the road between Paul and Evergreen—the environment was hazardous. Unpredictable events could occur. People with murder on their minds and evil in their hearts might erupt at any moment to attack and dispatch an old woman. A torrential rain could wash out the bridges. A man felling a tree could let it topple on a passing car. There might be a pothole that could wrench the front of a vehicle off the road into a ditch. A wind could blow them over, spinning them like chaff in a wheat field. Even a child, an innocent little child, might wander into the middle of the road and cause them to crash into an oncoming logging truck.

Oh, no. Diane would not be getting her to agree to leaving her land anytime soon. Cora Lee would have to be comatose and paralyzed for her daughter to gain that kind of control over her destiny.

After sipping a second cup of coffee Cora Lee went to the screen door and let herself out onto the front porch. She sat in the porch swing, pushing it in a soothingly slow rhythm that matched her heartbeat. She surveyed her corner of the world while the sun dropped low behind the piney woods. She found it an excellent place, nearly a paradise. Camellia bushes four feet tall bordered the yard from the road. They were in full bloom now, their double white blossoms dripping toward the ground because of their heavy fragrant weight. A mimosa stood near the drive, shading the mailbox. The black cherry tree Barry had planted was dying of some exotic disease, its bark crumpled and lichen-covered, but it still had a few sprightly flowers reaching out for the sun. Along the path to the driveway were Cora Lee's flowers and ferns. Tall stalks of gladioli, yellow and pink and plum-colored, white periwinkle, red hibiscus with blooms the size of dinner plates.

Off across the drive was a field Barry used to plant with corn and peas. Beyond that lay the woods, and they belonged to Cora Lee; they were where she often walked when she wanted a cooling breeze and a peace she could not always find inside the house.

On this land was everything Cora Lee had ever wanted or needed. She had chickens to lay eggs, a nanny goat for milk, an old dog who lay near the front walk, guarding against unwelcome visitors. She had two cats, independent cusses who came to be petted only when they felt the urge. This was an attitude she cherished in an animal, for it reflected back to her the way she felt toward her grown children—indeed, toward all the people who tried to force themselves into her life. She had a kitchen garden out back with rows of collard greens, mustard and turnips, onions, tomatoes, even garlic. She had five peach trees and two pears. She had her own well so that she knew the water was sweet and unpolluted, a butane tank filled by a truck from the city every month so she could run a stove and heaters in the wintertime, and a telephone, which often proved to be a nuisance because Diane used it too often to ring into Cora Lee's solitude, calling with one more reason why she should not live alone anymore.

Cora Lee looked out now over what God had, in His mercy, approved to give her, and she wondered why in the world her children would ever think she should leave it. This was sanctuary. This was a haven.

She would never forsake it.

* * *

The Shape of Its Absence

"Mrs. Robertson, your daughter asked me to speak with you. I hope you won't feel I'm interfering."

Cora Lee looked over the old gentleman in his pale gray suit and crisp white shirt with a jaundiced eye. "Speak to me about what?" she asked, though she thought she knew his purpose. He had come to talk her into going into a nursing home. That was all the business he could have with her if Diane had sent him.

"May I come inside? It's powerful hot today."

Cora Lee could see he was telling the truth. The heat did not bother her, but for some it was a killer even though this was spring, and spring in south Alabama was often mild. A droplet of perspiration slid down the old fellow's temple even as she watched. She thought it admirable he did not make a move to wipe it away. "Yes, come in, you're welcome to come in. I'm sorry I've kept you on the porch. Bless God, I should watch my manners."

He moved into the room like a big gray flagship motoring into its berth. He was slow and easy, finding the best spot on the sagging sofa to sit, spreading out one arm casually along the sofa back, resting the other on the sofa arm. Cora Lee still stood, but not near him. "Can I offer you coffee? I've just made some." She had been about to have coffee with a biscuit and honey before he came calling.

"I'm afraid coffee would make me hotter. Could I have a glass of iced water, if it's not inconvenient?"

"Certainly. I'll be just a minute."

In the kitchen Cora Lee dropped ice cubes in a thick, clear glass and ran water into it. She turned to pour herself a cup of coffee from the pot on the stove and discovered, to her dismay, the pot was not there. She turned to the sink, her eyebrows knotting close over her squinted eyes. Alarm shoveled its way through to her thoughts. Not again!

But yes. The pot was draining. She had washed it. She had no coffee made. How was she so often mistaken? It was beginning to gnaw at her. She couldn't trust her memory. Just as Diane said. Or was it that something kept changing and rearranging the thoughts in her mind, or else the events, even as she tried to sort them out?

259

But no. It was nothing. It didn't happen so much she should concern herself.

She took the glass to the living room and offered it to the man. "What is this about, Mr. . . ."

"Marcus Hornsby. Dr. Hornsby, Mrs. Robertson." He took the water glass and smiled slightly. Cora Lee wanted to be angry her daughter thought to trick her by sending a doctor to the house without warning, but the old man's smile was kind. It caused her to smile back. He might be a doctor come to talk her away from her home and land, but she could tell he was not a cruel, battering man, and if she refused him in a courteous manner, she was sure he'd not insist.

"Well, Dr. Hornsby, I suppose Diane told you I left a skillet on the burner. Simple mistake. I take a nap some days around noon, and I must have forgotten I meant to fry some potatoes. It's nothing a doctor needs to get out in the heat of the day to see about, I assure you. But it was kind of you to call, just to check."

"I was informed of the skillet, yes, but that's not what I've come to see you about. Your daughter mentioned that one of the reasons you don't wish to move into Evergreen is that you feel your life would be in danger once you left your home. Is that true?"

Cora Lee thought before she answered. There might yet be some trick the nice doctor had up his sleeve. "It's not about leaving just my home," she said.

"Pardon me?"

"I go outside my home all the time. I walk clear down to the creek bounding my property. Last Christmas I walked all over this land hunting just the right fir tree to decorate. And of course, I'm outside most of the day feeding the animals, working in my garden. . . ."

He cleared his throat. "Yes, uh, I meant your *entire* home. The land. You won't leave it—ever, for any reason—is that correct?"

Cora Lee nodded emphatically. "I *have* no reason to," she said.

"What about shopping trips? Or to see a doctor? You never leave for those reasons either?"

Now this was a little question meant to trip her up, she figured, but blast him and the devil take him if she'd let him succeed. Might as well admit it right out, get the interview over with, and send Dr. Hornsby on his way.

"Dr. Hornsby, my sister's son, Donny Jack, shops for what I need while he's in town buying supplies for his mother. I don't need a doctor's care. I have high blood pressure, and my prescription's filled at the pharmacy when it runs out. I have no need to run off to town and waste my time. There's nothing there that would please me."

"Indulge me, Mrs. Robertson. What if Donny Jack couldn't go to town shopping for you any longer? What if he moved or fell ill? What if you couldn't find anyone to take his place? What would you do then?"

Cora Lee cocked her head, thinking. That was a prickly problem, all right, one she hadn't contemplated before. Donny Jack was fifty-two years old and never was sick that she ever knew. He sure wasn't about to leave Paul when he had his mother to watch after. An old bachelor had nothing much left to do but care for his elderly parents. Where would Donny Jack go to? But pretend he did, that's what the doctor was getting at, she could see that clearly. That she had never thought of it made her feel foolish. My goodness, Donny Jack wasn't a young sprout. He could even die! That was possible. She wished the doctor hadn't made her think of it.

"And I couldn't get anyone else to go for me?" She pushed one hand into her apron pocket and fingered her snuff can. "No one? There's two or three old boys in Paul goes to town regularly. If I paid them, they'd pick up my groceries, I'm pretty sure of that."

"What if they wouldn't? What would you do then? Would you go yourself?"

"If I couldn't get Diane to go for me?"

He nodded.

"And if I couldn't get Daniel or Jerry or their wives or my grandchildren, if none of them would take the trip?"

261

"That's right."

Cora Lee drew down her eyebrows, upset that she couldn't find a solution to this puzzle. She set the rocker to rocking. She didn't like the doctor for posing such a difficult question. It felt more and more like a trick.

She blew out an exasperated breath. "Well, I guess I'd do without."

"You'd do without food from the grocery store?"

"Listen here, what's the point of questions like this? Donny Jack picks up my things, and that's it. I don't see what all this speculating has to do with me."

Hornsby drank a sip of water. He was a calm one, Cora Lee decided. Her sharp tone hadn't rattled him a bit. "Let me ask you a question," she said. "Are you from the nursing home in Evergreen? Is that why Diane sent you?"

That smile. Where before it amused Cora Lee, now it served to infuriate her.

"No," he said. "I'm called in on special cases, but I'm not on the staff there, no. My specialty is psychiatric disorders."

"Then what are you doing here asking me questions that set me to fuming and fussing over nothing? I don't have any disorder. I don't want to hurt your feelings none, but I have some chores to do, and I can't be bothered with riddles."

"I beg to differ, Mrs. Robertson. You *do* have a disorder, if I am to judge from what little you and your daughter have told me. That disorder is called a phobia. I'm considered one of the leading experts in this field, so I trust that you'll believe me. It's nothing to be disturbed about. A lot of people have phobias, anything from fearing snakes to fearing numbers or darkness or thunder."

"Phobic? Am I? Of what, may I ask?"

"Tell me if this is true," he said, spreading his hands over his knees and leaning out from the sofa toward her. "You won't leave your property. You fear what might happen if you do. You think something horrible, something possibly fatal might happen if you leave here, is that right?"

Cora Lee failed to respond. She felt anger boiling up from deep inside, and she thought the next time she saw her daughter she'd give her a thorough tongue-lashing for the travesty she was now being put through.

"There's a medical term for it, Mrs. Robertson. Other people suffer from it. It's called spatiophobia, and it's an irrational fear of spaces outside a certain confined place. It's a *self-confining* phobia. You've restricted yourself to an area. Beyond those boundaries you fear for your life. You do it to yourself, in other words. It begins gradually, but one of the aspects of this particular phobia is that it can progress rapidly. It is quite crippling, especially when it means you have confined yourself here, where you'll allow no one to stay with you, and because your memory is beginning to fail."

"That is pure-T bullcrap. I've never heard such non-sense."

"Is it? Then would you agree to a ride in my car? We'll drive up the road, no more than three blocks, to the corner store in Paul. Then we'll turn around and drive right back."

"Impossible."

"Why is it impossible?"

"Because I don't have time to waste," she said, ending the conversation and standing, going to the door. She stood holding it open for him. "Good-bye, Dr. Hornsby. I'm sorry you came out all this way on such a hot day."

He paused on the porch, turning to her. "Your daughter is worried about you with good cause, Mrs. Robertson. Unless you fight and overcome your fears, you are essentially imprisoned on your plot of land. With that in mind, I agree that you shouldn't leave your home. But at least you might think about allowing a caretaker to live with you if you don't want to leave."

Cora Lee lifted her chin. She didn't have to agree to anything with this stranger. He had one minute ago told her she was crazy. She owed him nothing. He was like Diane and all the rest. They badgered and worried her. They tore at her life, trying to shred it. She would not have it. If she had to, she'd lock the door and take up Barry's shotgun to keep them at bay, all these people who thought they had every right to tell her what to do, to take her apart and piece her together again, to categorically deny what she knew to be true—that the world past the border of her land was hell on earth, and a lady was not safe there, not for a second.

She watched from the door until Dr. Hornsby's car backed from the driveway and aimed itself down the road.

He was another ploy to get her out of her happy home and into the depressing confinement of a nursing home. As if she were too old! As if she were incapable of taking care of herself, a woman who had lived through five wars, two husbands, and three miscarriages. A woman who had picked cotton when forced to it to feed her fatherless children before Barry came to court her. A woman who had traded hen eggs for school tablets so her children could go to school. A woman who had lived the past seven years in silent rooms echoing with her beloved's voice calling sometimes in the night.

She had seen common transportation change from horse-drawn buggies to cars. She had witnessed a man walk on the moon, the world burgeon with technological progress. Miracles occurred daily in medicine. They had even transplanted a baboon's liver into a man! They had taken a boy born with one hand, and when he was in a car wreck and lost his good arm they attached the severed hand to the one arm he had left, and there he was, a left hand on his right arm! She had lived so long she had seen the world topple so that families were forced apart, children left on their own while their parents worked, crime and violence and drugs escalated into a maddening spiral that threatened to take down not only the poor, but also the rich, not only the uneducated, but also the cultured and refined.

A phobia!

Common sense, it was.

Trouble was people didn't know what was good for them. Cora Lee Robertson knew, and she would hold on to it for as long as she could. Let all the doctors in the world come to tell her she was crazy. Full of fears! Why, of course she was fearful, and what left her confused was why so many others weren't. How could they drive the roads and highways, shop in the supermarkets, visit one another as if everything was just as it had been in the days before all this tumbling madness had taken over?

She'd not let them pressure her or trick her. If they meant to take her away, they'd have to take her screaming and fighting.

She screamed and she fought until they plunged a needle into her arm. When she woke she was lying in a single bed in a small strange room that had one tiny window.

Diane sat near the bed in a plastic turquoise chair.

"Mama?"

"What have you done, Diane? What have you done to your own mother?"

"It's for your own good. I was so afraid something would happen to you."

"Something has happened to me. My children have betrayed me and made me a prisoner." At the thought of where she was and how far away her home was, Cora Lee began to tremble uncontrollably. The sheet covering her body quivered, and soon the metal frame of the headboard tick, tick, ticked against the wall.

"What's the matter? Mama? What's wrong?"

Cora Lee couldn't speak. Her tongue felt swollen and lodged in her mouth. Dizziness swarmed her senses so that she felt as if she were falling from a cliff, falling for miles and miles. She clutched the bed, holding on for dear life. Her breath came in ragged bursts, and her hearing was clogged because she could vaguely distinguish her daughter's face hovering over the bed, her mouth working, yet nothing came from her lips.

Bedlam set upon Cora Lee. The world, just as she had always suspected, was skewed and untenable. She didn't know how Diane managed to stay on her feet or how the walls kept upright or the floors from dropping into a crevice of the earth.

She shut her eyes, longing for home, for safety, for a way out of this horror that pinned her to the bed and stripped her of freedom. She knew she'd never see her flowers again, or sleep in her bed, walk the woods, pet her cats, feed her chickens.

A sudden crushing pain gripped her chest, and soon she swooned into unconsciousness, her last thoughts being: They shouldn't have taken me away, oh God, they shouldn't have done it.

Dr. Hornsby wrote in his notes the truth. Cora Lee Robertson died of fear. That couldn't be put on the death certificate, of course. The attending physician gave the cause of death as a massive coronary. But what precipitated the coronary was fear. Hornsby had warned the old woman's family to step lightly. His advice was to let her be, don't force her. Talk her into taking a hired nurse to live with her. But families often thought they knew better and acted accordingly. He tried to explain that phobias were quite real to patients suffering from them, and without careful behavior modification methods they could even prove deadly.

And he had liked the old woman. She would have been better off dying by some accident on her own property than being hurried to her death by trumpeting hysteria.

As he finished his notes on her case and tucked them into a leather folder he sat back in his chair and gazed around his office. At least, thanks to Mrs. Robertson, he knew it was true. Outside the safe places the danger was enough to throttle the heart. *His* self-confinement encompassed a larger area of ground than did Cora Lee Robertson's. He could move around the entire county without incident. But not one foot beyond it. If he was careful not to let his family know, if no one ever found out, if his excuses against travel were always accepted, then he would be all right.

At least when he was so old he couldn't care for himself they would put him into Evergreen's nursing facility. He had already made those arrangements. For he was old. Just like poor phobic Cora Lee.

And he did not want to die before his time.

CANKERMAN

Peter Crowther

AGAIN?"

The boy nodded, his face tearstained and screwed up as though at the memory of something unpleasant.

"Nasty dream," Ellen Springer said, stifling a yawn. It wouldn't do to appear unconcerned. She knelt down beside her son's bed and eased him back under the covers. The boy shuddered as his tears subsided. A shadow thrown by the hall light fell across the bed, and Ellen turned around to face her husband, who was standing stark naked at the doorway, scratching his head.

"Was it the lumpy man again?" he said to nobody in particular. The lumpy man was a creation of David's, and a particularly bizarre one. He had first appeared in the sad time after Christmas, when the tree was shedding needles, the cold had lost its magic, and already a few of the gaudily colored gifts deposited by Santa Claus in David's little sack had been forgotten or discarded. Only the credit card statements provided a reminder of the fun they had had.

Ellen nodded and turned back to finish the securing

exercise. "There, now. Snuggle down with Chicago." She tucked a small teddy bear, resplendent in a Chicago Bears football helmet and jersey, under the sheets. Her son shuffled around until his face was against the bear's muzzle. "All right now?" He nodded without opening his eyes.

Throughout January and into February David had woken in the night complaining about the lumpy man. He was in the room, David told his parents each time, watching him. He had with him a large black bag, and the sides of it seemed to breathe, in and out, in and out. The man posed no threat to David during his visits, preferring (or so it seemed) to be content simply sitting watching the boy, the bag on his knees all the while.

"Okay, big fella?" John Springer said, leaning over his wife to tousle the boy's hair. There was no answer save for a bit of lip smacking and a sigh. "We'll leave the hall light on for you. There's nothing to be frightened about, okay? It was just another dream."

Stepping back, Ellen smiled at her husband, who was standing looking as attentive as four A.M. would allow, his right hand cradling his genitals. "Careful, they'll drop off," she whispered behind him.

John pretended not to hear. "Okay, then. Night night, sleep tight, hope the—"

"He's still here, Daddy."

"No, he's *not* here, David." He recognized the first sign of irritation in his own voice and moved forward again to crouch by the bed. "He never *was* here. He was just a dream."

The boy had opened his eyes wide and was now staring at his father. "My . . . my majinashun?"

"Yes." He considered correcting and thought better of it. "It was your majinashun."

"He said he'd brung me a late present."

John Springer heard the faint *pad, pad* of Ellen moving along the hallway to the toilet. "He said he'd brought you a present?"

David nodded.

"What did he bring you?"

"He got it from his bag."

"Mmmm. What was it?"

"A lump."

"A lump?"

David nodded, apparently pleased with himself. "It was like a little kitten, all furry and black. At first I thought it *was* a kitten. He held it out to show me, and it had no eyes or face, and no hands and feet."

"Did he leave it for you?"

David frowned.

"Let me see. May I see it?"

The boy shook his head. "I don't have it anymore."

"Did the man take it back?"

Another shake of head and a rub of small cheek against the stitched visage of the little bear.

"Then where is it now?"

For a second John thought his son was not going to answer, but then suddenly he pulled back the bedclothes and pointed a jabbing finger at his stomach, which was poking out pinkly between the elastic top of his pajama pants and a Bart Simpson T-shirt.

"You *ate* it?"

David laughed a high tinkling giggle. "No," he said between chuckles. "The man rubbed it into my tummy. It hurt me, and I started to shout."

"Yes, you did. And that's what woke your mommy and me up."

David nodded. "You called my name, Daddy."

John looked at him. "Yes, I called your name."

"It scared the man when you called my name."

"I scared the lumpy man?" He moved into a kneeling position on one knee only and affected a muscle-building pose. "See, big Daddy scared the lumpy man."

David chuckled again and writhed tiny legs beneath the sheets. John felt the sudden desire to be five years old again, tucked up tightly in a small bed with a favorite cuddly toy to protect him against the things that traveled the night winds of the imagination. Then he noticed his son's eyes concentrating on something on the floor behind him.

"What is it?"

David shook his head again and pulled the sheet up until it covered the end of his nose.

"Is it something on the floor?" He turned around, sticking his bottom up into the air, and padded across the room to the open door, sniffing like a dog. There *was* a smell. Over inside the doorway, coming from the mat that lay across the carpet seam. It smelled like the rotting leaves that he had to clear from the outside drains every few weeks during the early fall.

There was a shuffling from the bed. "He went under the mat, Daddy. Lumpy man hid under the mat when I cried."

David's father turned around and stared at his son, who was now sitting up in bed. Then he looked back at the mat. Ellen wandered by toward their own bedroom and glanced at him. "Isn't it time *you* went back to sleep, too, Mister Doggie?"

John smiled and gave a bark. He lifted the mat and looked underneath. Nothing. He felt suddenly silly. He had looked under the mat more for himself than for David, he realized. It would have been easy to tell the boy not to be frightened; that a big man could not hide beneath a small rug. But just for a few seconds he had been frightened to go back to bed without investigating the possibility that there was . . . something . . . under the rug. But the smell . . .

"Has anything been spilled around here, Ellen?"

"Mmmm? Spilled? Not that I can think of, no. Why?"

"It just smells a bit weird." Actually, it smelled a *lot* weird. It stank to high heaven. He laid the rug carefully back in place and got up. "Nothing there." He turned around and snuggled David back into his sheets. "So off to sleep now. Hoh-kay?"

"Hoh-kay," said David.

John wandered out of the small bedroom and swung back along the hall to the toilet. Within a minute or two he was back in bed, his bladder comfortably empty, with Ellen complaining about the coldness of his feet. He lay so that he could see into David's room. The little mat lay between them, silent as the night itself, and despite John's tiredness, sleep was long in coming.

That was March.

David left them in September.

The problem was a Wilms tumor, a particularly aggressive renal cancer that showed itself initially as an abdominal swelling on David's left side. Ellen discovered it during bathtime. The following day the tummy aches began. That weekend David started vomiting for no apparent reason. By the following Tuesday he had shown blood in his urine.

The Wilms was diagnosed following an intravenous pyelogram, in which a red dye was injected into a vein in David's arm. It was confirmed by a singularly unpleasant session on the CT scanner, which looked like a Boeing engine and hummed like the machine constructed by Jeff Morrow in *This Island Earth*.

The prognosis was not good.

David had a tumor in each kidney. He had secondaries in lung and liver. The kidneys were removed surgically, but on the side that was worse affected they had to leave some behind because of danger to arteries. He went through a short course of radiotherapy and then a course of chemo. He felt bad, but John and Ellen kept him going, making light of it all each day and dying silently each night, locked in tearful embraces in the hollow sanctity of their bed.

The tumor did not respond.

David's sixth birthday present was for the consultant to tell his parents that it had spread into his bones. It wouldn't be long now.

Morphine derivatives, Marvel comics, and Chicago the bear kept him chipper until the end, which came just before lunch on the third of September in the aching sickness-filled silence of St. Edna's Children's Hospital. Both Ellen and John were there, holding a thin frail arm each. Their son slipped away with a sad smile and a momentary look of wise regret that he had had to abandon them so soon.

Ellen started back at school late. When she did return she had been sleeping badly for almost two weeks.

The cumulative effect of the long months of suffering, during which a life was lived and lost, had taken its toll. And though the grass had already started to grow on top of the small plot in Woodlands Cemetery, no such healing process had begun over the scarred tissue of Ellen Springer's heart. On top of that, she had inherited a difficult class at school.

Their lives were undeniably empty now, though they both went to great efforts to appear brave and happy, affecting as close a copy of their early trouble-free existence as they could muster. David's room had been redecorated, the Simpsons wallpaper stripped off and the primary colors of the woodwork painted over in pastels and muted shades with names such as Wheat and Barley and Hedgerow Green. The bed had been replaced with a chair and a small glass-topped coffee table, and on many evenings Ellen would sit in there supposedly preparing for the next day's lessons, though in reality she would simply sit and daydream, staring out of the small window into the tail ends of the ever-shortening days. Another Christmas would soon be upon them, and neither of them was looking forward to it.

The lumpy man and his black bag had been forgotten, though John still had the occasional nightmare. Ellen never mentioned David's dreams—in fact, she tried never to mention David—and John had never told her about his and David's conversation that long-ago night when the lumpy man had brought their little boy a late Christmas present.

The first night after the funeral had been so bad that they could not believe they had actually survived it. Despite a sleeping pill—which she had assured John she would be stopping soon—Ellen had tossed and turned all night. She had told John that David had been in their room watching her. John had tried to reason with her. It was the healing process, he had told her, the grief and the sadness and the loss. David was at peace now.

She had cried then, cried like she had not cried since the early days following all their conversations with doctors and surgeons. How they had begged for their child's life during those lost and lonely weeks.

Ellen did not stop the sleeping pills, nor did John try to

persuade her to do so. But her nights did not improve. Then, after five or six days, she had told him that it was not David who visited their room at night while she was asleep. It was somebody else. "Who?" he had asked. She had shrugged.

He had managed to get her to a doctor for a checkup. She had not wanted to go back into a medical environment, but she had relented. Too tired to argue, he had supposed. Or just too disinterested. John had spoken to the doctor beforehand and had persuaded him to refer her to the clinic for a full scan. The local hospital agreed to let her through—despite the fact that there was no evidence to support any theory of something unpleasant—because of her traumatic recent history. She had taken the test on a Monday, and they had the results by mail the following Friday. It was clear.

They celebrated.

That night John had a dream. In his dream a tall man wearing dark clothes and an undertaker's smile drifted into their bedroom and sat beside Ellen. He stroked her head for what seemed to be a long time and then left. He carried with him a huge, old-fashioned black valise, the sides of which seemed to pulsate in the dim glow thrown into the house by the street lamp outside their bedroom window. *Soon,* he seemed to say softly to John on his way out, though his misshapen lips did not move. John awoke with a start and sat bolt upright in bed, but the room was empty. Ellen moved restlessly by his side, her brow furrowed and her lips dry.

The following two nights John stayed awake, but nothing happened. During the days at the office he ducked off into empty rooms and grabbed a few hours of sleep. The work was piling up on his desk, but problems would not show up for a week or two. John was convinced it wouldn't take that long.

On the third night the lumpy man came back.

His smile was a mixture of formaldehyde and ether, which lit the room with mist, its gray tendrils swirling lazily around the floor and up the walls. His face was a marriage of pain and pleasure, an uneven countenance of hills and valleys, knolls and caves, a place of shadows and lights. And his clothes were black and white, a significance of goodness and non-goodness: a somber dark gray tailcoat and a white wing-collared shirt sporting a black bootlace tie, which hung in swirls and ribbons like a cruel mockery of festivity and inconsequence. His hair was white-gray, hanging in long, wispy strands about his neck and forehead.

Ah, it's time, his voice whispered as he entered, filling the room with the dual sounds of torment and delight. And as he listened John Springer could not for the life of him decide where the one ended and the other began.

Feigning sleep, curled around his wife's back, John watched the lumpy man move soundlessly around the bed to Ellen's side and sit on the duvet. There was no sense of weight on the bed.

The man placed his bag on the floor and unfastened the clasp. There was a soft skittering sound of fluffy movement as he reached down into the bag and lifted something out. John felt the strange dislocation of dream activity, a sense of not belonging, as he watched the man lift an elongated roll of writhing darkness up onto his lap. He laid it there, smoothing it, smiling at its feral movements, sensing its anticipation and its impatience.

Not long, little one, his voice cooed softly through closed, unmoving lips, and, leaving the shape where it lay, he reached across and pulled back the duvet from Ellen's body.

Ellen turned obligingly, exposing her right breast to the air and the world and the strange darkness of the visitor in their room. The man lifted the shape and, with an air of caring and gentility, lowered it toward the sleeping woman.

John sat up.

The man turned around.

And now John could see him for what he really was, a bizarre concord of beauty and ugliness, of creation and ruin, of discord and harmony. There were pits and whorls, folds and crevices, warts that defied gravity and imagination, and thick gashes that seeped sad runnels of loneliness. *Go back to sleep.* His voice echoed inside John Springer's head.

No, he answered without speaking. *You may not have her.* John sensed an amusement. *I may not?*

Cankerman

No, John answered, pulling himself straighter in the bed. *You have taken my son. You may not have my wife.*

The man shook his head with a movement that was almost imperceptible. Then he returned his full attention to Ellen and continued to lower the shape.

No!

Again he stopped.

Take me instead.

The lumpy man's brow furrowed a moment.

Surely it cannot matter whom you take, John went on, sensing an opportunity, or at least a respite. *You have a quota, yes?*

The man nodded.

Then fill it with me.

For what seemed like an eternity the lumpy man considered the proposition, all the while holding the shifting furry bundle above Ellen's breast. Then, at last, he pulled back his hand and lowered the thing back into his bag.

John felt his heart pounding in his chest.

The man stood up from the bed, his bag again held tightly in his right hand, and moved around to John's side.

John shuffled himself up so that his back was against the headboard. *Who are you?* he said.

I am the Cankerman, came the reply. He sat on the bed beside him and rested the bag on his lap. *And you are my customer.* John licked his lips as the lumpy man pulled open the sides of the black valise and pushed the yawning hole toward him. *Choose,* he said. John looked inside.

The smell that assailed his nostrils was like the scent of meat left out in the sun. It was the air of corruption, the hum of badness, and the bittersweet aftertaste of impurity. Gagging at the stench that rose from the bag, John still managed to hold onto his gorge and stared. There seemed to be hundreds of them, rolling and tumbling, climbing and falling, clambering and toppling over, pulling out of and fading into the almost impenetrable blackness at the fathomless bottom of the Cankerman's valise.

All were uniformly black.

Black as the night.

Black as a murderer's heart.

Black as the ebony fullness that devours all light, all reason, all hope.

Cancer-black.

Choose, said the Cankerman again.

John reached in.

They scurried and they wobbled, squeezing themselves between his fingers, wrapping their furriness around his wrist, filling his palm with their dull warmth, their half-life. They pulsated and spread themselves out, rubbing themselves against him with a grim parody of affection.

Big ones, small ones, long thin ones, short stubby ones.

All human life is there, John thought with detachment.

And he made his choice.

There, deep within the black valise, his arm stretched out as though to the very bowels of the earth itself, his fingers found a tiny shape. A pea. A furry pea.

He pulled it out and held it before the grisly mask. *This is my choice,* he said.

So be it, said the Cankerman, and he closed the valise and placed it on the floor. Taking the small squirming object from John's outstretched hand, he allowed himself a small smile. *No regrets?*

Just do it.

The Cankerman nodded and, leaning toward him, placed the black fur against John Springer's right eye . . . and pushed it in.

Pain.

Can you hear a color?

Can you smell a sound?

Can you see a taste?

John Springer could.

He heard the blackness of a swirling ink blot, smelled the noise of severing cells, and saw, deep inside his own head, the flavor of exquisite destruction.

Good-bye.

When John opened his eyes the room was empty. He lay back against the headboard and felt exhaustion overtake him.

Cankerman

Ellen's hand brought him swimming frantically from the deep waters of sleep into the half-light of a smoky fall morning.

"I let you sleep," she said simply.

"Mmmm." He licked his lips and squinted into her face. "What time is it?"

"After eight."

He groaned.

"Hey, I had a good night."

John looked up at her and smiled. "Good," he said. "I told you: Nothing lasts forever."

"You were right. But it'll take me some time." She stood up and walked over to the wardrobe.

"I know." He watched her sifting through clothes. On impulse he closed his left eye and saw her outline blur. "Love you," he said . . . softly, so that she might not know how much.

ENDURE THE NIGHT

Robert Weinberg

RALPH WAS JUST REACHING FOR THE BOX OF OLD CLOTHES when the lights went out.

Instantly he froze, his entire body rigid with uncontrollable fright. Immobile, terrified beyond comprehension, he could feel the wild thumping of his heart, pounding like a sledgehammer against his chest. The sound of blood rushing through his system roared in his eardrums, threatening to overwhelm his senses.

His eyes, popped wide open, strained futilely as they searched for a flicker of illumination in the pitch-black attic. But they hunted without any chance of success. There were only two small windows in the huge room, and both of these were covered with heavy-duty tar paper. Placed there to keep out the night, the tarp served equally well to hold in the darkness. Not a trace of moonlight filtered through the barrier. Ralph was trapped alone in a blackness he helped create.

Slowly, ever so slowly, he forced himself to take deep, long breaths. Each time he inhaled, some small measure of sanity returned. There was an emergency flashlight nearby—he had them stationed along with candles and matches at strategic points throughout the entire house. If he could maintain a tight grip on his nerves, all he had to do was take a few steps in the right direction, and everything would be all right. That was, if he could move his feet without going mad.

The bugs scared him. Huge, giant cockroaches. He knew they were lurking about somewhere on the floor. Though an exterminator sprayed the entire mansion every month, Ralph suspected that the monstrous insects were still alive somewhere, hiding, waiting for him to move. He cringed, remembering the feel of them crawling up the sides of his legs, the indescribable loathsome feel of them scuttling across his belly and genitals.

He felt a scream welling up inside himself. Desperately he forced it down. His mind was playing tricks on him. The bugs existed only in his mind. They were horrors of his childhood, not of today. Thinking of them only led to madness and insanity. The darkness gave them life. The only way to banish them back to the prison of his memory was to turn on a light.

Hesitantly Ralph slid one foot forward, inches at a time, half expecting at any second to touch something alive in the dark, something disgusting and frightening beyond belief. He encountered nothing. Biting his lower lip, he shuffled his other foot forward. Again he touched nothing. Little by little he skated across the floor, never once raising his feet, never moving more than a dozen inches at a time. It took an eternity that lasted five minutes until he reached the sloped roof of the attic that signaled he had gone as far as possible.

Kneeling, his hands trembling so hard that his fingers hurt, he groped around the base of the wall, searching for the elusive emergency flashlight. Ralph knew his fears were irrational, insane, but it didn't matter. To him they were very real. His entire world centered on his shaking fingers.

Finally one hand latched onto the flashlight. Ralph wrenched it from the socket and flicked on the light. Instantly a soft white beam of illumination flooded the room. The attic was again no more than an ordinary room topping the huge old mansion he called home. There were no bugs anywhere. All was exactly as it had been when the lights went out. He was safe.

Ralph stood up, stretching the kinks from his body. It felt as if he had been hit by a truck. The muscles of his arms, legs, and chest had tightened so badly that it hurt just to flex. His head pounded with the beginnings of a terrible headache.

Hastily he reached down and found the box of candles he kept close to the flashlight. He placed four of them in his pockets along with a book of matches. He was taking no chances that the charge on his flashlight might fail.

A tall, slender man with pleasant, distinguished features, Ralph Dresden was the author of six best-selling novels. Just under forty, he lived alone in a huge Victorian mansion in North Port, New Jersey, an hour's drive from New York City and his publisher.

He had bought the house soon after the publication of his second book five years ago and had lived there ever since. Popular with his neighbors, he was considered one of the mainstays of the community, contributing large sums of money to all of the local charities and schools. He even attended the high school football games—if they were during the daytime. For Ralph never went out at night. He was afraid of the dark.

It was an irrational fear, a phobia that bordered on insanity. Ten years of therapy had provided a little help, but not much. When the lights went out, Ralph froze. The darkness transformed him from a suave, sophisticated man of the world into a terror-struck child.

The root of his problem was a nightmarish childhood dominated by an abusive father who believed in harsh punishment for the slightest annoyance. A violent, drunken brute of a man, Tom Dresden had lived alone with his son in a ramshackle apartment in the worst section of Brooklyn. For the first ten years of his life Ralph had suffered there in a state of perpetual terror, never knowing when his father might explode over some imaginary transgression.

Too often those rages took place late at night, when his

father arrived home in an alcoholic stupor. The sight of a crayon left out on a table, a plate not washed from dinner would turn the surly Dresden into a raving lunatic. Screaming obscenities, he would rush into Ralph's bedroom, yank the sleeping child out of bed, and beat him unmercifully with his belt. Then, when he was done and his son whimpered in pain, Tom Dresden would do his worst.

He would take Ralph, a sensitive, timid child, afraid of the dark, and throw him into the hall closet. Oblivious to the child's screams of terror, Tom would then go to sleep— leaving his son locked in a pitch-black, narrow compartment a foot deep by four feet long. There Ralph remained until morning, trapped in a closet filled with old clothes and inhabited by hundreds of huge, extremely active cockroaches. Bugs that crawled all over Ralph, driving him to the brink of insanity. Somehow, barely, he survived.

Then, one day shortly after Ralph's tenth birthday, his father didn't come home. Instead a policeman showed up. A drunken Tom Dresden had taken the wrong step at the wrong time. He never even saw the truck that smashed his body to a pulp and thus released his son from constant torment.

Freed from his father's insanity, Ralph grew up into a normal, healthy adult. Except for one failing. He was terrified of the dark. Blackness brought back the closet— and the bugs.

So he slept with the lights on. And became a writer, so that he could work his own hours, in his own stable, safe environment that he controlled. A world where the darkness never intruded. Where the lights were always on and a flashlight was always nearby.

In time Ralph made his terrors pay. His books, horror novels featuring young children in peril from wicked relatives, grabbed the public's attention. Reviewers raved about the intensity of feeling in the stories, the raw emotion that dripped off the pages. The horrors of Ralph's childhood served him well, made him rich.

He frowned in annoyance. One of the advantages of wealth was that he had paid to have his entire mansion rewired with new electrical lines. The power should not have failed. There was a backup system, but the controls for that were in his study on the first floor. Even with the flashlight it would take him a half hour or more to summon the courage to walk through the old dark house. Still, he could and would do it.

The whisper of a man's voice caught him completely off guard. Burglars, was his immediate reaction. Anxiously he swung the flashlight around the narrow confines of the attic. There was no one there. Yet the voice continued.

After a second Ralph realized the sounds were coming up the old metal heating duct in the floor. The old pipes transmitted noise better than any radio. Someone was in the house, but he could be anywhere. Bending close, Ralph put his ear to the grate.

"Where the fuck is this loony?" someone asked in a harsh, nasal voice. "I thought you said this job would be a snap."

"It will be," said another voice, softer, more difficult for Ralph to hear. "This bozo's rich, I tell you. Look at this place. It's filled with stuff we can sell. Once we off the geek, we can tear the place apart without anyone being the wiser. This Dresden lives by himself. Nobody will suspect he's dead for days. By then we'll be long gone with the loot."

The first man laughed, loud and harsh. "But first we gotta find the jerk. What if he calls the cops before we grab him?"

"That's why we cut the phone lines," replied the man with the soft voice. "And stationed Max by the door just in case Dresden managed to slip by us and get outside."

Ralph squeezed his eyes tightly shut, as if trying to banish what he heard from his consciousness. But there was no escaping the truth. He was trapped in a nightmare with no chance of waking up.

"This Dresden ain't going to give us any trouble," continued the soft-voiced man. "I read an article in the paper about him last month. That's what gave me the idea of breaking in here. The poor sucker's afraid of the dark."

"Yeah, yeah," said his companion. "So you told me. If he's so damned scared, where is he?"

"Probably huddled in bed with a flashlight waitin' for the power to go back on," said the soft-voiced crook. "He won't be hard to locate. Just look for a room with a light."

Ralph jerked erect. He didn't need to hear any more. The stakes were quite clear. A gang of killers had invaded his home. Two men hunted for him inside the mansion while a third waited outside. The electricity and phone were both dead. Given the nature of his phobia, there was no chance of anyone stopping by to visit tonight. He was on his own. *In the dark.*

Ralph's hand tightened around the flashlight. He could not function rationally in the blackness. But the killers were aware of his fear. If he kept the light on, they would find and kill him. His survival meant enduring the night.

Wildly, he considered a dozen schemes that would enable him to leave on the light. He swiftly rejected them all. He could not stay in the attic with the door locked and hope the crooks would leave him alone. That only happened in fairy tales.

Nor would setting the bedroom curtains on fire guarantee his escape. He doubted any distraction would work. The two men in his house wanted him dead. The only way to survive was to beat them at their own game. Which meant he had to reach the study on the first floor.

Ralph drew in a deep breath, then exhaled slowly. He felt like a character in one of his books. Trapped by circumstances beyond his control, he had to fight back against a pair of insane killers. Unfortunately, he faced not only human monsters but the horrors of his own subconscious. And he wasn't sure which he feared more.

His whole body trembling, Ralph headed for the staircase leading down from the attic. He still held the flashlight tightly in one hand, its circle of illumination providing him with some brief measure of courage. Hurriedly he scrambled down the wooden steps to the third floor.

The door leading into the hallway was ajar, exactly the way he had left it. Ralph clenched then unclenched his fingers, striving to fight the panic building within him. He could postpone the inevitable no longer. With a flick of a finger he shut off the light.

Darkness descended like a shroud, covering him completely. The blackness was absolute, mind-numbing. In despair he sank his teeth into his lower lip, drawing blood.

The sudden pain served as an anchor, drawing him back to the real world. Three feet away was the door. He had to exit the stairway before the killers arrived. There was no time to hesitate, to build up courage. He had to do it now.

One step, then another, and finally the third. He was at the door. Then one more step and he was into the hallway. It was no better here than in the stairway. It was still pitch black. He froze in place, not able to move a step further.

Ralph's fingers curled on the switch of the flashlight. One brief flicker of light to orient himself was all he needed. Or so he argued mentally, trying to justify turning the flash back on. A few seconds, nothing more. But he knew that if the light went back on, he would not be able to shut it off.

"There are no bugs in this house," he whispered to himself, trying to draw courage from somewhere deep inside. "They exist only in my mind. Only in my mind."

Speaking aloud snapped the spell of fear that bound him. Reaching out with his left hand, he touched the far wall of the hall. The wood paneling steadied him, gave him a feeling of belonging. He was not a little boy trapped in a closet. *This was his house. This was his life.* He would not give up either without a fight.

Ralph closed his eyes, then opened them. Somehow the hallway seemed less dark. Straining, he could make out the other wall, even the chair outside a nearby bedroom. Looking down, he could see his feet, even catch a glimpse of the pattern in the carpet. Suddenly he realized what it all meant. Light was rising from the second-floor stairwell. Someone was coming up the steps.

The dim glow provided just enough illumination for him to function normally. Ralph hurried down the hall to a bedroom. There were three on this floor, all opening to the hallway. Moreover, each room was linked to the one next to it by an inner doorway. Thus the middle bedroom had access to both the first and third chambers. He could not be trapped inside it.

Ralph scrambled into the room, softly closing the door behind him. Again the blackness of the chamber threatened to overwhelm his senses. But he had picked this room for several reasons.

A small emergency night light, the type that went on when the power failed, was plugged into a floor outlet. It provided only minimal illumination, but that was all Ralph needed.

Hopefully, whoever was coming up the stairway would spot the open door to the attic and continue upward to investigate. Ralph cursed at his lack of foresight. He could have set a trap for the crooks. If only he had left a candle burning in the room above. He shook his head in annoyance. It was too late now to worry about what he should have done. Only the present mattered.

"Mr. Dresden?" Ralph recognized the voice of the harsh-toned man. "Mr. Dresden, it's the police. Where are you?"

Ralph nodded. What better line to use than that? Under normal circumstances he would have been rushing to greet his rescuers. Pressed hard against the inner wall of the bedroom, he remained motionless.

"Mr. Dresden?" the man called again. His heavy footsteps echoed on the floorboards. "We've come to help you."

A door slammed open. Ralph's head wrenched around as a glare of light shone from beneath the door connecting this bedroom to the first one.

"You in here, Mr. Dresden?" The hoodlum was in the next room. Death stood on the other side of the wall. "Nothing to worry about. I'm here to help."

Anxiously Ralph watched the doorknob to the other bedroom. If it turned, he was out into the hallway. If not, he intended to enter the room as soon as his adversary departed. Then, while the man searched the second bedroom, Ralph could be out the door of the first and headed downstairs.

An eternity passed in the span of five seconds. Then the light beneath the doorway disappeared. The thug was back in the hallway. Time for Ralph to move.

Gently he twisted the knob connecting the chambers. It turned, but the door didn't open. Not used in months, it was stuck shut.

"Mr. Dresden?" It was the harsh-voiced man, outside this bedroom. "You in there? It's the police."

Desperately Ralph pushed his entire body against the unyielding wood. With a whisper of air it swung open, sending him tumbling into the other room. Instinctively he closed the door behind him.

Whatever slight noise his passage made was drowned out by the entrance of the hoodlum into the second bedroom. "Anyone here?" the man asked loudly, sounding impatient. The light from his flash curled under the connecting door and licked at Ralph's feet. "Where the hell are you, you dumb son of a bitch?"

Ralph sucked in deep lungfuls of air as his enemy stomped about the room. There was no way he could make it to the stairs before the crook left the other bedroom.

A drop of sweat trickled down his back. The two men had evidently split up to search the mansion. He knew where the loudmouth was. But what of his partner, the soft-spoken one? Where was the mastermind behind the whole scheme? He might be waiting right now for his intended victim to stumble into his arms.

Cursing loudly, the would-be killer left the second bedroom. With him went his flashlight, plunging Ralph again into total darkness. Instinctively he whimpered in fear, his arms and legs locking tightly together.

If the hoodlum had heard him, he was a dead man. Ralph waited helplessly for a response, his back pressed against the door connecting the two rooms. The muscles in his chest tightened so hard that it was difficult to breathe. His arms and legs felt like they were tied in knots. Five seconds passed, then ten more. Nothing.

Down at the end of the hall the thug pounded on the third bedroom door. "You inside there, you stupid shit?" the man shouted. "'Cause it's the boogeyman, comin' to blow your fuckin' head off!"

Ralph was safe—for the moment. But he couldn't remain

in this chamber. Sooner or later the two thugs would find him. He had to get to the study, and the darkness, his worst enemy, would keep him safe.

Five shaky steps took him to the bed in the center of the room. Carefully he edged his way around it. In his mind's eye he located the doorknob, only two long steps from the foot of the bed. Grasping it, Ralph felt slightly more confident.

Even without lights he knew his way around the mansion. Gifted with an exceptional memory, he remembered the exact layout of every room in the building. In a house this size, that knowledge represented a major edge.

Ralph pressed his ear to the door. He didn't hear a thing. Given all the noise made by the hoodlum earlier, it seemed unlikely he was in the hallway. Either the thug was still in the third bedroom, or he had gone up into the attic. It was time for the stairs leading down to the second level.

Ralph slipped out into the hall. Now he could hear faint, muffled steps up above his head. The loudmouthed thug was in the attic. Once he realized the room was empty he would be on his way back down. Ralph had to be gone before that.

Six halting, shuffling steps took him to the stairs. Ralph grabbed hold of the railing with both hands. Usually he jogged down the stairway without a care. But that was with the lights on. In the darkness they threatened his fragile nerve.

There were a dozen steps. He took them one at a time. Slide a foot across the carpet and down. Then follow it with the other foot. Drag his hands along the railing. Then repeat the whole procedure. Again and again, never letting go, never losing contact with wall or floor.

He was halfway down the staircase when he heard someone coming. A thin beam of light ran along the second-floor landing. It was the other crook coming down the hallway. Ralph was trapped on the stairs with an enemy above and an enemy below.

Feverishly he pulled the flashlight from his waistband. Then, knowing he had no other choice, he pounded his arm into the wall.

"Huh?" The soft-spoken man sounded surprised. His footsteps approached the landing. "That you, Stan?"

Ralph grunted incoherently. He was six stairs from the bottom. Carefully, he knelt so that his head was level with the banister. The flashlight he held in front of his body, aimed like a gun at the base of the steps.

"What the hell you doin' coming back down here?" the other man asked. He was standing on the landing now. The light of his flashlight poked upward. Aimed at where his partner's body should have been, it passed directly over Ralph's head. Not expecting trouble, the crook stood outlined in the flash's glow.

Instantly Ralph turned on his light. Desperation guided his hand. Like a whip the bright ray caught the thug square in the eyes.

"You stupid shit," the man exclaimed, raising his hands to shield his face. Which was exactly when Ralph, leaping forward from the step, slammed into his chest.

Momentum carried them across the floor and into the far wall. The thug mewed in pain as his head crashed into the solid wood paneling. Together they collapsed to the floor.

Ralph landed on top. Knowing every second was precious, he allowed his opponent no time to recover. Brutally he rammed a fist into the man's face, catching him directly in the nose. Blood and cartilage sprayed across Ralph's fingers. The crook screeched in pain. Mercilessly Ralph hit him again. And again.

"Joey!" came a shout from the third floor. It was the other crook. The pounding of his feet in the hallway above hit Ralph like a slap in the face. Time was running out.

Scrambling off the battered thug, he snatched the flashlight from the floor as he rose shakily to his feet. Halfway down the corridor was the double set of stairs leading to the main foyer of the mansion. Once there, it was only a few feet to his study—and the emergency power switch that would restore lights to the whole building.

But fate wouldn't let go so easily. Before Ralph could take a step, two bloody hands grabbed him by an ankle and dragged him back to the floor. Though his face was a mask of blood, the soft-spoken crook was still conscious. He was determined not to let his prize escape. Clawlike fingers dug into Ralph's leg in an unbreakable grip.

"I'm coming, Joey!" bellowed the other crook, pounding down the stairs. "I'm coming!"

With all of his strength Ralph swung the flashlight against the other man's head. Metal and bone collided with a sickening crunch. The light went flying from Ralph's numbed fingers. And for an instant the crook's grip loosened.

It was just enough for Ralph to wrench his leg free. On his hands and knees he tumbled madly down the hallway, running for his life.

Grabbing the banister railing leading to the first floor, Ralph risked a quick glimpse back. The other thug, a big burly man with a bulldog face, stood bending over his wounded comrade. In his right hand the crook held a large pistol.

As if sensing Ralph's gaze, the hoodlum looked up, his eyes burning with rage. "You're dead meat!" he roared, and he raised his gun. Panic-stricken, Ralph leapt into the dark stairwell as the man fired.

Ralph almost made it to the bottom of the stairs. His feet hit the third step up and dragged for an instant. The collision caught him completely off balance. He grabbed for an unseen railing and missed. Angular momentum thrust him forward with sickening speed. Face first, he smashed into the first-floor carpet. Pain exploded in his left leg, and he knew without a doubt that he had sprained his ankle.

Clutching his wounded limb, Ralph rolled away from the steps. A rush of adrenaline muted the agony. Still, there was no way he could put any weight on his ankle. Grimly he started crawling on his stomach for the study door.

Any second he expected to hear his enemies thundering down the stairs, their guns belching death. His situation seemed hopeless, but he refused to give up.

Then his fingers sank deep into the plush carpet. It reminded him of the old winter coat he had worn as a child. The winter coat that had ended up on the floor of his closet prison. Without warning a flood of dreaded memories engulfed him.

The bugs swarmed over him. Clicking and clawing, they scrambled over his body, running up and down his legs, pinching at his fingers. He couldn't scream for fear they would run down his throat and fill his insides.

He dared not open his eyes, knowing that they would be right there, on his cheeks, waiting to squeeze his pupils to jelly. They burrowed through his hair, searching for his ears. Huge black cockroaches with shells as hard as walnuts; nothing could stop them. Ralph's whole body quaked in terror as the horrors of his childhood roared back.

It was the pain that rescued him. Thrashing about on the carpet, trapped in his nightmare, Ralph slammed his injured foot into the floor. Instantly an incredible jolt of agony shot up his leg, a lance of flame setting his nerves ablaze. He shrieked, nearly passing out, as his brain exploded in white-hot fire. And broke him free from his dreams.

Drenched in sweat, Ralph wriggled like a snake across the carpet to the study. Each move sent a fresh spasm of torment cascading through his body. But the suffering kept the bugs at bay.

He snapped shut the lock of the study door to the sound of his enemies coming down the stairs. An emergency night light in the room provided all the illumination he needed. The familiar sight of his desk lifted Ralph's spirits. Groaning, he raised himself to his knees and lurched into his easy chair.

Sitting, he could almost ignore the pain in his ankle. There would be plenty of time to take care of that later. Already the two thugs were at the study door. The bolt was designed for privacy, not protection. It only delayed the hoodlums an instant. Which was all the time Ralph needed.

The emergency switch was in the top left-hand drawer of the desk. He tripped it as the study door crashed open. The two crooks stood framed in the entrance as everywhere in the mansion the lights went on.

The bulldog-faced man, Stan, held a gun in one hand. He appeared off balance from kicking open the door. Leaning against him, half-supported by his arm, was Joey, the gang leader. Blood dripped in a steady stream from his smashed nose. His eyes were glazed with shock. A look of stunned disbelief crossed the crook's face as he caught sight of the .45 automatic in Ralph's hand.

Ralph gave them no chance to recover. His gun barked once. At this distance he couldn't miss. The big slug caught Stan in the chest and knocked him off his feet.

"If he moves," said Ralph, directing his comments to Joey, "I'll blow him away."

His voice was shaky but determined. "If you've got a gun, drop it. *Now!*"

Dazed, the smaller thug fished out a revolver from his coat pocket and dropped it to the floor. Swaying dizzily, he raised his hands over his head, a beaten man.

"Don't think of trying anything," warned Ralph. His gun never wavered. "I spend lots of time at a pistol range. Next time I'll finish the job."

He grinned savagely. "Don't give me an excuse—any excuse."

Calmly, almost coolly, he dialed the police, using the cellular phone he kept in the desk drawer. He was careful to warn the law officers of the third crook hidden outside. Though he suspected that by the time they arrived their approach would have frightened the man away.

"I can't believe this," said Joey as Ralph hung up. He glanced down at his partner, shivering in pain on the floor. "You beat the two of us. Alone. By yourself. And you're scared of the dark."

"You made one big mistake," said Ralph. Already he could hear the shrill cries of the police sirens in the distance. "Like too many people these days, you drew a conclusion based on one fact. And that's where you went wrong."

"Yeah?" said Joey, the blood dripping from his nose making a red stain on the carpet. "Whatcha talkin' about?"

"You never expected me to fight back," said Ralph. "But I did. You see, *it doesn't mean a man's a coward just because he's afraid of the dark.*"

THE OLD
STEEL-FACED BLUES

Dean Wesley Smith

DANNY WATCHED CYNTHIA'S FACE MELT AS HE SLIPPED THE diamond engagement ring on her finger.

Like so much hot butter, her pert nose, her thin eyebrows, her high cheeks, her full lips slid down her face and dripped from her chin. A pool of skin-toned liquid mixed with faint touches of pink lipstick, gray eye shadow, and swirls of blood formed on her skirt in her lap, then ran off onto the couch and down into the cracks between the cushions.

He watched what was left of her upper lip disappear before he dared glance back up at her face. Only pale blue eyes, two nostril holes, and a slit of a mouth remained on the smooth metal surface where her face had been.

He glanced around the living room of his apartment, stared at his stereo, his VCR, his coffee table to make sure everything else was still in place. It all seemed to be, except that suddenly the place seemed much warmer, almost like a sauna. It was a warm day in New York, but it wasn't that warm.

He took a deep, shuddering breath and then looked again

at her. Hard steel and no expression greeted his look. He had been afraid this would happen.

"Oh, Danny," she said, holding up her hand and admiring her new engagement ring. "It's so beautiful, but it's way too expensive. You shouldn't have."

She was right. He shouldn't have. The diamond seemed to glitter, almost as if it had a life of its own. He glanced down at the tip of her nose, melting on her lap like an ice cube on a hot summer sidewalk, then forced himself to look back up at her face.

"Are . . . Cynthia . . . are you . . . I mean, are you *feeling* all right?" He knew it wasn't really her, but he had to ask.

"I feel wonderful." Her hand grasped his, and she leaned forward to hug him. He barely moved his head aside in time to avoid the kiss and ended up feeling the cold steel of her face against his cheek. It felt as if he were leaning against the hood of a taxi on a cold morning.

She pulled back and looked at him, her once-beautiful blue eyes now cold and pale. No expression marred the cold surface. Was this the true Cynthia? Damn. Why hadn't he seen this before? Why hadn't his vision been working?

"Honest," she said. "I feel great. Why?"

He shook his head and turned his gaze downward at where her hand held his. As he watched, her hand turned into a steel claw, gripping his wrist painfully, holding him from escape. He was doomed. He just knew it. He again glanced around the living room as now the walls seemed to close in. He hated it when they did that.

"Danny. What's wrong?" Her tone was beginning to sound panicked.

He shook his head. No way he was going to tell her she had lost her face.

"You're having second thoughts already, aren't you? You can't even last ten seconds after asking me to marry you."

This time he kept staring at her steel-clawed hand and didn't even shake his head. No way was he going to look back up into that face. That coldness was not how he wanted to think of her.

"Damn you, Danny Eaton," she said, yanking her hand away from his, tearing skin as it went. "I should have known better than to think you could ever get married. Here's your damn ring back. I don't know why the hell you even gave it to me."

With a yank she tugged off his ring and threw it at him, hitting him in the chest. The ring bounced once and went down the same crack in the cushions where her upper lip had gone.

"I'm . . . I'm sorry. It's just that . . ." He was going to try to explain, but her face was back. Everything in the right place. All the skin, her eyebrows, her nose. Her beautiful face was back, and all he could do was stare.

She stood and glared at him, normal hands on her full hips, tears in her eyes. "Sometimes I wonder what I see in you." She turned toward the front door.

"Wait!" He stuck his hand down into the crack of the couch, searched for a long few seconds amid the crumbs and old popcorn kernels until he found the ring, then went after her. He caught her before she reached the front door, spun her around, and looked deep into her blue eyes.

"I love you," he said. "I honestly do. It's not what you think."

"Then what is it?"

"Fear," he said.

"Fear of what? Marriage? Commitment? Just what the hell are you afraid of, Danny?"

He laughed. He hoped this would be what she wanted to hear, because there was no way he could tell her the truth. He took a deep breath and looked her square in the eye. "To be honest, I'm afraid I won't be enough for you."

Her eyes glazed over for a moment, a puzzled expression on her face, then she smiled. At first a small grin, then a full, laughing smile as she pulled him close and hugged him. Her soft body felt so good against his; her kiss was warm, her lips full.

He tried not to sigh.

After a minute she broke the kiss and held him at arm's

The Old Steel-Faced Blues

length. "Damn you, Danny Eaton. How do you always know to say the right thing?"

He shrugged, took her hand, and slipped the ring back on her finger. Cynthia was Cynthia. He'd just have to get used to that. He loved her. From her he could put up with a lot of things. No stupid fear was going to keep him from marrying her.

She again held up her hand and stared longingly at the engagement ring. "I really do love you, you know."

He hugged her close. "And why is that?"

"Because you see me for what I truly am and still love me. Still want to spend the rest of your life with me."

"That's right," he said. "I do." She had no idea exactly how right she was.

Slowly her face melted again, sliding down the front of her dress and forming a pool of facial parts on the rug. He closed his eyes, leaned forward, and kissed her steel-cold lips. He'd get used to it. Or he'd learn to keep his eyes closed to her faults.

A moment later she pulled away, looked at him with cold eyes, and said, "And I can see you for what you are, too, you know. And I still love you."

He chortled and stopped a laugh.

She frowned. "Don't you believe that I really see you? Do you think I'm blind?"

He forced a concerned expression onto his face and looked into her steel-faced eyes. "Sometimes it is better not to see."

She pulled away, glaring at him. "You really don't think I know you. Do you really think I'm stupid enough to marry someone I don't know?"

He shrugged. "I just think it takes more time than we have had to understand another person."

"Well, I don't. And I'll bet you. Go ahead, tell me something about you I don't know."

"This is stupid."

"No, it's not," she said. He could tell she wasn't going to drop this. Maybe now was as good a time as any to clear some things up.

"So you want to bet?" he said, smiling. "Did you know about this?" Slowly his face melted, dripped off his chin, and formed a second puddle on the carpet beside her melted face.

"Yes," she said. "You lose."

"What?"

She pulled him tight against her, closed her eyes, and kissed him hard. The sound of metal scraping against metal filled the house.

It was a sound he would never grow used to.

PASSAGES

Karl Edward Wagner

THERE WERE THE THREE OF THEM SEATED AT ONE OF THE corner tables, somewhat away from the rest of the crowd in the rented banquet room at the Legion Hall. A paper banner painted in red and black school colors welcomed back the Pine Hill High School Class of 1963 to its 25th Class Reunion. A moderately bad local band was playing a medley of hits from the 1960s, and many of the middle-aged alumni were attempting to dance. In an eddy from the amplifiers it was possible to carry on a conversation.

They were Marcia Meadows (she had taken back her maiden name after the divorce), Fred Pruitt (once known as Freddie Pruitt and called so again tonight), and Grant McDade (now addressed as Dr. McDade). The best of friends in high school, each had gone his separate way, and despite yearbook vows to remain the very closest of friends forever, they had been out of touch until this night. Marcia and Grant had been voted Most Intellectual for the senior class. Freddie and one Beth Markeson had been voted Most Likely to Succeed. These three were laughing over their senior photographs in the yearbook. Plastic cups of beer from the party keg were close at hand. Freddie had already drunk more than the other two together.

Marcia sighed and shook her head. They all looked so young back then: pictures of strangers. "So why isn't Beth here tonight?"

"Off somewhere in California, I hear," Freddie said. He was the only one of the three who had remained in Pine Hill. He owned the local Porsche-Audi-BMW dealership. "I think she's supposed to be working in pictures. She always had a good—"

"—body!" Marcia finished for him. The two snorted laughter, and Grant smiled over his beer.

Freddie shook his head and ran his hand over his shiny scalp; other than a fringe of wispy hair, he was as bald as a honeydew melon. A corpulent man—he had once been quite slender—his double chin overhung his loosened tie, and the expensive suit was showing strain. "Wonder how she's held up. None of us look the same as then." Quickly: "Except you, Marcia. Don't you agree, Grant?"

"As beautiful as the day I last saw her." Grant raised a toast, and Marcia hoped she hadn't blushed. After twenty-five years Grant McDade remained in her fantasies. She wished he'd take off those dark glasses—vintage B & L Ray-Bans, just like his vintage white T-shirt and James Dean red nylon jacket and the tight jeans. His high school crew cut was now slicked-back blond hair, and there were lines in his face. Otherwise he was still the boy she'd wanted to have take her to the senior prom. Well, there *was* an indefinable difference. But given the years, and the fact that he was quite famous in his field . . .

"You haven't changed much either, I guess, Grant." Freddie had refilled his beer cup. "I remember that jacket from high school. Guess you heart surgeons know to keep fit."

He flapped a hand across his pink scalp. "But look at me. Bald as that baby's butt. Serves me right for always wanting to have long hair as a kid."

"Weren't you ever a hippie?" Marcia asked.

"Not me. Nam caught up to me first. But I always wanted

to have long hair back when I was a kid—back before the Beatles made it okay to let your hair grow. Remember *Hair* and that song? Well, too late for me by then."

Freddie poured more beer down his throat. Marcia hadn't kept count, but she hoped he wouldn't throw up. From his appearance, Freddie could probably hold it.

"When I was a kid," Freddie said, becoming maudlin, "I hated to get my hair cut. I don't know why. Maybe it was those Sunday school stories about Samson and Delilah that scared me. Grant—you're a doctor; ask your shrink friends. It was those sharp scissors and buzzing clippers, that chair like the dentist had, and that greasy crap they'd smear in your hair. 'Got your ears lowered!' the kids at school would say."

Freddie belched. "Well, my mother used to tease me about it. Said she'd tie a ribbon in my hair and call me Frederika. I was the youngest—two older sisters—and I was always teased that Mom had hoped I'd be a girl, too, to save on buying new clothes—just pass along hand-me-downs. I don't know what I really thought. You remember being a kid in the 1950s: how incredibly naïve we all of us were."

"Tell me!" Marcia said. "I was a freshman in college before I ever saw even a *picture* of a hard-on."

"My oldest sister," Freddie went on, "was having a slumber party one night for some of her sorority sisters. Mom and Dad were out to a church dinner; she was to baby-sit. I was maybe ten at the time. Innocent as a kitten."

Marcia gave him her beer to finish. She wasn't certain whether Freddie could walk as far as the keg.

Freddie shook his head. "Well, I was just a simple little boy in a house full of girls. Middle of the 1950s. I think one of the sorority girls had smuggled in a bottle of vodka. They were very giggly, I remember.

"So they said they'd initiate me into their sorority. They had those great big lollipops that were the fad then, and I wanted one. But I had to join the sorority.

"So they got out some of my sisters' clothes, and they stripped me down. Hadn't been too long before that that my mother or sister would bathe me, so I hadn't a clue. Well, they dressed me up in a trainer bra with tissue padding, pink panties, a pretty slip, lace petticoats, one of my fourteen-year-old sister's party dresses, a little garter belt, hose, and heels. I got the whole works. I was big enough that between my two sisters they could fit me into anything. I thought it was all good fun because they were all laughing—like when I asked why the panties didn't have a Y-front.

"They made up my face and lips and tied a ribbon in my hair, gave me gloves, a handbag, and a little hat. Now I knew why sissy girls took so long to get dressed. When Mom and Dad got home they presented me to them as little Frederika."

"Did you get a whipping?" Marcia asked.

Freddie finished Marcia's beer. "No. My folks thought it was funny as hell. My mom loved it. Dad couldn't stop laughing and got out his camera. This was 1955. They even called the neighbors over for the show. My family never let me live it down.

"Pretty little Frederika! After that I demanded to get a crew cut once a week. So now I'm fat, ugly, and bald."

"Times were different then," Marcia suggested.

"Hell, there's nothing wrong with me! I was a Marine in Nam. I got a wife and three sons." Freddie pointed to where his plump wife was dancing with an old flame. "It didn't make me queer!"

"It only made you bald," said Grant. "Overcompensation. Physical response to emotional trauma."

"You should've been a shrink instead of a surgeon." Freddie lurched off for more beers all around. He had either drunk or spilled half of them by the time he returned. He was too drunk to remember to be embarrassed but would hate his soul-baring in the morning.

Marcia picked up the thread of conversation. "Well, teasing from your siblings won't cause hair loss." She flounced her mass of chestnut curls. "If that were true, then I'd be bald, too."

"Girls don't have hair loss," Freddie said, somewhat mopishly.

"Thank you, but I'm a mature forty-three." Marcia regretted the stiffness in her tone immediately. Freddie might be macho, but he was a balding, unhappy drunk who had once been her unrequited dream date right behind Grant. Forget it: Freddie was about as much in touch with feminists as she was with BMW fuel-injection systems.

Marcia Meadows had aged well, despite a terrible marriage, two maniac teenage sons, and a demanding career in fashion design. She now had her own modest string of boutiques, had recently exhibited to considerable approval at several important shows, and was correctly confident that a few more years would establish her designs on the international scene. She had gained perhaps five pounds since high school and could still wear a miniskirt to flattering effect—as she did tonight with an ensemble of her own creation. She had a marvelous smile, pixie features, and lovely long legs, which she kept crossing, hoping to catch the eye of Grant McDade. This weekend's return to Pine Hill was for her something of an adventure. She wondered what might lie beneath the ashes of old fantasies.

"I had—still have—" Marcia corrected herself, "two older brothers. They were brats. Always teasing me." She sipped her fresh beer. "Still do. Should've been drowned at birth."

Her hands fluttered at her hair in reflex. Marcia had an unruly tangle of tight chestnut-brown curls, totally unmanageable. In the late 1960s it had passed as a fashionable Afro. Marcia had long since given up hope of taming it. After all, miniskirts had come back. Maybe Afros?

"So what did they do?" Freddie prodded.

"Well, they knew I was scared of spiders. I mean, like I *really* am scared of spiders!" Marcia actually shuddered. "I really hate and loathe spiders."

"So. Rubber spiders in the underwear drawer?" Freddie giggled. It was good he had a wife to drive him home.

Marcia ignored him. "We had lots of woods behind our house. I was something of a tomboy. I loved to go romping through the woods. You know how my hair is—has always been."

"Lovely to look at, delightful to hold," said Grant, and behind his dark glasses there might have been a flash of memory.

"But a mess to keep combed," Marcia finished. "Anyway, you know those really gross spiders that build their webs between trees and bushes in the woods? The ones that look like dried-up snot boogers with little legs, and they're always strung out there across the middle of a path?"

"I was a Boy Scout," Freddie remembered.

"Right! So I was always running into those yucky little suckers and getting their webs caught in my hair. Then I'd start screaming and clawing at my face and run back home, and my snotty brothers would laugh like hyenas.

"But here's the worst part." Marcia chugged a long swallow of beer. "You know how you *never* see those goddamn spiders once you've hit their webs? It's like they see you coming, say 'too big to fit into my parlor,' and bail out just before you plow into their yucky webs. Like one second they're there, ugly as a pile of pigeon shit with twenty eyes, and then they vanish into thin air.

"So. My dear big brothers convinced me that the spiders were trapped in my hair. Hiding out in this curly mess and waiting to crawl out for revenge. At night they were sure to creep out and crawl into my ears and eat my brain. Make a web across my nose and smother me. Wriggle beneath my eyelids and suck dry my eyeballs. Slip down my mouth and fill my tummy with spider eggs that would hatch out and eat through my skin. My brothers liked to say that they could see them spinning webs between my curls, just hoping to catch a few flies while they waited for the chance to get me."

Marcia smiled and shivered. It still wasn't easy to think about. "So, of course, I violently combed and brushed my hair as soon as I rushed home, shampooed for an hour—once I scrubbed my scalp with Ajax cleanser—just to be safe. So it's a wonder that I still have my hair."

"And are you still frightened of spiders?" Grant asked.

"Yes. But I wear a hat when I venture into the woods now. Saves wear and tear on the hair."

"A poetess," remarked Freddie. He was approaching the

legless stage, and one of his sons fetched him a fresh beer. "So, Grant. So, *Dr.* McDade, excuse me. We have bared our souls and told you of our secret horrors. What now, if anything, has left its emotional scars upon the good doctor? Anything at all?"

Marcia sensed the angry tension beneath Freddie's growing drunkenness. She looked toward Grant. He had always been master of any event. He could take charge of a class reunion situation. He'd always taken charge.

Grant sighed and rubbed at his forehead. Marcia wished he'd take off those sunglasses so she could get a better feeling of what went on behind those eyes.

"Needles," said Grant.

"Needles?" Freddie laughed, his momentary belligerence forgotten. "But you're a surgeon!"

Grant grimaced and gripped his beer cup in his powerful, long-fingered hands. Marcia could visualize those hands—rubber-gloved and bloodstained—deftly repairing a dying heart.

"I was very young," he said. "We were still living in our old house, and we moved from there before I was five. My memories of that time go back to just as I was learning to walk. The ice cream man still made his rounds in a horse-drawn cart. This was in the late 1940s.

"Like all children, I hated shots. And trips to the doctor, since all doctors did was give children shots. I would put up quite a fuss, despite promises of ice cream afterward. If you've ever seen someone try—or tried yourself—to give a screaming child a shot, you know the difficulty."

Grant drew in his breath, still clutching the beer cup. Marcia hadn't seen him take a sip from it since it had been refilled.

"I don't know why I was getting a shot that day. Kids at that age never understand. Since I did make such a fuss, they tried something different. They'd already swabbed my upper arm with alcohol. Mother was holding me in her lap. The pediatrician was in front of us, talking to me in a soothing tone. The nurse crept up behind me with the hypodermic needle. My mother was supposed to hold me tight. The nurse would give the injection and pull out the needle, quick as a wink, all over and done, and then I could shriek as much as I liked.

"This is, of course, a hell of a way to establish physician-patient trust, but doctors in the 1940s were more pragmatic. If Mother had held my arm tightly, it probably would have worked. However, she didn't have a firm grip. I was a strong child. I jerked my arm away. The needle went all the way through my arm and broke off.

"So I sat in my mother's lap, screaming, a needle protruding from the side of my arm. These were the old days, when needles and syringes were sterilized and used over and again. The needle that protruded from my arm seemed to me as large as a ten-penny nail. The nurse stood helplessly. Mother screamed. The doctor moved swiftly and grasped the protruding point with forceps, pulling the needle on through.

"After that I was given a tetanus shot."

Marcia rubbed goose pimples from her arms. "After that you must have been a handful."

Grant finally sipped at his beer. "I'd hide under beds. Run away. They kept doctor appointments secret after a while. I never knew whether a supposed trip to the grocery store might really be a typhoid shot or a polio shot."

"But you got over it when you grew up?" Freddie urged.

"When I was sixteen or so," Grant said, "I cut my foot on a shell at the beach. My folks insisted that I have a tetanus shot. I flew into a panic, bawling, kicking, disgracing myself in front of everyone. But they still made me get the shot. I wonder if my parents ever knew how much I hated them."

"But surely," said Marcia, "it was for your own good."

"How can someone *else* decide what is *your* own good?"

Grant decided his beer was awful and set it aside. He drank only rarely, but tonight seemed to be a night for confessions. "So," he said. "The old identification with the aggressor story, I suppose. I became a physician."

Freddie removed his tie and shoved it into a pocket. He offered them cigarettes, managed to light one for himself. "So how'd you ever manage to give anybody a shot?"

Passages

"Learning to draw blood was very difficult for me. We were supposed to practice on each other one day, but I cut that lab. I went to the beach for a day or two, told them I'd had a family emergency."

Marcia waved away Freddie's cigarette smoke. She remembered Grant as the class clown, his blue eyes always bright with ready laughter. She cringed as he remembered.

Grant continued. "Third-year med students were expected to draw blood from the patients. They could have used experienced staff, but this was part of our initiation ritual. Hazing for us, hell for the patients.

"So I go in to draw blood. First time. I tie off this woman's arm with a rubber hose, pat the old antecubital fossa looking for a vein, jab away with the needle, still searching, feel the pop as I hit the vein, out comes the bright red into the syringe, I pull out the needle—and blood goes everywhere because I hadn't released the tourniquet. 'Oops!' I say as the patient in the next bed watches in horror; she's next in line.

"Well, after a few dozen tries at this I got better at it—but the tasks got worse. There were the private patients as opposed to those on the wards; often VIPs, with spouses and family scowling down at you as you try to pop the vein first try.

"Then there's the wonderful arterial stick, for when you need blood gases. You use this great thick needle, and you feel around the inside of the thigh for a femoral pulse, then you jab the thing in like an ice pick. An artery makes a crunch when you strike it, and you just hope you've pierced through and not gouged along its thick muscular wall. No need for a tourniquet; the artery is under pressure, and the blood pulses straight into the syringe. You run with it to the lab, and your assistant stays there maybe ten minutes forcing pressure against the site so the artery doesn't squirt blood all through the surrounding tissue."

Freddie looked ready to throw up.

"Worst thing, though, were the kids. We had a lot of leukemia patients on the pediatric ward. They'd lie there in bed, emaciated, bald from chemotherapy, waiting to die. By end stage their veins had had a hundred IVs stuck into them, a thousand blood samples taken. Their arms were so thin—nothing but bones and pale skin—you'd think it would be easy to find a vein. But their veins were all used up, just as their lives were. I'd try and try to find a vein, to get a butterfly in so their IVs could run—for whatever good that did. They'd start crying as soon as they saw a white jacket walk into their room. Toward the end they couldn't cry, just mewed like dying kittens. Two of them died one night when I was on call, and for the last time in my life I sent a prayer of thanks to God."

Grant picked up his beer, scowled at it, set it back down. Marcia was watching him with real concern.

"Hey, drink up," Freddie offered. It was the best thing he could think of to suggest.

Grant took a last swallow. "Well, that was the end of the sixties. I tuned in, turned on, dropped out. Spent a year in Haight-Ashbury doing the hippie trip, trying to get my act together. Did lots of drugs out there, but never any needle work. My friends knew that I was almost a doctor, and some of them would get me to shoot them up when they were too stoned to find a vein. I learned a lot from addicts: How to bring up a vein from a disaster zone. How to use the leading edge of a beveled needle to pierce the skin, then roll it one-eighty when you've popped the vein. But I never shoved anything myself. I hate needles. Hell, I wouldn't even sell blood when I was stone broke."

"But you went back," Marcia prompted. She reached out for his hand and held it. She remembered that they were staying in the same hotel. . . .

"Summer of Love turned into Winter of Junkies. Death on the streets. Went back to finish med school. The time away was therapeutic. I applied myself, as they used to say. So now I do heart transplants."

"A heart surgeon who's scared of needles!" Freddie chuckled. "So do you close your eyes when the nurses jab 'em in?" He spilled beer down his shirt, then looked confused by the wetness.

"How *did* you manage to conquer your fear of needles?" Marcia asked, holding his hand in both of hers.

Passages

"Oh," said Grant. He handed Freddie the rest of his beer. "I learned that in medical school after I went back. It only took time for the lesson to sink in. After that, it was easy to slide a scalpel through living flesh, to crack open a chest. It's the most important part of learning to be a doctor."

Grant McDade removed his dark glasses and gazed earnestly into Marcia's eyes.

"You see, you have to learn that no matter what you're doing to another person, it doesn't hurt *you.*"

The blue eyes that had once laughed were as dead and dispassionate as a shark's eyes as it begins its tearing roll.

Marcia let go of Grant's hand and excused herself.

She never saw him after that night, but she forever mourned his ghost.

BIRD ON A LEDGE

Nancy Holder

OUT OF THE CAGE:

Snow fell on the ledge and made it slippery. It was six inches wide and made of old, crumbling brick. It hadn't been cleaned in years, and it was nubby and contoured with pigeon droppings.

But the snow rained onto it like goose down, like the purest of dove feathers, and hid the ugliness. Down it came, white and clean; and Amalia was sorry to step on it. She was sorry she was up here at all, in her billowing white pajamas and scuffy slippers. But it was the obvious choice; you had to learn to fly at some point, didn't you?

Didn't you?

She scarcely hesitated as she opened the window. The wooden frame scraped old paint. She crawled backward through the window, snow and wind chilling her ass. The reality of the weather shook her hard, like a frightened, angry parent. Ignoring it, she pulled herself up by the outside crossbar and stood, panting, with her face against the frozen glass.

The wet snow seeped through the holes in the soles of her

slippers. Without thinking she lifted her left foot up, murmuring, "Ay." Then she realized it didn't matter much, did it? It really didn't.

When you are little you dream so many things. Dancing on a stage, directing traffic, living in a big house filled with gleaming tables and sofas dressed in silk. You dream of riches and babies. You dream of one special man.

You dream.

But no snow rains down on you.

She tried to catch her breath. The horns and din of the traffic below echoed as if from a bottomless pit; it was snowing so hard that the noises were muffled. No one would be likely to see her in her swan clothes of white. But her skin was dark, and her hair was black—that much they might see. That much they had always seen.

Amalia didn't know how to turn around. Should she just let go now and tumble backward? She took deep, hard breaths as she considered. It seemed cowardly, somehow, not to face it. Not to openly acknowledge what she was going to do. One giant leap for womankind. She smiled grimly.

Then she cried out as a swarm of pigeons flocked and landed on the ledge. Their guano stank; their wings brushed her ankles. She wanted to scream. But if she did that, if she freed herself too much, she might do what she wasn't yet ready to do.

One of the birds flapped its wings, taking flight and soaring across the back of her head. Nausea ripped through her; she was going to vomit; she flailed at it once, then clung to the window, for if she touched it, if she so much as batted her little finger against one of its wings . . .

Evil, they were evil. She shuddered hard. Why had she done this to herself? Surely she had known there would be birds. Yes, of course she had. That was why. The final punishment. The last humiliation.

She held fast to the window and tried to listen to the traffic. There had been no pigeons when she'd opened the window. Of course not. Now that she was dreaming the last dream they had come to peck at it, fly off with it.

* * *

When she was a baby, barely walking, the cousins had come, for some reason, and the aunts and grandmothers. And Papa's eyes were red and swollen. Everyone so sad. On the wall her mother's paintings of the little bird sellers in Mexico, a boy and a girl, in yellow and blue and purple. Big-eyed and sad. Dark, with doves and parrots in cages they carried on their backs, held in place by thongs across their foreheads. Enormous burdens. Mamacita had started drinking because the medicine she had to take made her hands shake, and she hadn't wanted to frighten her children.

Their two yellow parakeets were sick. Their bottoms were coated over with infection, and they couldn't poop. The bird doctor had said that they would probably die.

Amalia sat in her black dress, staring at them, utterly fascinated. They moved like cartoons, jerky and unnatural; and as she watched, her uncle, her Tio Pablo, came up behind her and put his hand on her bottom.

"So beautiful," he whispered, and she knew he was talking about the birds.

"They're going to die," Amalia whispered back.

"Everything dies in this house." He drew her onto his lap, and she cried. Her mother, ah, she remembered now. Her mother was dead. Her body was lying in the front room in a box.

One of the birds made a tiny peep and fell off its perch. Amalia screamed and screamed and screamed.

And Tio Pablo laughed, slow and deep in his throat.

Now, on the ledge, the gray birds huddled close to Amalia, and she wondered if she kicked at them, would they be stunned and fall? Or would they catch their balance and soar away to safety? The snow fell so hard; didn't their wings grow icy, like those of planes and jets? Did they crash-land? She shut her eyes against images of pigeons twisted and bleeding, their guts strewn across the snow, pulsing bits of lungs and hearts. The eggs, caviar for the dead.

Bile rose in her throat. She licked her lips and shook her right foot carefully. The merest brush of a feather sent shock waves through her. God, get them away!

Bird on a Ledge

Steve Dahlton had had a pigeon coop. She couldn't remember what miracle had led her to his house, nor how he had come to show her his birds, to actually speak to her at all. He was blond and muscular, and when they were older he would surely play football and date cheerleaders. He lived in a huge brick house, and his father did something very important; and he never wore the same thing twice.

Steve's pet pigeons fluffed their breasts and cooed. He had rows and rows of them. She was afraid of them; there were so many, and they were his. The sounds they uttered were like sighs, promises.

"Hold this one," he told her, unaware of her terror. A large dark bird plumped between his hands as he gathered it up. It cooed and jerked its small head to the right, to the front.

"Oh," Amalia murmured. Her throat lumped, but she took a breath and held out her hands for the bird. Steve's fingers ran over hers, and she wished desperately that he wouldn't let go.

The bird was much heavier than she had expected. The feathers much smoother. The claws scratched daintily at her, and a thrill of fright rose inside her. It was alive. Blood pulsed through it, and it had a heart that beat. It could die. She could kill it.

But she could never kill anything that belonged to Steve.

She had turned away at one point because he didn't know how much all this meant to her. To be here, to hold these supernaturally living things; to have him speak to her kindly, one kid to another, maybe even one boy to one girl.

She had only been mildly hurt when his mother had poked her head inside the coop and said, "Steve, do you want to invite your friend to dinner?" and he had asked, "Who?" Because she understood he wasn't used to thinking of her as a friend.

Amazing that he *had* asked, though. A maid had served Amalia, a strange expression on her face: Why are you sitting there and not helping me? And *Brava, chica!* that you *are* sitting there. Amalia had been confused by all the silverware, but she watched Steve and did as he did. They ate chicken, pulling the flesh off the bones with knives and forks, not holding the pieces in their hands as they did in Amalia's home. She thought of the pigeons outside, and she was revolted by the piles of bones on the table. Saint Francis loved the birds and animals; she vowed she would be like him and become a vegetarian.

Steve had leaned sideways with a leg bone in his hand; a little white dog had leapt at it—

"Steven, no!" his father had said, in a deep voice like Tío Pablo's. "Bosworth will choke on that!"

"Will not," Steve murmured under his breath. He put the leg back on his plate. Later, as Amalia was leaving, she saw the dog in the yard, the bone between its front paws. She worried about it all the way home.

The next day she walked to school in her best skirt, just a little patched, and brightened as the yellow school bus passed. Steve and his friends hung from the windows. She raised a hand—

"Wetback!" one of them called.

And Steve did, too. "Wetback!" he shouted. He shook his fists at her and laughed. "Wetback!"

There was no embarrassment on his face, no sense that he was giving in to the prodding of his friends. It was as if he had never seen her before.

She stood still as the tears welled and prayed to the Virgin Mary that his dog had choked to death on that chicken bone. And that the pigeons got sick and couldn't poop—

—and maybe even she herself would die—

—then she had doubled over because deep inside her, in her private places, pain roiled and streamed through her; it had something to do with death, and something else with loss and betrayal, and a lot to do with rage.

Her father hadn't even noticed that she had stayed home from school, and it wasn't until the truant officer called that she went back.

Steve Dahlton didn't notice either.

And later he *did* become a football player.

Now she stood on the ledge, and somewhere in this house

the walls were filled with her paintings of birds. Amalia the artist, imagine that. Parrots, doves, pigeons, and peacocks.

Ravens. Hawks. Vultures.

Her foot slipped from under her. She gasped and clung to the wooden crossbeam. The traffic noises geysered up, louder and more insistent. Sweat poured down her face, freezing instantly. She began to hyperventilate.

How could you live when you were so afraid of something so insubstantial?

It was the baby bird that had sent her here. She shut her eyes, trying not to see the memory of it. She had been standing in the den, watching the snow, and spied it, hopping in the slush by the hedge, peep-peep, a beautiful spring-sky blue. A tiny yellow beak and beady, miniature eyes that stared straight out from its head. Its leg was broken; it held it up like a stork, tried to hop, fell over.

And then a yellow cat broke through the hedge, shaking the snow from the small hunter-green leaves. It walked slowly, languidly, no need to hurry, was there? That helpless baby bird was going nowhere.

The bird began to peep in a paroxysm of terror. The cat sat before it, tilted its head.

Amalia beat on the window. "Shoo! Go away! Go!" she shouted, in English and Spanish. *"Vete!"*

The cat hunkered down on all fours. The muscles beneath its fur shifted like water in plastic grocery sacks. Its chest and paws were white, pure white.

"Go!" She tried to open the window. It was stuck. She pounded harder. "Shhhst! Bad cat!"

The bird screeched. The cat watched it.

She should go outside. She should run and pick it up—
—*pick it up*—

But she couldn't. The mere thought made her dizzy. She held her stomach to hold her heart inside her body. To touch it; to make contact with that bird—

She could bring the cat inside. Or kill it.

Kill it.

Amalia burst into tears. Why did that seem the most

313

reasonable course of action? She had held Steve's birds, so many years ago. Why couldn't she touch the little baby now? What had happened in the intervening years?

Why were her paintings of dead birds, bleeding, pecked by other birds or shot by hunters?

The cat advanced on the baby—

She couldn't bear it. She couldn't stand the fear inside herself, so impossible, so ridiculous, so—

—the ledge. But first:

—the place. The aviary, where all broken birds were healed; where their wings were sewn back on, and all their shit could flow out freely.

But something had happened. Yes. And now, God bless the ledge. Here she would spread wide her arms and soar, and finally she would become birdlike and understand; transcend—

"Good God, Janet! Stay where you are!"

She almost let go then. She wanted to, but her hands were so frozen she couldn't move them fast enough.

The man grabbed her around the waist. Her head fell backward; her back arched; her feet slipped off the snowy mounds of droppings. But it didn't matter; he had her, and he dragged her through the window and into the room. The other woman was there; she held Amalia's arms as she struggled to free herself.

"Janet! What were you doing? How did you get out?" the man said. He raised his hand but didn't strike her.

"Janet," he said again.

She thought of the baby bird. Surely the cat had gotten it by now. Her fault. Coward. Longingly she looked over her shoulder at the ledge.

"My name is Amalia," she told him.

The man traded looks with the other woman. Amalia slumped, suddenly exhausted, and the man nodded to someone across the room.

Another man came forward. He was carrying a large white jacket, a huge, flapping thing like an albatross—

She shrieked. "Don't make me do that!" She flailed her arms, her legs, her torso. But the woman held one arm, the

314

Bird on a Ledge

man who had dragged her back into the room, the other. They pulled her between them—make a wish—and the second man jammed a sleeve over her hand, slid it up her body.

. As they wrapped the sleeves around her and tied them in back she thought of the baby bird. She saw the cat with feathers protruding from its sated pink lips. Blood on its nose.

"Janet, we're going to have to—"

"My name is Amalia," she repeated firmly. She trembled. Three cats, and she was wounded.

Perhaps the little bird had hopped into the cat's mouth, just to get it over with.

"What happened?" the man asked her. "Why did you do this?"

"The cat was coming. The cat," she said, trying to make them understand.

The man said, "There are no cats here."

They walked her down the hall. They led her into the darkened room.

In the corner she saw the cage, and remembered, and began to scream as loudly as she could. Someone would come, someone who was not afraid; someone who had the courage to touch birds. Someone, please, someone—

They strapped her into the chair. The man said, "I don't think we need to shave her. Her hair has barely grown."

The woman and the other man crossed to the wire cage and hefted it between them. A dozen yellow birds hopped and peeped inside it.

"What is your name?" the first man asked her.

Tears streamed down her face. "Amalia."

He sighed. "You know we're doing this to help you. You know what you were like when you came here."

She wept on. She had no memory of having come here. They said this was a hospital. Sanctuary, at last, from the advancing tigers. But *they* had told her her name was Janet. Hadn't they?

"You *do* know. You *do* remember."

Which was better, to tell the truth or to lie?

315

"What is your name?" he asked again.

She paused. "I—I—" It was a trick. They knew she was Amalia. That she was a painter. They only wanted to see if she would break.

The man looked at the other two. Nodded.

She clenched her jaw and fists. They lifted the cage over her head, removed the round seal from the floor, and positioned the exposed hole in the bottom over her head. It bit into the skin on her forehead and scalp, scraping at the scars and flesh that had just begun to heal.

She heard the flutter of wings, a peep.

And then, oh, God, as it flew down and landed on her head—

Through the shrieking she heard the woman ask, "How long, Doctor?"

"This time a few hours, I think."

They left the room.

Shrieking, struggling.

Another bird landed.

Another.

Amalia. Amalia. Amalia.

They pecked at her head, which was shaved every day; they pecked and pulled the flesh from her skull. Their sharp needle-nosed beaks rammed through the flaps and the sores, rooting for the worms of her thoughts, her supposed delusions.

The cage, and the jacket and the room and the questions.

They pecked and bit and chewed. After a time she stopped struggling and weeping; she felt each claw tapping on her head, kneading the barriers. Each beak rooting away more, more, more.

Mea culpa, all of it, my grievous fault, but I am Amalia, I am—

The baby, consumed by now; the cat had swallowed the canary. Her fault, her fault, her grievous fault.

Everything that had ever happened (peck, peck, peck) her fault.

Then they gathered in a flock and began to bite at the center of her head, digging for the worst meat, the worst

memories; out spewed her brains, the thoughts flying away
as the birds tried to catch them, snap! snap! Fluttering after
them, slamming themselves against the cage as Amalia's
thoughts escaped through the bars. In their frustration, the
birds digging deeper, finding new, uninjured places between
all the sores, until it hurt so badly that she couldn't take it
anymore; she just wanted to jump.

Free herself, free! She gripped the ends of the chair, and
then, with a gasp, she sailed from the ledge.

Through the snow and the fog she hurtled herself with her
arms spread wide, a perfect swan dive—was this a terror
birds felt, trusting themselves to fly? Did they live in horror
that their wings would betray them, and they would be
smashed into pulp?

Down she tumbled, heading for the pit as the noise and
the shouts shot up to meet her.

"Amalia," she whispered.

And she landed on a heap of bodies of birds, broken,
bleeding, that cushioned her fall. And lying there, wondering, she touched the wings and hearts of her feathered
saviors, covered with snow. In the distance the cooing of
pigeons, the screech of a raven.

They were not so bad. They weren't bad at all.

The pain in her head throbbed; it was the snow raining
down upon her, so hard and cold, so unending, so infinite.

—Perhaps her name *was* Janet, and she was here because,
because—

Because maybe she had never been a little girl, nor
dreamed. Maybe all that had been the worms, going in,
going out, for the little yellow birds to find.

Maybe she had been born with a cage upon her head, a
bird vendor selling dreams; oh, Tio Pablo!

"Tio Pablo," she whispered, growing distressed. Tio
Pablo and his hands, and death.

Her mother . . .

But if she were not Amalia, had she had a Tio Pablo?

And if not, was there any reason to fear the birds? They
were only clearing a way for the eggs to hatch.

For more to hatch. Happy thoughts. Silver birds.

Oh, thank you, Doctor, so wise, so good. Not a bad man, not crazy himself, as she had once believed.

Back inside the cage: Blood streamed from her head and into her eyes, dripping across her lips so that she tasted what life was like. The snow rained down very hard, gouging holes in her skull, thrusting snowballs into her brain.

Yet fear melted from her. It was all right now. All right, wherever she was from, whoever she might be. She might have been evil, a murderess, mea culpa.

Tio Pablo.

A killer of birds. But she was free now, free as a bird. The past, whatever it was—

—A memory fluttered within her, of her paintings of decapitated vultures, ravens with their eyes pecked out. The pretty pictures of the bird children her mother had so loved—

Fiercely she shook her head.

With half-closed eyes she looked at the broken bodies all around her and whispered, "Sail on, sweet dreams, sweet silver birds, take flight and soar."

Far from the madding place, and the cages, and the cats.

MATTERS OF SUBSTANCE

Robert Sampson

At the Hanneckers' party Ed Carleson had two or three drinks. Or perhaps a few more, for he saw his wife, Helen, glance toward him with all expression smoothed from her long face, her eyes slightly widened, the familiar signal of warning and reproach. He retreated to an upstairs bedroom that contained a colossal bathroom self-conscious in egg-yolk yellow and white. The air smelled deliciously of lemon. The room, Edward thought as he washed his hands, was entirely too decorative for the performance of the less mentionable human functions.

At that moment he noticed that the bedroom door had somehow drifted shut. The lining of his throat hardened. Dropping a yellow-striped towel, he hurried from the sink across a prairie of pale-blue bedroom carpet. Already it was too late. As he reached for the doorknob his body recoiled. He found himself across the room, heart pounding, his thoughts incoherent. The door radiated menace. Not the door itself, but the intensity of waiting concealed behind it, an immense pressure concentrated upon him. Its presence was palpable as fire. Around him the air thickened with imminent disaster. This time, he realized, he would not escape. So many times before he had dodged catastrophe by luck, by accident. But not this time.

Remote behind this churn of fear, a mental voice from some calmer time remarked that if he opened the door, he would see nothing. A well-lit hallway. A cream-colored wall fussy with mounted photographs of the Hanneckers, in all their generations, cheerfully hailing yesterday's cameras. Nothing else.

But he could not open the door. He could not concentrate the moral courage to approach the door. A revolting ball of whiskey soured his stomach. He remained trapped in the bedroom, dry-mouthed and staring, until the doorknob unexpectedly clicked. Helen's faintly fretted face peered into the room.

"You've been so long."

"I was just coming."

Once the door opened, the menace evaporated. As always. He walked, faintly shaking, into the coolness of the hallway. From below came the sounds of voices and music. He felt the desperate lightness of escape. The door beneath his fingers was a door only, not a permeable screen for fear.

How these fears had come to him, he could not remember. More than anything, he thought, they resembled a cancer of the emotions, growing silently until the first lethal spot of blood presented itself. The door of their first house, small and dove-gray on Saxton Avenue, had been a solid wooden slab pierced high up by a lean glass crescent. He had lifted Helen across the threshold traditionally enough, his new bride laughing as he carried her inward to her changed life.

Light from the window above the door struck a bright crescent across her forehead. Clasping his neck, she said, "I don't intend to let you slide away, Mr. Carleson."

Looking down into her face, he was ridiculously touched. "Say it three times, I'll believe you," he told her.

Arms engaged, he pushed the door shut with his foot. No fears then. Not of doors.

Over the years they had had three daughters, two of them now married. They moved to a larger house built of pale red brick. The yard was too large and spattered by dandelions. At the rear the lot tilted to pines thick among gray chunks of limestone. Helen spoke distractedly of snakes, and he constructed a high wooden fence through which the boulders loomed dimly, like shapes glowering from a mist. He experienced no difficulty with doors. Like his death, that problem lay in an unrealized future.

The fence stood for years, its gray boards slowly fading to warm silver. Finally a February storm flung down a pine that scattered limbs and fifteen feet of fence across the sodden yard. Edward borrowed a chain saw, whose violence frightened him, and sliced the tree apart. The fence took longer to repair.

Things broke, he thought. Things wore out. The fence, like windowsills and family automobiles, required constant maintenance. He had squandered his most productive hours fighting the inevitable erosion of things.

He piled the logs for later burning. Somewhere he had read that marriage killed love. Supposedly it substituted bonding and personal regard, and perhaps that was correct. Regret grayed the edges of his thought. Marriage, like other substantial things, also demanded regular maintenance. Even marriage eroded. What a distance he had traveled with Helen since those days of bright affection when every emotion seemed a warm new toy to be shared and whispered over.

The pine logs, when burned, coated the interior of the chimney with tar that had to be expensively removed. Every action had an unforeseen consequence, often painful, invariably costly.

One evening he stood in the living room of the brick house, listening to the thin voice on the telephone that was the least impressive part of Dr. Harrison B. Wiston, director of BBW Engineering Labs. Wiston was a diffident man of high technical accomplishment. In the director's office Edward held the ambiguous title of chief executive assistant and applied himself to that glassy flow of management

reviews and staff papers that are widely believed to determine the course of engineering projects. Dr. Wiston was
inclined to defer decisions and required extensive and
repetitive briefings. Annoying as that habit was, Edward
regarded him with more than usual admiration and respect.

"Yes," he said into the telephone. "Yes, sir, Dr. Wiston.
Yes, sir. I can do that, sir."

Looking up, he saw Helen staring fixedly at him, her eyes
lucid with disbelief and embarrassment. Immediately he
understood that she thought him fawning. His mind turned
like a key in a lock. He heard the shocking tones of his own
voice. That unctuous self-betrayal stunned and confused
him. He averted his face from Helen's eyes. But it was less
easy to excuse himself to himself.

He hung up the phone and did whatever he had told Dr.
Wiston he would do, sir. The incident remained in his
memory as a tiny ulcer, never healed. For that humiliating
telephone call coincided, in some way he did not understand, with the shifting of his marriage to a less happy level.

Their oldest daughter moved to Houston with her new
husband. After that time it seemed to him that Helen drew
around herself a kind of self-contained remoteness, as if
conducting her life from a nearby hill. Some benign structure between them had shattered. He sensed that she saw
him as diminished. It seemed capricious. He could not
understand. He could find no way to reestablish that easy
intimacy when they shared nothing but each other.

She took a part-time job in an art glass shop and hung
their front windows with vivid parrots and flowers sparkling
along metal stems. Voice grown authoritative, she spoke of
foiling, lead cam, grozing pliers. Across the gulf he stood
mute, listening.

In October Edward's father died. Walter Lewis Carleson
had spent his adult years as a consulting petroleum engineer. The streets of the Near East and Mexico were more
familiar to him than the rooms of his own home. To Edward
his father seemed unapproachably foreign. Years of sun in
distant places had evaporated his American habits. His
habitual gestures, the sudden outward fling of his hands, the

unexpected tilt of his heat-dried face in conversation, established him as an outsider from volatile lands. A dry odor accompanied him, like the smell of hot sand. His eyes, narrowed by intense sunlight, were merciless.

He retired to an elderly house in Huntsville, Alabama. Perhaps his chilled eyes drew the life from Edward's mother. In less than a year she died. Two years later, amid southern humidity and the artifacts of the space age, Walter Carleson also died. In the desert he might have endured another fifty years. Alabama softened and destroyed him. He had managed to outlive all relatives and most friends.

"He spent his whole life away," Edward said. "When he came home it was like a visit from a family friend."

"Hard on your mother," Helen said, selecting her words with care. She had not liked Edward's mother, who embraced her with soft cries of affection and afterward discussed her failings with the neighbors, voice regretful.

"It made her possessive," Edward said. "She was always after me. Be careful. Watch out. Don't do whatever."

Helen's hand executed a gesture of mild annoyance. "That's mothering."

He said, "Till I was a teenager I was afraid to go outside without a hat."

"Well, that explains a lot," she said.

The night after the funeral they slept in his father's house. Next morning they composed lists of things to do and exchanged telephone calls with the lawyer, whose air of relaxed competence annoyed Edward and caused him to mispronounce simple words.

Thrusting away the telephone, he walked heavily into the front room. There his youngest daughter, Joyce, squatted before packed bookshelves, dubiously inspecting the spines.

"Find anything?"

"Just technical junk. Boring."

"I imagine your grandfather paid fifty dollars apiece for those books."

"Still boring."

She tugged languidly at a wedged volume, a narrow girl, all legs and tumbled pale hair, with her mother's long face and an air of dissatisfied competence. He left her bumping books into a box and wandered glumly upstairs.

In a severely neat bedroom, smelling dryly of his father's presence, Helen arranged clothing from a dresser into systematic piles.

"We might as well give it all to Goodwill," he said.

"It seems such a waste. It's all perfectly good."

"You know," he said, "I haven't been in this room for years. Mother kept it closed when Dad was gone. When he was here he shut the door."

"That's your family. Hearts on their sleeve. Why don't you see what's in the closet?"

Edward approached his father's closet. Across the door stretched a relief map of the Mexican Gulf Coast. Examining it, he became aware of a dull discomfort in his chest, an acceleration of the heart, as if he had brushed a weakly charged wire.

He said, scowling at the map, "I really don't like this room much."

"Well, now, my dear," she said briskly, "when it comes down to that, you don't like anything much."

He barely heard her words, his mind intent on the past. "I came running up here one time. Dad'd just come home. I'd found a snake skin I wanted to show him. Pushed the door open, and there he stood absolutely stark naked. Didn't he shuffle me out in a hurry."

"Did he look at the snake skin?" she asked, quietly disapproving.

"I never showed it to him." Not that the incident had happened quite that way.

"That was mean."

Edward looked distastefully at the map of Mexican beaches. He felt strongly disinclined to open the closet.

"Well, what did he know about being a parent? Spent most of his life in Saudi Arabia." His temples ached. Speaking of his father made him edgy. "One time I snuck a tomato out of the garden next door. He got me by the belt and hauled me back over there to apologize. He said if I did that in Iran, they'd cut off my hand. They're a cruel people."

"That's a really hateful story, Ed."

"I didn't steal tomatoes again," he said, and he violently jerked open the closet door. Rows of white shirts faced him. Neatly shined shoes lined the closet floor. The smell of the old man's body surrounded him. He would not have been surprised to see his father staring from behind the shirts, his hollow face mercilessly disapproving. A melancholy, transient grief passed through his chest. He pulled down shirts and carried them to the bed.

"Don't put them there," Helen said.

He stared down at the neatly arranged clothing on the bed, thinking with sudden anger that he should throw it on the floor. Then he should put both arms around her. However, he did not. She did not like being touched while working.

For months afterward he exhausted himself clearing up his father's estate. It was no simple process. The smallest action generated a maze of complexities. By some disquieting analogue, the fears that had troubled him in his father's room now returned, like puppies become snarling dogs. They raddled his thoughts. They darkened and branched in fantastic patterns, and one day he found in himself a powerful resistance to opening doors. That innocuous act created apprehension so virulent he was left dry-mouthed and shaking.

It was absurd. More than absurd. It was sick.

With an effort he snatched open the utility room door to frown at the water heater. It stood placidly, muffled in a thick white wrapping to reduce heat loss. His heart jarred. Brooms and dust mops angled against the wall. Nothing else. Of course, nothing else.

He closed the door and flattened his hands against the paneling. Through the frail protection of the wood he seemed to sense vague disturbance, as if something shaped itself from the dark. His body, briefly uncontrollable, recoiled. From a thing that existed only in his head. This sick thing. This foolishness about doors.

Not every door. Not really. Not doors with glass or doors with screen, or partly open doors, or doors he had no intention of using. Precisely otherwise. Those doors he must use, closed doors solidly protecting his shirts or shoes or water heater—those profoundly upset him. As if opening them would free that predatory thing, substantial and overwhelming.

These feelings deeply embarrassed him. They recalled childhood nights when tainted darkness lay under his bed, and he knew positively that if his hand slipped from the protection of the covers, something would bite.

Now the same fears rose again, untouched by daylight. Facing the closed door, he felt his body shake.

"What is it?" Helen asked. "Are you getting sick?"

"No, no. I'm fine."

"These things *do* have to go to the back room."

He loaded his arms with boxes. Said with guile, "Get that door for me, will you?"

She said, exasperated, "You are so strange, Edward."

At the BBW Engineering Laboratories Dr. Wiston retired, lauded and feasted. His replacement, Dr. Boyle Fitzharris, a younger man with a vaguely sinister look, spoke meaningfully of reducing layers of staff fat and slouched blank-faced in his chair during Edward's presentations.

It was a clear warning. Change grumbled in his future. He scheduled lunches with friends in aerospace contracting. While eating he praised BBW's management and the company's luminous opportunities, acknowledging nevertheless that a more challenging position might well engage his interest. The circuitous protocol of these negotiations required that he show no spark of need. At night, sitting crumpled on the bed, he stared forward into black time, where all opportunities had withered.

By some hateful natural rule, one problem gestates another. He discovered that Helen felt compelled to close all open doors. On bad days he had to face a shameful struggle before ripping open his closet, tasting fear, feeling his body cringe. On really bad days he could not even approach the door.

He could think of no simple way to ask her to leave doors open. Not without exposing his contemptible weakness. Shame silenced him. Just as shame of his vulnerability at work silenced him. He could not force himself to tell her that, either.

How could he possibly expose the enormity of his failure to secure their future?

Already she faced problems enough with Joyce, who had chosen this time to uproot herself and go live with Kemmie Harron. He was years older, and his truculent confidence was not supported by the age of his truck or his work in the less skilled fringes of construction.

"Kemmie looks so nasty," Helen said. "A man that age. Without any education. I thought we raised her better."

"I think it'll work out."

"Men always think it's going to work out," Helen said.

Nearly six weeks later he drove to Joyce's apartment, following a threadlike road that wound back among trailers. Finally the road widened to a street of small houses, front lawns strewn with plastic toys.

He parked and walked toward a low gray building, its windows studded with air conditioners. From the landfill, half a mile away, came a faintly sour smell. Joyce, in apartment B, gestured him in. Her body conveyed the undesirability of physical contact.

"Kemmie's still at work," she said. "I just got in. I'm on half days at Mega-Mart. I'm their outside plant girl."

Grime showed under her unpolished nails. The living room, narrow and hot, smelled of used furniture. Blue ties restrained cheerfully flowered curtains. On the television lay a pair of magazines, edges carefully squared, and one of his father's engineering books, its formal binding clashing with the worn furnishings.

He said bluntly, "Look, we still love you. We haven't forgotten you or anything."

"I'm all right," she said, sharp-voiced. "What'd you think? I was starvin' to death or something? We're doing fine. Kemmie's fine."

"Listen," he said, "we worry about you."

"Well, don't," she said. "You don't need to worry about me. We're doing fine."

This information he relayed to Helen, who considered it

with sardonic eyes. A half glass of wine sat on the table beside her.

"She'd like to come home and doesn't know how," Helen said. "That's what that means."

She tasted the wine, eyes remote, as if no longer thinking of Joyce. Increasingly Helen seemed to be living in a distant place. She seemed no longer quite aware of his presence. Having become manager of the glass shop through a series of labyrinthian upheavals, she now spoke confidently of quarterly tax payments and contracts for stained glass windows. Two or three nights a week she visited friends in the south of town. Often she came in after he had gone to bed. But not to sleep. As she flung back the covers he smelled the sharp odor of whiskey.

"It's late," he said.

"Oh, God," she said, rolling away from him and pulling the sheet tight across her shoulder, "we get to gossiping like a bunch of old women, and pretty soon there you are."

The falsity of her explanations terrified him. Things deteriorate, he thought. Things crumble, and there's no repairing them. He allowed himself to accept her absences as he accepted his torment before doors. It was shameful. He could not bear to face what he must face. All day he lived with the knowledge that he was a coward and a fool and was certainly going crazy.

The doctor scrawled a prescription to help him sleep. "You all right otherwise?"

"Perfectly fine. Yes."

How could he tell the doctor that craziness occupied great pieces of his life? That he could no longer force himself to open a paneled door? There was nothing he could do. Or anyone else. Nothing whatever.

Late one afternoon as he revised a manpower graph he was called to the director's office. Fear slashed through him, gouging a frigid abyss behind his heart. As yet he had received no formal job offers. In the director's suite an exquisitely polished secretary led him into a beige room filled with wood and leather. His mind, quite still and clear, observed papers heaped by the computer, the massive

African violet in the north window, the shadows angled across the untidy bookcase. Dr. Fitzharris, more affable than usual, shook his hand and offered him the management of the BBW Resources Office. The raise was modest; the increase of authority, substantial. He returned home faintly dazed by the collapse of his fears.

"That's so nice," Helen said. "That's such good news."

"It's one of the key jobs," he told her, gingerly testing the extent of his elation. "The last two people who had the job are senior executives now."

"I'm so glad for you," she said.

When he returned home the next day she was gone.

On the kitchen table lay a typewritten note. This required endless rereadings, the sense melting from his mind each time he neared the bottom of the page.

> Things get messed up. How did it happen? It just got away from us, and here we are. This means I'm a bad wife, and I'm ashamed of that. You just go on and on, and when you look around it's all different. Then there's somebody I'm fond of, and that wasn't supposed to happen either. It's all a mess.
>
> I'm going off to see if I can think about it. I will be safe and nothing bad or anything.
>
> Congratulations on your new job. You deserve success.
>
> It's not brave to tell you this way, but you would argue, and there's nothing arguing would do except make us both unhappy. I've thought about this a long time. I never told you. But you knew already, didn't you? Both of us watching it all fall down.

He flung himself through the house. He felt not quite focused, as if sleep stunned his body. As if he watched a not particularly credible television drama. His mind denied her absence.

In their bedroom he wrenched open closets, threw back doors. From room to room through the house he traced the shape of her absence. Her new luggage was missing, a few clothes, her shoes and jewelry, her family photo album. Her coats from the hallway closet.

So few things.

The rest of her possessions remained behind. She had abandoned them all, familiar things in familiar places, wreckage along the highway.

In her blue and white kitchen, orderly, neat, he made fresh coffee. He felt intensely aware of Helen's presence, just out of sight. She might have diffused into the air, so that every breath drew her into him. Her favorite teapot, gay with tiny red flowers, waited on the pantry shelf.

He closed the pantry door. Then, eyes intent, he opened and closed the door again. Far off in the unexplored darkness of himself he felt a dull recoil, a distant sense of movement, as if smoke trickled from an exhausted fire.

Once more he opened the door and slammed it viciously. During his confused, blundering search through the house he had explored every closet, plunged into every room, opened every door. Without fear. Without emotional punishment. In the brutal shock of his loss he had forgotten to feel afraid.

Closing his eyes, he tested the deep economy of his body for panic. Far off he sensed that familiar heaviness. But grown small, driven back, leaving behind a sort of dull ache in the hollowness it had occupied.

A kind of numb anguish slipped across his mind. For the moment, he thought, Helen's flight from him overwhelmed all lesser problems. He had traded one thing for another. This was stern knowledge, and cold. He had exchanged his wife for the ability to open doors.

Standing in the neat kitchen, he watched coffee stream into its receptacle. He did not feel real. He hung suspended in unreality. The sense of her nearness flooded through him. Soon she would enter the kitchen. He must wait. When she came he would ask her nothing.

She did not return. No word came. After several weeks a lawyer called to speak of dreadful matters in a voice that made such agonies routine.

"I will not contest," he told the voice.

"She doesn't want a settlement," the lawyer said, professionally disapproving. "I advised otherwise. She said she wanted nothing. There is, however, the matter of the house. . . ."

Time passed. His new job devoured his days. Out of sight his lawyer talked with her lawyer, and papers passed between them. He signed his name frequently.

As it turned out, the fears crept back. Behind doors, menace again thickened. Now, however, he possessed a weapon. Although it eventually became humiliating to him, the memory of that frantic search through the house gave him power of a fragile sort. It sustained him. With struggle, with time, fear might have an end.

In time it did.

One Friday night Joyce telephoned:

"Listen, since Mom moved out I guess you've got a lot of room, haven't you?"

"Plenty of room."

"I need a place, if that's okay."

"What about Kemmie?"

"Never mind about Kemmie. He really makes me really sick."

She spoke at length about Kemmie and his crimes. Afterward two friends, both male, helped unload her station wagon packed with boxes and carried them to her former bedroom.

"Well," she said, surveying the familiar walls, "I see nothing's changed. Nothing much."

Her eyes slid from his. "I mean I'm sorry about Mom and all."

"So am I."

"Did I tell you I was thinking of going back to school? I'm thinking of going into engineering."

"Fine. That's fine."

Warm emotion rose and pierced him. He saw the vulnerability behind her assurance and realized how much he loved her, how he wished to protect her from future pain.

She said, "You got to do something besides stay at home and have kids, right?"

"I think," he said, "it's about time we sold Dad's house. He wouldn't mind it going for education. He'd probably like having another engineer in the family."

The following day, Sunday, began gray, with low clouds spitting single fat drops against the windshield of the car. They parked in the driveway of his father's house. The lawn needed cutting again. Joyce shoved open the door, and they walked into the forlorn smell of unoccupied rooms.

"God, look at all the dust," she said. "Are you going to sell the furniture, too?"

"Guess we'd better."

"Gotta get this cleaned up."

She began to drift through the lower rooms, eyes calculating. Edward climbed the stairs to the second floor. How many years ago had he carried the snake skin toward his father's room? Tentatively he extended one hand toward the door, alert for emotional change. Foreboding flickered behind his heart, the ghost of former terrors.

"Not again," he said sharply. "Not again."

For an instant a channel lighted in his mind. He felt that he stood in some ancient place where meaning flowed like a liquid, where doors and sorrow and anger, failing jobs and failing marriages glided together. To this place he always returned. It was as if he walked a complex of roads, circular and interconnected, with only a single entrance and no exit at all. He understood perfectly how his deepest concerns transformed themselves to fears and the face that menace wore as it yearned for him behind a closed door. He could not hold this knowledge long. Abruptly the brief lucidity dimmed and glided away. Leaving him oddly satisfied, as if some harsh surface had been smoothed.

Pushing the door open, he stepped into the bedroom. Here he had stood, so many years ago, the mottled snake skin in his hand. There, at the bathroom door, his father had stood, quite naked, a blue-striped towel trailing from his hand.

"Didn't she teach you how to knock? Out of here, you little fool."

Downstairs Joyce sang in a tuneless contralto and

bumped something heavily across the floor. Edward moved slowly to the bathroom. It was empty of his father's presence. But when he opened the closet door he could still detect a trace of the old man's odor, the smell of Arabian sand and sun-scalded cloth.

He stepped into the closet and turned, looking out into the room. Over the years he had grown taller than his father. The overhead shelf touched his hair. He felt abnormally fragile. Experimentally he tugged at the door. It swung almost shut, leaving a vertical bar of gray light. As he looked out into the room he could see the bed frame and a section of windowpane dotted with rain.

Here he could stand and wait. He closed his eyes. The odor of sand and cloth surrounded him.

Eventually Joyce would call. He would answer. When at last she opened the closet, there he would be, looking out at her with loving eyes.

BRIDGING

Rick Wilber

IT IS THE DYING HOURS OF THE TWENTIETH CENTURY, AND
Paul Doig would rather be home in the Florida sunshine to
wait out the epochal madness than be standing here in the
rain where he is tired, wet, and cold. Only Julia, even in
death, could have brought him here.

He began this odyssey with an afternoon flight from
Tampa. After two plane changes and that dizzying false
night of travel over the Atlantic he caught a taxi from the
Glasgow airport to his hotel. A few hours there for a nap,
and then it was time to drink a cup of wretched and
overpriced coffee and come across to Edinburgh for Julia's
funeral.

To clear his head he didn't take a taxi but, instead, took
the risk of walking through several dangerous blocks of
miserable Glasgow poverty to Queen Street station for the
train across to here.

On the way he was nearly caught by some endtimers, four
young toughs dressed in monk robes and carrying staffs so
they could cudgel anyone they could catch into donating to
their cause.

Bridging

Paul was dressed down to avoid trouble. He wore blue jeans and an old rain jacket, but something about the way he carried himself or perhaps the way he checked street signs for directions gave him away as an American, and the endtimers zeroed in on him as soon as he stepped into the Sauchiehall Street pedestrian precinct.

He carried a stasprod and might have used it to stun all four of them, but several policemen were walking the beat together near Buchanan Street as Paul rounded that corner, and the endtimers pulled to a halt when they saw the police. There was some jeering and yelling, but Paul got to the station easily enough after that and was on the five P.M. train when it pulled out. He treated himself to a first-class ticket and sat alone, avoiding any conversations.

He wasn't sure why the endtimers were out to get Yanks; certainly life in the States was just as miserable for most people as life in Scotland these days. If they were going to beat someone up out of sheer envy, they should take on some German or Japanese tourist. Or beat up an Englishman; at least there was history behind that sort of action.

Still, he wasn't about to argue points of economic logic with four of that sort, so he counted himself lucky as he settled into the seat for the fifty-minute run over to Edinburgh.

The train guards checked his credentials three times during the ride, making sure he was legal to carry the stasprod, which was powerful enough to kill if he set it that high. He had it on the middle levels, though, and had his papers straight as well, so there was no problem. Truth was, he had owned the stasprod since it had first come on the market, five or six years ago now, and had never used it once.

From Edinburgh's Waverly station he caught a taxi that avoided the worst of that dying city's danger spots by weaving through the narrow streets of Old Town to eventually bring him out here to tiny little Cramond. They crossed several bridges on the way, and now he wonders how Julia managed crossing them for all those years. Her fear of bridges, her terror of them, was legendary. There must have been other ways for her to get here from the city.

He watches the black hulk of the taxi disappear around a corner and shakes his head. The driver had tried to get him chatting three or four times, and Paul's ignoring of the remarks didn't seem to work. Finally Paul asked him to please be quiet and then had to suffer the driver's foul mood for the final mile or two. It is good to be out of the noisy, smelly old taxi, nasty weather or no.

Paul turns and walks to the guard box where the letter from Julia's daughter will get him through the newly bricked city walls and down into the village for the service. He has never met the daughter and hasn't seen Julia in fifteen years, not since the one time he came here to visit.

He wonders what kind of service it will be. Julia's eccentricities were famous, so almost anything at all could take place this evening—a High Mass, a loud party, a quiet gathering. Who knows?

Nothing would surprise him, not after what he knows of her and what he's read about her in the magazines—the reclusiveness, the bitter hirings and firings of her staff, the manic jet-setter parties, the binges with alcohol, the paranoia and the phobias. There was so much pain that accompanied her success.

He thinks of her fear of bridges. That one, at least, he understands. He was there when that began for her. Her rise and his decline started on that terrible day.

He shoves that memory aside, doesn't want to think about it. Instead he prefers to remember the years with her this way:

Those small, perfect breasts that rose and fell in rhythm as she moved above him. Beads of sweat on her upper lip, though the window unit labored to cool the beach cottage bedroom. She would smile that slight smile that started at pale blue eyes and gathered together those high cheekbones, the upturned lips, the almost open mouth. She would arch her back to ride him as they moved together in waves that crested with her cries of passion and joy. They were nineteen and very much in love.

The comfort of a shared life with her as they made the long drive through the American West, listening to bad pop and country on the tape deck and stopping to climb the peaks and walk the valleys.

Once, at a place called Mosquito Pass in Colorado, they drove their beat-up old Volksie bus up the jarring narrow gravel road nearly to the top before the engine ran out of air and the Volksie stalled.

They got out at the entrance to an abandoned lead mine there, and Julia, always the one in good spirits to contrast with his dark moments, told him it was fine, just fine that the bus gave out. They weren't meant to go over that pass, that was all. Fate.

A four-wheel-drive rescue jeep came by, and two women got out. "You two okay?" one of the two women asked Paul and Julia. And Julia laughed. "Of course," she said, "why wouldn't we be?"

"We heard someone went over the edge up there about an hour ago," the woman said. "Tough winds today, gusts to eighty. You were smart to stop here with that thing," and she hooked her thumb toward the unstable old Volkswagen bus.

Julia said nothing as they drove back down from the pass. She just stared at him, and smiled, and nodded her head. Fate.

Or the time, years later, toward the end, when he was pitching for that semipro baseball team in the championship finals of their summer league.

It was a miserable Florida August day, unspeakably hot, with no breeze from the nearby Gulf of Mexico, no hint of shade from clouds or the thin palms. Just heat.

In the top of the ninth, up by a run, he had to get through the last two hitters to win it. The first grounded out to short on the second pitch, a flat slider that Paul was lucky to get away with.

The second was stepping in when Julia pulled up in the little Toyota they shared, beeped the horn, and got out waving a piece of paper in her hand.

Paul took the sign, nodded, and went into the windup as Julia ran from the car and headed toward the field. The pitch, a tired fastball, reached the plate as she ran out from behind the backstop. The batter, swinging under it, tipped it almost straight back, and Paul watched in horror as the ball arrowed toward Julia's smiling face.

At the very last moment she saw it enough to begin to duck, and the ball grazed her left temple instead of hitting her full on the forehead. She dropped like a sack.

Paul ran to her, yelling in fear, afraid for her life. When he reached her she lay silent, eyes closed, and he thought for a single insane moment that she'd been killed and it was his fault. Then she opened her eyes, smiled, and said, "You've got to see this. Look."

It was a letter from *The Atlantic Monthly.* "We are pleased to accept 'Greggie's Cup' for publication in . . ."

Her first sale. The start of everything for her. The start of nothing, of his collapse, for Paul.

A few minutes later, while she sat with ice on her head, he got the last man to fly out to left, and they won the championship for the summer league.

That night they toasted each other. He for his championship, she for her sale. It was, he realized now, about the last time he'd won anything. For her, it was barely the beginning.

She was a wonderful lover, taught him everything at age nineteen. They met at college in Tampa, sat one desk apart in a creative writing class. The professor wrote stories for *The New Yorker,* and Julia thought him wonderful. Paul thought he was a pompous old fool, and *The New Yorker,* which Paul despised as unreadable, pretentious drivel, deserved him.

They argued about it after class, then took the discussion to a local bar. A week later they were making love, and a week after that he was reading the professor's stories while Julia lay next to him and watched approvingly.

Bridging

That, too, she said, was fate. He'd write for *The New Yorker* one day; they both would. And *The Atlantic*, and the *Paris Review*, and novels and poetry . . . she just knew it was their fate.

It was the start of five years of heaven. That's how he thinks of it now. It was heaven, and he didn't know how special it was, thought it would always be that way.

He was drifting into newspaper work by then; someone had to pay the bills for them, and he was good at it, from news to features to columns. He liked it, too, when he admitted it, though he never told her.

They were good years, fine years. They talked about finally getting married, having children.

Then came that day on the bridge, when so much of it died.

Standing there, just inside the city walls, cold rain on his face, he remembers how that happened.

He'd been late at the paper, finishing a piece for the Sunday feature section, a story on the area's growing violence, the steady march toward a big-city crime rate.

She had come by to pick him up at ten, and they'd gone home, parked the car, and then walked out to the beach for drinks and a late meal. It was a safe, pleasant one-mile walk across the Bayway bridge to the Seahorse bar, where they had grouper sandwiches and a couple of Heinekens.

Paul remembers parts of this in agonizing detail. Thirty years later, and still he recalls the details with startling, painful clarity. The beads of sweat on the green Heineken bottles. The sound of the waves against the restaurant's seawall. Julia's hair against the backlighting from the bar across the room. So beautiful.

On the walk home their timing was bad. That was how the police put it. Just bad timing.

A sailboat just returning from a month in the Keys putt-putted up the channel, signaled for the bridge to open, and then slowly moved through while the bridge was up.

A single car waited for the bridge. Inside were three young men in their early twenties, two of them in the backseat.

339

They were high, giggling, bouncing around in the seats. They had just robbed a gas station convenience store a few miles up the beach, had shot the attendant and left him for dead. Their world was hilariously simple, was all theirs for the taking, as they waited while the center span opened and raised itself high. There were no other cars coming from behind.

Paul and Julia walked along the bridge's sidewalk, coming up close to the draw so they could watch the sailboat pass by below. They were arm in arm as the boat passed beneath them. They waved at the man at the helm, who waved back.

Paul was just telling her about his feature story on the victims of crime when they were attacked.

Paul's memory is sketchy on this part of the night. There are hazy images of a beating, fists into his side and into his cheeks. Boots kicking into his ribs. Not much pain, really, not then.

He was sitting on the sidewalk, watching, helpless, as the two from the backseat dragged Julia away and into the car.

Paul tried to rise and then discovered the pain. Still, he managed to get to his feet, managed to step over the metal barrier that separated the sidewalk from the road, managed to take four steps toward the car, his arm raised.

The two in the back, busy raping Julia, paid him no attention at all. Their friend in the front opened his door, stepped out, said "Stupid fuck," and shoved Paul back over the barrier and onto the sidewalk. He lost consciousness at that point.

Another minute or two later, no more than three, the span came down; they tossed Julia out the car door and drove off. The bridge tender, an elderly man, could see Paul and Julia then and phoned for help.

The whole thing took a few minutes, a fraction of time from a lifetime of fifty-five years, thinks Paul. But Julia never crossed a bridge again without knowing what her various psychologists and psychiatrists and counselors and friends all called that "irrational" fear.

Paul didn't find it irrational at all.

* * *

Bridging

It was all so long ago.

The rain is light but insistent. He pulls up the hood on his jacket, and it focuses his sight on the road ahead, the peripheral vision nothing but gray plastic. That is something the wise person never does these days, close off the side vision. The wise walker keeps an eye out for trouble, for the proddy boys with their joysticks, the druggies needing cash, the endtimers with their profitable fervor, the simply vicious.

But this village is walled and guarded; he feels safe enough. And though he has only been here once before, years ago, and can barely see the buildings that line the road, he knows this place well enough. This is where he came to beg, years after she left him.

That memory hurts, like a lot of them. She was always reminding him of their past, using him. He's seen himself in dozens of her stories since those early days, known himself in four of her novels. He saw himself there all the time and hated her for it, the way she made him into the hero he wasn't that night when she needed him.

As he walks, through the gray plastic and the rain he recognizes landmarks from her stories and poems.

On his right is the old church, Cramond Kirk, where she had her hero, him, finally kill the madman who'd pursued that poor woman through three continents and a handful of time zones.

Beyond that is Cramond Inn, where that same hero two books later sat in the dark corner by the fireplace and hatched the plan that saved the world and rescued the kidnapped heiress.

He laughs. She made him a hero known all over the world, a dashing figure capable of winning through against all odds. Handsome, talented, rich beyond all need, this make-believe man grew more popular each year even as the world declined into depression and violence and fear.

But the real man, the figure on which all this is based, can only smile at that image. He is a lonely columnist for a local daily paper, nothing more. He writes about local politicians and greedy business executives and how it's the little people who always get hurt.

He is very good at this, and very popular. Not many people know how solitary a life he leads. He is handsome enough, tall, a bit thin, bookish with his reading glasses. But he dates only when he must, so women think him gay or asexual. He almost wishes that were so; the first would at least be companionship, and the second a relief.

But it isn't so. He is, instead, isolated; can't seem to reach out. He finds ways to ruin any relationship he might drift into. A shrink he spent two years visiting said that he was into self-defeat and needed to work through why that was.

Paul smiles at that thought. He has come to accept that only through his column, through the safe distance of words on recycled paper, can he reach out to people, talk to them, try and know them.

And he is, at least, very good at that. He is popular, well-read, well-known in the city. Successful in his own way.

But it isn't what he thought he'd do, not back then with Julia, back when they planned the future.

Once, talking to her on the telephone, listening to the weird satellite echo that repeated his anger, he tried to defend himself, to tell her that he'd won a prize that year for his writing, and at least what he did was write about reality, at least it wasn't the invented pabulum of the cheap thrillers that she'd turned to writing.

She laughed at him, agreed. Just cheap thrillers, she said. That was all. Millions and millions of them.

Paul walks into the churchyard of the old kirk. A low stone wall there marks the ruins of a Roman fort from the second century. The rain is easing off, and as Paul pulls back the hood of his jacket the sun pokes through the clouds, and there is a moment of almost warmth.

In "Hope as an Element of Cold, Dark Matter," a story she wrote that won her prizes, Paul read of himself walking into this same place, walking along the same low stone walls that were the farthest extent of Empire, the very edge of Rome at its height of power.

Bridging

He stands now atop the wall that once held the armory and looks to the north and west, where the mean waters of the Firth of Forth, the mountains beyond, and the simplistic brutality of the Picts just didn't seem worth it to Septimius Severus in the second century when he, emperor of all Rome, came here to visit. This, thought Septimius, was far enough.

The sky is clearing from the northwest, and there, its great girders rising over the hills, Paul sees the rail bridge over the Firth of Forth.

It was the wonder of the world in 1890, the greatest achievement of the age, a symbol of an empire's power and might at the height of its influence.

Paul wonders why Julia chose to live almost in the shadow of the bridge, why she would want to see it daily, this thing she never dared cross, this ultimate horror, this reminder.

"The bridge?" he hears a voice say from behind him. "I think she actually enjoyed seeing it out the front window. She once said that because she could see it she always knew where her enemy was."

Paul turns, and a young woman is there. Julia at twenty, he thinks for a crazy moment, and then he realizes it must be the daughter, the one who called him two days ago in Tampa, telling him of her mother's death.

This girl is beautiful. Not her mother's beauty, not really, he decides as he looks at her. She is darker than Julia's pale beauty, and stockier in build, more athletic. But the short, dark hair suits this girl, and the smile seems genuine enough, given the grief, and the eyes are her mother's, pale blue and haunting, perceptive.

He's never known much about this daughter, never met her until this moment. He remembers that the girl's father —Julia's first husband, the one who came within the year after she left Paul—died a few years ago in a boating accident. This poor child is alone now.

"Hello, Angela," he says. "I came as quickly as I could."

"Thank you," she says simply. "I'm glad you could come all this way on short notice. Mother made it clear that you were the first I should call after she died."

She walks over to him, takes his two hands in hers, holds them for a moment. "Mother told me a lot about you."

"She was a wonderful woman. A wonderful writer."

"She was a hack, actually," Angela says, smiling. "That's what she always said, just a hack grinding out novels to make a living."

Angela shakes her head as if to clear it of that kind of memory, drops Paul's hands, turns toward the water, points to it. "Beautiful view when the sun's out, isn't it?"

"Yes, beautiful."

"She loved this place. The village, this old ruin. She hated leaving it when she had to tour. Toward the end she even had me go into the city for her when she needed things."

Angela turns. "It was awful, Paul. Toward the end. The wasting away. That vital woman, eaten away like that."

"You were with her?"

"I was with her the past year. Quit my job and came home when she called and told me how it was."

There are no tears as Angela says this. Paul suspects the tears have already come and will come again later. Now she is being strong, lucid. She needs to tell him this. He listens.

"She's left me plenty of money, Paul. And two manuscripts, too. That's something we have to talk about, the manuscripts."

"We have to talk about them? Why? Surely she left instructions on when to publish."

"She asked that you be involved with them, help cut them down to size. She said you're a wonderful editor, and that you understood her, and the work."

He laughs. Now? To ask this?

"You don't need me to do this, Angela. Hire someone, or just let her publisher handle it. I won't do it. I can't."

"It's not charity. She says this is something she should have done long ago but couldn't. She didn't tell me why."

Paul knows why, of course. The bridge. When he couldn't save her, couldn't help. She knew, in her head, that he did the best he could, couldn't have been expected to do more. He knows it, too.

But in their hearts, for both of them, he is to blame.

Bridging

And now this is Julia, asking for a kind of forgiveness. She reaches out to him from wherever she is now, crosses that thing that divided them for all these years.

He smiles. "I'll think about it, okay?"

She nods. "It will be getting dark in another hour or so. That's when the funeral procession will take her to the cemetery. She asked me to take you for a walk first. A little stroll along the shoreline. Is that all right?"

"Fine," he says. "Down this way?" And he looks toward the shore. There is a path there, he can see it from here, edging along the Firth of Forth. In the distance is a ruined castle, remnant of other violent times. They head that way.

First there is a ferry across the River Almond. The ferryman lives on the far side, in a small brick home. Angela rings a bell to summon him.

A face peers out the front window. Angela smiles, waves.

"Thomas will be here in a minute or two," she says. "He makes it a point never to be in a hurry." They both laugh, almost nervously.

They say nothing, the silence a strain, as the front door creaks open and the ferryman comes out smileless, turns to slowly shut the door, and then walks down the low ridge to the dory that serves as a ferryboat.

"It's a new ferryman," Paul notes. "Fifteen years ago it was an older man. Looked a bit like Popeye."

"That was Jordan," Angela says. "He died a few years back. Bad heart. This is his son, Thomas."

In five long, slow minutes Thomas has the boat over and, in another equally slow five, takes the three of them back to his side of the river.

Paul thinks that Thomas is every bit as slow-moving as his father was but doesn't voice the thought. Instead, as they walk along, the rain returns, spitting at them, cold despite the calendar.

He shakes his head. "I never understood why she lived here, Angela. She could have lived anywhere, her own private island in the sun somewhere, or Canada perhaps, or, hell, anywhere but here."

He waves his hand vaguely in the direction of Edinburgh.

"Why did she feel she had to live like this? God, the place is getting outright dangerous. Glasgow's fallen completely to pieces; Edinburgh's not much better. Hell, I avoided London entirely, too many gangs, too much violence. The whole U.K.'s a mess."

Angela picks her way over a fallen log as they enter a small woods. The leaves drip but block the worst of the rain. "It's like this in the States, too, isn't it, Paul? That's what our nets tell us, that it's even worse over there."

He nods his head. "A lot of places, yes, it's worse. Some places, like where I live, it's not too bad yet. Other places"— he shrugs—"it's anarchy. The government has given up completely in some of the big cities."

"You know she liked to face things head on, Paul. She always told me she liked to see the enemy, know where it was, and then she could deal with it."

Which is a lie, Paul thinks, but he says nothing. Some things, maybe, she faced, like having that damn bridge out her front door to stare at each day.

But other things, no, she dodged them as the rest of us do. The big things, the ones that really hurt. She stayed away from those if she could.

Angela leads the way, and they emerge from the woods onto a small stone beach. A large stone outcropping sits there in the tidal pools.

"She wanted me to make sure you saw this," Angela says, and she walks carefully around the pools to stand by the side of the outcropping. She points.

"That's said to be a Roman eagle carved into the side of the rock."

Paul walks over and looks at it. Perhaps. Worn away by two thousand years of miserable weather, but yes, perhaps it is an eagle cut into the stone. Some Roman, or a mercenary tied to Rome by profit only, spent the hours here to carve that, a symbol of how far the Empire had come.

"Remember in *Words of Praise* how the hero came here and saw that eagle?" she asks him.

He nods. Another book where she made him the hero.

"And then he traveled to Rome, found the drug lord and killed him, rescued the girl he loved. Yes, I remember it."

She laughs. "Silly stuff, I suppose. But it pleased millions of people, Paul. It made them happy for a time. That's all she said she wanted."

He nods.

An hour later they are at Julia's home. It is a small stone cottage that sits on a bluff overlooking the firth. To the west is the rail bridge. To the north is Fife. To the south is Edinburgh.

The cemetery is in the small churchyard in Cramond, where Paul's evening began. They will return to it with a two-mile walk along the old main road. Halfway there, crossing the River Almond, is Cramond Brig, the old stone bridge over the river.

It took death to make it happen, Paul thinks when he hears Angela explain the procession, but at last Julia will conquer a bridge, cross one calmly, easily, and reach the other side.

It is dark outside when they leave her home. The casket, in a horse-drawn hearse, comes first. Angela and Paul are next, walking behind it, and friends and admirers fill in behind. They all hold candles because Julia wanted it so. In *The Compass* there was a funeral procession like this, and now is her chance to make that scene real.

The rain has slackened again, but a fog rolls in from the firth as they walk along the old macadam. Paul can see the casket in the glassed-in hearse ahead, can see Angela next to him, can hear the muffled footsteps of the two dozen or more behind, and that is that. Things twenty or thirty feet away are invisible, or brief murky snatches of them appear and disappear in the swirl, a dark branch of a tree, the shadowy form of a small house, the hulk of an automobile.

In the five years he was with Julia he saw things clearly, felt them sharply, knew their edges. Not like now, here, where everything is hidden and muddy, obscure in the damn mist that swirls and hides and confounds.

His life is like that, he admits. Muddy. Obscure. It is his job to make things clear for five hundred thousand readers of the paper he works for, four times a week, fifty weeks a year.

That is what he does. Clarify.

But he has never met another Julia, and now he never will. The clarity he gives to others will never be his. Ever.

There are shouts from up the road a bit. Yelling, muffled in the fog. Paul peers forward, moves to his left to see past the hearse. The horse is shying away from the clamor ahead, trying to pull up.

There are torches. It is past eight P.M. on the final night of the millennium, and the endtimers are on the march, perhaps a dozen of them, two dozen, marching straight toward them.

The hearse jolts forward onto Cramond Brig, the driver clucking and urging the horse onto the stonework of the old bridge. On the other side, waiting, are the torches and the quiet group of endtimers. No one is saying anything. The people behind Paul and Angela don't know yet what is happening.

"Endtimers," Angela says. "They're out early. I thought they had a rally planned for the High Street at eleven to get ready for the end of it all."

"They might be here for us. It'd be easy to know we'd be here," Paul says. "I read about this funeral in the *Glasgow Herald.* It was probably in the *Scotsman,* too. They were no great fans of hers, you know, these endtimers."

"She hated them," Angela says. "Talked about them all the time in interviews, said they were just using the millennium as an excuse for violence and thievery."

"She was right, for what it's worth," says Paul, coming to a halt as the hearse finally pulls up to a stop halfway across the bridge.

The torches come forward.

One of them—a teenager, a kid, really—speaks. "Tonight's the night, you lot. You shouldna be here. You should stay at home or get down to the Tron for the hour to come."

348

"Out the way, lads," the hearse driver says in even, quiet tones. "This is a funeral. There'll be plenty of time later for the New Year."

"It's not just the New Year, you stupid cunt, it's the almighty end," the endtimer says. He raises up his torch to see the driver more clearly. "And we think you should turn this thing around now and go back. We won't let you cross this bridge."

"You *must* let us across," says Angela, walking past Paul before he can stop her, and then moving around to the side of the hearse as she speaks to them. "This is my mother's funeral. You must respect that, even you."

"Well, well," says the endtimer. "Look at this," and he walks toward her, holding the torch high.

"That's her daughter," says one of the others from behind him.

So, Paul thinks, they did know what the funeral was about. This is a planned confrontation.

"And a beautiful thing she is, too," says the endtimer by the hearse.

The group from behind the hearse is caught up by this time and beginning to make comments. There are several prominent people in the group, and many of them have personal phones on them. Paul knows the police are probably already on the way.

On a normal night the police would arrive in a few minutes. This isn't the States yet, where the police might or might not arrive at all.

But this is no normal night. This is the end of the millennium, and the crowds in the city might already be in full riot. Paul wonders how long it will take for the police to get out here to Cramond to help. He wonders if he can stall these crazy young endtimers for that long, long enough to get Julia across this bridge in peace, finish the funeral procession, get on with the next thousand years.

Then the endtimers answer the questions. The one in front, the one doing the talking, walks up to Angela, holds his torch up high, and says, "Why don't we just celebrate right here, eh, daughter?"

And he grabs her by the right arm and starts pulling her back to his side of the bridge.

The hearse driver and Paul react at the same moment, both yelling and starting to come to Angela's aid. But the driver suddenly staggers, jolts upright, and shakes. A bolt protrudes from his leg, and a thin wire trails back to the endtimers—someone has a wire stunner and has used it on the driver. The electric shock might kill him if it goes on for long, and Paul knows he can't do anything about it except try to sever the wire.

Angela, meanwhile, is yelling for him, and the crowd from behind is starting to yell and scream as well, some of them running past the hearse and throwing their fists in the air to threaten the young toughs.

But threats won't work here. Paul sees one of the people from the crowd slip on some gloves and start to tug at the wire from the line stunner, and that frees Paul up.

He runs hard at the endtimer with Angela, who now has two friends with him who are holding her down on the ground, where she is kicking and struggling. The endtimer is pulling down his pants. A few more endtimers are coming up to watch.

It is all chaos and shouting and murky shadows in the flickering light.

It is violence and screaming.

It is Paul not stopping, not slowing down as he runs full tilt into the endtimer whose pants are half down. Paul throws a cross-body block into him, and the endtimer's left knee pops as Paul rolls through him, and there is a howl of pain.

Paul, landing on all fours, scrambles to his feet to take on the other two. He is crazy, insane with fear and rage, ready to take on anyone, do anything, kill them both if he has to. He has completely forgotten the stasprod in his coat pocket.

He gets to his feet, is ready for the two of them, but discovers there is only one. The other is on his back, and Angela leans over him, her arm pulled back. A vicious stab forward and blood spurts from the endtimer's nose. Another howl of pain.

Bridging

Paul thinks of the stasprod, pulls it out, holds it forward to show to the final endtimer. This one holds his hands up, palms out, and mumbles something incoherent about just having some fun before turning to run.

Paul and Angela stand together and look toward the other endtimers. There must be twenty of them, maybe more, standing there at the end of the bridge, torches in hand, staring at them.

Paul starts walking toward them. Behind him Angela has walked back to take the horse by the halter and lead him forward. The hooves clop against the stone bridge.

"We're coming through," Paul says, simply. "Just step aside now, we're coming through."

And they do step aside, pulling their wounded with them. The funeral procession passes through them, crosses the bridge.

At the cemetery the ceremony is simple, brief.

Later, as the crowd walks down to Cramond Inn, the fog rolls back, disappears into the firth, and a full moon seems nearly blinding by comparison.

Paul Doig, walking beside Angela, sees the old Roman fort clearly as they walk through it on the way to the inn. In the distance, reflecting the moonlight, is the huge shadow of the rail bridge.

Tomorrow, he thinks, the sun will rise on schedule, and the endtimers will have to find a new excuse for living. For himself, this clarity right now is enough. It is hard earned. It is years in the making.

The Contributors

JERRY AHERN and SHARON AHERN are the authors of nearly one hundred novels which have sold more than twelve million copies worldwide. This is only their third short story. Their previous work has appeared in *Grails: Quests, Visitations and Other Occurrences* and *Confederacy of the Dead.*

ROBERT BLOCH's recent projects include his autobiography, *Once Around the Bloch;* a collection of his pulp-era short stories, *Robert Bloch's Tales from Arkham;* and the editing of the original anthology *Monsters in Our Midst.* His short story "Yours Truly, Jack the Ripper" and his novel *Psycho* are among the most influential works of twentieth-century literature.

RICHARD LEE BYERS was born and raised in Columbus, Ohio. After receiving a master's degree in psychology from the University of South Florida, he worked for more than a decade at an emergency in-patient psy-

The Contributors

chiatric facility, leaving the mental-health field in 1986 to become a full-time writer. His works include the novels *The Vampire's Apprentice, Dead Time* and *Dark Fortune*. His short stories have appeared in several anthologies, including *Freak Show*.

NANCY A. COLLINS' novels include *Sunglasses After Dark,* winner of the Bram Stoker Award, and her short fiction has appeared in many leading anthologies, including *Under the Fang, The Ultimate Werewolf* and *Confederacy of the Dead.* Her scripts for DC Comics' "Swamp Thing" have been among the most popular in the history of the long-running series.

PETER CROWTHER, through a capricious twist of fate, was born an Englishman on the fourth of July. As a result, or so he believes, he has since espoused all things American. "Cankerman" is the nineteenth story he has sold within the past twelve months, a period which has also seen the completion of *Escardy Gap*, his collaborative novel with James Lovegrove, and two volumes—*Narrow Houses* and *Touch Wood* —of an anthology series based on superstitions. He is firmly convinced that the confrontational nature of the truly horrific holds the answer to everything that ails us.

GEORGE ALEC EFFINGER was born in Cleveland, Ohio, and attended Yale University. He has been writing professionally since 1970 and has published twenty novels and about 150 short stories. For the past twenty-one years he has resided in New Orleans.

VALERIE FRANKEL is an editor at *Mademoiselle* and the author of the Wanda Mallory mysteries, including *A Deadline for Murder, Murder on Wheels* and *Primetime for Murder.* On the nonfiction front, she is the author of *The Heartbreak Handbook.* She lives in

354

The Contributors

Brooklyn, New York, and is working on her fourth Wanda Mallory mystery.

RICHARD GILLIAM's writing career includes more than twenty years of free-lance nonfiction, a dozen short stories and the editing of several well-regarded anthologies. Richard is possibly the only person to claim both *Sports Illustrated* and *Heavy Metal* among his credits. He is the film critic for *Horror* magazine and a contributing editor for *Pulphouse*.

CHARLES GRANT has received three World Fantasy Awards, two Nebula Awards and the British Fantasy Award. His novels include *Raven, The Pet* and *For Fear of the Night*, while his hundred or so short stories have appeared in a wide variety of magazines and books. He also writes as Geoffrey Marsh and Lionel Fenn, the latter of which is used for his successful Kent Montana series.

MARTIN H. GREENBERG is a professor of international relations at the University of Wisconsin at Green Bay and the author of several well-regarded texts, including *The International Relations of the PLO*. He has edited more than six hundred anthologies, and serves as an advisor to the Sci-Fi channel.

JACK C. HALDEMAN II lives on a farm in rural Florida surrounded by cows, sheep, dogs, cats, chickens . . . and alligators. Though trained as a research biologist, Jack has been writing short fiction full-time since 1971. His latest novel, *High Steel*, is a collaboration with Jack Dann.

JON A. HARRALD is the pseudonym for the husband-wife writing team of Harold Schechter and Jonna Semeiks. Currently living in Paris, they are at work on their new novel, *Outcry*. Harold is also the author of the true-crime classics *Deviant* and *Deranged. Depraved: The Real Life Horror Story of Dr. H. H. Holmes, America's First Serial Killer* will be the next book in the series.

NANCY HOLDER has written three horror novels: *Making Love* and *Witchcraft,* collaborations with Melanie Tem, and *Dead in the Water,* her first solo horror novel. She has also sold more than fifteen romance and mainstream novels. The author of more than forty short stories, Nancy received the 1992 Bram Stoker Award for Best Short Story from the Horror Writers of America for her story "Lady Madonna." She has also written game fiction and comic books, and has been translated into more than sixteen languages.

ANDREW KLAVAN is the Edgar Award–winning author of six novels written under his own name and under the pseudonym Keith Peterson. A former radio and newspaper reporter, he is a graduate of the University of California at Berkeley. His more recent novel, *Animal Hour,* was optioned for the screen by Demi Moore. Currently working on his next novel, Mr. Klavan lives in London with his wife and two children.

EDWARD E. KRAMER's credits include more than a decade of work as a music critic and photojournalist. Recently directing his talents toward writing and editing fiction, he has hosted both regional and national literary conferences in his hometown, Atlanta, Georgia. He is also a licensed consultant to the psychiatric and educational professions.

J. M. MORGAN is the author of four novels, including *Between the Devil and the Deep,* and eight other novels of suspense and horror under the pseudonyms Morgan Fields, Meg Griffin and Meredith Morgan—for suspense, historical and horror—and Jessica Pierce, for her young-adult novels. Her seven short-fiction sales include an appearance in *Freak Show* and the upcoming *Stalkers II.* "Heaven Sent" is dedicated to her mother in loving memory.

BILLIE SUE MOSIMAN is the author of five novels; the latest, *Night Cruise,* was nominated for the Edgar Award. Her short stories, totaling more than forty-five, have appeared in magazines and anthologies such as *Pulphouse, Ellery Queen Mystery Magazine, Psycho-paths* and *Predators.* She lives in the country, where whippoorwills call while she writes her next novel.

KATHRYN PTACEK has been a full-time writer since 1979, with twenty novels and three anthologies to her credit, in addition to numerous short stories and nonfiction articles. She edits *The Gila Queen's Guide to Markets,* a monthly newsletter that lists opportunities for writers and artists. Kathy's best-known novels include *Ghost Dance, The Hunted* and *ShadowEyes.*

KRISTINE KATHRYN RUSCH has received numerous nominations and awards for her short fiction. Kris has four novels in print, the latest being *Heart Readers.* She also edits *The Magazine of Fantasy and Science Fiction* . . . and has a deep-seated fear that she won't have enough time to sleep or eat. . . .

ROBERT SAMPSON's writing career began toward the end of the pulp era, although it was not until his retirement from NASA that he devoted himself to writing full-time. The author of nine highly regarded books about the history of magazine fiction, Bob won an Edgar Award in 1986 for one of his own stories, "Rain in Pinton County." "Matters of Substance" was completed shortly before Bob's death in October 1992.

DEAN WESLEY SMITH has received three Hugo nominations from the World Science-Fiction Convention for his work as an editor. He won a World Fantasy Award for founding Pulphouse Publishing, and has written more than fifty short stories, innumerable essays and two novels.

S. P. SOMTOW was born in Bangkok, Thailand, and was educated at Eton College at Cambridge, where he obtained his B.A. and M.A., receiving honors in both English and music. Following a successful career as a composer, he turned to writing, producing such highly acclaimed novels as *Vampire Junction, Moon Dance* and *Jasmine Nights.* His writings for younger readers include *The Fallen Country* and *Forgetting Places,* which was honored by Books for Young Adults as an "outstanding book of the year."

BRAD STRICKLAND has been writing fantasy and science fiction professionally since 1986. In addition to the *Moon Dreams* fantasy series, he co-authored two novels with the late John Bellairs, and has written the popular young-adult fantasy adventure *Dragon's Plunder.* Brad has also written more than sixty short stories, along with hundreds of articles and book reviews. In everyday life he teaches English at Gainesville College. He lives in Oakwood, Georgia, with his wife, Barbara, and children, Amy and Jonathan.

KARL EDWARD WAGNER has edited fifteen years' worth of the venerable *Year's Best Horror* series, and is the only person to have won the World Fantasy Award as both a publisher and a writer. He is an M.D. by training. "Passages" tells why Karl chose to specialize in psychiatric medicine.

The Contributors

LAWRENCE WATT-EVANS is the author of *The Nightmare People* and numerous other works of horror, fantasy and science fiction. He does not suffer from fear of flying, but only from a vivid imagination. He lives in Maryland, near the nation's capital, with his wife, a son, a daughter, a cat and a parakeet. The only one who seems to have any problem with flying is the parakeet; it's probably just lack of practice.

ROBERT WEINBERG is the author of the novels *The Black Lodge* and *The Dead Man's Kiss,* as well as numerous short stories. An expert on the history of pulp-era fiction, Bob has twice received the World Fantasy Award.

WENDY WEBB's short fiction has appeared in such anthologies as *Confederacy of the Dead, Women of Darkness* and the *Shadows* series. Her many varied credits include acting in film, television and on the stage. She received a master's degree in biology education and is a registered nurse currently on the editorial advisory board of *Nursing News Today.*

RICK WILBER's short stories and poems appear regularly in mainstream and science-fiction magazines, as well as major anthologies. He is the author of the textbook *Magazine Feature Writing,* and is a professor of journalism at the University of South Florida. He edits "Fiction Quarterly" for the *Tampa Tribune,* and edited the anthology *Subtropical Speculations.*

JANE YOLEN is the author of more than 130 books for children, young adults and adults, as well as close to 100 short stories and poems. A past president of the Science Fiction Writers of America and a twenty-year veteran of the Board of Directors of the Society of Children's Book Writers and Illustrators, she is also editor-in-chief of Jane Yolen Books, an imprint of Harcourt Brace. She has won the World Fantasy

Award, the Kerlan Award and the Regina Medal. Her books have won the Caldecott Medal, the Christopher Medal, and have been nominated for the Nebula and National Book awards. Her poetry has been nominated for the Pushcart Prize. She has no phobias, except she cannot abide snakes and she's not really great at heights.

"A totally original thriller. A hurtling joyride into a
nightmare world of horror and dread...."
—Jonathan Keller

THE
ANIMAL
HOUR

A NOVEL BY

ANDREW
KLAVAN

Author of the Edgar Award-nominated
Don't Say a Word